THE SIGNPOST

THE MACMILLAN COMPANY
NEW YORK · BOSTON · CHICAGO · DALLAS
ATLANTA · SAN FRANCISCO

THE SIGNPOST

by

E. ARNOT ROBERTSON 1903 –

NEW YORK
THE MACMILLAN COMPANY
1944

PRINTED IN THE UNITED STATES OF AMERICA
BY H. WOLFF, NEW YORK

To
the *good friends I am*
about to lose
in Eire

CONTENTS

THE SIGNPOST

CHAPTER I

EFFORT

His housekeeper came into the room where the Air Force pilot who had just been decorated sat in angry apprehension, pretending to read, waiting for the telephone to ring.

She fidgeted about, making little duties for herself, until he looked up unwillingly. It seemed to him too great an effort, for the sake of such peace as he could now know, to tell her to leave him alone: everything, lately, had become a disproportionate effort.

'I'm sure I congratulate you, sir.'

'Oh. Thank you, Mrs. Mott.' Because of a daylight raid, the investiture at Buckingham Palace had been adjourned from the courtyard to a shelter inside. It seemed odd that men who had won their honours for courage should receive them hiding below ground: but personally Fairburn was thankful. This was early September 1940; the attacks on London were becoming more and more vehement by day as the first great air test between the fighting nations developed.

'I'm sure Mr. Mott will be sorry he wasn't at home to come round and tell you himself.'

'Will he, Mrs. Mott? Well . . .' Kindly woman, very close to tears: if only she would go, leaving him with his fears and his trapped anger.

'Mr. Fairburn, it was a wonderful thing to have done!'

Yes, he might have said. An act of appalling endurance. By someone else. A man so different from me, to-day, that I have nothing in common with him but the decoration. 'Oh, I don't know,' he told her, envious of the past, not more than six weeks away, when he would have said easily, 'Run along, Mottie, and don't be silly.' Now with uncomfortable understanding he felt the decent longing of herself and her kind to put into words their gratitude towards the men behind whose tired bodies and nerves they sheltered. Only — fortunately — the words would not come.

'Mr. Mott will be back later to-night, of course,' she said with the surprised expression she always wore when repeating this formula:

I

it had become familiar to Fairburn after two years of her services in peace-time: she looked as though she wondered why she used it. 'Never been away for one night since we were married, Mr. Mott hasn't. This was the inevitable end of the formula.

'No? Really?' he said once more, thinking lightly, to steady himself, how impossible it was to imagine Mott boasting about this fact, which may have been technically true but was true in no other sense. Mott, a drunk who lived by his wife's industry, was notably unfaithful. How odd it was that men and women apparently spoke the same language when their pride and their desire, their lies and their truths lay so far apart. If everything to do with an emotion which both of them agreed to call 'love' could be known by different names, according to the gender of the speaker, what misunderstandings it would save, he reflected, destroying the hampering belief that people were talking about the same thing when they used the same words . . . From the release of fancy, his mind swung back to panic as the telephone bell rang. He looked at her beseechingly, and she went out. He let it ring for a moment. Now. Now they would start: the hearty good wishes of acquaintances who would not like to congratulate him on being still alive; because so very soon he might not be: as soon as his sick-leave was up, in fact, he had been discharged from hospital ten days ago, with the bullet holes in his arm healing well. For something to say they would probably ask what it felt like to get away with bombing the wrong target. (The horror of chemical fire, added to the surprise and terror of the attack, for the workmen in the big industrial plant he had discovered by accident, in enemy territory . . . His mind, in its present state, sickened at the memory of the night for which he had been rewarded. How many men had been trapped and burnt to death in that one building — enveloped, a few seconds after the first stick of bombs went down, in leaping, almost incredible flame? More, probably, than he had been instrumental in killing in any other raid.)

Friends who knew him well would congratulate him straightforwardly on being alive.

He had been given another objective for the night's raid, but had failed to reach it: his navigator was wounded, as they crossed the enemy coast, by a shell which also damaged one engine. Instead, he had found the unsuspected chemical works when he had just turned for home, with the stuttering engine threatening to cut out altogether. It was an excellently hidden plant, observed on this occasion only because he was forced to fly low, and the slant of moonlight threw a rectangular shadow on the ground where no such shadow should have lain.

Not in the moments of action, but later, came the appreciation that down below him then there were men, helpless like himself, caught up in the machine of war — Dutchmen or Czechs or Poles, possibly, among the Germans — but men, in any case, waiting for the ghastly end which he had made certain. No reluctance to kill could make itself felt at such moments. Had any remained in him, it would not have survived the difficulty he met in keeping the machine steady, mainly on one engine, with the other firing intermittently. After the first lucky hit, the bomber's whole load had been put down accurately into the raging, many-coloured fire, which was spreading swiftly when he left.

A few miles nearer home, the low-flying plane was hit again, and he himself shot up slightly. 'George', the auto-pilot, he found, had been damaged and would not function. With the controls heavy he grew tired by the time they neared the coast; dizziness came and went; he could take little avoiding action when they ran into heavy flak. The port engine cut out finally. The starboard engine coughed and spat throatily for so long that he ordered 'abandon aircraft' — they were over France now: there was always a small chance that the crew might get home from here. He pushed the signal button and saw the wireless operator help the navigator to bale out, and then follow him. He pushed futilely at the button, cursing with pain at the rear-gunner, who did not acknowledge. With an enormous effort Fairburn ordered his muscles to lift his legs off the rudder bar, and noticed with detached approval that though slow, they behaved better than the rear-gunner, who had still not acknowledged. He was right out of the pilot's seat before he realized that the rear-gunner was too badly injured to move. He had climbed back, and nursed his one damaged engine to England, where, as he lost control, his plane had crashed on landing, killing the other wounded man. It had been quite useless, the last and most exacting part of that feat. The bomber had been wrecked and burnt out, but he had been dragged clear in time.

He took off the receiver. 'Hallo?' Now.

'Is that the fishmonger? I should just like to know why you haven't

sent round my order!' A woman's voice came through high pitched
with indignation. 'I should just like to know why, that's all!'

'Madam, I'm sorry . . .' He thought it was laughter which prevented
him from going on. He had grown accustomed to this mistake in the
days of peace, when he shared the flat with a friend, while Mrs. Mott
looked after them both; he could even remember the number which
the caller really wanted, it had a nine in it instead of the five in theirs.
On an average he had told strangers that he was not the fishmonger
about once a month for two years.

The caller was furiously giving a name and address. ' "Sorry!" What
good do you imagine that is? I gave the order in plenty of time. I said
specially it was to be round by twelve. For lunch. And do you know
what the time is now?'

'No, I don't.'

'Quarter to three,' said the voice triumphantly. 'I suppose you're going to say it's on its way. Well, if your boy delivers it now you'll have
to take it back!'

All at once, for him, the sum of human endeavour became no more
than this — the death of an air-gunner whom he had liked — his own
horror of the future — a quivering awareness of other men's endurance
— no more than this; the voice of an unknown person, urgent with
self-importance, strident about something that no longer mattered.

'I shall bring it round myself!' she said.

'If you do,' he told her, in a sudden access of rage, 'I shall be standing just inside the shop. And I shall hit you on the head with a had-
dock.'

He heard her gasp before he put the receiver back and sat with his
sound elbow on the table, still under the impression that he was shaking with amusement. It was a few seconds before he realized that he
was not laughing.

The telephone rang again. People knew the time of the investiture,
and that he had been given sick-leave. They would expect to find him
in by now; he could not hope for another wrong number.

He left it ringing and went out of the flat, stopping at the fishmonger's to forestall a complaint of insolence, in case some assistant
were sacked, and then climbed with great caution to the top of a bus,
the first that came by, going he did not mind where. He was irritated

by the excessive care he took of himself nowadays; a little jolting did not hurt his arm, but he could not help the precautions to avoid any sudden movement.

Seated behind him, two jolly office-cleaners got into conversation over the morning raid. They discussed their places of work, and the war and its leaders circumspectly, neither wishing to venture an unacceptable opinion.

'Did you 'ear 'Alifax on the wireless, dear?'

'I did. What did you think of it?' The Foreign Secretary of the time had recently made a speech on policy, of which two-thirds had been devoted to his belief that God would not countenance defeat for the country — though it fought alone — which officially championed Him, like England. There was a pause.

'Beautiful, wasn't it?' said one tentatively.

'So dignified,' said the other, and there was a second, longer pause, in which Fairburn could feel them measuring each other.

'The Finns were very religious, too, weren't they?' ventured the first, as though this had no bearing on what had gone before.

'*And* the Poles!' said the other, as they burst out into understanding mirth. Fairburn half-turned to look at them. A mail-van swept by the bus. Recovering herself, wiping her eyes, the one who was having most trouble with her loose teeth read out the war-slogan pasted along its side, ' "If you must talk, talk Victory" — D'you know how my daughter puts that? — ' Her voice was lowered in consideration for the man in uniform two seats in front, but it was still audible to attentive ears. 'She says, "If you must talk nonsense, talk Victory!" ' and they roared again.

A grand couple, he thought warmly. Without hope in this world or the next; having no need of hope. The best of the people of England, like the men he fought alongside, the gunners and observers and wireless operators, were wiser and stronger in desperation than their leaders would ever credit, with their anxious talk of confidence when no reasoned confidence was possible.

But if he, too, could go on without personal hope — must go on since there was no alternative — in other ways he needed more than they did: a belief that when his own existence ended, something good would remain, though he had no part in it; some future for the world, worthy of the bright and careless devotion, the cold achievements of valour which he himself had seen over and over again in the air during the last six months above the ill-served airfields of France and in raids on enemy territory. Day after day, of late, the same courage had flamed into new intensity in the fighting over the English channel or the English countryside.

Yet even that assurance of mind was denied him. What chance had mankind of living in anything but an armed camp, for at least the lifetime of everyone now on earth? Whichever side won, even if the improbable happened, as all but the best of the people pretended to themselves to believe — even if England came through the war — what trust could there be between nations after the desperate betrayals and tragedies of the last year? And without trust, how falsely echoed the statesmen's talk of rebuilding a fitting habitation for the soul of mankind. For that, armour and only armour would remain.

But if the gesture were useless, together with gentleness, tolerance and trust in the essential goodness of men, still it was necessary that those who had lived by these things should prove that they could die as faithfully as those who denied them any value, in a world of barren and meaningless savagery.

One of the two jolly women recognized a friend in the street below, getting into the cabin of the bus. They hurtled off the top to join her, everything about them agape and flapping with spirit, from their battered handbags and the plaquets of their straining skirts, to their laughing mouths, which remarkably retained loose plates; these flapped, too, in the gale of their merriment about the funny hat worn by the friend.

He remembered irrelevantly a French Air Force dentist remarking to him with awe that fifty per cent of the teeth in England, real or artificial, seemed to be held in place by native loyalty alone. In France, a logical country, the dentist had insisted, they would fall out with so little support . . . A logical country, France; and there, more important things than teeth had given way — it did not help in war to look logically ahead, either at the personal chance of survival or the use of surviving in the world to come.

Alone on the top of the bus, he sat for a few seconds as he had sat at home, with his head on his hand, his elbow on the back of the seat in front of him. And feeling himself shaking, he thought, this time, that it was not with laughter — to find again, with surprise, that he was wrong. He gulped with sudden laughter, uncontrollably: it was so funny, about the nation's teeth and what the dentist had said!

So this was what it was really like, to lose one's nerve, he thought, one part of his mind aghast while the rest laughed on helplessly at a stale joke which had not seemed very good even when it was first made. He had supposed, before, that he knew all there was to be learnt about the process of losing one's nerve — It was a curious relief to think of this horror in the form of words: 'Losing one's nerve' . . . This had been in the period of long-distance night flying which had ended with his being hit. Then he had imagined that it only meant being aware of fear, to the point of torment, for long stretches of time, whether he happened to be in actual danger or not. (Looking back, this stage seemed almost as remotely innocent as the time when, along with everyone else in the training camp except the instructors, he had thought of losing one's nerve as something that happened to other men, poor devils.)

He gasped for breath, recovering from his laughter. Now that he was out of hospital, with three weeks separating him from flying again, he knew. It meant having this stranger in absolute charge, amused or angry when he was neither, but using his voice for these feelings; as soon, the stranger might be using his body, when he had gone back to his job, dictating to it through terror.

He had a very short time, it seemed to him, in which to rid himself of this stranger. To the urgency of his personal problem it made no difference that those three weeks were likely to settle, as well, the amount of freedom to be known by the world for the next few hundred years, by swinging the mastery of the daylight skies towards one of the two combatants. His enemy had changed, and come too close for him to think of any other.

He had taken for granted the idea that he would spend his sick-leave in London, doing what everyone else did, pressing as much pleasure as possible into the time that remained, except for one week-end with his parents in Cork. Nothing but pity for two people who were anxious about him, with whom he had little in common, had made him agree to go back on a war-time visit, exasperated as he was by the attitude of the country towards neutrality. But now his heart turned longingly not to his home, nor to anyone he knew, but to a place which he had hardly remembered for years; he had not been there since he was a boy. Then he had been happy: at Kildooey, in Donegal. What was that famous letter which a young Irish prisoner had written, long ago, to his girl, so movingly that the judge — also an Irishman, of course — had let him go free when it was read to him by learned counsel? Fairburn could not remember more than a phrase or two: 'I am in a far place . . . but there is a gap in the blue hills through which I can see the sea. And it's there I do be looking the whole day long, for it's more like yourself than anything I can imagine.' In Kildooey there was indeed a gap in the blue hills, and through it shone the sea. It would be nearer to the sweetness of the world he had loved — and life had been very good to Fairburn — than any other place he could hope to find. In Ireland, he knew — grateful at last for her fantastical quality — he would feel further away from the war than he could have done by travelling half-way across the world in his three weeks' reprieve.

He prepared to push his way off the bus against a knot of oncoming passengers. They had reached the stairs first, hampered as he was by the needless wound-caution imposed on all movement by the stranger in charge, against whom he tried once more to make his muscles rebel, and failed. The people coming up saw that one arm was out of the sleeve of his tunic, which bore wings; and they backed away from him with exaggerated concern. A fat man with a red neck passed embarrassing, throaty remarks. (Opposite the bus-stop a newsvendor's blackboard said: 'R.A.F. Lunch-Time Score 48 Nazi planes for 11.') Thank heaven in that other place, he thought, if he let his voice slip back to its childhood's accent, the breathy, sharp Cork tone, almost everyone would consider him a plain fool for getting mixed up in the wrong fight; if not, indeed, a bit of a traitor. It would be very refreshing.

He climbed down like a child, one foot at a time, clinging to the rail, scarlet with anger against himself and the fat man who said 'God bless you, lad', as he passed. But with more inward composure than he had known for days, now that the idea of Kildooey was firmly in his mind as something to which he might look forward, he reflected that so far, at least, he had met better luck in coming to earth, from any

kind of vehicle, than most of his colleagues. One of these had been
mobbed and kissed by thirty-seven damp laundry girls when his plane
crashed in their drying ground: while another, a Czech speaking gut-
tural English, had been peppered in the leg by an excitable farmer
with a shot-gun before he could get free from his parachute. Over
half the pilots with whom Fairburn had trained were already dead.
But he was still alive, and the late summer sun shone on him warmly,
and soon he would be rock-fishing for pollock from the headland at
Kildooey. Desperately, without cause, but because he saw no other
salvation, he centred all his hopes upon Kildooey. In Kildooey, alone,
he would get the better of his cringing, clamouring physical self. The
stranger should let go: enough, at least, to allow him to behave as he
wished, for as long as might be necessary.

Fairburn took a taxi to the office of the Irish shipping company,
making a great effort — knowing that no boat-train left before evening
— to refrain from telling the driver to hurry.

CHAPTER II

FEAR

At the counter, he stood below a pre-war poster suggesting that he
should visit Dublin (where two of his friends were interned, after a
forced landing) and had his new hope crushed at once by an apathetic
clerk. The man seemed more interested in his own fingernails than in
Fairburn's desire to put forward, by a fortnight, the date of the permit
for Eire which he already held. It seemed that the formalities involved,
in passing from England at war into neutral territory, were such that
it would take rather more than a fortnight to alter the papers. Fairburn could put out no further effort at self-control for a while. He
raged in vain, hearing a man, whom he could not stop, making the
kind of scene which had always seemed to him incomprehensible: the
customer with a grievance being rude to an underling not responsible
for the regulations.

'Even with my parents domiciled in Eire?'

'Ah, it makes no difference at all,' said the clerk in a rich Northern accent, while he bit at a piece of loose skin. 'Why do you not go to Ulster, instead, if you are wishful of visiting Ireland?'

'Because I loathe all Six Counties,' said Fairburn. 'Full of bloody Scots.' He suspected the clerk of being an Ulsterman, but this outburst of pure ill-temper acted, surprisingly, like a charm.

'It's the only way, if you are wishful of visiting Ireland immediately. I shall be going in myself that way in a little while.'

'I'm not "wishful of visiting Ireland!" ' Hearing his voice charged with fury, Fairburn looked at the man with apology, but the official face had not altered. 'I just wanted to go to Donegal.'

'Is it the town, or the county of Donegal, you mean?'

'What's it to do with you, if I can't get in now, anyway?'

'Ah, nothing.' The clerk sidled from behind the counter as Fairburn turned away, and caught up with him at the door, where they were out of earshot of the other clerks. 'I'm from Donegal myself: the town.'

'It's Kildooey I had in mind.'

'And I related to half the people in the place! Isn't it the strange thing; as soon as you said "Donegal", I was wondering, can it be Kildooey, if it isn't the town itself? Will you give my regards to Mrs. Sullivan? Three of that name there are, three sisters-in-law. And many more Sullivans besides, unmarried. But Mrs. Mary Sullivan, that's the one. If you forget the name, it's she who saw the ghost, re-member. Tell her, love from Shamus. Now why should I think of Kildooey as soon as you said that about the Scots infesting the Six Counties? When it might just as well be Killibegs or Kilcar you wanted, or anywhere else in Donegal.'

'I couldn't say. But how do I get in?'

'You go by Ulster, amn't I telling you all this time?' said the clerk, irritable in his turn. 'The frontier's closed each night after six o'clock, mind, on the Ballinfaddy road.'

'Closed?'

'Closed. The guarda goes home then. Only a small road it is. There's little traffic by day. Not worth keeping a man by night at the post.'

'So after six, you mean, I just go straight through?'

'Meaning that. Many's the crack I've had with my aunt Sullivan, over the times we'll be seeing when we've pushed Union over on those fat-farming Scots in the Six Counties, and they'll be forced to share and share alike with us at last!'

Fairburn, after another session at the counter, went out with his heart lightened and tickets for the late night train and the next day's boat safe in his wallet. It was true that even for Ulster his papers could not be ready in time, but Shamus was telegraphing to official friends along the route, most of them ex-I.R.A. men, Fairburn gathered, who would be delighted to see that a British officer on leave was not delayed in getting into that part of his own country which they particularly grudged to him. It was like being in Ireland already, he thought.

'You are for Union yourself?' insisted the clerk, accompanying him to the door for the second time. Another newsboy, also with a blackboard for a poster, was shouting the figures of the day's air battle, in the life-and-death struggle of the civilized world.

'I don't give a damn: I'm not an Irishman. I just don't happen to have liked any of the Scots I've met in the North. But it doesn't seem to matter now who owns the Six Counties: you or I or they, except for the ports.' He softened the words with a grin.

'Then why are you visiting Kildooey if you're not one of us?'

'I once spent a week there when I was a boy, and I want to go again. That's all. I know it's the centre of the Gaelic Revival and all, but I'm going to fish for pollock.'

'If I'd known — !' said Shamus, grinning back. 'But I'll let you through, now. So many get in by that road, who shouldn't, that one more won't matter. If you fished trout in Loch Corrib, instead, you'd be breaking your line, half the time, round a German agent. It's better at Kildooey, where there's only the lads at night, drilling in the bogs. *Eire le h-aghaid na eireannacthal!*'

'Not with my help. But thanks. And I'll let Mrs. Sullivan know you're as loyal as ever.'

'Do, now,' said Shamus, and hurried back to the job of random obstruction.

Mrs. Mott's distress, when Fairburn asked her to pack for him at once, was lessened by the siren which sounded while she was reciting the list of people who had rung up to congratulate him. 'It's fidgeting, coming so often, there's no denying that,' she said, listening through

the dying wail to the footsteps hurrying a little — but only a little —
as they passed in the street below the open window. Few people in
London went into shelters by day, even while the air attack was at
its height. 'I dare say you're better away from it all for a bit. Though,
mind you, Mr. Mott won't like your having paid me a share of a whole
year's housekeeping for doing nothing but a bit of dusting. "Can't feel
the money's really earned, can we?" he always says. And now, when
you're out of hospital, I shan't be able to look after you — I don't know
what he'll say.'

('Has the chap left any whisky?' almost for certain, Fairburn reflected, and made a mental note to lock up his drinks for her sake
before he left the flat.)

Did she really believe her respectable myths about her worthless
man? He could not tell, but that she yearned to believe them was
obvious. While all that Mr. Mott required to think about his wife, for
his own self-respect, was that she cooked well and was comfortable
looking, which happened to be true — Men and women's deep mis-
understanding of one another's needs, Fairburn thought again, trying
to keep his imagination from creeping under the skins of the approaching German airmen. They were attacking London in the brilliant,
cloudless weather which he had learnt to dislike on his own account.
From the direction of the Thames estuary, in which his window faced,
came the sound of anti-aircraft guns. Little white puffs, swiftly dis-
solving, appeared in the blue sky, chasing planes too high to be seen
without glasses.

What were they feeling as they came, the men who flew them? No
effort to keep his mind impersonal would succeed now. For the past
fortnight they had been losing a high proportion of their strength in all
daylight raids; but they came, wave after wave, because they had been
ordered to come, just as he had been ordered in the past to sustained
and desperate attacks. And would be again: for this reason alone he
must not think like this. None of them was a free agent. The duller
reverberation of bombs came, land-borne instead of air-borne like the
sound of the guns. He turned from the window. If there were among
them men like himself, capable in moments of action of great nervous
control, and paying for it, in between, out of all proportion to the release of those moments, at least they were in the grip of that ghastly

exaltation now. It did not do, in war, to feel with the other side. It was utterly idiotic at present, with death falling from the air into the London streets. But knowing and hating the job they did, he could summon no anger.

'What'll the I.R.A. do to you, Mr. Fairburn, if they catch you?' asked Mrs. Mott, helpfully, bringing him back to his plans.

Perhaps in Kildooey these thoughts would not come. 'They? Oh, they'll do the same as they did in the Troubles, years ago,' he said. 'Invite me into their houses. Feed me better than they can afford. And tell me stories of killing English soldiers by treachery. Expecting me to see their point of view. And to understand, of course, that if they'd had five minutes' chat with the victims first, they wouldn't have done it, so I'm all right.'

'Why should they do that?'

'I couldn't tell you,' he said, 'I was brought up in Cork, but I'm not really of the country, you know. Still, that's what they'll do, Mottie; don't worry. It's what they did when they burnt my uncle's house while I was staying there. They made up beds for us in the nearest cabins— I was eight, and was nearly torn apart, with everyone wanting to play host.'

'And suppose there's a German invasion while you're there?'

'Well, I can always pass as an Irishman. I'll join the local inhabitants falling over each other in their rush to be kind to them. It'll be your best defence, that hurry. The Germans will look hot and tired when they land. They'll want to know which is the road for Dublin, and is it far? And we'll wave them amiably down the dead-end that stops at the peat-cutting in the bog, saying "Ah, 'tis no distance at all!" Because that'll happen to be the way they're facing, and we won't like to disappoint them by saying the town is fifty miles away in a different direction. Better let their heavy vehicles get bogged than be troubling the poor sweating gentlemen to turn them round.'

'Then they'll come back and shoot you all,' she said, not certain if he were serious or not. Animation had suddenly returned to his voice, and as suddenly died again.

'That'll probably be the quickest way of getting a real understanding with the Irish. Speaking a language they know. Don't put in anything I can do without. I'll borrow the fishing gear. I shall probably be buying a cheap second-hand car to sleep in while I'm over. There's no hotel at Kildooey, you see, nor anywhere near. So I'll want as few things as possible, for the sake of space.'

'Now, that's a dreadful idea, Mr. Fairburn! You camping out; not even with a proper tent. Well, if I told Mr. Mott he simply wouldn't sleep of nights, for thinking of you, trying to make do like that.' Having faced for nearly a year the likelihood that Fairburn would die in the cabin of an aircraft, she became volubly horrified by the notion that he should sleep in a car. Fairburn spent the rest of the day outside the flat, in news-reel houses and a theatre, among small audiences thinned out still further by successive air-raid warnings.

The attendance dwindled less and less on each occasion. Theatres, playing at a loss, were about to stop their evening performances. It was as if, with the approach of night, determination grew among the populace not to be deprived of whatever solace their money could still buy. From an afternoon cinema-audience of about fifty people, less than ten went out, but fewer still from the revue audience of about three hundred, though by then the night raiders were over, coming punctually with the dusk, and in the quieter moments of the show explosions were heard, for the first time that day in the heart of the city.

As the hours of darkness crept on in London, he sensed the mounting fear of the town, now helpless against attack. No enemy planes had yet been brought down in these night raids. Not till an hour or so before dawn could there be hope of respite.

Worst of all, at this period, was the uncertainty in everyone's mind as to how much the bombing could be intensified, beyond what was going on already, night and day. It was the first time Fairburn had been there at night since the full air-attack on the capital began. Elsewhere, on leave during night raids, he had known a pleasant feeling of security, shared with other Air Force men, in listening to anti-aircraft fire with whose efficiency he was not personally concerned. This evening his mind kept harking back, during the leg-show which could not hold his attention, to a fantasy of H. G. Wells's, *The Time Machine,* which had once seemed enchanting to a mechanically-minded boy. It did not seem enchanting or fantastic any longer: it had become madly parallel to the real world, where comely and defenceless creatures fluttered about — the young girls in their summer dresses, who had charmed his eyes all day — laughing while the sun shone and they owned the bright

surface of the earth. In the darkness, whose coming they had tried to
ignore while they could, the unspeakable horror was loose again among
them, to reach out and choose its prey at random — at leisure — at any
moment during the next six or seven hours of listening and waiting.
From them, or others of these changed and anxious people around him,
it would select a handful at a time, night after night, no one knew for
how long, nor how quickly its appetite would grow; and till the daylight returned none of them would know any security save that of the
hunted beast in the herd — the chance that death, when it struck, might
make its blind choice of someone else. 'The people of the upper earth',
Wells had called them: the boy who had delighted in that story had
never day-dreamed of himself among them.

It was like a smell, he thought, this feeling of apprehension rising
from the city to the skies, where the enemy planes droned remotely,
hour after hour, above the tents of brilliance which formed and re-
formed before his eyes when he went out into the darkened street during the interval — the searchlights groping in vain, occasionally lighting up a barrage balloon but nothing more. The anti-aircraft shells
planted the tops of the tents with clusters of golden stars from time to
time. A curiously beautiful effect, he noticed, when seen from the
ground, but not otherwise impressive. London, sprawling over so many
miles, was impossible to miss for the bombers: if they were not picking
their targets in detail there was no need for them to come low enough
for the few guns or searchlights to matter; and the people knew it. It
was disturbing beyond expression, the emanation of close-packed, controlled fear from millions of human beings cowering in shelters, in
cellars, keeping up a fine pretence of indifference in their own homes,
nervously carrying on with gaiety or trying to sleep, if they were work-
ers who must sleep, with vaselined cotton wool in their ears, or their
bedclothes over their heads, or their windows closed in the stuffy night;
striving to shut out the noise of death which was all that they could
shut out.

As he came back into the foyer, a middle-aged man said, 'That's a
German', to the pulsing beat of a twin-engined plane floating down to
them. It was very curious, this strolling in and out of a theatre, with
women in evening dress about, moving at a step into the utmost savagery
of war.

'There's no way of telling by sound,' said Fairburn with authority, noticing, in the dim light, the apprehension on the face of an elderly woman beside him. 'We've got some new twin-engine fighters. It might be one of our patrols.' He had forgotten that he had changed out of uniform, and was heatedly snubbed by the middle-aged man, whose brother-in-law, it appeared, was in the Air Ministry and had taught him how to tell the difference.

As if to back up his claim, a bomb crashed about quarter of a mile away in the next few seconds. The man darted a nasty look at him. 'That couldn't have been from the plane we heard,' Fairburn began. 'Too close. Don't you see that if he wasn't diving — if he was just cruising at about a hundred and eighty miles an hour, say fifteen thousand feet up, he wouldn't hit anything within a radius of —' and then noticed that the frightened woman had gone. He stopped, mumbled something, returned the truculent look, and went back to his seat — pleased to find, for once, that he was neither unbearably irritated nor wanting to laugh. He could not really be in as bad a state as he feared, one part of his mind pleaded with the other. He had behaved sensibly, under fair provocation.

In a moment he knew why the trivial incident had not stirred him like the events of the earlier day; he was prey to a new and overwhelming anxiety. Would his train run, despite the raid, and could he reach the station in time? He must get to Kildooey, without delay.

Though it was still an hour too early, and his bag was already at the luggage office, he left the theatre at once and walked to the Underground; some of the stations remained open though all the lifts had stopped working. On the way he passed through a silence that seemed unbelievable in the midst of nine million breathing creatures.

No taxis and very few private cars were feeling their way along the dark caverns of the streets. At this period London was not yet putting up its costly barrage for the poor comfort of its people, longing for the noise of something being done even if that something should prove ineffective; and the raiding planes still husbanded their loads, dropping bombs only at long intervals as they cruised with their engines throttled down almost to stalling speed. For each machine to achieve its greatest effect, in disturbing the yet unseasoned nerves of industry, the pauses in the attack were as valuable as the long-awaited crash of explosions. Aware of the absurdity of what he did, Fairburn found himself trying to walk more and more softly along the deserted pavements; it was as if he were the only living thing for miles which was not holding its breath.

Throughout the long wait at Euston, until the express actually pulled out, he was sure that the departure would be cancelled, or that there would be a direct hit on the station. For distraction he started up a conversation with another traveller to Ireland who had arrived too early, and regretted it for the rest of the journey: the man turned out to be the most tiresome type of Irishman abroad, who acted himself for the other's benefit, telling long and whimsical tales of his own inconsequent behaviour. There was one, which seemed to Fairburn to go on all night, about a bootshop in Dublin and the Irishry of the narrator's feet in refusing to take the same size shoes; he got into Fairburn's carriage in order to finish it. No sleeping berths were available; the two sat up side by side all night, Fairburn aware that the other kept a wakeful eye on him, ready to burst into reminiscence again whenever he stirred.

At Liverpool he received, with a feeling of triumphant anger, the news that the day-boat service had been temporarily suspended. He might have expected this; Kildooey was not to be reached so easily. Enemy submarines were reported in the channel between the Stranraer passage and the Bristol minefield, and survivors of a torpedoed ship were rumoured to be landing that morning in the docks; the risk of sailing before dark could not have been justified, and in any case the shipping company was acting under Admiralty orders in interrupting the service; but he loafed about the town all day, seething to himself about the mismanagement of public utilities, devising phrases which might have appeared in letters signed 'Pro Bono Publico'; and the realization of how pompous they were in no way lessened his indignation.

Killing time, he made a game of avoiding the company of the friendly Irishman, merciless in pursuit of an audience. Twice during the day Fairburn felt impelled to take a tram back from the town to the shipping office in the docks to make sure that the time of the evening embarkation had not been changed; the bored amusement of the clerks in the office grew more and more humiliating. On the last occasion he was caught by his train companion, whom he greeted with overdone cordiality to make up for former curtness. He could not shake the man off again. Inability to be firm took over from the mood of unwilling rudeness, with which it seemed to alternate, at a time when rudeness would at least have set Fairburn free from the miserable pretence of being amused, in a state of loneliness more intense than anything he had yet known.

They queued up together to go on board. With two shiploads of passengers to accommodate, the boat would be crowded to the limit allowed by war-time regulations. As they moved slowly towards the ship's side, Fairburn burned with exasperation through a sequel to the boot-shop story, in which the vagaries of the Irishman's shoe-fittings led to even quainter extravagances of word and situation. There was a pause when they reached the gang-plank. Fairburn was aware of someone immediately behind him, and the need to make a return, conversationally, for the man's attempt to interest him. He half turned, and out of the depths of wretchedness produced the remark, 'As far as I know my feet are exactly the same size', to find that he had made it to a stranger, the Irishman having gallantly stepped back for a woman to precede him.

The woman stared at him blankly. Fairburn stared back, incapable at the moment of accounting for a statement of such startling idiocy. It shot across his mind that probably she had not even noticed that someone else had been talking to him. Then she laughed, at the appeal in his look; and they moved on, to be parted by the crowd in the ship.

CHAPTER III

AT SEA

ALL anxieties took on the same importance. Dread of the future, and the probability that someone on board, whom he was not likely to meet again, considered that he was mad — neither of these mattered more nor less than the clearing of the night sky, which had been overcast up till the time of embarkation, so that when the moon rose, as it would during the crossing, the ship must become visible as a target for attack from air or sea.

He had given no thought until now to the risks of the sea passage, so small in comparison with those to which he had grown — not hardened, because one did not grow hardened to the shadow of death, lying between oneself and the things in the sunshine. (As the spirit tired, the shadow grew colder, and its touch less endurable.) But familiar with it he was, at least, and until now he had always been able to weigh one hazard reasonably with another. He knew from his own experience the difficulty of hitting a ship from the air, even by day, and for hours he had been fulminating to himself against the giving of any consideration to the other possibility — attack by submarine. If the navy were doing its job, with the cooperation of Coastal Command — this was the gist of all the pursy letters he had composed during the day — these narrow coastal waters should be adequately guarded. Considering the chances taken daily in other essential services, what was a sea passage of eight hours, that the Irish boat should not run to schedule?

Yet, in spite of this, the atmosphere of the ship took hold of him, soon after coming on board: it was one of furtiveness and anxiety. To most of the passengers the crossing was only a brief danger to be borne and finished with before daylight. To the men who ran the vessel it was part of a strain and responsibility which was increasing, now, week by week, as the attack against the ports and shipping grew fiercer, but no one yet felt that he had the full measure of the enemy's strength. This was the heart of all fear throughout that summer — the doubt whether the known worst were anything to compare with the horror and suffering which might be freed upon the country, from one moment to the next.

Twice lately the Irish packet had been bombed. The time of sailing was kept secret until the moment when she left the dock, to the wail of the port sirens heralding the regular evening raid, by which people in the town maintained that they had learnt to set their watches. She slipped into the Mersey several hours after the embarkation at dusk. No last minute preparations for leaving had been noticeable, either from the quay or on board. Through long hours of waiting she had been kept ready, with men lounging near the hawsers; and when she was about to sail the only sign was that the passengers were shepherded below decks. It was the one way of ensuring that no landsman used a pocket torch on deck, started a pipe carelessly, or opened a door which might let out a gleam of light.

With a double load on board the passengers could not find enough seats below-decks, and stood packed in the lounges and smoke-room. Though all the cabins had been booked up in advance, so that Fairburn failed to get one, no one seemed anxious to turn in, despite the fact that this end of the passage, being the darker, would certainly be safer than the other, in the moonlight. The attentive Irishman had found some other exiles returning home; Fairburn was able to edge his way out of their circle unnoticed. It was perhaps the one excuse for the exist-ence of nations, he thought, that people were much nicer where they felt sure that they belonged. Having no one to be typically Irish at, with Irishmen all about him, the man who had been such a nuisance in the train was telling a good and un-Irish story exceedingly well when Fairburn drifted away.

He was very tired; he had had little sleep in London except by day since he came out of hospital, and almost none during the previous night in the train. But it was impossible to get out of range of four or five conversations going on in the press around him: Sentimental con-versations, 'All in the front line equally now . . . Everyone in London behaving like a hero.' Knowing conversations, 'Simply a feint in Nor-way.' The new mythology of the war, 'They say you can't hear the whistle of the bomb that's going to hit you.' Angry conversations, where people fresh from the bombed areas were working off their sudden release from tension, 'Do them good in the country to get some of what we've been having in town. They think this war's no worse than the last!'

This remark was from a middle-aged couple, aware that they had formed a ring of hostility round them by trying to bribe a steward to get them chairs more comfortable than those which they already oc-cupied; much older people were perched on suit-cases; and mothers, worn to an ineffectual scolding, stood on guard over their restless chil-dren, lest they should be trampled, lying on the floor.

'It's ridiculous,' said the woman of the pair, 'herding us down below like this. Suppose a bomb came through that ventilator, eh?'

Getting no response from the people nearest to her, she bent forward and addressed her indignation to a half-turned back. A tall woman was leaning against a nearby settee which two nuns had managed to secure for themselves. (They were sitting bolt upright, telling their beads, getting no benefit from the coveted back-rest. He might have been in Ireland already, Fairburn thought again, judging this time from the number of black-habited figures of both sexes about him, not quite making the most of the only comfortable places.) 'What do you say to that, eh?'

'To what? I'm sorry, I didn't hear —' The tall woman turned and Fairburn recognized her as the person he had astounded with fatuous information about his feet. He had a ray of hope: that she might have taken no particular notice of his face, and would not know him again.

'Suppose a bomb came through that ventilator?'

'I shouldn't give it a second thought!' the tall woman said lightly. It was a grim joke and neither of the pair to whom it was made saw the special implication of the words.

'I think you have not had experience of bombing!' the man said ruefully, shaking his head.

She started to reply and changed her mind, smiling instead. Her eye caught Fairburn's in understanding. She had a curious brief smile which pulled down the corners of her mouth and, in a second, had left no trace on the very fair, thin face. A woman of about thirty, not well turned out, he thought, her clothes were creased with travelling; he did not realize till afterwards that it was only because they had once been extremely expensive that she kept so much as an air of crumpled elegance; they were put on without interest. She was not even freshly made-up. The paint on the lips was there by habit, and wearing thin on the inner side; but it occurred to him that he had rarely seen a face which had more of a quality he could not name for a moment, and then the word came to him: serenity. It was not a quality he looked for in the ordinary way; the setting of the moment made it more admirable to him than any other.

It was hot in the saloon; he wore his overcoat loosely over his shoulders, so that it hid the damaged arm, and would not take it off, believing that even in civilian clothes the injury brought him glances of interest or sympathy. He began to make his way out, passing close to the tall woman. When he had gone a few steps beyond her he turned back. The look of serenity was just exhaustion, he realized from nearby. He had learnt to know that glazed, aloof mask on men's faces.

'There may be some way of getting on deck,' he said, 'in spite of the regulations. I'm going to try, anyway. Would you like to come too? It'll be cooler out of here, anyway.'

She nodded and followed him. As a small boy, crossing several times a year to school in England, he had made himself a nuisance to the stewards and crew by exploring their private domains; he remembered the internal lay-out of these ships. Down to the lowest deck, along to the pantry and through, when no one was about, into the crew's quarters, and then up to one of the forward entrances not used by passengers, and so left unfastened; it was not difficult while the harassed stewards were engaged in trying to satisfy the people clamouring for service in the dining-room.

The freshness and gloom outside seemed very welcoming. Towards the open sea the sky was lit by the flashes of the shore batteries, firing back, over the ship, at the planes attacking the docks behind them. In the shelter of the hatchway, where they remained very still to avoid notice, they were invisible to one another. He found himself counting, after the flicker from the guns, to get the range of their firing, feeling his muscles tensing involuntarily at about 'eight, nine, ten — ', waiting for the burst of the shell. He must remember that, for the moment, it meant nothing to him. He would think comfortably, instead, of his small escape; obviously this woman could not have identified him with the imbecile who spoke to her on the gang-plank, or she would not have come with him.

He took off his coat, glad that he could do so without drawing attention to his empty sleeve, and insisted that she should use it as a cushion.

'And how are your remarkably symmetrical feet?' she asked. He could feel the swift-passing smile in her voice, and the hot blood starting to climb in his face, and then all at once the incident fell back into perspective. It no longer mattered as desperately as everything else. It no longer mattered at all. One anxiety, at least, had died.

'I was hoping you hadn't recognized me,' he said. 'I'm sorry — '

'Not at all,' she told him, with a curious gravity of indifference. Her voice was at variance with the lightness of the words, the trivial jokes current between strangers at this time. 'It's a pleasant change to start a conversation without the usual bomb-doodlery that has to be got over first. Before anything interesting can be said.'

'All right.' He smiled back at her in the darkness. 'Then we won't tell one another about our bombs, and how close they came. I could explain why I spoke to you like that.'

'You don't need to. Standing in that queue, I heard quite a lot of the boot story!'

'Well, my feet are doing nicely. But if you'd care to share the coat I'd sit down, all the same.'

She spread it out for him, and a feeling of intimacy grew between them, because, sitting cramped together in the hatchway, it was necessary to whisper. Once or twice figures came close to them, and they flattened their backs against the woodwork, holding their breath lest someone should be going below by this entrance, but the figures passed on. There was much activity on deck; the ship had recently been armed, and hoped for the chance to reply if she were attacked again.

It troubled them both that they could not smoke. She was friendly and easy to talk to, but as time went on the feeling of intimacy became, not more real, but less. It was like the darkness of the shores between which the ship made her way skilfully, turning by almost invisible marks on the black tide. From the look of them, these banks might have been part of some lost, dead, featureless land, yet under cover of the blackness, he knew, almost within hail, thousands of men were at work, along some of the busiest wharves in the world. The deserted air of the shores was an illusion, like the warmth of her voice and her nearness; they were all illusions.

I might be talking to a ghost, he thought; sure, somehow, that only part of her mind was answering him. Even so, it seemed better company at the moment than most people's full attention. At least one could say anything to a ghost.

She observed, 'It's funny, one's got used to the black-out in London. In a ship it still seems odd, doesn't it? — such lit places.'

'Do you travel much?' As he asked it, this seemed to him an absurd question to put to a ghost. 'I mean, did you before the war? In what I still think of as "real life"?'

The range of the anti-aircraft guns shortened till the red stars were gleaming almost overhead; but the noise of their own engines drowned those of the plane, for which searchlights were now groping; the dead shores had abruptly sprung into life.

'Yes.' The raider was flying on: the bursts were feeling through a further patch of sky. 'I think it's rather a dull and laborious way of getting to know people one couldn't meet otherwise. I don't enjoy travel for its own sake, but just for the people. I can't imagine travelling to see places. For the sake of half a dozen remarks, heard on the way to India — remarks which wouldn't have been made on any other trip — well, it was worth going to India.'

The guns roared as a battery abreast of them came into action.

'Shells. Going up,' he said quickly, through the rustle and whine that she might so easily mistake for a falling bomb. He felt impelled to add, apologetically, 'But I'm sure you didn't think it was anything else'. What odd courtesies one paid women in these days!

In the ensuing silence, his mind followed sickly, 'three, four, five — '. A three-mile range. She said, 'As a matter of fact I didn't think that was a bomb. Although I haven't heard gunfire so close before — which is strange. In a way. I expected to — .' She stopped abruptly; he could hear the intake of her breath in the quiet before the next salvo. 'You see, I was in Paris when most of us still believed the town would be defended, and instead we — welcomed them in.'

'We?'

'We, the French. I know I don't sound it, but I'm French.'

'Oh!' At the time of which she spoke, the German entry into Paris early in June, he had been flying, four or five times a day, from a French army airfield where his own and two other hard-pressed squadrons had taken over most of the work of its escadrilles. The Commandant of these had announced, with immovable logic, that they would now fly twice a day — 'Puisque c'etait leur devoir' — but not more — 'A quoi bon, puisque tout est vendu?' (During their two flights, the French airmen had done magnificently.) It was their airfield, they had insisted to the last. Remaining behind when it was evacuated, they alone were to be responsible for demolition. Hangars were being blown up when Fairburn took off from the cratered ground for the last time, too drunk with lack of sleep to care. Later he had narrowly escaped being shot down by what he took to be a friendly machine, recognizing it as one of theirs. Later still he heard that sixty French aircraft on the ground had been left behind intact. A man with a light-pistol — and plenty of these were among the abandoned stores — could have destroyed them all before he left by walking along the lines, firing one shot each into the tanks. They were being refuelled as Fairburn climbed into his own plane. This must have saved the Germans at least two hours in putting them into action against the retreating British infantry.

That, and so much more, lay between the strangers talking; in the careful evenness of her voice, trying not to sound bitter, saying 'we — welcomed them', and the abruptness of his 'Oh'. And yet it was nothing; the sharpness on his part had been without intention, a mixture of gaucherie and surprise — she had such a thoroughly English voice. Still more it was the result of weariness of mind and body; he could not bring himself to search for words in which to explain, to a stranger, that in his opinion there should be no sense of responsibility between individuals for the acts of nations. It seemed to him that this must be so obvious, to any reasonable person, that it need not be said; and by anyone unreasonable it would not be understood or believed, however plainly put.

She said: 'In the old days I often wondered at my Jewish friends. They would go ramming the fact of their Jewishness down other people's throats. Particularly if it wasn't noticeable, lest they should be accepted as something they weren't. I used to think it was silly of them, and rather tiresome. Because nobody minded either way, among the people I knew. But I do the same thing myself, now, about being French. To porters, and shop assistants, and you.'

'Well, I certainly don't mind.'

He thought again of the sixty planes. On personal grounds it would be far more sensible to throw her overboard for that than it was for the young Germans in the sky to be killing hotel clerks and typists and their families who happened to be in Liverpool, now several miles astern of this creeping ship. At the moment some cheerful companions of his own were probably on their way to kill other irrelevant people, who chanced to live too near the unfortunate railway junction at Hamm; it was a fine bombing night. Soon it would be his turn again.

Another wave of raiders was almost overhead. Hoping to escape notice, the ship would not fire unless she were directly attacked, but the shore batteries were opening up again. He wanted his companion to talk; of anything not connected with the war, but could himself find nothing to say. As if she knew this, in the intervals between the salvos the disembodied voice beside him went back to the remote experiences of a peace-time traveller in search of humanity. It was a curious conversation and, at the moment, exactly the conversation he wanted. 'I once shared a table for three meals a day, several weeks on end, with a saint. A real saint. That was on the way to India. A bustling little Scotswoman whose conversation flowed on without a pause, and was made up of statements that East, West, Home is Best; and there's nothing like a nice cup of tea, is there? Also it's just as well to be prepared for everything, though there's no sense in meeting trouble half-way. They were all made with an air of bright discovery. It wasn't till just before we landed that I found out what she did: she'd been working for eighteen years at a medical mission, dealing with over a thousand cases of ophthalmia a year, mainly among the native children. It wasn't reticence that had kept her quiet, she just wasn't interested in her work by that time. Neither the medical nor the missionary side. And once she'd started talking about it, she managed to be as uninspiring about that as about everything else. But she went on with it in the same way that if she'd been a secretary or a dressmaker, for eighteen years, she'd certainly have gone on being a secretary, or a dressmaker. Never wondering whether there was any point in what she did. Some time before I met her she'd had one eye infected, and been home to spend six months in a dark room. On our trip she was coming back from a second bout. Both eyes had been despaired of, but some of her sight had been saved. Enough to go on with. Unless she caught it again, which would mean permanent blindness. I gathered that the work she did was almost entirely useless, and she knew it. Most of the children got reinfected within the year, when the next fig season came round. You see, latex from the figs — '

The shattering roar of the guns came again — 'latex from the figs', said the uncaring voice out of another world, 'is the best possible germ-culture for this particular type of ophthalmia. On the working-reverse of the principle we were told about in childhood, "Wherever there's a nettle you're sure to find a dock-leaf nearby to take the pain away" — wherever you meet a particularly filthy disease, you can count on the perfect carrier being just around the corner. The children got latex on their fingers and then touched their eyes, crawling with flies, and sixty per cent of reinfected cases were hopeless from the start. My saint didn't even like the Indians — feckless people, she said, and so cruel to animals. She was just a saint. Much more memorable than any temples I saw later. I went on to Ceylon —'

'Look here,' he interrupted. 'I must warn you, we'll be getting shrapnel down in about three minutes. Not from the guns here; the ones ahead. The angle from their last shoot was just right. This hatch wouldn't be proof against it. Oughtn't you to go below for a bit?'

She treated this as a kindly spirit might; it was a courteous idea of his, but had no practical importance. 'Oh, I don't think so,' she said, and went on with her infinitely remote conversation. This was not courage; at the moment, he felt, she could not possibly be afraid; and the phrase came into his head, 'Nothing to lose'.

'Ceylon ought to be memorable for all sorts of things. So it is when you see it through someone else's eyes, or a camera. A lovely country. But it was there I overheard the shortest and most mysterious conversation which has ever bothered me. And it's bothered me for years. I still can't think of any explanation of it. I was sitting by my hotel window on the first floor, and two middle-aged Englishmen were going by in the street below. Government officials or respectable business people, I imagined, from what I could see of them; they couldn't see me. One said, "Charming woman. Charming". And the other said, "Pregnant, of course?" And then they were out of earshot. Whenever Ceylon comes into my mind, that's what comes first. It shouldn't be, I know. And wouldn't be, in any mind that could be broadened by travel. But mine can't, and it is.'

'Could they have been doctors?' he suggested, laughing with her. 'That would make sense.' (But this did not make sense at all, this further lightening of the load of fear because someone talked nonsense to him, scarcely attending to it herself; the living ghost of a woman socially adept, accustomed to entertaining, exerting herself by habit to amuse a companion.)

'I thought of that, too. But they weren't doctors. I'm certain. There isn't any profession except schoolmastering that stamps a man so clearly, is there?'

They waited, and the shrapnel missed the ship, which was lifting now to the first of the channel swells. In a little while they were out of the area of the raid. The conversation drifted back to something she had said: the reversal of a childhood's law; and on from that, taking suddenly a different tone, to the reversal of all laws, all reason, all ordinary values in war.

'People got accustomed in the last war — more or less — to the idea that for a man to be young and fit meant that he was more likely to die young. To be sure of survival, then, he needed to be sick or mentally defective. But this time — this war — it's so ingenious, the number of new things that have been turned inside out. Even among the simpler moralities. Down to the trivial point that those who looked on their servants as human beings, in peace-time, refused to live in houses with basements. And now, in all the bombed towns, they're at a disadvantage with those who didn't care, and so have underground rooms to sleep in. Where, if they aren't safe, at least they're safer from flying glass, which makes the worst wounds. That's trivial, but it's also typical.'

'The idea of appeasement,' he said. 'That's been turned inside out too. The word smells now in all decent noses. Appeasement as between nations. But nations are sets of individuals, and between individuals it means kindness; and understanding to call out kindness and understanding in return. It can't mean anything else. The best way of dealing with other people; in fact, the only reasonable way. But now it smells.'

It was as though both were thinking aloud, not helped by the other, but so certain of understanding that there was no need to stop and see whether they were in agreement. He had not known that exciting experience before. She said: 'Telling the truth as one saw it — I suppose that was the thing which used to seem most worth-while. Fundamentally worth-while. To people who thought at all, that is. Telling it in various ways, with art, science, personal integrity. To-day it must hardly ever be told. Not in entirety.'

'That isn't a new thing in war.'

'No, but surely there's never been a war in which it was essential for more people to believe in more lies. "It's better for the masses to be fed on deception" — that was the principle which anyone with a head as well as a heart struggled against, in peace, because it seemed the greatest possible betrayal of everything good in humanity; well, it's come into its own now. It *is* better. Encourage the people to believe in a God who has allowed this horror to break out again, and will now take sides in it. Our side. He's a valuable antidote to panic. Just over a year ago I don't think I had a single intimate friend who didn't regard religion as one of the mischievous things with which there could be no compromise: a prop of social injustice, the self-respecting reason for leaving bad conditions as they are. (Why not leave them as they are, with heaven and all its compensations waiting just round the corner? To be won by sacrifice here below.) But I fancy all those people would agree that God's too useful as propaganda even to be laughed at, for the moment.'

Fairburn thought of the two gay women on the bus. They wanted no support from grave pretences. But they were the strong element in the population. And even the strong might not always be strong. He thought of letters received from mothers, in answer to his miserable efforts at sympathy, when brother officers were killed. For the time being it was indeed better to let them imagine that the pleasant lads they loved had not ended for ever in the mess of broken bones or burnt flesh of which he knew. Many such letters spoke of reunion, but whether the writers really looked forward with hope, after the first intolerable weeks of grief, he could not guess. Only one woman, whom he had seen personally, had pressed him for his own view of the possibility of personal survival, and of course he had lied.

He said: 'I think most kindly people have always felt that it was more forgivable to lie to the old and the middle-aged than the young.'

'But now, if it makes it easier for them to die, it's become right to lie to the young, too. Probably it's easier for the young to die deceived about all sorts of things. Purity of national motives — if the black is entirely on one side, and the white on the other, the issue is so much simpler. And about the fate of their cause in the hands of those who survive. And the safety of the people they leave behind.'

She said that; it was he who added: 'And they've got to die. Some of the things for which this war is being fought — they're important

enough to be worth anyone's life. Freedom of thought; a certain kindliness — perhaps kindliness above all — a chance for the world to grow
up, and not be arrested at the mental age of a blood-thirsty boy scout.
For the rest, we're fighting for a good deal, I take it, that neither you
nor I like at all? Privilege, tradition, superstition. We mayn't be still,
by the end of the war, but we are now, at least in many people's minds.'

'For the last six weeks I've been working in Stepney,' she told him.
'Till the local authorities found I was a foreigner. (Or rather till I
impressed it on them, against my will, as I did on you. And then they
had to tell me I couldn't go on because of the Aliens' Restriction Bill.
Not as the law stands at present, that is. And we were all very sorry
together.) I scrubbed floors among professional lovers of the poor, and
listened to them repeating bits of contemporary folk-lore, like "Every
Londoner a Hero", and saying that slum-products must have a fairer
deal, after the war, because they're such grand people. Nonsense. The
worst of the London poor are bestial, scarcely human. Such people
mustn't exist, nor the conditions that bred them. That's why there's
got to be a fairer deal. Because the human results of extreme poverty
are disgusting. Not because they're lovable. I know it's absurd to be
irritated by anything so small as a national catch-phrase. When Britain
really is fighting for a good many of the things she says she is, and
those do happen to be the ones that matter most. But it's just another
upside-down aspect of the war that the professional lovers of the poor,
like God, are really doing useful work in some places. (In Stepney they
kept the shelters more or less sanitary, some of them, anyway.) And
so they mustn't be discouraged till afterwards. When the good they
do will certainly be outweighed again, by the harm they do in holding
up any really drastic change.'

'Yet you say you didn't want to leave the job?'

'No. I wanted to go on working. But I've no complaint that the
authorities wouldn't let me, though I very much needed something
to do. For my own sake, that is. This thin, high shrieking of the
intellectual press about the treatment of aliens in England — the waste
of their good intentions — in war it's idiotic to fuss too much over
the less awful kinds of waste. Any more than you would if a bird
used your hat for the wrong purpose in the middle of an earthquake.'
(So ghosts could laugh at their own plight. How pleasantly they could

laugh. And how reassuring it was to laugh with them.) 'I'd have had no complaint if they'd interned me,' she said, in the tired, far-off voice that laughter warmed for so short a time. 'Instead of advising me quite gently to go away, which is what I'm doing. (You, though? You're on leave from the Army, I take it?')

A brilliant flash lit up the distant shore: something considerable, probably an ammunition store, had been hit. The guns fired again astern of them. The question remained unanswered. Let her think that; it was near enough.

'As an outsider,' she went on fairly, 'I do know that about one-third of the East End population are behaving magnificently. Better than anyone had any right to expect. Another third, just as you'd guess. More calmly than most Germans or French in the same position. But not as toughly as most Spaniards or Finns. And one-third as badly as possible. They've never had control of anything in their lives — certainly not the conditions in which they exist and work — so why should they control themselves now, at a time of terror? Having got into the best shelter that's going, why should they make room in it for anyone else who can be kept out? Or leave anything so that it can be used again by others? They don't, that third; I know because so much of my time was spent in cleaning up after them. Listening to the news-bulletins, these days, I wish I could believe the R.A.F. consisted wholly of people too young to know anything of the lives for which they're losing their own.'

'Most of them wouldn't care whether the people they die for are worth preserving,' he told her. 'You needn't worry about that! I've heard a man say, "To think they *pay* us for doing this!" — a fighter pilot; he's been killed since — he meant what he said, too. It wasn't to a girl, or to impress anyone. It was said in a kind of ecstasy, to another pilot in a bomber squadron. The other man agreed at the time.'

'You mean, "And is also dead?"' she asked, a certain horror in her voice making it more alive than he had yet heard.

'No, we don't all die so soon!' he told her aggressively, angry because she had brought him back to his own affairs, the cage from which he had escaped.

'Oh — I didn't realize — !' Her voice trailed off, shaken.

In the silence between them he strained his ears across the water for the sounds of danger, but there was nothing to be heard now besides the noises of the lightless ship creeping watchfully over the dark water. Forgetting that she could not see, he smiled at her in remorse. ' "We" in my case — as you gather! — means one of the people who mustn't be told the truth — the flying men less than anyone else, I take it, while this particular phase of the war is on?'

'I ought to have thought — but I guessed, "Army", and you didn't contradict — I'm sorry!' She sounded more distressed than he had imagined possible for someone so withdrawn. ' "Army" is so blessedly non-combatant — just at the moment, anyway! It's rather horrible, finding you're in the R.A.F. after what we've been saying. And, I suppose, the pilot who agreed . . . ?'

'Yes.' Harking back, he said: 'Mustn't hear the truth, or tell it — ' and was talking again to a ghost before he realized how much he had longed for this moment.

'The worst times are never in the air, of course, but on the ground. In between flights. Waiting to be briefed, knowing you'll be up in six hours. Piloting a bomber at night — a lot of it's too inhuman and mathematical to be anything but cold-blooded. Except at intervals, and they're short, compared with the waiting. Actually, up there I was always quite absorbed in the mechnical routine. And I'll be able to manage that again. But on the ground — ' Irrelevant thoughts came into his mind, and were spoken as they came.

She did not say anything. 'Isn't it absurd, that brought up in Ireland during the Troubles, I've never been able to take violence seriously? At least, I've never felt that it ought to be taken seriously. A uniform's still something that if a man has to die in it — well, it seems an undignified way for him to go out; in fancy dress. I suppose that'll change in time; the feeling, I mean. I once had to say embarrassing things to the ground staff about fighting to the last man and the last round in defence of the airfield. I was anxious that nobody should ask me what to do if the two didn't coincide. Ought I to say that the remaining three or four men should toss up for the last round; but what could the final survivor do if he saw no chance of using it before he was captured: swallow it? (Nobody did ask me, of course. I suppose I shouldn't have felt so isolated if they had.)'

She put her hand out to him, and felt him jerk away from the touch on his strapped arm.

'Oh, that too! I hadn't noticed — with your coat on — '

'You didn't hurt,' he reassured her. 'It's quite old, as these things go. And the jump is mostly habit on my part.'

She questioned him and was given baldly an account of the journey home and the crash; he kept to himself the firing of the chemical works, about which horror had built itself subsequently in his mind. He was still not quite sure of her — would she regard it as something of which he was secretly proud, even while he spoke of it with revulsion?

He said: 'Our wings are albatross wings, they have to be called "the sparrow's arms", among our lot. They *always* have to be called "the sparrow's arms", do you understand? (And I'm thirty, too old for this job, I think — though some of our best pilots are older.) That sort of habit — "sparrow's arms", "I've got my fingers crossed, in front of my mind" — it sticks, as you noticed. Even when it doesn't come easily, at first, it sticks after everything that fits in with it has got lost. There was a lot of excitement for me in the idea — just the idea — of flying for a purpose, in war. (Because I'd flown a lot in civil life, for fun.) The glamour of it carried me through my training. Well, it had to, or I shouldn't have got through. There's no nun in Ireland more carefully tested for a vocation, in the novice state, than a pilot — ' He stopped and with his sound arm groped for one of hers, moved over and linked his with it.

'Gliding was my hobby in peace-time. It's got nothing to do with flying, in the sense of hurling machinery about the air by force, with a lot of noise. It's much more like sailing, only about a thousand times better. The most delightful thing I've ever known — yes, still the most delightful! It would be again, I think, if I could go back to it now — nothing to do with mechanical flight, in my mind; the perfect preliminary training for it, in everyone else's. The gliding clubs — well, in the four I belonged to I don't think there was a single member who wasn't down for the R.A.F. by the end of September last year. It'd have taken a lot of moral courage not to be. In fact I don't think it was considered by any of us, unless there was a doubt of being up to the physical standard — eyesight or something. The only question you heard discussed was how much it could shorten our training, what we already knew. (It shortened it quite a lot. At least half of those lads are dead, because they got into action before we out-armoured the German machines.) I was considered particularly lucky, I'd got a civil flying Certificate A. I'd gone in for it to see whether I liked that side of flying (and decided I didn't, much). But mind you, I didn't actually dislike the prospect. I wasn't a martyr. There was a lot of glamour. I suppose in the early stages I saw myself a bit through other people's eyes, too. As I say, enthusiasm lasted just long enough.

'Then I flew into real war and loathed it. I was surprised to find I hated it so soon. I was frightened (of how much I hated it. At least, that was what it was at first). And I had to go on doing it and making a good job of it. Everyone round me still assumed that flying was the one thing worth doing; and the one thing I wanted to do. There wasn't anything much said about this. There never is. It's taken completely for granted. As a matter of fact, when do you ever hear people say that breathing is essential to living; but then you don't meet anyone who doesn't think so, do you, so why discuss it? Well, it's like that.

'I'd expected to be alone at times through fear — I knew all about that; I'd been scared stiff, gliding, over and over again, in a convection cloud — I'll tell you what it's like some day,' he said, forgetting that when this voyage was over he could not expect to see her again. 'But then we hadn't any responsibility for anything but ourselves, the cloud and I. It was our affair entirely when the cloud suddenly chose to stop chucking me around, or I decided to get out of the lift. There was no need to go on when I didn't feel like it. I hadn't expected — I don't know — "the sparrow's arms" feeling. Of being right out of touch, after a bit, with the boy who said, "To think they pay us for doing this", because it was such bliss to kill in the air. With his successors, that is, because he didn't last long enough for me ever to disagree with him. But he's got plenty of successors. Even when I found I couldn't honestly agree any more, I thought it wouldn't matter. I could pretend, and manage the same line of bright talk — "Oh, it's an old English custom, bribing the mercenaries." And be all right by myself. There didn't happen to be anyone of my own kind where I was stationed. Or if there was, I didn't discover them — daren't — "the sparrow's arms" for ever. One or two I thought might be. But they got smashed up or disappeared, before we really talked. There was one gunner—' He stopped again, still unable to speak, even to a ghost, of the man whose life he had not managed to save.

'To be entirely by oneself among desperately gallant children — yes, I do understand. Go on.'

'Children who'd managed to keep what I'd lost. Much decenter as children than I was an adult — do you understand? But I went on with the job all right for a bit. Through the part you were talking about — the collapse of France, and the Dunkirk period. Then in the normal way I was sent to a convalescent camp in Scotland. For ten days. To rest. The Air Force is extremely understanding. Extremely adult in some ways. In direction, for instance. (The motive is to get better flying, of course.) Air-crews are being reconditioned all the time in quiet spots like Lennick. Not because they've been ill or anything. But the change will make them more efficient. The official attitude's roughly this: an aircraft lost is nothing; we've thousands, and we're getting more. A heavy bomber is just a thirty-five-thousand-pound way of getting a crew and a load of bombs to where one can leave the other, most usefully. But the pilot has had a long training, and probably he's got some months of experience behind him; same with the other men. And experience can't be replaced so quickly. The bomber must be good enough to get them back, whether it's almost shot to bits or not. That's why it costs what it does, for the return journey. The machine matters even less than the men as men; and that isn't much. But it must fetch home all that valuable training.

So the air-crews are well looked after; they're precious. People saw me off to Lennick. Rather casually, of course. But saying, "Good-bye for now", and "Give my love to the blonde in the station kiosk", with all the jokes about her being tattooed "As patronized by your father", because Lennick was a rest-camp in the last war. There was a careful pretence that I was going to have no end of a good ten days. That was altogether artificial, and everyone knew it. All the time, alongside it, there was the real ghastly assumption that I regarded Lennick as rather a waste of time. Just something that had to be got through before I could come back, to fly again.

"So the convalescent period was fairly awful, too. If I let myself go

at all I'd start sweating with sickness as soon as I began to enjoy anything, realizing I'd be back in a week's time — three days — whatever
it was. And that I'd go on flying.

'The train journey back — it took eight and a half hours — so hor-
ribly short after the first few minutes. Were you sent to boarding
school as a child?'

'I? Yes. Why?'

'Did you hate it at first?'

'Not more at first than I did all the time. Well, not much more. A
French child, sent to an English Public School for Girls — what do
you expect. (My accent's the fruit of those awful five years: the only
fruit, and not worth it!)'

'You remember the first term then? Your parents probably came
over for half-term? Mine did, from Ireland. And there was a point
where you realized — wasn't it in the middle of the last meal with
them? When they asked the waiter, as unobtrusively as possible, to
order a cab for the station? — you knew the process had started that
was going to land you back, alone, in a ten-year-old's hell; there was
nothing you could do about it. And the best reason for not making a
fuss was just that it wouldn't do any good. Well, it was rather like
that, intensified, in the train. Except that the school rapidly became
bearable. At least, mine did; but the airfield remained the same.'

'My father being a Roman Catholic priest,' she said, 'it wasn't like
that for me! He'd just become one, after a happy bereavement, when
I was sent abroad. Newly-ordained priests don't tear themselves away
from the arms of the Bride of Christ, in order to see daughters at
school. Inconvenient daughters, at that. I just stayed there — holidays
and all — from twelve to seventeen. So I didn't share all the usual
experiences. But there are other ways of knowing what you mean. I
can imagine the journey. And after it, when you flew again.'

'I was all right, the first two spells after Lennick. The third time —
the last time — I did the bravest thing I've ever done. Probably the
only really brave thing I've ever done. I went to my C.O., all nerved
up, and said, "I'm extremely sorry, sir, but I just can't go on flying.
I can't stand it". (Funny formal words one uses "extremely sorry".
For that state of mind. I remember thinking it sounded idiotic as I said
it.) He was very nice. We discussed that point, about "extremely

sorry" and other forms of understatement, and very little else. I hadn't known how pleasant he could be. It seemed that plenty of people had felt the same as I did. Not after a crash or anything. I've wondered since whether I've talked "sparrow's arms" to lads who'd have given anything for five minutes' relief of this sort.

'Anyway, he arranged things, the C.O. Transferred me to the administrative branch where I could have a comfortable office-job, awarding ten days C.C. to ill-behaved aircraftmen. While other men flew. I'd hear them go up in the evening. Perhaps seven from our station, taking off for Hamburg or Essen. If I guessed it was Essen (when you're not detailed for the job yourself, of course, you shouldn't know, but actually you very often do) I'd work out whether the moon would show up the bend in the canal by the time they got there, supposing they went in from the north. Or if they'd be likely to make it north-east, to be sure of the coastline, because there might be ground haze. And then I'd turn in to a warm snug billet. And wake when they came back, to listen to them landing. Six machines. If mine had been the seventh, and I'd been up instead of young David, who used to be my second pilot — so young, he was absurdly wary about flak on the way over, and then turned reckless on the target — well, I thought there might have been another five men clamouring for eggs and bacon at the moment, instead of more jelly or cinders lying about some bloody German field. It's mostly luck, but it mightn't have been then. I was much more experienced — those years with gliders, I suppose they did tell. It's as I said, getting back is what's wanted.

'Everyone was very nice about my new appointment. Too damned understanding, I thought. I was sure there was a lot of head-wagging going on behind my back. Actually, I don't suppose there was. Because you're forgotten, in the R.A.F., as soon as you're round the corner. Any sort of corner. It's got to be like that. It wouldn't be possible to go on, wondering what's happening to So-and-So and all the others who haven't shown up for a bit. They're in rest-camps, or they've been promoted, or killed, or got posted overseas; anyway, it doesn't matter, and they'll only be remembered if they do turn up again. Then everyone'll be very glad to see them. I wasn't part of the squadron any more, and the squadron minded its own business. But I can't stand pity. I never could. I don't want you — please — to talk about all this when I've finished telling you. I just wanted to tell you, or somebody. I thought I saw pity in the eyes of everyone I met in the street. Not just everyone I'd ever had a drink with. Every newly-joined aircraftman seemed to take one glance at my wings and then saluted as if he was thinking "So that's him. Poor chap. Lost his nerve, they say." It didn't make the least difference, my knowing from my own early days just what he was actually seeing: something he had to salute, and how he hoped he was doing it right, and nothing else.

'After a bit this became worse than the other. I volunteered for flying duties again, and put on an act that convinced the interviewing board, and got back. Some time ago I was shot up, as you found out. Not badly, and it's pretty well healed.'

CHAPTER IV

KILDOOEY

'There's really nothing more to be said about my affairs,' he told her again, 'because I'm going back so soon. Just, thank you for listening. D'you want to sleep? If you do—' he disengaged the arm which had taken hers and put it round her shoulders, pulling her against him '—better this way. You're awfully tired, aren't you?'

'Yes, I suppose I must be.' She sounded surprised, as though she were rediscovering a forgotten fact, somehow irrelevant to the position. It was irrelevant, he knew now, to the sense of withdrawal wrapping her so completely that still, having told her so much, he could ask her no questions which mattered. He had thought of her quality at first, how serene. And then: But it's only that she's worn out. Now it was plain to him that more lay behind this remoteness than the uttermost weariness of the body; and once more the thought came into his mind, he could not tell why, that she had nothing more to lose.

For much of the passage they slept or half-slept, she propped against him in the narrow hatchway, her head lying uncomfortably on his shoulder.

Once, when she stirred, and he knew she was awake again, he said, 'Where are you going in Ireland?'

The moon was lifting, brilliant and a little past the full, from the edge of the sea. It would be up for the rest of the night. The light, at that angle, seemed to lever the ship higher out of the water.

'I thought I'd stay in Belfast a bit, and then perhaps go on to Londonderry. I don't know. What's your name?'

'Fairburn. Tom. Whyever Belfast and Derry? They're the two dreariest towns in the whole Six Counties, and that's the dullest part of Ireland. Have you friends there?'

'No. I've never been to Ireland before. My name's Denyse Messagère. It was turned into "Mrs. Messenger" in the Stepney first-aid post. That's how I was allowed to stay so long, in spite of the regulations for aliens. No one suspected me of being one. (Engaged, as I was, on work of the greatest national unimportance, unlike all the other aliens you read about in the papers!) Most nights I just walked miles and miles, conducting bombed-out children to underground lavatories. They'd never waited for me, of course. And when I was on duty by day, as you know, I scrubbed in the wake of their parents. It got me through time, anyway. They've no regulations against employing aliens in Ireland; not at present, at least, and I must do something; that's why I'm travelling now — not to see people! I thought, in Belfast or Londonderry — they're both manufacturing towns, aren't they? — there'd be canteen work, or something like that.'

'Is that why you chose them?'

'From a guide-book,' she said sleepily. It struck him first that this was absurd; and then that it was almost the forlornest thing he had ever heard said without emotion.

She made him laugh by another remark, produced at their next waking with all the severity of someone half-roused by a recurrent discomfort; her head had again slipped off his shoulder; he had already retrieved it twice. 'Why do writers talk about "sleeping in someone's arms"? You can't sleep in someone's arms. It's just what you can't do — sleep.' And then, more resentfully, 'Human bodies don't fit when they're relaxed.' She sounded as cross as a child.

'Not when relaxed,' he agreed, half asleep himself. 'They don't do too badly at other times.'

She grunted at him, and he protested, 'I didn't design them', and both dozed off uneasily for a while.

He woke her by running a finger round her chin. 'Listen,' he said gently, 'I'm afraid they're after us now, all right! Go below.'

'What?' She was dazed with broken sleep, and when he pulled her to her feet, stood blinking in the light that streamed into the hatchway from the high moon, showing the silhouettes of men hurrying along the gleaming deck.

The gun aft sputtered. He pushed her down through the hatch into the lightless passage, and followed her, before the stunning, crescendo roar of the diving plane enveloped the ship. They stood braced against each other and the walls on either side as the ship heeled to violent steering. Two bombs missed her, the impact through the water shaking the hull so that Fairburn felt Denyse stumble out of his hold; he could not find her again in the confusion, the noise of the raider's machine-guns, spraying the deck, drowned that of running feet. Men collided with them, cursing, struggling by in the dark, forcing them further apart. The racket died as the plane circled away.

The opening of the pantry door let a beam of light fall on Fairburn. One steward seized upon him indignantly; someone else must have shepherded Denyse Messagère back to the passengers' proper quarters; he did not see her again that night. His steward bawled inaudibly about the enormity of such straying, easing his nerves by official anger, while they progressed towards the dining-room together in short rushes; the movement of the ship was wildly erratic again, the plane was returning and the ship's gun-crew were firing rapidly. There was the lurch and concussion of another fairly near miss after the shattering ordeal of the dive, followed by more machine-gun drumming, and then silence, nerve-wracking at first and only very slowly turning into reassurance. Mysteriously, to the passengers—feeling trapped and helpless down below—the ship resumed her normal course and no further attack was made on her throughout the passage.

No one knew why the plane had suddenly made off. Had she been hit, finished her ammunition, or seen better quarry? To Fairburn the mystery seemed a fitting preparation for his landing in Ireland, a part of the gigantic idiocy from which Kildooey must—it must! It would!—provide him with relief. Two skilfully constructed things, a ship and an aircraft, had engaged in mutual destruction, and broken off that contest for no apparent reason. But at Kildooey men would be catching fish, and women would be cooking them, and children would be playing with the scales that came off on their hands when they went to help in pulling up the boats. There was sense in such actions, which would not cease because of wars. However ignobly its peace had been bought, Kildooey itself stood for all the good things that remained, and his heart ran ahead to it in hope.

Landing in the morning, he looked for Denyse Messagère in the Customs Shed. A few passengers had been slightly hurt when they were thrown off their feet or hurled against the ship's furniture. They were taken straight through the Customs into waiting cars, their baggage left behind to be dealt with later. She was one of them.

'Nothing serious!' she called to him, limping between two stewards. He could not reach her on the other side of the barrier. A minor official was making trouble about his papers: the type of conscientious northern-Irish Scot whom he had cursed to Shamus. One of Shamus's friends, of senior rank, turned up to extricate him in time, but by then she had smiled and waved to him, and disappeared.

Still, at six o'clock or thereabouts, he knew, on the Eire side of the frontier, the guard would be sauntering home from the post on the Ballinfaddy road — nothing else could matter to Fairburn at the moment. He spent a delightful, busy day in Belfast, very different in spirit from the day of waiting in Liverpool, though of the two towns he still disliked Liverpool the less. He had his arm dressed at a hospital for the last time, and for the first time got it into a sleeve again.

To sleep in at Kildooey he bought a car so battered, though the engine seemed sound, that even the second-hand car dealer did not pretend it was only a second-hand car. ''Tis an experienced vehicle,' he said eagerly when he heard why the customer wanted it. He ran a hand over a front tyre, in a way which suggested that he had once been a horse-coper. Fairburn mentally took ten pounds off the price at once; recognized a Southern accent, remembered what he owed to Shamus, and put half of it back again; although convinced that he was about to be swindled.

'Many's the time this car would be bringing me safely home, with the road turning difficult on me, and it a Saturday night.' The phrase, with its literary flavour and beautiful lilt, came shortly after the man's admission that he had no idea of its mileage; it had not been long in his yard. At some stage in its decline from an expensive family saloon, the car appeared to have been used as a milk float; behind the back seat, which had been prised loose and could be lifted out, there was now an opening and a tail-board. The rails had been removed under the seat beside the driver's; it slithered about somewhat when the car was moving, unless wedged in some way, but it could also be lifted out easily and this suited a camper; there would be room to stretch at full length, with the feet under the dash-board. The wings sloped inwards at a surprising angle, giving the whole thing a knock-kneed air. 'It would be a grand lepper?' said Fairburn, using the phrase reserved in the South for a horse with nothing to recommend it as it stood. The dealer agreed absently, and insisted on throwing in, for the price of £15, an old primus stove and a screw-topped can for water, a frying pan and six eggs from his own hens. Fairburn drove off, to buy blankets and more stores, wondering just how he had been swindled. The car turned out to be in superb running order; he never discovered what the dealer imagined was wrong with it, apart from the appearance, to which no one in Ireland would object.

And on the Ballinfaddy road the slanting sun of the late afternoon covered with golden charm the tarless Irish dust which took him, in spirit, straight back to all the roads of boyhood. It lit up the closed frontier post, and the various notices in both languages about contraband and the penalties for infringement of the law. Fairburn drove happily from a world at war into neutral territory, without stopping and by no man's leave. The light was remarkable, turning vivid with menace; the brilliant, fickle light of an Irish day changing almost without warning into storm. Everything stood out in it with great distinctness, as though possessed of a tremendous new significance of its own.

If a frontier post, unguarded, between peace and war, meant danger to his own side, as indeed Fairburn knew that it must—if enemy agents came along this road, as Shamus had almost said that they did (and certainly they would be stupid not to use it; Ireland was a comfortable home for spies at this time) even so, this was something which no member of a more efficient race could hope to enjoy, a precious idiocy. If not security there was at least consolation to be found in a world where, at any cost, the keeper of a belligerent frontier went home to his tea at six o'clock.

The mood of satisfaction with everything that he saw stayed with Fairburn, while his improbable car bore him over the green hills with the bog-purple heavy on their summits, swinging him in and out of valleys where the white cabins lit their lamps early, because of the sudden darkness of approaching thunder and rain. Brightness spilled out carelessly over their half-doors, when the swirling black clouds had eaten up the last of the after-glow. He had not expected to be so moved by seeing again the light of men's homes, shining without fear in the dark. It was cheering in the same way as the empty official post.

Even while he laughed at the illusion, the impression was strong upon him that every lit room contained a great sum of human happiness — the impression so hard to discredit for anyone out and alone by night. What effect would it have, he wondered, on those in the countries at war, to be deprived for so long of the means of believing in this simple, pleasant untruth: that human contentment gleamed from nearby windows?

He would have liked to stop at some of the cabins, to inquire about the way, when he knew; or to ask for milk, of which he had plenty, in order to be bathed in lamp-light at a door once more, to be invited inside by soft voices; but the car ran as if by magic, seeming equally anxious with himself to get to Kildooey; and though that would be impossible to-night, when he was too tired to drive long, he had marked a spot on the map which he intended to reach. It was just about half-way. For a few miles the road wound round the brow of the hills; there would be stonebreakers' quarries with their backs to the wind from over the crests. In his experience, a good quarry, looking to leeward, was the best chance-found bedroom in Ireland. He had enough food with him for supper and breakfast: tea, bread and butter, and the deluded dealer's eggs. He was anxious to get the car backed in, the loose front seat out, and stowed on the carrier under a ground-sheet, and himself snugged down inside with the primus going, before the rain in the clouds now covering the sky came roaring out of them with the thunder. Already this was muttering ahead: the wildest night was threatening.

The sheep, leaving the higher slopes of the hills, felt its approach. They crouched in ditches, and under the banks along the fenceless road. As he drove up into the high, uninhabited places, the beam of his headlamps picked out their eyes; it showed nothing of the animal except the eyes — red eyes making an avenue of fiery points which extended suddenly as the car rounded a bend, and the red points clustered thicker along the road ahead. It was a little eerie with the storm coming on, and the solitary night before him. He was somewhat exalted with it all, and the lack of sleep.

A man stepped into the road, held up his hand and asked for a match. It was plain from the way he put his head in at the driving window as soon as his pipe was going, and settled his elbows on the top of the door, that it was not the match he had really wanted. After a few minutes of complimentary conversation ('A fine car you have there. You would be a great traveller?') Fairburn recognized the signs: there was one thing which the man intended to ask eventually, it would not be for money or a lift, but for information of some kind. And in the courteous way of the country, it would be twenty minutes, probably, before the real subject could be reached, unless Fairburn himself could guess it beforehand and volunteer what was wanted.

The rain suddenly sluiced down over the man's back, and the night grew darker. Twice in thirty-six hours Fairburn found himself held like the wedding guest by the merciless local politeness. He was now aware that he was yearning for something to eat as well as for sleep. The quarry ahead took on the allure of a long-sought haven. The man was not interested in the war, in Fairburn's identity or his destination, though all these had to be touched on vaguely; he did not mind the rain, he wanted to know about the countries Fairburn had visited. It became evident that the core of his curiosity lay somewhere in this direction.

Fairburn's trips abroad in peace-time had been few, and were disposed of easily; each in turn, as he mentioned the name of the country, was dismissed with the comment that indeed the visit must have been very interesting. Feeling about for a clue, knowing that he would not escape until he found it, Fairburn began questioning in his turn, but made no progress; polite question merely drew forth polite question in return; they got on to topics in which, it was plain, neither of them was interested at all. The man was a sheep-farmer, with all the long night at his command. Had Fairburn's family, he asked, also been about the world?

The exaltation ran out of the evening for the tired traveller while he related as much as he could remember of his father's adventures in Egypt, and drew a gentle blank. Must it not have done the old gentleman a power of good to meet so many beguiling sights? Fairburn reminded himself that this was exactly what he had come for; the woman in the boat had been right: one travelled to see people, not places. The well-remembered look of Ireland he carried with him anyway; it was to the people that he had returned with longing; and here was one of them doing just what he had hoped that they would do for him again: allow him to hear language used with Elizabethan freshness, as though each word had never before been yoked to its companion. 'Beguiling sights' — it was the best possible description of what his father, always at pains to meet no one, had actually seen in the Middle East. How right she was, the serene woman: one learnt little from countries, they could do no more than beguile the passing eye.

There was nothing to prevent him from driving on, as there had been nothing to stop him from silencing the other Irishman in the train, except the overwhelming weight of Irish manners. These softly herded his conversation back to the path of foreign travel whenever it strayed or flagged, while the thunder rolled about them, almost continuously now. The farmer was bent on getting his own way, whatever that might be. Glumly Fairburn recalled for him an aunt who had nearly met her death in the Mississippi floods of the last century, and another who had fished in Jamaica throughout the riots of 1938. 'The obstreperous ladies! Grand tales they must have had for you,' he was told, unconcernedly.

There was a pause: Fairburn had no more travelled relatives. Lightning lit the farmer's face; it looked almost coy. 'Ah, now, I mustn't be keeping you,' he said for the second time, but made no move to take his head and shoulders out of the driving window. 'A fellow was after telling me — at Mrs. Hogan's it was. Mrs. Hogan away over at Ardrinath,' he added, with an air of explaining the urgency of his curiosity.

'Well, he was telling me there's worse storms than this in the hot places . . . ' He glanced away, as if with embarrassment. ' . . . In Africa, now?'

It had taken nearly ten minutes to reach the land of his interest. In another five, by eliminating gold mines, Table Mountain, its tablecloth and its funicular; jungles and big game, with the help of an imaginary uncle Fairburn was able to trace the heart of the matter to the Karoo. Had his uncle been across the Karoo? — the Little Karoo, it was called, according to the fellow who had set the farmer's curiosity on fire.

'Certainly,' said Fairburn. His uncle had spent years in the Karoo. The thought of bread, butter and tea — he would do without the eggs till to-morrow — seemed all that a man could desire in this world. Except sleep. And he would also like to think a little of the serene woman; though he was quite certain now, with small memories of her face and her voice fitting together like jig-saw pieces, that her air of security was only that of someone too unhappy to care what happened. Perhaps he would also do without the tea, if it took too long to make, when he had reached the quarry.

The man settled himself further in at the window, his eyes shining, too, in the sudden flash which lit a red vista from sheep beyond the range of the headlamps. Was it true — the words came from him at last in a rush through the thunder — that the Dutchmen there bred a fat-tailed sheep, with a tail so heavy it had to be supported on a plank with two wheels under it? Lashed to a little carriage of its own, as it were? Or the poor beast could not void its dung and died?

'The breeding rams, yes,' said Fairburn, who vaguely remembered having heard of this.

'Glory be to God, then it was the truth he was telling!' said the farmer. 'Good night to you,' and he disappeared into the ringing darkness.

The rain-lashed night in the quarry he found, a few minutes later, was the best that Fairburn had spent for many weeks; he slept without dreaming, and did not know when the storm bellowed itself into peace. Drowsiness overtook him half-way through the second chunk of bread and butter. He had been soaked by a fierce squall while lifting out the front seat. It had taken him some time to manage this, more or less one-armed as he was when it came to shifting weights; and getting in

again he had only wriggled off coat and shoes before reaching for food
and huddling down among the blankets on the floor, resolved to blow
up the air mattress and arrange the bed more comfortably later. He
found some of the slice under his cheek at about eight o'clock the next
morning and went on eating it despite the accumulation of blanket
hairs. A small child was leaning in the window and patting his sound
shoulder, wanting to give him some fresh milk.

'Thanks, but I've got plenty.'

'Ah, it'll be stale from last night. We saw you come in.'

'Really, I won't want it. I'm sure what I've got hasn't turned. It's
very good of whoever sent you, but — '

'My mother says you're to have it,' the child told him firmly, poured
some into his shaving mug and went away.

These people were the kindest and most ruthless in Europe, bar none,
he thought, driving on towards Kildooey after an excellent breakfast;
past ambush-places in the lanes, marked with the crosses of the gunmen-
patriots who had fallen there. The men commemorated by those crosses
had died to keep alive and free the fighting spirit of Ireland; and by
dying in sufficient numbers they had achieved the present fantastic
situation, by which fighting Ireland stood aside from the war which
would decide her future (except in so far as she hampered, by the reservation of her ports, the side on whose victory she depended for all
hope of liberty). Would his own death be somehow as fantastic and
useless as that in due course, he wondered, and pulled his thoughts
away swiftly; Kildooey was only a few miles ahead.

He would think instead of small, precise comparisons — the kindest
and most ruthless people, the most charming personally and the stupid-
est politically. The Germans were the race nearest to the Irish in this
mixture of domestic softness and collective hardness; and a male race
where the Irish were female. If they took the helpless land and bred
from the Irish, they might almost produce the type of sentimental-
callous supermen, of whom they dreamed, to be the future conquerors
of the world. Keeping his thoughts carefully in trivial ways — on comparisons and definitions — pushing the anxiety lest Kildooey should
fail him into the bottom of his mind, he reached the lovely coast round
Shane Head, and with it a mood in which he felt curiously content to
fight Ireland's battles for her, as though he had been blarneyed into it

by a woman, whose sayings and doings were appalling to remember in absence, but they were pleasing when one looked at her, because in their stupidity they distracted so little attention from her beauty. The sea on his right was intensely blue, white-edged with surf, and the mountains on the other new-washed with colour — surely in no other land did the earth glow after rain as though the light were not falling on the surface, but came from inside it? Even the rocks themselves had lamps in them that day. She was a bitch and a bore, all right, was Ireland, as one of her own poets said of her. But what a lover to come back to, he thought, when head and heart were tired, and only the body wanted life. Cheerfully keeping up the idea of this comparison, he even stopped and had a shave in her honour, at a place where a track up to the peat cuttings allowed him to run the car some distance off the road. Shaving on a car-camp had two good features, the water was really hot for once, because the tin mug could be kept on the primus all the time, and the driving mirror was small enough to make the result look very gratifying to the shaver — much better than it was likely to be, in fact.

A donkey, passing with peat-panniers on his back, stopped to rub a neat haunch against the squared-off end of the car, and unhitched the loose stern-board which Fairburn had only propped in place and not fastened. The piled-up contents of the back of the car — kettle, empty water-can and many tins — fell out around the beast with an alarming noise. He gave Fairburn a look of mournful reproach before cantering down the track, out of sight along the road towards Kildooey. A bare-legged girl in attendance, almost a child, smiled up at Fairburn out of wonderful blue eyes marred by sandy lashes. She accepted his offer of a lift in the car, in pursuit of her beast, with the graciousness of a great lady bestowing patronage.

'You have no need to be hurrying. He'll stick to the road, that one. He always does. Finish what you're doing first.' She repacked for him while he went on shaving, and settled down comfortably on the step to watch. 'We've no man left in our cabin, so, do you know, I've never seen that before!' she told him, to put him at ease when he apologized for keeping her waiting. She added quickly, 'And I to be married too!' and laughed, lest he should think her what indeed she was, as young and fresh as the morning.

'You? Already?' he said. He had taken her for about fifteen. She was snub-nosed and absurdly freckled, not a pretty creature save for her sea-coloured eyes, but very sweet with her manner of knowing no half-way measure between the shy and the supremely assured. 'Ah, not for years and years', she said happily. 'But it's all arranged. Though I wouldn't care, for myself, if I wasn't married at all. I'm not like Helen. My sister, she is. Would you believe it, she's after travelling all the way home from America to marry her old sweetheart in Kildooey? You wouldn't find me coming back for any man if I could get so far. Do you just waste all that soap, now?'

He passed on the information that Queen Victoria had been fascinated by the process of shaving, as demonstrated by the Prince Consort.

'Why wouldn't she be?' asked the girl composedly. 'A very amusing spectacle,' and Fairburn was tickled to find that his pride was slightly hurt by her choice of a word; she might have said it was interesting.

He discovered by indirect questions that this was Bridie, a niece of the Mrs. Sullivan who was aunt to Shamus. A bold one, that Shamus, said Bridie; still, he was a Sullivan relation, and she was glad therefore that he had done well for himself in London. She asked particularly if he had mentioned when he was coming home, but all that Fairburn could remember was that he had said 'soon' in speaking of getting in through Ulster by the Ballinfaddy road.

'Maybe he won't come,' she said thoughtfully. 'It must be very exciting over there, with England at war. And even if he came to Donegal, there'd be plenty for him to do, in a town, without traipsing over to Kildooey.'

In the car she was too nervous to say much unprompted. Fairburn gathered that this was the first time she had ridden in anything but a cart. She made only two observations: 'We have a new signpost in the village — "To Dublin" it says. None of us had been thinking before of that old road leading to Dublin. Fancy it now!' And with the abrupt confidence of the shy she turned to him just as he drew up beside the grazing donkey: 'Helen's glad when the wind's in the west like this. Because then it blows from over the sea. She said so this morning. You wouldn't think she'd feel like that, when she's new home to this country. New home this week!'

She insisted on filling his water-can for him, in return for the ride, from a pump in the garden of a house which stood outside the village. Of grey composition stone, it was hideously superior in structure to the rough-built Donegal cottages. Little pieces of coloured glass had been let into the door jambs and gate-posts, in squares and lozenges. The elaborate front gate appeared to be stuck fast, as though no one ever used it. Bridie, exquisite in movement, climbed over the wall. Fairburn was left holding the donkey's halter through the driving window, the captured beast gazing at him still more reproachfully; the girl had raised clouds of dust out of him, with two otherwise ineffective thumps.

'Your house?' he asked when Bridie came back with the can. It was depressing to find concentrated ugliness in a countryside where the dwellings, as a rule, were a perfect part of the scene.

'Dear, no. Mr. Wallace, who owns the shop, he built it for himself; we've only an old cabin. Do him good to give something for nothing for once, the old crow. Even if it's only water.' She stood in the road, looking back at the pretentious house, herself alive with the wild-legged grace of a young animal. 'But isn't it the beautiful place!' she said wistfully. 'I suppose, now, in the big towns — in Dublin — there are many more beautiful houses?'

He agreed, and drove on, the top of his mind and all his senses alight with pleasure as he came in sight of Kildooey, lying exquisitely in the low green lap of the shore, between great knees of land that jutted into the sea.

The two irregular lines of thatched cabins, just as he remembered, lay one on each side of a shallow stream, with the bridge across it forming the background for all communal life — everything was exactly the same: except, as Bridie Sullivan had said, that the new signpost now stood by the quarry, away up the hill, on the further side of the village. He drove through and stopped there. The turning it marked was no more than a lane, running inland, but in the way of Irish signposts, in country places, it gave the road's remotest and least-needed destination. Fifty miles nearer the capital, where travellers were more likely to be looking for the way to Dublin, the signposts bore the names of the nearest villages, which could rarely be identified on a map. But the quarry had not even been deepened, he thought; except for the dreadful house, out of sight behind the headland, scarcely a new pig-stye could have been built in the place in the last fifteen years. And the people were the same in their welcome. They came on foot or in turf-carts, to see the new arrival, protesting, 'Ah, 'tis no trouble at all!' as they shifted mounds of rubble, so that his car should stand level. Every-one pretended to find nothing extraordinary in a visitor's desire to sleep in such a place, and by an even greater stretch of goodwill, they claimed to recognize him as soon as he mentioned that it was not his first visit.

'Wasn't I wondering who it was himself had put me in mind of?' Mrs. Mary Sullivan looked round triumphantly. 'And isn't it, of course, the boy he used to be?' She had arrived among the first, on a passing tinker's van. He had no recollection of having ever met this moun-tainous woman, but she took charge of the levelling operations and his general settling-in, sending nephews and nieces running for things that he did not particularly want, and getting in first with the inevitable in-vitation that he should come down to the house for the evening.

In the next twenty-four hours, the Kildooey lads took him trolling for pollock in their boats, and lent him hand-lines when he wanted to fish alone from the rocks, while others dug for him more lug-worms than he needed for bait. The priest walked up affably to pass the time of day, and following him came the owner of the one shop, Mr. Wal-lace from the hideous house, whom Fairburn suspected of being the local gombeen-man; ostensibly he came to ask for orders but actually he seemed more interested in finding out what the priest had said. Fairburn had luck with the fish, and no dearth of hearths, smelling ex-cellently of peat, by which to sit and talk; or listen to conversation bet-ter than his own, while the various Sullivan women cooked his catch for him. There was the usual stream of small, touching presents, brought along to the car at all hours, mostly by Bridie: a duck's egg, some butter, or half a dozen gooseberries at a time; it was as difficult as ever, without hurting anyone's pride, not to live off the country and its almost penniless inhabitants.

And at the end of this period he knew that his return had been a failure. He had come alone, wanting no associations with the deadly present, to a place which held for him only happy memories; and it was the memories that became unreal to him, the good things on which he had depended for help; the friendliness of strangers and the slow rhythm of life that turned on the tides and seasons. He walked in the sun, seeing beauty, apprehending none of it, his mind in England where night and day the German air attack went on, his heart sick with his own thoughts. There was no escape, it seemed.

In a few hours, by furious driving, over roads which would have shaken the life out of a more reasonable car, he was across the frontier again and back in the dreariness of Belfast, starting out early in the morning to inquire at hotel after hotel, trying to trace Denyse Messagère. He had nothing to go on except for one casual interchange, some time in the strange conversation between them. It came when she was talking of the depths of human degradation by poverty, forced up to the surface of national consciousness by the war: 'We who've always been sheltered by money —'

'Speak for yourself!' he had told her, against the background of gun-fire. 'My income's only been of the sheltering kind for the last five years. In fact, since a vehemently Protestant aunt died. Rather than let a Catholic get hold of anything, she left it to the nearest atheist. I was just beginning to believe in the shelter when all this happened —' He made a gesture of the hand, knowing it would be outlined against the flashing horizon — 'And it stopped being sheltering! I take it then, that you've got lots of money!'

'Lots.' They had both laughed at such a curious question and answer between strangers.

'Still? Now that you've left France?'

'Well, no, probably not,' she had said, as though this, too, like her state of extreme weariness, were something she had not yet seriously considered. 'To tell you the truth, I don't know.'

Some habits of luxury, however, died hard: he was sure that while she had anything left she would stay improvidently at the most comfortable hotel.

But she had also said that if she did not like Belfast — and he was equally sure that she would not like Belfast — she might go on to Londonderry. He had done his best to put her off Londonderry. In that he had probably succeeded, he thought now, as he turned away from the last of the probable hotels on his list, and began doggedly on the seedy ones. Expensive hotels in Belfast were rather shabby, the second-rate places were so uninviting that he knew she would not be there; but it was easier to go on looking than to accept the probability that she had already left for some other town, also chosen at random. In that case there was no chance of finding her, and she was all that remained of hope; he could talk to her.

In the anxiety of the search he had not thought out exactly what it was he meant to say, to ask of her, were he successful; but not more than this: that she should let him stay near her, wherever she chose to be, for some part of his leave. She could decide the terms.

When he had exhausted the impossibly inclusive list he had made, he went back for a meal to the first hotel at which he had inquired, telling himself that while he ate he would think of other places where she might be staying — knowing there was none, unable yet to admit defeat.

He saw her as he crossed the hall, several seconds before she saw him. She was coming slowly downstairs; her eyes on her hand, which was playing with each of the knobs of the banisters in turn, making the same four movements every time, carefully exact in touch, as something to do while her body passed aimlessly from one place to another. The look of tranquillity was so transparent now on her face, that suddenly he wanted from her not consolation, but the opportunity to give it.

Her gaze shifted slightly and they stared at one another for a second, standing still, separated by the flight of stairs. Her whole figure came to life at the recognition. It seemed to him, in some odd corner of his mind, shocking that a face so deeply controlled should light up with such relief at the mere sight of someone who was not wholly a stranger. She could not know that he had come back to find her; a dozen reasons might have kept him in Belfast.

He said her name and went up and kissed her, under the eye of the reception clerk, not like a man welcoming a lover, with a wild certainty in his heart, but as one greeting a wife of long standing after an unimportant parting. The clerk, unconcerned by such apparently normal behaviour, was fussing about him before he let go of her, explaining that when the gentleman had said 'Messagère', it had not sounded to him like Messagère (but like some other name which, as the clerk said it, sounded exactly like Messagère, or so Fairburn thought, only now he did not care enough to curse the man).

Over tea together Denyse told him, 'Yes, I'll come to Kildooey with you'. All modesty of demand had evaporated out of his mind as soon as he kissed her. (Days later he remembered to tell her that he had not come back intending to make love to her; by then, this seemed so funny.) 'I'll put it no politer than to say I don't mind. Because, just literally, I've nothing better to do. And you're nice.' Her smile took the grudgingness out of the words.

'Never say I asked a woman to share that car!' he told her, happiness creeping into him by degrees. 'Remember, you've practically suggested it yourself. That sounds ungrateful—but you haven't seen the car.' And later: 'The guarda at the post on the Ballinfaddy road goes home at six o'clock; if we're to get through to-night, to save being held up for twenty-four hours, we'll have to go out and shop now, and then start at once. Two tin plates, one cup; knife, fork and spoon, and another cushion for a pillow—or do you want two? Can you think of anything else you'd like as a wedding present? Would you like a separate bowl for washing up? I've made do with the saucepan so far. Just pouring hot water over the plates.'

'I don't mind about that. I'd rather have plenty of saucepans. Have you only got one?'

'It's enough. With a frying-pan. On one primus. There's no room in the car—'

'I'd like four. And a second stove. But one saucepan can be a steamer, which would count as two. As long as there's another that'll do as a *bain marie*. I'm probably the best cook you've ever met.'

'But Denyse, we couldn't get all that into the back. Not comfortably. Not with two suitcases, and another blow-up mattress. We've enough blankets, already, but there'll have to be a bigger water-can—'

'Then hang them outside. We aren't going to be comfortable, anyway.'

'They'd clatter.' The sweetest assurance in the world lay in bickering about such trifles now.

'All right. Then they can clatter. I don't mind noise. I can't get really interested in ways of washing up, either. You can stop shaving for all I care. As long as your beard meets in the middle. The last days in Paris gave me a down on the aesthetic type; I'll tell you why, some time. And their hair always seems to grow in tufts. But cooking is just something else again. If you want me to come, the price is four saucepans, assorted sizes. It's years since I've been able to cook without a professional thinking I oughtn't to be prying about in her kitchen. Except for eleven days on the road to Bordeaux last June. And then, of course, I couldn't get anything to cook, along with thirty thousand other refugees.'

Soon, now, as they both knew, she would tell him what had been held back during the hours of stress in the ship. The English school — travel — the incongruous work in London; about all these things she talked freely enough. He sensed that there was something else which had happened to her in France, just before the flight along the refugee roads to the sea — something which was not yet in the past for her; and for the moment he did not want her to tell him anything more; not until after to-night, which they would spend somewhere on the road. He guessed already that there were other arms in which she would rather be lying. Till to-morrow they would talk of trivial things.

They drove out along the Ballinfaddy road with everything Denyse had wanted stowed somehow in the car.

She would not be amused, as he was, by the routine of the guarda who went home to tea. 'We had all that sort of whimsicality in France,' she said as they drove into Eire. 'Seen close to, as a background for invasion, it all at once stops being funny. And for ever. Tell me what they're like, the people at Kildooey?'

'Ordinary, nice peasants,' he said.

'Do they know you're not married?'

'No. Luckily for you. Remember, they're a fanatically chaste people. Irish love-making's famous the world over, but it's mostly verbal; at least, so far as my observation goes.' He swerved to avoid a goat and kid lying asleep in the middle of the road; spies were evidently not plentiful on the border that night. Towards everything that inhabited this absurd world, which could include him and them and Denyse, he felt, for the moment, nothing but an overwhelming goodwill. He hoped that if there were any foreign agents about they would not be in a hurry, lest they should run over the animals.

'But you were twenty-four hours in Kildooey!' she said. 'It'd be the first thing you'd be asked in a French village — "Et votre femme, Monsieur? Vous en avez?"'

'This is a politer race, I suppose; that's all. With a lot of different taboos which you'll just have to learn. Otherwise I'll be forced to go round the houses apologizing for the fact that my dear wife has no manners, and explaining that it's because she comes from the Continent. Then they'll say consolingly, "Ah, 'tis only to be expected. Born so far away, among the terrible disthurbances they do always be having in those parts".'

'What are the taboos? I'll try and remember,' she said laughing at his voice. It was very good to hear this woman laugh, breaking the dead quality of her mood of acceptance and control. It was like a protest, a sudden insistence from the spirit within that she was alive still, and young still; and it was not she but her world which had broken. He wanted to hear it again.

'Oh, that you mustn't get at what you want by the shortest route, like a straight question. And you mustn't forget that Cromwell's day was only yesterday hereabouts, and as an Englishman I'm personally responsible for everything that happened then, even if you're not. And you'll hear them say, "God save all here" to one another, maybe, when they're crossing a threshold, but if you say it, it'll be resented, even if they think you're a Catholic; because you're a stranger. Never forget you're a stranger. They'll try to make you. That's essential in their hospitality, but they'd much rather you didn't. And don't misunderstand Irish flattery. It isn't meant to deceive — this is where people go wrong so often, they say it's unconvincing. The whole object is to make you feel cosy, thinking how blatantly someone is willing to lie to please you.'

'And, of course, it does make you feel cosy?'

He nodded. 'Pleased with the good intent, like a saint with a candle.'

She gave him the reward he wanted, the sound of her chuckle.

He said in a different tone, 'What I said just now — "Terrible disthurbances, far away" — that's all they feel like to-night, don't they — the things we both know?'

'Yes.' She moved nearer to him in the car, which rattled behind them continuously and sounded very friendly. They were driving into a primrose-yellow sunset along that part of the road where the sheep had lain with eyes on fire. But now all the weather omens were good: the beasts were cropping high up on the crest of the hills, moving black against the bright sky; it would be a glorious night. (After a year of war he knew how quickly, faced with the large, simple issues of living or dying, men turned to the oldest forms of belief: in luck, in charms, in the lore of clouds and colours and the movements of animals. Men had accepted omens before they accepted gods, and trusted them more enduringly. This association which was about to begin — he had an idea that somehow it would be as simply important to him as the question of living or dying. He was glad that the omens were good — as he had always been before raids; his mind incredulous, his nerves reaching out for the most foolish promises of security.)

She was saying, 'But I can't think they'll believe you had a wife all the time, whom you just didn't mention!'

'I can only promise you, they will. If not, you might be hurled off the rocks into the sea. With me after you.'

'Chastity and lack of suspicion about other people's morals — they don't go together!'

'You mean in France. Where the sun shines a lot, and the people as a whole haven't been badly under-nourished for several hundred years.' It was the heart of enchantment to talk so distantly, remembering every bend of the road which led to the quarry, that excellent bedroom just ahead. 'Well, here they have. Not much food, plus not much sunshine, equals not much sensuality. Other sorts of energy, like the mystical and political — but not that. It's a sort of natural equation. And one doesn't suspect other people of wanting to do what one doesn't want to do one's self. Malnutrition and grey skies, combined — that's what's given the Church her fiercest hold over Ireland.'

Both of them knew that their thoughts had none of the cool impersonality of their words. A figure appeared, hurrying across a field as if to intercept them on the road ahead: it might or might not be the sheep-farmer, a prey to further doubts about travellers' tales heard at Mrs. Hogan's. In no mood to be delayed again, Fairburn put his foot down on the accelerator and raced him out of sight.

'I was wrong just now,' he said soberly — it was the last sober thing they said that night — 'when I told you the people of Kildooey were nice, ordinary peasants. That's how I've been wanting to see them. You know — funny Irish types. They seemed better props for me that way.'

'Because types don't get hurt, like people?'

'I suppose so. I didn't want to face any more feeling, for myself or anyone else. That's something you've already done for me; made it possible to look at people again. They certainly aren't just nice, ordinary peasants at Kildooey. And they certainly aren't funny, except in the superficial ways which don't count — the ways in which they might find either of us funny — you for being French, say, at such an unsuitable moment in history! — me for volunteering again for the job I'd got out of. I think there's a thin skin of funniness over most desperate human affairs, and peasant life in this country can't ever be very far from the grim, whatever it looks like on the surface. In Kildooey — ' his voice lit with the interest of discovery — 'well, I've been there alone just long enough to know that there's one rather evil and fascinating old woman — the one who saw the ghost; she'll tell you! One wretched man forced by his conscience into doing wrong — into doing something cruel: that's the priest. Yes, and another man who can do harm without caring, for the sake of power. (Do you know what a gombeen-man is? Well, you will.) A young man living on the idea of an Ireland that's dead. And another — oh, several other people, who've been bewitched by a signpost. That isn't such a rare spell as it sounds, not in these parts. The land reeks of stagnation to the young, if they've any sort of vitality. I knew all that—gathered it by myself — but couldn't realize it, somehow, without you. People couldn't get through to me — oh, my darling Denyse!'

'And now,' he said, 'they can all go to hell. This is the quarry.'

CHAPTER V

GHOST STORY

'WASN'T it on that very road where the signpost stands, my dearest —' Sitting in her own cabin with her relatives about her, Mrs. Mary Sullivan was warming up to the retailing of her great experience, for the benefit of Denyse as the newcomer. 'Wasn't it in the shadow of the quarry itself that the figure of the gunman appeared?'

'Ah, now, I could never make sense of the whole happening,' put in her sister-in-law. This was another of the Mrs. Sullivans of Kildooey, a complaining woman, Mrs. Agnes; thin and insignificant where Mrs. Mary was fat and commanding. Mrs. Agnes, it was recognized in the village, had also seen the ghost, but by superior verve and position Mrs. Mary had made it entirely hers by now.

Within ten minutes of the car's reappearance at Kildooey, Bridie had arrived beside it, breathless with running, bearing her aunt Mary's offer to bake the visitors a cake of maize bread, to be ready by the evening — 'when maybe, she says, you'll both be coming down to her cabin?' Denyse was accepted without question.

Now the flat round of bread, just lifted from the pan on the hearth, was filling the cabin with a smell which mingled gloriously with the smell of peat. More Sullivans came in from neighbouring cabins and sat down by the fire; they kept watch on the pan in which Mrs. Mary's own bread was baking, changing the smouldering turfs piled up on the lid, as the red died out of them. Everyone expected Mrs. Mary to ignore practical matters in her own cabin when talking of old times. Others fetched her tea-things, running next door for extra cups, or found stools for the later arrivals to sit on, while she occupied most of the settle undisturbed, and waved away Fairburn's thanks for the bread as if it had been her due. Actually, he learnt from Bridie, it had been baked by Mrs. Agnes, from maize supplied by Bridie's mother. (This was the third sister-in-law, Mrs. Kathie Sullivan, sweet-faced and anxious.)

All the family must have known the tale of the ghost by heart, but they listened with grave attention. Only Mrs. Mary interrupted her own narrative at intervals to lean back and keep a puffy eye lifting over her half-door, so as to see the bridge beyond and anyone who might be passing over it, from one half of the village to the other — 'Sean, tell Father Keith there's a cup of tea waiting for him here when he's done with Mrs. Clancy. It's Mrs. Clancy he's on his way to, for certain; she with her girl just off for a nurse to England. Run the short way, boy, between the houses.'

The 'boy', Sean, was about twenty-five, with an ardent face thin with dreams.

'I don't understand that woman either,' said Mrs. Agnes plaintively. 'Always wanting the priest's support, but letting her girl go off to live among strangers, where she'll not be with those of her own faith.'

'You that expect to understand everything!' said Mrs. Mary Sullivan in comfortable contempt. 'Didn't you always. Weren't you talking to me that night, coming home from the dance at Ardrinath. (Young things we were then. Still unmarried, and not expecting to become related, either. Twenty years ago, it was, with the Troubles raging.) "Now there must be some *reason*," you were saying, Agnes, "for the Black-and-Tans to go breaking up the shop of the only man in these parts to serve with the British Army!" (So they did. Mr. Wallace: you've seen him?) "And why should they have a reason?" I said — and then we saw the figure. Just where I'm telling you. In the very place your car is standing at this moment. He'd his hat over his eyes, and the sort of raincoat our boys were mostly wearing. (The I.R.A., do you see, for this was a great stronghold of theirs. God rest them, those that fell, but their sacrifice will not be wasted.) The moon was behind them, shining down over the lip of the quarry, the way it will be late to-night. "'Tis a gunman, Mary," said Agnes. "And what will we do," she said, "for he's holding the road against us? He's none of the boys we know."

' "We'll go straight on, and past him," I said. "Gunman or no gunman. Talking as if we didn't care." For that was my way in those days. In any case, not another road would lead us back to our homes.

' "Maybe he'll shoot us in the back when we're past," said Agnes.

' "Maybe he won't," said I — but I was just as frightened myself, I tell you now.

'So talk we did. Of a girl we were in service with in Ardrinath, who'd come in one night with a terrible story. Telling us how she'd been set upon by three men, and tied to a tree, and showing us the wounds she had in her head. And didn't it turn out in the end that she'd done it all herself — Now there was something for Agnes to understand! It wasn't a good subject for us to be talking of — attack. Putting it into his head if it wasn't there before. But we couldn't think of anything else. And we got as close to him, my dearest, as I am to you at this minute. He looking at us all the time, out of his eyes deep in the shadow of his hat. With his gunman's coat close round him, and his hands in his pockets, and not a word out of him all the while. We went right up to him, and when we were just past, it was worse.

The fear of him, I mean. Amn't I right, Agnes? Wasn't it worse as we came down the road away from him?'

'It was worse. For then we were thinking — '

'For then we were thinking' (by raising her voice slightly, Mrs. Mary Sullivan took back the narrative) 'we might be getting a bullet in the back at any moment. 'Tis a terrible feeling, that,' she said, looking from Denyse to Fairburn for appreciation. 'Never knowing, from moment to moment, when you may be shot!'

'Indeed,' he said with restraint, 'it must have been most upsetting.'

'We've never been so frightened since!' she said nostalgically. 'Close on twenty years ago, and I have it with me still, the sensation between my shoulders. But he let us get safely to the turn in the road, nothing done and nothing said, only for the way he looked at us out of those eyes we couldn't quite see in the moonlight. And as soon as we were round the bend, Agnes and I, we knew it wasn't a gunman at all we'd passed, but a ghost! Not a word had he said the whole time we were coming, and going by, and leaving him standing like that in the moonlight!'

The little group of relatives, drinking tea round the hearth, stirred and murmured agreement. This was the accepted end to the anecdote, satisfying like a familiar story to a child.

'Come in, my dears, come in,' said Mrs. Kathie in her troubled voice to a girl, pretty in a bright, townish way, who stood smiling over the half-door with a heavy young countryman behind her. 'This is my other daughter, Helen, from America. And her man.'

They made an incongruous couple; and behind them came two old shawley-women, still more out of keeping with the frilly girl, who smoothed out the creases in her dress with care as she sat down. The old women took their places self-effacingly, away from the fire, in the shadows. Poorer looking than any of the Sullivans, they were the dependants of Helen's young farmer, his mother and aunt.

All were welcomed in to evening tea — and to that still more precious thing, the sound of strange voices — with what, thought Fairburn, was really lavish hospitality, even for Ireland. Mrs. Mary's ascendancy in Kildooey was entirely due to personality; her cabin was bare of all but necessities and she lived on invisible means, reputed to be a pension from the I.R.A., because her husband had been accidentally killed in a shooting affray.

'But I don't see why you thought it was a ghost?' Denyse was saying. 'Why couldn't it have been a gunman after all?'

Mrs. Mary Sullivan turned on her triumphantly: 'Is there a living man in the length and breadth of Ireland,' she demanded, 'who would have let two pretty girls, as we were then, go by without a greeting on a moonlight night?'

'That's easily the most convincing ghost story I've ever heard,' said Fairburn hastily, frowning at Denyse.

'It's no story,' said Mrs. Mary Sullivan, unmollified.

'I mean, the best possible proof of a ghost,' he said. 'But you see, my wife, being French, didn't quite understand.'

Bridie, sitting hunched up in a corner with her chin in her cupped hands, gazing at her sister, turned her curious eyes to Denyse. 'Is it that you are!' she breathed, as though it were almost too much, in one gathering, to be able to look at Helen, who had shaken her heart with the glamour of return from far places, and also at someone who had not only seen but belonged to another land and people.

Mrs. Kathie Sullivan, always apprehensive, stroked away at the small social difficulty with nervous words. 'You must be longing now, my dearest, for them all to stop fighting in Europe, so your poor country can recover herself.'

Helen gave a quick, hard little laugh. 'As if stopping the fighting was all that was needed to set France where she was before! — that's how they see the outside world in Kildooey!' She appealed to Denyse with eyes much softer than her voice, they were frightened; apologizing for her own contempt, as well as for the ignorance of her mother's remark. 'Have you been to America, Mrs. Fairburn? I'm just over from there, you know.'

'Yes, I've been there. Not for a long time, though, and it was only a short visit.' Denyse tried to draw the young farmer into the conversation as well as the girl. Eager to get Helen's attention, he was slow and clumsy in speech; and as soon as the girl discovered that Boston was one of the places where Denyse had stayed she ignored him altogether, in her longing to say over, like a lover, the names of streets and landmarks and stores; for three years these had consti-

tuted for her a world of excitement and unimagined civilization. 'I'd
never been so far as Dublin before! Not even to Dublin,' she repeated.

'Dublin!' said Bridie. 'I'd be content if I could see that!'

'You'd want to be back from there soon enough!' Mrs. Agnes spoke
sharply. 'Irish people are always wandering, and wishing they were
home again. Father Keith says it's better to know too little than too
much of most towns, and our own Dublin's not above reproach, Father
Keith says—'

But the girl was not listening; she had heard all this too often.
The yellow-fringed eyes, staring out into the September dusk, were
seeing no city that could ever have been built by human hands, but
the legendary Dublin of the poets and saints, the famous beauties and
wits.

'Bridie, child, don't be looking along the bridge for the moment,'
said Mrs. Mary, who had just been doing this herself, 'or you'll catch
the eye of Mr. Wallace (the one I spoke of, my dearest. Him from
the shop). If he doesn't stop in passing I'll not be asking him in, for
he and Father Keith see everything differently, so they do, and I've a
strong hope that Father Keith will be over presently. He was never
one to refuse a cup of tea.'

I must remember this moment, thought Fairburn, glancing round
the warm, sweet-smelling cabin. In bad times it will be something
to have enjoyed. Here is Denyse. And even if it is only an illusion,
here is the sense of security and peace: people still wholly engrossed
in their small private affairs. He looked with care, to memorize details
which were already familiar, at the blackened bread-pans on the open
hearth, and the hearth itself; at the tiny lamp burning before the
coloured print of the Christ of the Bleeding Heart. There were no
other pictures on the walls, stretching up without ceiling to the cob-
webs under the thatch. The built-in dresser with its few, unmatching
crocks, and the bed in the alcove; the trodden earth floor, and the
effect of dignity and space in a room without ornament—all these
things could be duplicated in a hundred other cabins where he had
been made welcome in the past; but here, even more than usual, the
sweet smell seemed less of peat and new bread than of the graciousness of the people.

He looked with conscious pleasure at Bridie, entranced, grave with her desire for something she could not put clearly into words — the further side of all blue hills, the place of ultimate enchantment, which she had chosen to call Dublin, because the road from the quarry led towards that town. Named on the signpost, it did not seem to her so wholly unattainable as other far places. Part of her attention followed her eyes, dutifully turned from the bridge to the fire, and played there with visions; part was given with delight to the conversation between Helen and Denyse; one-sided as it was, at least it had another great city for subject.

'— do you remember in Boston, Mrs. Fairburn — Oh, do you remember — ' It was plain to Fairburn that Denyse was only pretending to recall the details of a place she had not seen for years, out of kindness to the excited girl who was already homesick for its pavements. The young farmer tried again to intervene in the conversation, with a pointless remark of which only Denyse and Mrs. Kathie took any notice. He repeated it louder. Mrs. Kathie agreed with him in a hurried, soothing tone which made him appear still more ill at ease. She darted anxious glances at her daughter, absorbed in showing Denyse the bangle on her wrist and the brooch at the neck of her cheap, fresh blouse, telling the older woman where these treasures had been bought, and how much she had paid for them. 'I was earning good wages, do you see. Plenty of money, I had, while I was there.'

Fairburn turned back to Mrs. Mary Sullivan. So this shapeless wreck of a woman, with only her eyes and her tongue still lively, was not much more than forty. She could not be, if at the time of the Troubles she had been only a young thing in service. And pretty, too, like Helen perhaps, though there was now no sign of that. He looked from her ungainly bulk to the girl; would a few years of strict Catholic marriage do as much for the slim young figure, alive with the recaptured joy of wages to spend, window-shopping and nightly walks in the city streets? — All these were things which the village priest, if he came in now, would certainly condemn as 'worldly temptations', to be forgotten by one who was about to take on the sober duties of a wife.

Mrs. Mary's eyes ran about the company maliciously. 'Anyone would think,' she said to Denyse, 'that it was you Helen had come back to marry, instead of Michael!'

Helen's man reddened, and for a moment he could not find the words he wanted. Then he said sturdily, 'Isn't it natural enough she should miss what she has given up?' and it was as if saying this, in her defence, opened his eyes to the truth of what he said. Sorrow seemed to strike him suddenly with the realization that he would be poor consolation to his sweetheart for what she had lost. Looking round, he tried again to find something to say to them all, to show that he understood the position, and would not hold it against her if she looked back at times with regret for her freedom. He turned to Denyse. 'It's as I told himself—my father died, do you see. And I have the farm. So after a bit the priest wrote to her to tell her we should be married now. I am no hand with a pen. (But Helen can write a beautiful letter, so she can. One every week, she wrote, for us to share, the way we knew how it was with her all the years she was away.) We had it arranged, before she went, that we would get married when my father died.' He made no further attempt to intervene in the conversation, and after a second or two, smiling at him with contrition, Helen went on talking to Denyse about the places they had known in common, as though there had been no interruption.

No, thought Fairburn, there were things in this room which would not be good to remember, later on.

'If we hadn't been so young and silly,' said Mrs. Agnes plaintively, picking up the story which she never managed to share, 'we shouldn't have been scared of the ghost while we thought he was a gunman.' It was as if she grudged even the bygone fear so greatly enjoyed by Mrs. Mary. 'We knew it couldn't be any of the Black-and-Tans, for they wouldn't dare come in these parts alone. So why should he shoot us in the back if he was one of our own boys, we both being good friends with the I.R.A.?'

'Didn't we marry two of them before the year was out? Aye, and weren't we widowed of them both before the fighting was over? Though one, at least, died in his bed.'

'Mary!' said Mrs. Agnes, low and warningly, under cover of Helen's chatter. 'Be quiet now.'

'Sean's out. Didn't I send him myself after Father Keith?'

'There's others.'

'I forgot. I'm getting so fat —' Mrs. Mary spoke in a normal voice again, and laughed — 'I can't be turning round all the time to see who's in the cabin and who's not.' She hesitated, as if wondering how to explain this exchange to Fairburn, the only person who had overheard, and then took the masterly line of explaining nothing. 'Reason!' she said, returning to her surprise that anyone should expect causes to be connected with events. 'Would you still be looking for reason from a man with a gun in his hand? It's not the way things happen.'

'Not to you!' said Mrs. Agnes. 'Or so you're pleased to think.'

Helen got up, still aware of no one but Denyse. 'I could fetch my photographs for you? Just picture postcards they are. But I chose them carefully to show all the finest streets. It's no distance to go for them. Our cabin's only the other side of the bridge. Then you'll remember how Dominion Avenue runs — the great, broad street it is! You must remember. Will I fetch them now?'

Denyse said that this would be very nice, and as the girl went out, slid her eyes round to Fairburn. He grinned unsympathetically; serve her right if she now had to look at masses of picture postcards of Boston; it would teach her that in Ireland, if she lied for kindness' sake, she must do it thoroughly.

But Helen did not come back that night. Her troubled Michael followed her out, unaware that he left in the middle of one of Mrs. Kathie's nervous sentences. The two old ladies went too, apologizing for him, their manners courtly, their faces noble with the gaunt beauty of their race in old age, their bare ankles above broken shoes showing traces of the cow-byre. 'A terrible lad he is for worrying over his farm,' they said. 'A terrible lad that way. He'll be after remembering that some of the bastes were left out from the afternoon milking, we were so taken up in showing Helen the stock. We must give him a hand now, or they'll be feeling the burden of waiting.'

'Milking now!' exclaimed Denyse in a shocked voice. 'Don't you keep fixed hours for that?' In the cabin this evening Fairburn realized how deeply French she had remained at heart, and felt an even greater thankfulness for this than he knew at mealtimes, when she produced marvels from almost nothing out of the saucepans he had grudged her. Death and destruction she had seen in plenty on the road to Bordeaux, but she, a townswoman, knew that cows gave less milk if they were tended irregularly, and she could still be astonished by fecklessness in practical matters, as distinct from human life. He had already noticed that she stressed one aspect of brutality which would not have impressed an Englishwoman, in referring to the German machine-gunning, from the air, of the cattle in the fields of France. 'They were practically *their* cattle by then, too! The *fools*!' Money, as a symbol of power, meant little to her, but the good things of the earth must not be wasted. In time, he knew, this strong-rooted, practical attitude would bring her fully to life again, more surely than anything he could do, even by needing her.

'We do be milking when we do be thinking of it, my dearest,' said the most beautiful of the old ladies, gently shocked in her turn that a fellow guest should question an excuse on a social occasion. Their going broke the spell that had been on Bridie; she spoke her thoughts to the fire as though nothing had passed, neither time nor other conversation, since she talked of Dublin. 'Father Keith says that mostly the City people have a mean, hard side to them — a man would hardly stop to tell you the way if you asked him. But wouldn't you say, maybe Father Keith was unhappy in Dublin, when he went as a lad, because he didn't know what to expect? I think if you saw it was just they were busy, you wouldn't mind.'

The priest says . . . the priest says . . . He himself, reflected Fairburn, would not have known how best to set about discouraging the ambition of this eager young creature, had he thought such a course necessary for her salvation, except that it would not have been by urging that dance-halls were wicked and Dublin full of them, or that danger lurked in the shadows of the Liffey water-fronts, where ships came in from the furthest corners of the world. Primed by the priest, her elders could find no better arguments than these to bring against her. Even Mrs. Kathie became short with the girl when she asked difficult questions! 'Oh, Father Keith — !' said Bridie, 'aren't all the priests the same — apt to be thinking men terrible sinful everywhere? Did you ever hear one say that we had no need of repentance here in Kildooey?'

'He is a good man,' her mother reproved her, 'and you wouldn't be understanding the half of his reasons, Bridie!'

Bridie smiled the confident, secretive smile of a child. Would they keep from her the glory of distant scenes — the anxious priest and the anxious women? They should not keep it long!

'Only the other day he was telling us' — Mrs. Agnes pointed her long, wizened nose at the visitors in turn, with quick, birdlike jerks, but she spoke at Bridie — 'he was telling us, the drinking among the foreign sailors is worse now than it has ever been, on account of the war. He has it from his brother who works among them, and brave work it is. "God forgive them", he says, "it's knowing the perils of the way home that sends them to making beasts of themselves ashore".'

The settle creaked as Mrs. Mary leant forward and gave words to the wisdom that went so strangely with the malice she showed at other times. 'Good man that he is,' she said boldly, 'he speaks too much of forgiveness.'

'Mary, how can you! In the cruel days we have now!' There was a chorus of protest.

She turned impatiently to the two strangers and talked as to equals, excluding the others with a wave of her hand. 'If a man is at rest in himself, doing the best he can before God and man, what need has he to be always thinking, "Is it for you to forgive me? Is it for me to forgive you? Is it for God to forgive us all, and for what?" Where there's no judging on one side or the other, there's no forgiveness wanted.'

There was a gasp of disapproval from those not addressed. ' 'Tis a demeaning relationship for all concerned, a forgiveness!' she said as a summing up, and grinned wickedly at the look of resentment on Mrs. Agnes's face.

'But, Mary, you know that Father Keith would say — '

In his absence, a clear picture of the priest could be built from his own speech, as reported by people who loved and admired him. Narrow, ignorant, dogmatic, jealous for the dignity of his Church, he and Mr. Wallace of the shop, as Fairburn had suspected, disputed between them the position of village-adviser in all things. Both liked to be consulted over all land-purchases and inheritances; and expected to have the arrangement of marriages and quarrels; but there was no doubt that Father Keith won in almost every battle.

A country boy, he had been sent through Maynooth by the proud

sacrifice of his family, who were also Donegal people, known with awe
by Mrs. Kathie. To the visitors, listening to her praises, he appeared
to combine all the qualities of the worst of the Irish priesthood, even
to a lack of compunction in using, on people simpler than himself,
the tricks of sarcasm and rhetoric taught him as a defence against the
more formidable enemies of his faith. His ruthlessness with Helen was
something which Fairburn had already realized; only Bridie remained
unaware that her sister had not wanted to come home. It seemed that
Father Keith dealt implacably with any rebellion among the younger
members of his flock against the pronouncements of the Church, such
as the recent edict for the discouragement of dancing. No understanding had been shown of Bridie's aspirations, nor of those of the
other young people who turned their eyes towards wider fields of
living; it was his habit to invoke against them the authority of the
older generation, anxious to hold on to their children. Yet, oddly
enough, Bridie seemed to be fond of him.

'Ah, but you should hear him speak of the signpost!' said Mrs.
Agnes with satisfaction. ' "As if it is not hard enough to keep our young
folk where they'll be safe, without Mr. Wallace putting up legends
to turn their heads." That's what he says. Mr. Wallace? Oh, yes,
it was he that persuaded the Donegal District Council to let him erect
it, he having the building trade in his hands hereabouts. Just in order
to annoy Father Keith, he did it.'

'But does the lane by the quarry really lead to Dublin?' asked Fairburn. 'It looks more like a farm track.'

Bridie glanced up, waiting to speak.

'Oh, I wouldn't put it past going there,' said Mrs. Agnes sourly.

'It does so,' said Bridie eagerly. 'Sean says it does.'

'How would he know, and he never further from home than Sligo?'

'There's a big map of all Ireland the guardai showed him in the
station at Sligo, when they questioned him about the drilling. And
it has our lane on it, you could follow it right to Dublin, he said,
getting bigger all the time. There's other roads run into it, do you
see, swelling it as it goes. Sean is on your side in the matter — as you
well know! — he would have the signpost down, if he could. So he
was particular to notice if the road does what it says. And he wouldn't
tell me till I asked him.'

'A new thing, for anyone to hear you quoting Sean!' said Mrs. Agnes, worsted.

Bridie gave the happy shake of the head which Fairburn remembered from their first meeting, near the peat diggings, when she had told him that it would be years before she was troubled with marriage, though it was 'all arranged'.

'Father Keith says,' put in Mrs. Kathie, 'wouldn't it be the reasonable thing for the guardai to pay more heed to the potheen that's made in the hills, and leave the young hotheads to do no harm at all by themselves in the bogs!'

'Instead of having them up to question, if they hear so much as a squeak from a rusty bolt on a rifle so old they wouldn't be daring to fire it themselves.' As the mother of Sean, Mrs. Agnes spoke with indignation. 'Father Keith has the rights of it.'

Fairburn had seen the priest only once, for a few minutes, and remembered nothing but a thick-set figure, a twinkling eye, and an invitation to come and use the wireless at any time if the visitor wanted to hear the news: 'A poor set I have, but the only one in the place. If you bar Mr. Wallace's, and he's away out beyond the spur. You wouldn't want to go thraipsing up the hill to get the English version or the German version alone on his grand machine. When on mine you can have Athlone, a bit muzzy, maybe, but giving them both, one after the other, with a fine impartiality! Sometimes the one put first, and sometimes the other! It will send you back to England with a proper view of our neutrality!' A typical country Father with a pleasant native wit, Fairburn had thought, on first impression. Now he was really interested in the prospect of meeting the man, and discovering what was the quality by which his people were drawn to him so strongly; no hint of it appeared in their accounts of his acts or words. It was disappointing to hear, on Sean's return, that Father Keith could not leave Mrs. Clancy. The wretched woman, it appeared, was in a great taking over the return of her daughter to a hospital in the West of England which had already been bombed once. He sent a message that he would look in at Mrs. Mary's the following evening. 'So you will have to come again, then, to meet him!' said Mrs. Mary, delightedly, to Denyse.

Information about the Clancys was showered upon the campers;

Father Keith had opposed the girl's going to England in the first place;
Mr. Wallace, it was, who had advanced the money on a property-
mortgage which had enabled her to be trained as a nurse. Did it not
serve her mother right, sorry as everyone was for the poor woman,
to be laden at the moment with anxiety? This was what came from
following the advice of Mr. Wallace instead of taking that of Father
Keith. Mrs. Kathie suggested that it might even be the presence of
Margaret Clancy in the hospital which had brought the bomb on
the place. Mrs. Mary thought otherwise; hadn't Father Keith said
himself that now she had her training, it was her duty to use her skill
for the people in the afflicted towns?

'In any case, as she wasn't killed by the bomb,' began Mrs. Agnes,
'it wouldn't be reasonable —' She caught Mrs. Mary's contemptuous
eye, and stopped.

'You'll be coming in, for sure, to-morrow night?' Mrs. Mary clutched
at her principal visitors with friendly hands as they rose to go. 'To
see Father Keith. Ah, you will now, you will!' She was like a child,
who at the end of one treat has found a reason for demanding another
the next day. Company was her greatest pleasure, and she always resented its dispersal; but a slight feeling of awkwardness had come
over her little gathering — because Helen had not come back with her
pictures. Mrs. Kathie rose, too. 'Bridie and I must be joining Helen
at home,' she said. 'Maybe she discovered, when she'd found what
she wanted, that it was too late to be worth coming over again. Even
though it's only a step beyond the bridge.' The worried face belied the
soothing words as usual.

'Oh, Tom, the lights!' said Denyse, catching her breath with surprise
when they stepped outside into the September night. 'The lights of
the other houses!' From the further side of the stream they shone,
a row of unshielded windows, pouring their unconcern into the darkness. In Mrs. Mary's cabin, too, the lamp had been lit during their
visit, and there were no curtains to be pulled, but only from outside could the effect come full upon them of the peaceful glow of
men's homes.

He took her arm. So to her, as well, the bright, confident windows
were intensely moving. Twice, before going back to the car to sleep,
they walked the entire length of the village street, over the bridge

and back again, basking in the patches of light that fell on them, smiling when these came high enough for them to see each other's faces.

CHAPTER VI

FATHER KEITH

THEIR days, they found, tended to be arranged for them, unless they made efforts to assert themselves against this friendliest of tyrannies; most of the time it was pleasanter to let themselves be coaxed, provided for and directed.

Not only Mrs. Mary felt that she had established some prior claim on their company (she attempted to inveigle them into her cabin, on one pretext or another, every evening of their stay). Bridie, as their first contact in Kildooey, considered herself to be their appointed messenger, and ran errands for them. She appeared before breakfast, on Denyse's first morning in Kildooey, with the usual gift of milk and the information that Danny Hughes and Peadar McQuire had holed the boat which they owned together, the one that himself had borrowed before. 'But it doesn't matter,' she said, 'because Sean will have his boat waiting for you by the time you have eaten; and bait is already on board. In case there's no luck with the spinners this morning, for the water is unkindly clear. Ken Clancy had some worm from yesterday, so we sent him word for it. That way you can get rock fish if the pollock won't bite, and you needn't wait till midday, when the tide will be down, to have the worms dug for you. It would be too late.'

'Too late for what?' asked Tom.

'For you to have some hours at the fishing before you go to Father Keith's for the news. It is read at twenty to one and quarter to six and ten past nine; they read it out from Athlone, every day at the same time. Except Sunday which is different. I know, because Kenny has looked in a paper to see for you. Father Keith was after saying last night at Mrs. Clancy's he wouldn't be back from Ardrinath till eve-

ning. Only he hoped you wouldn't be taking that into consideration
at all. Sean can show you which is the house and where is everything,
when he brings you back from the fishing. Have you enough spinners,
now, or will I be fetching some of Danny's, seeing he can't use his till
the boat is mended? — not that he wouldn't be glad to lend them anyway — '

'Thank you, I've got two. Peadar gave them to me. That'll be enough,'
said Tom, feeling himself unequal, so early in the morning, to the
strain of defending his freedom from the communal goodwill.

'Maybe I could come in the boat too?' suggested Bridie, dropping
her gaze from their faces, and speaking in a very small voice. 'That
is, if there's room?' They were never able to make out what caused
her unexpected lapses into shyness.

Sean, however, appeared unwilling to take her, when she accompanied them to the beach. 'You have no idea of trimming the boat
and you move too suddenly,' he told her — brusquely for Kildooey —
and only relented on their intercession.

The sea looked very deep that day in its smoothness, and as though
it might at any moment well up over the sides of the curragh of
tarred canvas and withies, and engulf them without a sound. Like
all typical Irish craft, Sean's boat appeared too frail and too patched
to be trusted far out to sea in a dead calm; actually, as Tom knew,
it would be at its handiest in a considerable jabble, buoyant as a cork
and able to ride a short curling sea which would founder a heavier
boat. In such transparent water the fish did not bite well, neither
spinner nor worm would lure them, but the conditions were too lovely
for anyone to care.

Bridie took her turn at the oars. Light as she was, and only half-
matured, she was more sturdily built than Sean, and rowed well.
Showing through the limp, shrunken cotton dress, the lines of the
young figure were a delight to watch as she moved, and her whole
being glowed with the pleasure of the day. 'Have I tar on my face
again, that you look at me like that?' she asked, and before they
could answer, began to laugh. 'Oh, the last time I was in the boat —
do you remember, Sean? A new patch was tacky on the inside, and
I touched it, not knowing, before pushing my hair back from my
eyes. Never a speckled hen has carried more bars of black around her

beak than I took home that day! And I walked through the village thinking, Surely the world has gone mad at my approach!'

'I was hoping you'd lay an egg for my tea if I didn't disturb you with an explanation,' Sean said. 'More like an old hen than anything, you looked.'

'Well, there's no smudge there to-day,' said Tom. 'I was just thinking how very rare it is to see eyes that are really the colour of the sea; and yours are.' Bridie blushed violently at what was probably her first adult compliment.

Sean added quickly: 'With eyelashes like that damn yellow sea-weed — the sort that's slippery over the sharpest rocks, and parts, and holes your boat for you!'

'Now for that I will tell them something against you!' It was plain, however, that Bridie was not really affected by anything he said. Brought up to the bickering of Mrs. Agnes and Mrs. Mary, the young people had fallen into much the same kind of relationship. 'See that Sean doesn't get you late to Father Keith's with his grand patriot's watch —'

'Leave off that, now!'

' — The one they served out to him at the time of the raid across the border into Cavan. When the boys from the bogs nearby were sure the whole of Eire would rise with them —'

'Bridie, leave off that, do!'

'Oh, 'tis not supposed to be known, but told far and wide, of course it is! Just a handful of police chased them all the way back again.' Bridie bent double with amusement, her oars in the air, and rocked the boat so that Sean called to her angrily. 'The bold invaders!' she said. 'And weren't they forced to lie up all the light hours of one day in the wettest part of the bog, and creep home in the dark, and the grand watch has never got the better of that experience, what with the damp and the disappointment. Sean will be telling you, "I have the time exactly, for by now it is two and a quarter hours fast." But sometimes it is only two hours and sometimes it is all of three.'

'Sounds like one loop of the spring hitched over the next, doesn't it, Tom?' said Denyse, 'if it's taken to going as fast as all that.' The day was too good for such scrapping; obviously nationalism was a subject on which Sean could stand no chaffing.

'Yes, it does,' Tom agreed. 'If so, it's quite simple to put right. I could do it for you with a pin.'

'No, thank you, though it is kind of you to think of it,' said Sean. 'I have it worked out by now, how far ahead it has got at every hour of the day. I set it each morning, you see. It is easy to reckon when you are used to it. Bridie is just being silly.'

'He wouldn't be letting a man from England look into his grand patriot's watch,' said Bridie mockingly. 'And it racing through time to bring the end of Partition the nearer!' Denyse was forced, for the sake of peace, to break the conversation in the boat in two, and take charge of Bridie's end of it, distracting the girl with travellers' tales of great cities, Paris and Rome, Delhi and Colombo; to these she was always ready to listen for hours, wide-eyed and silent with longing. No other place, however, was as stirring to her imagination as Dublin.

They landed with only three fish between them, but the sense of a morning well spent; even Sean was willing to admit, 'There's something to be said for the poor, small farms we have in these parts. Instead of the great rich ones in the Six Counties. Here, a man can take his pleasure in the morning with a clear conscience, for it makes so little difference if he works or not'. The scene on the beach was exactly as Fairburn had imagined it before he came to Kildooey. Children rushed down from the bridge and the stream where they had been playing, and splashed knee-deep into the sea to meet the returning boat, handling the catch, and commiserating on its smallness in sweet, sing-song voices. They helped to lift the curragh out of the water and bore it up the beach beyond the hightide mark; the younger ones, arriving late, flung themselves on the bow, clung to the gunwale, and lent only their moral support to the carrying of the boat by swinging their feet off the ground, while everyone with a free hand slapped amiably at any part of them within reach. The boat left the sea encrusted, as with barnacles, with these ecstatic little bodies.

Sean's time-keeping may or may not have got the visitors punctually to Father Keith's house; Bridie's promise, that he would show them where everything was to be found, turned out to be over-optimistic. Neither he nor Fairburn could discover how the priest's wireless worked until after the principal news had been given. They missed the figures of the latest air losses over Britain.

The room itself was the ordinary room of a busy country priest with more than one village to look after — untidy, as much an office as a place for leisure; it held very few books or other personal things, and it gave no idea of the man who lived in such colourless surroundings. Yet the impact of his personality was immense when they met him later in the evening at Mrs. Mary's. It was surprising to realize, soon after he had settled down to his cup of tea in the cabin, how little he tallied either with the first impression he made or with the picture which his flock combined to present of him; or rather, how misleading both these ideas were, although true in detail; but they left out his essential quality. Here was a mind uncertain and afraid, tormented into rigidity lest at the least yielding the whole structure of his life should fall in ruins about him.

All the Sullivan relations and in-laws were present, except Helen and her young man, and on their absence no comment was made. Fairburn asked about the secret drilling at night in the bogs, of which everyone seemed to know; and the flaming spirit in Sean leapt to answer in words of a passion which was new to Denyse, except by hearsay. She listened incredulously, her heart sick with recent memories: France in collapse and the way to final victory left open, it seemed, to the conqueror; while here men spoke hopefully of civil strife.

If the traitors in Ulster were to admit conscription, even for the Six Counties — if Dev or another in his own good time should call the people, the one and inseparable people of Ireland, to unity — 'Ah, be done with the "if's" now,' said Sean. 'It's "when" I'm saying! When — ! And it will be no mere raid this time.'

'Let them have their dreams!' said the priest, in reply to Fairburn. 'They might have worse.'

'Worse?' echoed Denyse. 'What dreams are there, worse than those of pointless killing?'

'As to the point, it's a matter of opinion. And surely,' said Father Keith, 'in these days men do, and think, many greater evils than killing?' He turned the talk to the strange but harmless plague of voles with which the district had been infested during the summer. It seemed a curiously trivial subject, after the fierce self-consciousness of Sin Fein, but it was not trivial to him.

'The eared-owls came over from Norway, and bred here. All the way from Norway, they said so in the papers! A great number of them. We saw them everywhere here, and in a few weeks they had dealt with the thronging of the voles. Now is there any material means by which they could have known, before they came, of what was waiting for them beyond the sea — the riches of food for their young? There was none; of course there was none. And there are those who claim that man can understand everything on this earth, as well as beyond! And when the owls had reared their young, didn't they all go flocking back, across the sea again? Never before, in my lifetime, has there been this great concourse of owls.'

He knew little more than most country-dwellers would know of the habits of birds and beasts, but they meant much to him. 'The clean things . . . the innocent ways of them . . .' For him, the world of men ran sickeningly with the sores of sin and shame. He turned his eyes aside with relief. It was not possible to hear him speak in fervent praise of those whose activities he approved — 'the dear people who are bringing back our ancient language . . . a handful of teachers in our schools, who are striving to make the best of the past live again for the children!' — without realizing how implicit in all praise is condemnation by contrast; the greater the admiration, the lower by inference must be the level of normality, from which the thing praised stands out in virtue. In his despairing view the most that could be hoped from human activity was that, like the revival of Gaelic, it should be harmless.

Forgiveness — there was little his mind could rest upon which did not seem to him to cry out for this most holy and precious attribute of the God he served, with constant searching of conscience; the loving God who required of him so much severity. He was a lonely and touching figure, and the visitors' hearts went out to him, like those of his flock — even the young ones, understanding instinctively more than their owners knew. Face to face, it was impossible not to like Father Keith.

His pleasure in Mrs. Mary's company was plain to see, though the two were always at cross purposes; he and she were the quickest witted people in the community; and, as a tough and unregenerate character, she could be reproved as often as he believed necessary without fear that what he said would have any grieving effect; or, indeed, any effect at all, beyond that of bringing on him an immediate, small revenge. Twice, by directing several people to attend to his cup, she got into it double the amount of sugar which he allowed himself, by strict rule, in pandering to an immoderately sweet tooth.

'I shall cut myself down for a week now,' he said, half irritably, sipping with an air of luxury. 'You know it is not right, at a time of suffering and privation abroad, for any of us to indulge ourselves.'

'This war, do you see,' said Mrs. Kathie as an aside, with her air of excusing something, 'it is constantly on the mind of all the people of Ireland. Not a chicken is run over on the bridge by Mr. Wallace's cart, as it was Wednesday, but someone will say, "These terrible times are making everyone careless and hard of heart". We do be always thinking of it.'

'Ah, now, Father, let you tell your housekeeper to put no sugar on the table,' said Mrs. Mary complacently, 'and the poor silly creature will forget. Then you'll help yourself without knowing. May it do you good, body and spirit, the one through eating it and the other through thinking you haven't.'

'Mrs. Omaney looks after me very well, and if I tell her —'

'Why wouldn't she look after you. Knowing there's not a soul in the place, having tasted her bread, would give her employment but you, out of charity.' Mrs. Mary was very proud of her bread-making by proxy, and had already offered to teach what she called 'the knack of it' to Denyse.

'It is not charity. And yourself would be hard put to it, Mary Sullivan, to know that sweet quality if you met it, having so little!'

Bridie, lighting the lamp with deft movements, screwed up her shining eyes in delight, and waited for further thrusts and parries between the old antagonists; any dispute between them nowadays was likely to lead on to talk of the new signpost and all it stood for; Mrs. Mary would defend it in the circumstances, so that for a while Bridie might hope for a friend at court. But Sean was not to be diverted from the wrongs of Eire by owls and voles and scruples about sugar. He launched out again into vehemence.

'It may well be in all our minds, this war! Of all the countries blockaded, we who are neutral are the one most squeezed! Because it so pleases the big nations fighting for their own lands. For all their fine words, that's what they're doing, no more; fighting for themselves. Fighting for the freedom of small nations — that's what England says! Isn't Ireland a small nation? Aren't the Six Counties part of Ireland, and doesn't England keep them from us? Is that fighting for the freedom of the small?'

'Isn't Ulster even smaller than Eire?' asked Denyse, genuinely uncertain on this point. But Sean went on, oblivious of the awkward question.

'And it suits England and Germany to stop our trade! Because we will not be drawn into quarrels that are none of our choosing. What right has either of them, I'm asking you, to stop our own ships from fetching the things we need from wherever they may be found? But oh, no —'

'Not even an Irishman can argue with a well-laid minefield,' said the priest, with a smile.

'If they think in London to starve us into giving back the ports, let them starve us and see!' The fanatical voice rose. 'There's not a thing to choose between these protectors of small nations. So say we!'

'Now, Sean!' said Mrs. Mary, getting to the only aspect of the subject which interested her. 'Maybe Mr. Fairburn is in the English Forces, for all he speaks like a man from further south?' She threw a pleased glance round the cabin; no one else had thought of this way of asking the newcomer what he did at home.

'Yes, I am, but it doesn't matter. What Sean's been saying, I mean.' He gave Mrs. Mary's curiosity no further satisfaction. 'I was brought up on that quarrel about the past. Only long before I was his age, it had struck me that the future was a lot more important than the past. To everyone. And a lot more interesting to me personally,' he added softly to Denyse, under cover of Sean's heated assertion to the whole company that no Irishman who had lived through the Troubles in this part of Donegal could ever be willing to ignore the past, while the old injustices remained. 'Even if he happened to be scarcely more than a baby in the Bad Times. Like myself,' said Sean. 'Remembering nothing of them but what I was told afterwards.'

A little silence fell in the cabin, and then every one of the Kildooey people talked at once. Father Keith and the three older women spoke of thankfulness that the worst days were over for Ireland; though Mrs. Mary sounded less heartfelt than the others, in her hopes that the Bad Times would never return. 'There was always so much going on in the Troubles,' she said wistfully. 'But maybe it was only because we were young, then, that fighting seemed to accomplish more.'

Bridie contributed, in her lilting childish voice, the news that a man was after telling her that very day on the Comines road: the war would be over in a matter of weeks now. Out of thoughtfulness for the guests she did not add the reason which he must have given, since it was what all Ireland believed: that Britain was already beaten to her knees.

The conversation swept past the visitors into a historical and religious controversy between Sean and the priest, agreed on the need for ending Partition, and differing merely on the grounds of their belief. Denyse and Fairburn might have been alone for all the attention paid to them at the moment; it was one of the charms of cabin society in Ireland, that people were always capable of being interested in the conversation of those to whom they had talked for years, to the complete exclusion for the moment of something as precious as a newcomer.

'The future was just about at its best when I was Sean's age!' said Fairburn. 'Before there were any rumblings in the distance, that people like me could hear clearly. In the days, in fact, when the future was a purely personal matter, made up of convection clouds and civil engineering.'

Denyse said, under her breath, 'So that's what you were, in what you once called "real life" — civil engineer?' It felt strange, talking together in the momentary seclusion of other men's passions; and stranger still to be learning elementary facts about one another at this stage of friendship. They had as yet had very little time alone together; Kildooey had seen to that.

'Yes.'

'Did you like it?'

'Very much. Why? Does it sound so dull to you?'

'No. I really don't know what it means. I vaguely supposed it had something to do with putting up municipal washhouses!'

'Well, that among other things! It's just my bad luck that I can get a lot of fun out of putting up most things, and none from blasting them down. Mostly I've had to do with bridges. In peace, I mean. They don't happen to have come my way as bombing objectives. I can't tell you how it'd go against the grain to destroy a good span.'

She touched his hand unobtrusively. About them flowed, with eager unreality, talk which seemed to belong to an age in which expediency had no place.

'It is well enough for those on England's side to hold that the past had best be forgotten.' Sean could not leave the subject.

'Until we have put our own house in order, it is not for us to be taking on the quarrels of others.' This was the priest's view.

'There's some would have us believe nuns and priests are ill-treated in Germany,' said Mrs. Agnes. 'If so, God help them, and the day of reckoning will come. Maybe a hundred years from now, with none of us here to see it. But come it will.'

'If you have children it will be easier for you to understand how it is with us.' Father Keith drew them back into the conversation. 'You wouldn't wish others to interfere with your management of them; we want no foreign influence on the Irish conception of duty. Either national duty or personal duty.'

'You don't *want* — you're standing on the side of a volcano, saying you'd rather it didn't blow up!'

'But we don't mean to be mixing up with any more troubles at all, do you see,' said Mrs. Kathie. 'It's little enough peace this country has bought with all she's suffered. We want the world to forget we are here. You wouldn't be blaming us for that?'

'Aren't we small enough?' Mrs. Agnes echoed her son, adding grudgingly, 'even if Ulster is smaller.'

'And if conscription came to Northern Ireland it would be the Catholics only that would have to march,' said Mrs. Mary. 'With the Protestants filling all the reserved jobs. Did you know, my dearest, not a Catholic will they take in the A.R.P. or the Fire Services.'

'Yet the Ulstermen think we should hand them back the ports. It isn't sensible!'

'Ah, Agnes, will you never let go of your hopes of sense on this earth!' Mrs. Mary sounded more annoyed by her sister-in-law than by the Ulstermen.

'Praise be,' said Sean, 'that Dev took the bold line with everyone about the war from the outset.'

'Like a tremulous girl at her first grown-up party,' said Fairburn. 'Actually daring to drink lemonade instead of something stronger! What do you think would happen to your bold independence if we lost, with your help?'

'We should be no worse off than under England.' Sean's sombre eyes shone with such impersonal hatred that there could be no question of giving or taking offence. It was assumed by everyone in the friendly, hospitable group that national feeling was beyond resentment. Mrs. Mary's interjection about Fairburn and the English Forces had been merely a social effort to get the information she wanted, and not a serious warning to Sean to be careful of his words.

'You unutterable fool,' said Fairburn wearily, in the same spirit.

'Whoever comes here, we fight.'

'You mean you'll go on play-acting at soldiers in the bogs, till just too late.'

'You'll see if it's only that — one day. And those across the Border too.' Sean smiled, like a saint over thoughts of heaven, and at Bridie's prompting, bent down to pick up a live turf for the visitor to light his pipe, lest he should be put to the trouble of stretching for it himself.

'Ah, look now,' said the priest, unruffled. 'There is also to be taken into account the practical aspect of our position.'

Fairburn, who had tried for ten minutes to get this considered, merely nodded and watched Denyse battling with a desire to laugh. Indeed, she was coming most beautifully to life if already it cost her an effort not to show what she felt. He wondered why he had ever thought her face impassive.

' — But I can't talk to a man without calling him something. What is your name?'

'Fairburn — I'm sorry, I thought you knew.'

'I knew that. Your other name?'

'Tom,' he said, surprised.

'And yours?'

'Denyse.'

'Look now, Tom and Denyse, if we were to help England, there'd be terrible revenge taken on us at once by the other side. No matter what he says, this young bomb-maker here, we've neither the tanks nor the planes to defend our own land, and when you hear from the Dail, "Ireland has doubled her armament", isn't it in the coils and recesses of the politician's mind that we've found another gun under a haystack, where it's been since the Easter rising? We cannot rely on England to protect us; indeed, she has enough to do, by all we hear. And she has shown little inclination to help: not a weapon will she sell us to protect ourselves. Neither she nor America!'

'There now, Agnes, are you listening?' exclaimed Mrs. Mary. 'You fretting to make sense of the ways of ordinary people. When there's no reason at all, it seems, in the heads of the great states!' Having returned the conversation comfortably to personalities, she felt that the interest of neutrality was exhausted, and ran on, herself, through a list of people in the locality, whose behaviour seemed to her pleasantly inexplicable. Very richly peculiar they sounded, like the girl who bashed her head open, before tying herself to a tree — Bridie, try as she would, could not get her aunt and the priest into another argument about the signpost.

'— And Mr. Wallace, now. There's a puzzling one! What cause could you find for his saying it was a shame to bring Helen back from America?' She looked sidelong at Father Keith, who was gazing steadfastly into the fire. 'Not a letter of hers had we ever shown him. Eh' — she turned to Denyse — 'they were full of innocence, and the names of lads that must have been shouldering one another aside for the privilege of escorting our little Kildooey girl! Judging by the numbers of them that were mentioned from time to time. Not but that she wrote of them in all simplicity. Saying the young people of Boston were showing her much consideration, knowing she was far from her own place. It put me in mind of how it was when Agnes and I were young. (Younger than Helen, for we were married a year or so earlier.) Though in our day we never thought it was consideration the lads were so full of! We mayn't have travelled so far as Helen in our time, but we didn't stay so simple, either.' She shook and wheezed with laughter and then grew serious again. 'Yet, "it's a shame", he says! And no advantage for him if she stayed out there and had her fun. While there's always money to be picked up by a man in a shop when a couple sets up a home here. Even when it isn't in a new house like the one Sean will be building, but just an ordinary marrying into a family, with the place ready and waiting from the death of the old ones.'

This was the first that Fairburn and Denyse had heard of Sean's intention of building a house, or of any activity of his, beyond the occasional night's drilling.

'It was her duty to come home,' said the priest, not lifting his head. The life of argument went out of his voice; it was suddenly old. The cold of the night seemed to creep with his words into the soft summer air drifting over the half-door. Denyse's eyes sought Fairburn's, and were troubled. Considered against the background of the war, and the vast suffering of ravaged lands, this village tale would lose its significance, and become no more than a small, sad story of individuals who scarcely mattered; but in the atmosphere of the cabin it was not possible to see it in that perspective.

'You know it was her duty,' said Father Keith, though no one had answered him. 'And she knew it, too, or she wouldn't have come.'

Outside, under the first stars, the hills moved closer as they lost their contours, and grew into towering velvet-black shapes. The feet of warriors and martyrs had trodden closer here than anywhere else on earth. Generation after generation, Ireland, of the yielding manners and self-torturing heart, had sacrificed her young to her fierce visions of right and wrong.

'And you yourself, Agnes,' said Mrs. Mary, still enjoying the splendid disorder of the human mind, the seeming tracklessness of its ways, 'didn't you surprise us all by saying she should have her freedom for a year or two yet, before you would agree to calling her home? "For we can only be young once!" you said. Ah, you did that, when Father Keith wasn't around, so you did! It was that delayed us, in agreeing to ask Father Keith to write. Till the day she sent us a photograph, taken by someone out there; and Kathie thought to please you by saying it was so pretty, the way she smiled, it put her in mind of you when you were even younger than Helen. And true enough, I told you the same. It had something of a look of you in your best days. Before you married the first time. When you were eighteen or nine-teen.'

'Helen was twenty-three when that picture was taken!' said Mrs.

Agnes, in a tone so implacable that the feeling deepened for the visitors of being close to an evil and a grief which was not only of this time and place. Here was all the envy of middle-age looking at the freshness of youth, glad of its brevity. She turned her craggy face to Denyse and Fairburn. 'I was nineteen when I married for the first time, and trouble came thick on me then. I'd nursed two husbands, one after the other, and lost the fight to death with them both, before I was twenty-three! And reared a sickly child through it all, as well; and another that died on me later. That's enough to take the glow out of any woman's looks.'

'Ah, indeed it is,' put in Mrs. Kathie, the only one of the three who had kept some remnants of her prettiness.

'I didn't look like Helen at twenty-three,' said Mrs. Agnes. 'As if never a care had blown my way! You said yourself, Mary, I might have been thirty. Only my hair I kept the same as ever. Yes, I kept that.'

'And from the day the photograph arrived, you said it was high time that Helen knew there was more in life than gaiety, and took up her responsibilities!' Mrs. Mary chuckled with pleasure at such apparent lack of motive.

'It was high time,' said Mrs. Agnes, folding in her thin lips. To annoy her sister-in-law, she gave a warm welcome to the head of Mr. Wallace, when it poked round the upper half of the door.

'Come in there. Come in!' she said, effusively for her. 'Hasn't Mary had a cup of tea waiting for you this last hour?'

Slightly more of Mr. Wallace protruded at a curious angle from the door-jamb, and he smiled sideways at everyone.

Bridie, discoursing on life in Kildooey during her visits to the quarry, had already drawn the campers' attention to the peculiarity of Mr. Wallace—he never appeared squarely in any opening, whether doorway, quarry entrance or car window, but approached as if he were really making for somewhere else. Coming into the cabin now, he gave the impression that gravity did not pull him in the same direction as other people, and the effort required of his tubby little legs was to detach him from the door, rather than to carry him over the threshold.

A mean-looking man, Fairburn thought; it seemed strange indeed

that he should have had a generous impulse to stand out against the
conscience of the community over the enslavement of a girl. A high
proportion of his sentences began or ended with 'Really, — ' or ' —
seriously, now!' suggesting that for the rest of the time Mr. Wallace
spoke only in fun. But never in her lifetime, according to Bridie,
had he been known to make a joke.

To-night he talked awkwardly of many subjects, and Father Keith
fell silent. Everyone made it appear that Mr. Wallace was welcome,
but seemed less at ease because of his presence. To the campers, he
said, 'You'll not let yourselves be disturbed, in the quarry, by Sean
coming to dig for the material of his house? No, no, for I've told him,
I can let him have the stone cheaper and easier than he could get it
out himself. Seriously now, it would be better stuff too, for here the
quarry runs only to small stone.'

'I dug a bit, the morning the car drove away,' Sean said, almost with
apology. 'Just loosened some of the stone, but I didn't take it away
in time. I didn't know, you see, that you'd be coming back.'

'Good heavens, Sean, it isn't our quarry!'

'*I* knew you'd be coming back,' said Bridie contentedly. 'I said,
"Himself has only gone to fetch something, depend on it. There's no
telling what a man with a car might want. You've waited so long,
Sean", I said, "there's no hurry to start building the house to-day".
But he would; and now the little he dug is lying under the bank
behind the car, where he can't get at it.' This seemed to amuse her
exquisitely. Everyone, even Sean, who laughed wryly, appeared to think
that it was a good joke against him.

'Of course' — Bridie turned to Denyse with her smile of sudden,
deferential shyness — 'we couldn't guess himself had gone to fetch his
wife. Now we know why it was he came here first by himself — to
see if Kildooey would be suitable for you. And we're very pleased he
thought it was.'

'A place doesn't have to be as beautiful as Kildooey to be good
enough for me!'

Bridie, still shyer and pinker, nodded towards Fairburn. 'But no
doubt he thinks so.'

Fairburn and Denyse discovered, through Mr. Wallace, what the
rest of the village had not liked to let them know before — Sean's

plans, which their presence was hampering. Though the quarry had been almost untouched for fifteen years, Sean had been intending for a long while to build a new cabin, a little way outside the village, on the road to Mr. Wallace's. It was to be a leisurely business, taking perhaps a year or more before the walls of piled stone were up and ready for the roof. Considering everyone's advice about the site, and various other preliminaries, had already taken nearly a year. But he had been ready to set-to with his donkeys, collecting the material, carrying a few stones at a time from the quarry, just at the moment of Fairburn's first appearance. The car had effectively blocked the entrance to the quarry. Probably, as it was such a slow project, it was only the knowledge of an obstacle which then made Sean want to start work in earnest, and at once.

'I'll get the car out of the way and give you a hand to-morrow,' said Fairburn, the injury to his arm forgotten.

'Ah, no,' said Sean, echoing Bridie. 'There's no hurry at all with the house. This year, next year — I wasn't reckoning to put in more than a half-day or so in the week. To-morrow the weather may be better for the pollock. You should go fishing.'

In a few minutes Mrs. Kathie took Bridie away with her; Sean left with his mother, and the priest rose to go, the visitors with him. The friendly atmosphere of the cabin, which had survived the bickerings of the others, had been destroyed merely by the coming of Mr. Wallace. He and Father Keith had exchanged no words, except on the non-committal subject of the wild snapdragon, which bloomed in profusion along the lower ledges of the bridge. It grew near the water, where the children leaning over from the top could not reach it easily. Mr. Wallace spoke of it deprecatingly. 'Only the natural kind we have here, of course. Just seeding by itself in the crevices of the old stonework. But it's a danger to the children, I think. "Now God keep your heads from the bottles and bricks in that stream", I say to myself each day, as I see the row of them up-ended on the top of the bridge wall, striving to pick the flowers.' The grocer's concern for the welfare of the Kildooey children sounded unconvincing; they were his enemies, invading his shop and fiddling with the stock for the fearful joy of being shouted at. Father Keith, to whom they were precious souls, expressed himself honestly: 'One or two fall over into the stream every year, and get a bandaged crown for it. But it teaches the others to let the plants alone for a bit, and it's just as well, or there'd be none left. Lovely, they are. Sweeter than garden flowers, I think. For no hand tends them.' (Pure . . . pure. . . .)

Mr. Wallace scurried away, aware that he was breaking up the gathering. Sidling out in the manner of his entry, he popped his head in again, at the same improbable angle, to repeat to the campers the invitation which the priest had given — to use his wireless if they wished to hear the news. 'But let me know,' he said, 'so I may have the house left open for you.' Father Keith smiled in the triumph of poverty, needing to make no such arrangement; his door was un-locked at all hours. In the whole of Kildooey only Mr. Wallace, living in the expensive house which nobody visited, ever thought of fasten-ing anything except the pens of the domestic animals; and these were for ever escaping.

'Now why can you not treat your sister-in-law with decent Christian kindness?' grumbled Father Keith as he took his leave of Mrs. Mary. She had come lumbering to the door after her last three guests, in an effort to keep them with her to the last possible moment. 'Remind-ing the poor woman in public that she took the wrong side in a family matter!'

'I — Father! — Is it unkind to Agnes you mean? Because she wouldn't recognize at first the duty to Helen? Wasn't I her best friend as a girl? And didn't I persuade her rightly in the end over that very matter, by what I said of the photograph? Decent Christian kind-ness — ' Mrs. Mary's incoherence was that of a deeply wounded woman. Plainly, however, her mind was on something else: there must be a means of retaining her little court a few seconds longer. 'You should ask her, rather, what grounds she has for her hatred of me in these days!'

'Mrs. Agnes has no such feeling in her heart! She does her best, according to her lights, to live in peace with all — '

'Eh, and I'll tell you myself.' She smiled toothlessly at the priest, dismissing his remark for what both of them knew it to be, an out-break of his official manner, unworthy of further notice. 'Few of the women in this village but have been more blessed than myself in the way of family ties.' A wicked eye cocked upwards between rolls of grey flesh, to note the effect of her words. 'So they are privileged to devote their whole lives to the service of their dear ones. Now I'm a poor, fat old widow, with no man to look after, and no child to look after me when I reach my pitiful last days; and by all the laws of sense they go hankering after — especially Agnes! — I ought to be envying them their children and their consciences, that do them credit alike! And look at me. And look at them. The miserable worrying creatures they are, for the most part! They'll never forgive me contentment, with so little to be content about! Not Agnes, anyway.'

She stood chuckling and panting with the long aftermath of her laughter, in the lamp-light of the doorway, calling gaily after them as they tore themselves away by force. 'Come back soon. Come back to-morrow, my dearests!'

CHAPTER VII

A STRING OF FISH

'THAT dear woman's tongue!' said the priest, as the darkness folded round them. 'There's nothing I can lay a name to at the moment, has caused one half the distress and trouble in this place! Her tongue, and her manner of thinking there's no connection between the words running off it and the harm that follows them around. Yet she was justified just now, when she asked, what has she left to be so cheerful about? Nothing but a curiosity like a child's, to see what each day may bring. And to such simplicity, I think, it must be as hard for God as for man, not to forgive everything.'

The campers' way back to the quarry lay across the village bridge; Father Keith came a few steps of the road with them, just to the centre, where he leant over the parapet like one of the Kildooey children, and pointed out to them eagerly, by faith alone, the places where the snapdragon grew most plentifully in the stonework. The night was now too dark for them to see anything. 'The lovely wild things . . . Many of the bunches not even the children's hands have reached.' Obsession with the defiling quality of mankind came through his praise again. Fairburn had thought of reasoning with the priest, if the opportunity arose, about the harshness of the summons to Helen: a pitiless summons which went out from many Irish villages every year, to devout young people on the other side of the Atlantic; they broke their hearts when they obeyed, coming back to squalor and poverty, and the memory of wider horizons, forever shut away from them. He had met them before, in his home county, fretful and resentful, or else resigned, and growing drearier at heart because of their resignation. A few were happy, but a very few. The nagging of lost opportunities remained in their minds.

But with Father Keith, Fairburn was sure that if he spoke, he had no chance of doing more than airing his own resentment of cruelty; this man would not listen, dared not listen; and now, suddenly, he felt too tired to begin the argument.

Moved by his own thoughts, the priest said, 'I am always humbled and amazed to see in what unlikely crannies of circumstances human happiness can seed itself, like those flowers!' and listlessly Fairburn agreed, quoting three lines of modern verse which said much the same thing. (It was by the young poet who had described Ireland as a bitch and a bore.)

The older man's hand grasped his shoulder. 'Where is that from?' A heaviness which had been in his voice from the moment of leaving the cabin disappeared in an instant, before a rush of intellectual excitement.

Fairburn told him; and refrained, with a grin in the night, from quoting further.

'I had no idea you were a man of books! If — if it is possible for me, it would be a rare delight to come up to your quarry from time to time, and talk of such things again. The people of these parts —' He dropped his tone. Standing where they were, on the crown of the bridge, with the burble of the stream below them, they could not be heard from the row of dwellings on either side: yet the cabins, mostly dark and sleeping by now, gave the impression of crouching together and listening intently. ' — I am of the same stock as themselves, a peasant working among peasants: and I have no right at all to feel that I have been alone here for twenty years, because in one small patch of my life, at college, I knew a different society. But so it is with me at times, God forgive me. If you are a lover of books — '

He stopped, till the pause grew slightly awkward. His hand dropped from Fairburn's shoulder.

'But perhaps you are not staying more than a few days. How long will you be in Kildooey? I ask because — ' He stopped again, all pleasure gone from his voice, and in its place once more the heaviness of age and uncertainty. 'You may have wondered, both of you, that I used your first names in the cabin. Possibly I shouldn't be caring at all for your opinion of me, but I wouldn't have you taking the Donegal priests for a mannerless lot on my account. So I ask you to believe I'm not usually as free as that with strangers. But do you see, if I said "Mr. Fairburn" to you, I would be bound to call your lady "Mrs. Fairburn", and that, I fancy — I am almost sure — she is not. It would have been wrong of me.'

He waited: no one spoke for a second. The directness of the man made it demeaning to lie to him.

'With great thankfulness,' said the priest, 'I will ask you to forgive this insult if I am wrong.'

'But you aren't wrong,' said Denyse. 'And even if you had been, we shouldn't have been insulted. I would like you to understand our point of view, just as you wanted us to understand yours, a moment ago. To us there's nothing sanctified or unsanctified about human relations; they're good or bad according to the attitude of the people concerned. We believe that what we do is right. And if it wasn't, marriage wouldn't make it any better.'

'What you have just said,' answered Father Keith, with the honesty which was so disarming, 'seems to me such nonsense that I can only give you the reply which you will not accept: it is not for you to judge of right and wrong.'

'Why did you think we weren't married?' asked Tom.

'You forgot yourself for the moment in the heat of the bit of argument we had, about Eire and the war. I said you would see our way more clearly if you had children, and waited to hear. Instead of answering, Tom, you looked the question at Denyse, to know what to say if I pressed you. Now I never knew that ignorance in a husband, and he living with his wife! I wouldn't have noticed, maybe, but I happened to be watching you. Priests dare not be as blind as you think them, no doubt! When strangers come among our people we are always wary.'

'I see.'

'These are my people — my dear people, even if at times I grow impatient with their shortcomings. I ask you not to stay long among them. I ask it against my will — ' He spoke haltingly, with deep anxiety. 'Knowing what it would have meant to me to come in touch again, through you, with things that I have missed so long — '

'We shall be gone in ten days for certain. I've got to be back in England after that.'

'Ten days — well — it is not long. And I ask, too, that you will not let anyone here know how it is with you.'

'Naturally. We shouldn't have done that in any case.'

'No, no. Of course. I needn't have asked you that. It was only, if you had happened to grow specially friendly with some of them, and they had guessed — it is more important, because you will be greatly liked. Both of you. If it were not for that — but evil must seem less evil, seen for the first time in the guise of a friend, whereas in fact it is doubly dangerous. For the young people, particularly; it would be terrible if they knew. Above all, I think, for Bridie, who loves you already for coming from afar.'

'They shall be no worse off, your young people, through anything we say or do,' Denyse told him.

'Unless you consider our presence here a pollution in itself?' said Tom.

'On that, I cannot tell what to think. What you have admitted is vile. To me so appalling that I still stand astonished. You who seemed — who still seem — yet I know such things are common enough in the outside world. You are not of our Church, nor have you, it appears, any conviction of sin. Without that — without the way of grace open to you — who can say in what degree of grave peril you stand yourselves, or what danger you are to others, save by open example? It is beyond my judgment.'

' "Neither do I condemn — " You're a good man, Father Keith. It's true, we shouldn't agree on much. But I can see that.'

'No, no, you mustn't say such a thing,' protested the priest in distress. 'I am far from being that. And I tell you frankly, if I had known how things were before you had won personal regard among my people, I should have had you hunted from Kildooey. Your car would have been stoned out of the place. But now the memory of you would make your way of life less evil to all those unwilling to think harshly of you. It is only that consideration which moves me —' he stopped. There was a moment's silence and then they heard his footsteps receding swiftly along the dark road.

They went on towards the quarry, not speaking much, Tom with his arm round Denyse.

'It would take more than a miraculous tip to the owls of Norway,' she said, half lightly, half seriously, 'to reconcile me to a god that could drive a man so hard!'

He grunted agreement. 'A curious end to an odd evening — curious, and most unpleasant for you, I'm afraid. I'm sorry I'm such a bad actor!'

They laughed ruefully. 'It is upsetting,' she admitted, 'to see filth being made, in another person's mind, out of something one knows to be good.'

'The filth was there, ready and waiting. It wasn't made out of our relationship — that's much too recent. It was made out of all the man has learned or imagined, in sixty years or so, about the side of life that's been denied to him. Out of every normal instinct he's seen in action, except those of voles, owls and snapdragons, I fancy — if that's any consolation to you?'

'I suppose it is.'

'You do mind, don't you, Denyse? More than I thought. I am sorry!'

'Well, it's the first time anything of the kind has happened to me. I daresay you're more used to it.'

'I'm not used to being caught out by country priests!' he protested, and added irrelevantly, 'You know — poor chap — a man must be pretty far gone in starvation for the things of the spirit, when a stray airman represents the highest possible contact with culture! Along with a woman whose most noticeable feature is a kissable mouth. An extraordinarily beautiful mouth, my dear. I've never really had time yet, have I, to tell you what I think about the details of you — the rest of your face, for instance? There's been so much else to do and so many people about! It was very interesting in the cabin to-night, looking at you more or less for the first time with leisure to notice things.'

'Come to that, I didn't know you had such blue eyes. Oh, Tom, it was a good evening while we were there, wasn't it, except for one thing?'

'That I have blue eyes?' He did not want her mind to return to the conversation with Father Keith.

'No, I don't mind that! But Helen — that was a horrible moment, when those two hideous old women talked of the photograph with the out-of-date likeness. They made my skin creep, between them. (They usually do, old women.)'

'I rather hoped Helen would come in to-night with her pictures. That she wasn't really avoiding us.'

'Of course she's avoiding us. It was just that while she was talking about shops and streets she forgot something — that now she's got to spend the rest of her life here. And as soon as she got outside she remembered. All the rest of her life, on a farm where the old women go about fouled with cow-dung. Which must seem to her, now, so much worse than it does to us. Why should she torture herself more than she need, talking about America? I shouldn't have come back either, in her place.'

Half-way up the hill, where the road turned, they stopped and looked down on to the dim huddle of the village, asleep beside the faint silver of its stream. Denyse said, 'Somewhere there, I expect, she's still awake. I keep seeing the back of that frilly little blouse which won't wash well, and can't be replaced, and the girl inside it with her head down on her arms, at one of those grand, solid tables like Mrs. Mary's — the sort she'll never be able to admire, because it isn't modern American — Helen forgetting to cherish what she's wearing, so that it shan't look crushed before it must — and eating her heart out for all the things in America which I didn't particularly want when I was there — the frilly blouses, and the crowds of window-shoppers. But why shouldn't she have them, if they mean so much to her? Well, I hope I'm wrong, and she's asleep already; and won't be missing anything again till to-morrow. Which is one day nearer to not missing them quite so badly. But I don't think so, somehow. Tom, how could you say of the priest that he was a good man? That one! Unhappy, and deeply sincere, of course. But "good" — we can't mean the same by "good".'

'That's quite likely. He's tolerant, compared with most of his kind. I suppose I really meant that. You don't realize how surprising it is that he's willing to let us stay; putting his feeling for his people before the idea of duty. Looking at expediencies for once.'

Linked by his arm, they walked on towards the quarry; while small things scuttered from under their feet and squeaked in the grass verge.

'Father Keith's voles, are they?' she asked.

'The few who've survived the visitation of the owls, I suppose.'

'You know, I didn't feel he liked the voles as much as the owls, did you? It's true they were lowly enough to breed without offence, but they weren't directly inspired like the owls. There was no kindly intervention of Providence for them. They were merely inspired-owl-fodder.'

'Like us!' he said. 'Judging by the little we really know of each other, I think we both tend to look at things from the voles' point of view. That's why it's so difficult for us to understand the owl-minded, like Father Keith. "Kindly intervention" as seen by the owls, is bound to turn into "bloody favouritism" in the eyes of the voles — bloody favouritism, and the feeling "Why pick on us?" The cry of almost all our generation, incidentally.' How good this woman was to talk to! He could go on thinking aloud, as he had in the ship; and gradually, gradually begin to feel, as he did to-night, that it was his own voice speaking; his own voice, which would not suddenly change into that of the stranger, against his will. 'As I told you to-night, the future was at the top of its form a little while ago. Not only for me, though: for most people my age. We were doing very nicely (just like the voles; harmless little creatures, a bit inquisitive) till Father Keith's inscrutable god decided it was time to fetch the owls to us, and let the killing start. There's been an awful lot of nonsense written and talked by distinguished men, since the war started, about the years from 1918 to 1939 — "The uneasy peace" . . . "An ugly interlude between wars" . . . "A time of strain and foreboding." Well, it may have been all that for them, if they really saw trouble coming from such a long way off. But it wasn't for us, the ordinary, short-sighted voles. It was a very good time.'

'Oh, I read a lot of books in France, too, during the last year. Telling me how unsatisfied and unhappy I'd been without knowing it. Longing for spiritual regeneration. (It was the best period of my life, actually, the three or four years before Munich.')

'There was a lot of happiness. I doubt if there was ever so much happiness in the world before. We were doing so very nicely, we unimportant voles! By the way, I'd better know for future guidance — officially, have we got any children?'

She turned on him suddenly and fiercely. 'This is the one subject I don't even pretend to be reasonable about — say whatever you like to other people; but to me, nothing at all about my child. I left her behind — I had to. In what's now occupied France. Safe enough, physically, in a pro-Nazi household, and I suppose I should be thankful for that. They'll bring her up a dutiful little Gretchen, admiring everything that I think is contemptible. She's so small — four — what chance has she got against them, if they're kind? And if they're not kind — ! I left her to that because I couldn't get her out safely, and I'm still glad I didn't try. Plenty of children died in the last rush to the ports. And if I'd stayed with her she wouldn't have been safe.

'I know what the Germans can do to children, body and spirit. I've seen. The planes that mowed down the refugees when they attempted to turn back — when we were being herded cleverly down the roads to jam them against the French and English troops — and sometimes for no reason at all but the pleasure of killing; they were flown by boys, those planes. The girls those boys go back to — they must have been trained to appreciate just this sort of spirit. That's what I've left her to, unless the world's fuller than I dare believe of men like you who can hate what you do, but go on; or Reynaud was right — "S'il fallait des miracles pour sauver la France —".' She did not finish that sentence, but said instead, 'Yet I'd rather be here, with you, than there looking after her, turning a baby into a child for others to turn into something bestial.'

He took her in his arms and held her, feeling more helpless with her than he had ever felt with anyone, and more profoundly moved by the longing to help; but he could not summon up for Denyse words which he did not mean — conveying faith in some mystical advantage siding with justice, decency and hope, or any belief in a future which would give her back her child. He could only hold her closely till the moment of intensest feeling was over, murmuring endearments, waiting till she grew less rigid in his arms; and know gratitude to her, even at present cost, for being someone to whom he could offer no unworthy consolation.

'I won't always feel like this, I know. It's the same for me as for Helen,' she reminded him wryly as they went on. ' "L'eau coule, le temps passe, le coeur oublie." A bit, anyway. I may even have another child one day, by you or someone, and it won't be quite so bad, thinking of her. But just for now, you mustn't talk about my child — as you see! I'm sorry I was so vehement over it. I'm not given to hysteria. But just for now —'

It passed through his mind that all over Europe this was what lovers were doing for one another, this was all that they could do, holding one another closely, waiting for the worst moments to go by, and whispering very old words: 'My dear — so dear to me — very lovely — perhaps some day —'

A still figure grew visible, leaning against the glimmering white shape of the new signpost, as they reached the top of the hill and approached the quarry. For a fraction of a second, against all reason, both felt a stirring of the mind, in response to something more natural to this soil than reason — it was where the spirit of the gunman had stood, in Mrs. Mary's story. Then the figure came forward, to be recognized as Sean in the faint light rising from the moon behind the hill. 'I brought you some fish,' he said. 'Chased out of my mind entirely, they were, by the grand exchange of views we had in the cabin. Or I'd have given them to you before. Will I clean them now, and they'll do for your breakfast?' He held them up against the lightest quarter of the night sky: four fine pollock with a string through their gills. Tom already had a couple, from the morning's catch; the previous day, Bridie had commandeered for her campers, from someone else in the village, two illicit young salmon-peal which they had not yet eaten; the supply of fish was threatening to become a glut: but as these particular pollock were evidently in the nature of a peace-offering, they were accepted with warm expressions of pleasure. Though everyone else expected national sentiment to run high but remain impersonal, Sean must have felt some doubts about the argument after the gathering broke up — possibly because he himself was more touchy than the rest of the family.

'It's very good of you to bother about us so late,' said Denyse.

'Ah, as to that,' Sean told her, "tis truly no bother at all!' He crouched in the light of the headlamps, cleaning the fish on one of the flat stones destined for his house. 'The moon'll be up to-night, and I'm on my way down the bog, where there'll be more than me besides! He knows the rest.' Rising with the gutted fish, he hit Tom a friendly blow, narrowly missing the damaged part of the arm, and hung the string of pollock from the signpost. 'The best use for that damned notice!' he said, with less than his usual heat. 'Don't forget them, now, when you go to bed, or the gulls will have them.'

'The signpost seems to be causing a lot of ill-feeling,' observed Tom mildly, wondering what would have happened if Sean had landed a little higher: involuntarily, in his present state of nerves, he would have hit back as hard as possible. Sean's fisherman's-knife was in his hand. As things were, it might take no more than an Anglo-Irish kill- ing, whichever of them succumbed in the subsequent fight, to start up something very much like the Troubles in these parts, and Donegal could be relied on to do her best to embroil the rest of Ireland, with help from enemy centres in Dublin.

'It is that,' said Sean. 'Shouldn't the people of this country be willing to serve her wherever she's chosen to cradle them? And not be wear- ing out their wits, thinking of places too busy in the trade with England, to give her more than a blessing on St. Patrick's Day. (For that's what I've heard of Dublin!) Or maybe a shot or two when the rust is threatening the rifles, so they have to be cleaning them any- way! But we mustn't be starting on that again, with you wanting your rest. May the fish taste sweeter than you'd get it in Dublin!' He went off into the night, and in a moment returned, less at ease in manner, a little breathless. 'Let you not be putting up with Bridie hanging about you here, if she comes to be a nuisance.'

'But we're very fond of her. She's a most amusing visitor.' This, though the truth, was not the whole of it. Bridie was a charming com- panion, like most of the people who came up to the car in an almost endless stream during the day, to bring some small token, and chat for a while. (A regular tariff of conversation against presents seemed to have established itself: milk entitled the giver to stay hardly any time; an egg might mean half an hour's talk.) There were moments, however, when they would have been glad of fewer gifts and more privacy.

'Tell her to go when you wish,' Sean insisted. 'A young girl — you wouldn't be wanting to listen to her all the time. Or to be talking to her either. She shouldn't be here so much.' He took leave of them again, and did not reappear.

'Now what's behind that?'

'I don't know. Unless it's jealousy?'

'Over Bridie? He was paying no attention to her this evening. Or any other time that I've noticed.'

'No, but he's the man she's to marry in due course, all the same.'

'Oh, no, Denyse, I hope not! Our Bridie! He's not worthy of those really extraordinary eyes.'

'All the same, Mrs. Kathie told me, it was arranged long ago. Favoured by Father Keith. With Mr. Wallace, of the shop, seeing to the practical side, so that none of the family should have the embarrassment of comparing the value of one field with another.'

'But they're cousins. A priest-made marriage wouldn't be so close.'

'They're not, unluckily — I think she's too sweet to be wasted on anyone with only one idea. There's nothing I couldn't tell you about Sullivan relationships after this evening. Sean's by the first husband, and he isn't really a Sullivan. There's no blood connection between him and Bridie.'

'Pity. I always supposed vaguely it was Shamus she meant, when she said it was all settled, but she was in no hurry herself. He's also a connection of sorts, and also a fanatic; but he must have a lot more human graces — that's judging by the trail of devoted friends he's got, strung out all along the line from London to Belfast.'

'And he isn't part of her background, the way Sean is, and has been since childhood. There'll be even less excitement for Sean and Bridie in coming together than for Helen and her man. I should think it'll be unpleasantly like the brother-and-sister affairs we get sometimes down in the very deep country near our summer place. One of the farmers explained to my husband why he lived with his sister, which was causing a bit of scandal; he said, "I only do it between flax-gathering and the grape harvest, if the weather's bad. There's nothing to do out of doors". Poor Bridie, I hope it won't be quite as dreary as that for her — only noticed when there aren't any plots to be hatched for Ireland's sake!'

Through the window of the car, in which he was unrolling the sleeping kit, Tom could see Denyse's face, curiously lit by the bluish primus flame, as she knelt by the stove in a sheltered corner of the quarry. It had the look of votive intentness which she wore whenever she cooked. He wondered if she realized that this was the first time she had mentioned her husband.

They had already fallen into a routine of small chores. Denyse, while she talked, was boiling up the stock-pot which stood on the roof of the car by day, out of the reach of stray animals. The contents, a kind of bouillabaise, were what Tom called 'gluey', in highest possible praise, and appeared to be inexhaustible; they would each have a mugful before going to bed. He was blowing up the air mattresses with the foot pump of the car, before spreading out the two sleeping-bags which Denyse had made into one. Whatever mental reservation she might still have, beyond his knowledge, there were certainly none physically; it was her suggestion that they should do away with 'all this bundling'.

'So it's for Bridie the new cabin's to be built!' he said, 'and not just for Sean to have some place of his own, where he needn't live with Mrs. Agnes? I thought that was quite a good enough excuse for building.'

'No wonder they don't seem in a hurry, either he or Bridie.'

'Well, I don't burn with the same pure spiritual flame as Sean.' He got out of the car and went over to her. 'If that blasted soup's not ready yet, let's leave it and go to bed.'

'Ungrateful —'

'I'm not ungrateful!'

CHAPTER VIII

MORNING

GULLS, screaming over the signpost where the fish hung, disturbed them with a wild clamour in the dawn; they had forgotten Sean's advice.

The whole string of pollock was too heavy for any one bird to lift, and dangling there, under the board, the fish were difficult to attack separately. The beating white wings seemed to fill the world with light of their own, as the birds swirled down out of the morning haze. A few discovered the stone where Sean had cleaned the fish, and made off with the bits left on it, but others came to take their places about the post and the cloud of fighting grace grew denser.

The campers sat up to smoke, and watch the gulls, and the gradual parting of air and water on the misty horizon, where the pale sea began to shimmer, between the paler reflections of tall clouds. If the fish were lost it did not much matter: this moment, poised between night and day and alive with the magic of wings, was worth the price of an unwanted gift. One pollock, buffeted about by the birds, fell from the string to be torn to pieces in a few seconds under a mound of gulls, and borne away.

'They know what flight should be,' Tom said, following with his eyes the effortless soaring of a white body swinging out over the head-land to meet the air currents from the sea; it turned rose-hued as it drifted up into the first sunlight without movement of wings. 'I'm what I am—and exactly where I am now I suppose—because once, when I was a boy, a particular gull flew inland at a particular moment, over a hill near Cork. I was lying there on my back in the grass, watch-ing to see which of three bits of thistledown floated out of sight first, till I forgot about them, looking at the gull, and thinking, "That's how I want to fly. If it's possible". I didn't know then whether it was possible—I knew a fair amount about mechanical power, of course. Most boys do at 16—but not if a man could really inhabit the same world as a gull, using the movement of air. I'd never heard of it being done. I don't think there was any gliding in Ireland at the time. When I read, later on, that other men were experimenting along the lines of my dream — experimenting successfully, too! — I think it was the greatest shock of excitement I've ever had. Four years between that moment and the first time I went up, and the dream hadn't faded at all. It was everything I'd hoped, the first lift—and then not as satisfying as some of the experiences that came after. Being "drunk with happiness" really can mean something, you know. (Yes, of course you know. You must be getting very bored, hearing me talk about gliding. Well, you'll get a lot more tired of it in the next few days.') She smiled and shook her head, but he had not waited for an answer. He became much younger, speaking of anything he had liked. The edge of strain went out of his voice. 'Perhaps it was worth everything which has followed because of that moment on the hillside — just to have got drunk on knowing what it's like to be a gull. Knowing it with a human power of enjoyment, I mean. I'm not sure.'

He turned on one elbow and put his lips to her bare shoulder. 'I got you too by way of that gull. I'll think more kindly of it in future. More kindly than I have done lately, that is.'

She took him quickly in her arms, kissing his cheek as he lifted his face from her shoulder, surprising him with the warmth of her affection. This was something new to their relationship: they had been amiable strangers, who made love, both needing the same physical release. Intimacy had been of the mind and the body; not, on her side at least, of the heart. In a moment they had become something which, looking back with amusement, he could only think of afterwards as 'friends'.

'I like it when you turn into a gull again,' she said. 'I think I've picked up just enough of the technical side of gliding to be able to follow, in my mind. Suppose you took off the headland — it'd be lovely now, wouldn't it — where would you make for? Take me with you, if you can. For once. Or would that spoil it, not being alone?'

'No, not just for once,' he said, and laughed at her diffidence.

'That's a convection-cloud, isn't it? The towering one, turning red.'

'Yes, it is. Good.'

'Well, if we wanted height, and went in this side, we'd lift slightly before we reached it,' she said, looking at him for confirmation. 'Be-

cause the sun's on it. But inside — inside, blind in the fog, we'd be
rushed upwards as if we were being dragged off into outer space.'

'And incidentally shaken silly, and probably turned upside down,'
he said. 'It's no cloud for a first visit. I'd flick you out the other side
as soon as possible. The cold side, so we'd drop. But because of the
way Kildooey lies between the hills, there'd be a steady updraught
we could depend on over there. And hay-stacks, look. You must always
keep an eye open for hay-stacks. You'd be surprised from what a
long way above you can feel the air rising over them. He took her
drifting in imagination about the sky, while the clouds reddened one
by one, and grew in glory through the thinning haze, turning
the silver sea dun and purple in their shadows. The gulls still wove
their exquisite patterns about the fish, and succeeded in detaching
another.

'Surely everyone has known a moment when the world changed
because of something trivial,' she said, when he had plotted a course
back to the headland, giving her detailed technical advice on how
to land. 'A bird flying past for you; and for me, one word altered in
a sentence when it was repeated — "you" instead of "we" — '

She took one of his hands and played with the articulation of the
fingers for a few minutes, before she let it drop and stared out unsee-
ingly at the gulls, now battling round the third fish. 'I was very happily
married: French marriages are mostly successful; on every level,
whether she's a café patronne or a femme du ministre, the woman
has so much to do with the man's career. They have their interests
in common. Only we had so much more than that. Nearly everything:
political views, taste in art, and liking the same people — there was
just enough difference to make discussion of everything worth while.
I still think Paul made the best jokes I've heard. I daresay he still
thinks the same about me. Not that they were really so witty, perhaps,
but they were our sort of jokes. The irreplaceable things. We always
thought the best holiday was just to be alone together in the country;
I think I told you, we had a house there. But we lived in Paris most
of the time, and we did a great deal of entertaining. I don't mean the
sort of large, stuffy dinners-with-a-purpose that bankers' wives usually
have to give. In some ways we were both too ambitious to bother about
his becoming important as a banker. Banking, in France, is very often

a half-way-house to politics. In the end he would have a political career, so why waste time—and my housekeeping—on people who weren't interesting in themselves? We had friends among journalists and research chemists and painters, and diplomatic people, and I oughtn't to have been so vague when you spoke of civil engineering, because there must have been a good many varieties of engineer among the people we invited to the house—Paul brought in acquaintances very casually—only no one was asked because of what they did, but for that they could contribute in talk, so I wasn't always aware of their jobs. Paul had that knack of making other people seem brilliant, which is so rare in people who talk well themselves. It must be the most endearing trick in the world. We could manage a pretty international table, because though his English wasn't as good as mine, he was better in German, and he'd picked up a smattering of Spanish in Madrid during the civil war. When he went there on what was officially banking business, but it was also Government negotiation—one foot was already where we wanted it to be. We were both Republican in sympathy, which fitted in with the rest of our views. "Intellectual left" I suppose they'd be called in England. Though I think above all you'd have said we were extremely civilized beings. Oh yes, that above all. Munich was a nightmare to both of us, and the inevitable creeping on of war. War was the ultimate horror. Not only on personal grounds, but it was a personal one, too. Paul was of military age. He'd done his service—it's worse for French wives; or suddener, anyway—the way the men are taken. There's no long interval of training, for turning a civilian into a soldier; no time for the woman to harden a bit to the idea. A Frenchman's trained: war comes and he can be taken, pretty well straight out of the office, and sent up the line. But international finance became so important when there was no more hope of peace, we both knew he'd be reprieved for a while. Only for a little while, though. He said, after the Declaration, "I'm not going to pull strings". But he wasn't called up. All the faces we liked best disappeared from our table: except very occasionally, when people came back on leave. We worked out different ways of not thinking all the time of what was going to happen. He made an effort of detachment, which I couldn't manage—put in very long hours at his job, and refused to talk about the war when he came home. I busied myself looking after political refugees. We knew a lot of these personally from before the war.

'We didn't see a great deal of each other. For the first time there wasn't much to say, when we were together: so many things seemed to be barred between us. All speculation about the future, beyond the next day or so. Just one remark of his, right at the beginning, terrified me at the time — very odd now, to think I was frightened by that! But I was easily frightened then, I had so much to lose. He said, "If they're all wrong, our Maginot-minded generals — if the whole of France goes, this time — well, there's bound to be somewhere outside, where the men who are left can get together and still fight. From the colonies, or from England."

'I took the child down to our country place, and was there through the winter when nothing happened — arranging for the house to be turned into a convalescent home in case it was needed. He wrote me the most bitterly amusing letters from Paris, about the war-reactions of Big Business — so much more afraid of Stalin-cum-Blum than Hitler. Still worried about dividends to the exclusion of everything else. I was appalled once or twice when I went up to see him and met some of our old friends — everyone seemed to have turned so trivial: the great thing was to give tea-parties on Sundays because three days a week, by the new regulations, you couldn't have alcohol, and three days a week you couldn't have cream, so Sunday was the only day you could enjoy baba-au-rhum — and it seemed to have become tremendously important. Paul said that sort of thing was inevitable in war: it was the only way people could keep sane. If it didn't disturb him I thought it oughtn't to disturb me. He knew more than I did about how things were: he knew France didn't want to fight; we were both part of that France which had grown up to dread war and be awfully aware of its futilities.

'I was persuaded by the organization I worked for, the refugee reception people, that our place would be more useful at the moment as a home for political exiles: it looked as if hospitals were never going to be wanted. But a few liberal-minded men were still getting out of Franco-Spain alive, and there were Czech socialist leaders and scientists and Polish dons, and anti-Fascist writers escaping somehow, and reaching France by roundabout ways. Some of them Jews and some not. A lot were interned and pretty badly treated. What France has done to the men who trusted her! Others were waiting for visés for the States, and had friends to vouch for them, and were luckier. But generally they hadn't enough to live on, and nowhere to go in the meantime. Our country place was actually my house, you see — Paul's wedding present: the deeds were in my name. He said, "You'll never get these people out if you let them in, but if you're mixed up with them already, go ahead and please yourself. It's your affair."

'The place was crammed at the time of the break-through at Sedan. As soon as I heard rumours that the armies were rolling down on us I took our child back to Paul, in Paris. It seemed safer; and I wanted his advice about the people in my house. There were men there who mustn't fall into German hands again. The journey took five days instead of hours; refugees from further north were already on the roads. Louise and I had to go across the stream, not with it. That ghastly delay solved the problem by itself. I've never heard what happened to those black-listed men in my house. I'd warned them and given them money before I started, so they could try and escape again. If they could think of anywhere to go! But even if they weren't trapped there — two of those who'd been in concentration camps were still sick men. They couldn't have travelled far, as things were. And as I expect you know, in the end our police carefully rounded up such people, to be handed over to the Germans, with their dossiers.

'Paul wasn't concerned about that. He was right, of course, in saying there were bigger things to think of — the possible collapse of the whole country. Part of him seemed just dazed and went on attending to Government banking matters. He told me the head of the vast corporation he worked for had heard of my activities, among what were called "undesirables" — "*types déséagrables*". Some days before, he had called on Paul personally, which still counted as an honour. (The Germans were on the Somme then.) To talk about "unfortunate connections" and suggest other forms of war work, which Madame might find just as interesting. And more suitable to her husband's position. For instance, he said, his own wife was an indefatigable worker for the International Red Cross. Well, now the Germans were reported on the Loire. We'd just heard that Paris wasn't to be defended. It had always been said that it would be, at any cost. I remembered his remark about other places besides France, where Frenchmen could gather and carry on the fight. I said, "Paul, it's time we left!" and looked at a stranger who said, "Yes," and then repeated, "It's time you left". And went on talking about my staying with an American couple we knew who lived in England. Very nice people; he had their address and could send me money there.—Just talking to fill up the silence, I think.

'They were people I hadn't seen for some time. His friends more than mine. I'd never been on such terms with them that I could expect them to take me in, indefinitely. And perhaps he wouldn't be able to send me money; but none of that mattered. It was just something to say, which we could pretend to believe. He said, "After all, my job's here". In English you could take that in the war sense: "Here lies my duty". Although, of course, it didn't: I told you, didn't I, he was 32? But in French it's just literally "my job"—the way I get my living.

'I was in Paris 24 hours more, making up my mind to go. So stunned, it was very difficult to think. Louise was there, and I was lucky to have got her safely as far as that. She couldn't go on. We clung to that way of saving each other's face; the people I could stay with. As it happens, I heard afterwards that they'd already gone back to the States. We could have found that out from a cousin of theirs in the Embassy, if either of us had thought it worth while. But they were very useful to discuss; these friends waiting for me in Bibury; with the Cotswolds well out of the way of air-raids. When the war was over—in a few months—Paul could come across and fetch me. Such a cosy end to the journey that we didn't have to discuss the journey itself. I couldn't look at the truth with him, you understand. I couldn't. This was someone I loved—that I suppose I still love. Five years of happiness aren't wiped away by one sentence. The mind can say "It's all over," and be right, long before the heart. Also, I believed he was someone who loved me. Indeed, I still believe that too. It was partly my fault: out of pride; after the first shock of hearing him say "you". "It's time you left." If I'd made him understand what it had been like, getting through as far as Paris, I think he wouldn't have sent me out on that other journey alone. We both talked as if it was only a question of driving to Bordeaux, and I'm an experienced driver. "Once you're through the crowds and can get into the side roads—". I knew the state of those roads already and he didn't. He could have guessed, of course, but he didn't want to. And I didn't make any effort. If I'd said some-thing to bring back that other mood of it not being the end, when France fell—But I suppose it was a kind of shame that stopped me. He mentioned a Hungarian exile who'd left my house some time before, a man who'd suffered hell in Germany, and asked: "Did you know he'd gone back, as a spy for France, and been caught?" I said I'd sus-pected where he was going when he said good-bye to me. I knew he was a very brave man, but I carefully hadn't inquired. He said: "Who's going to believe, when these things are looked into, that you 'carefully hadn't inquired'? If you stay, and I'm 'out on the street' through sus-picion—and there'll be plenty out for less!—who's going to provide for the child, under Nazi rule?"

'The Germans were actually in the northern suburbs when I started. Coming in through Neuilly and the Bois de Boulogne, I was told, and I drove out south-west. It was quite good going for about 20 miles. The crowds were on ahead.'

The mask had fastened again on Denyse's face. 'That's a personal picture of how France went down, and why,' she said. 'Business men—Intellectuals—Do you remember, in the ship I told you, I'd no desire left for the company of aesthetes?—Oh, but it was more than that, of course. A whole generation bred sick of war. Men brought up on their fathers' stories of mud and blood and the uselessness of slaughter. Brought up as every reasonable race must bring up its young—to despise killing, not only to fear it. I see no solution to that problem—how civilized men are ever to meet the barbarian on equal terms, when killing is the meaning of life to him, and not to them.'

'They're meeting him now, round about Kent and Essex,' said Tom, and regretted the words as he spoke.

In-shore, under the shelter of the land, the pale pearl-tints still lingered in the sea, but a tide of deep blue crept towards them from the horizon as the sun, rising behind the hills, reached down over the land to wake the water. Currents became visible where it darkened, still lanes twisting through the glitter of little waves. He could remem-ber no morning which had broken more movingly. It was almost in-credible in this scene, at this moment, that not far off amiable lads, some of whom he knew, were killing and being killed in the clean, bright air.

'I know,' she answered quickly. 'I think I said that only in excuse for my people, and for him.'

'Do you know what's happened to him?'

'Oh, yes — through that "indefatigable worker for the International Red Cross", the wife of his ex-chief. And the Nazi-controlled Paris press. He's sometimes mentioned, always with approval. He holds quite an important post, under the Vichy government. One of the coming young men of the New France. Working for what's called "closer understanding with the Reich" as the country's best way out of a bad situation. He's got his wish — our wish. He's doing as well as both of us thought he would, in politics — now!'

The last of the string of pollock had been knocked from the post some time ago by the noisy gulls. Wheeling round in spreading circles they were satisfied that nothing more was left. One by one they flew out to sea.

Heavy autumn silence closed in behind them: the thin sound of cocks, crowing below in the village, seemed to be something felt, not heard; full day had come. The campers settled down to doze again for a little while, if they could. It was chilly in the quarry, even on a fine morning, while the dew was still thick. Tom heard Denyse move restlessly and spoke to her, feeling again his helplessness to comfort. 'Can't you sleep, sweetheart? Don't think about the past any more.'

'It was only three months ago,' she said, as if he might reasonably resent the time which love could take in dying. 'Paul's still so near to me. It's as if my child had done something which hurt. I could be angry, but only as I might be angry with myself. He's still the person I care for most. I'm sorry — I can't help that. Five years is a long time. Perhaps it'll be different in that "one day" we talked about last night. One day, when it isn't the same world, or we aren't the same people.'

In a little while she said, 'What a ridiculous leave you're having, Tom. You should have picked up something like Bridie, who'd only have broken her heart when you left. Instead of timing it so inconveniently beforehand!'

'Oddly enough, I'd still prefer it to be you, just as you are,' he told her, 'and that's the bloody-silly truth!'

'How nice you are,' she said, considering him with serious, beautiful eyes, turning his face about by the chin to look at all aspects of it. 'How very much the nicest person I know, I think. Much nicer than Paul, but that isn't the point.'

Presently she slept, and he lay looking at his new friend, learning carefully the delicate shape of her cheek and forehead, outlined against the pillow of his rolled-up coat. Then she turned further from him, still sleeping, and he could not see her face. Without disturbing her he opened the door beside him, and shifted so that through the opening he could watch the village, with its white cottages glowing in the early sun, and observe the order in which the chimneys gave a spurt of grey smoke as someone threw turf on the embers of the hearth — everywhere in Ireland, the first sign of the day's stirring.

It was so enchanting, lying in the car high up in the quarry, with the village and the sea spread out below, that he forgot the pain that had spoken beside him in the dawn. There was no past and no future, only this infinitely precious now. Neither of them had yet considered what she would do when his leave was over: nor, at the moment, could it matter. To-day was still unused. As soon as Mrs. Kathie's fire was kindled he made chirruping sounds at the figure beside him, impatient as a boy to be off to the fishing.

'Bridie'll be along with the milk soon. You mustn't lose another minute of my grand pollock morning.'

CHAPTER IX

WATER FROM A TAP

PARTLY from awe, partly from modesty, Bridie was always at her shyest if she came with the first present of the day and found Denyse still in her underclothes — they were much finer than any dress the girl had yet seen. It happened almost every morning during their stay, for Bridie got up, went into the byre and milked off a few cupfuls for them as soon as she woke; then leaving the cow for Mrs. Kathie to finish, she hurried with her crock to the quarry, eager for the time when her campers would talk again of the world beyond Kildooey.

Himself might even speak of Dublin: it was a source of great regret to the girl that Denyse had not been there too.

On the occasions when she arrived too early she stood leaning against the side of the car, facing the sea, discoursing into the air until it seemed fitting to turn round and beam. Men, in her opinion, needed no such consideration; their underclothes were less impressive, and if it were only Tom dressing in the quarry she walked past him unconcerned, to reach for the milk-jug which was kept on the roof beside the stew. 'Braces, now; why would they be taking six buttons when three would do?'

The throwing away of yesterday's milk was a ritual against which Denyse protested in vain. Told to leave it unless it had turned, Bridie smiled amiably but would not even pander to them by sniffing it in the morning: overnight milk was not to be drunk by her campers, whatever they said. After pouring it out on the ground she loosened the grease from the rim of the jug with a handful of stone-dust, before rinsing it under their private cascade. There was no shortage of water near the quarry; several clear little streams trickled down the hillside within a hundred yards, making mossy puddles by the side of the road.

To-day, addressing the sparkling view, she told them the local news: of the sickness of two of her mother's hens and that Sean had repassed the car while it was still dark, on his way home from the drilling. 'I heard him on the bridge and I looked out of my window and asked, were you sleeping as he went by? And he said, yes, you were both sleeping, with the moon full on the face of herself. How you could rest so, it beats him! And me too. Aren't you afraid?'

'Of Sean and his gang?'

'Oh, *no*!' Bridie's amusement disposed of their importance. 'Of — well, now — other things.' She grew confused. 'Bats, and such. Maybe they wouldn't come into a car, though.'

Bridie, they discovered, half believed in the Shee, the spirits which rose like mist out of the hills at night; and wholly in her aunt's story of the ghost seen at this spot: but also, with another part of her mind, that such foolishness was not really fitting in one who should deserve to visit Dublin.

'Get me the coffee, there's a good girl,' said Tom. 'It's in the back of the car. I'll make it while herself is dressing. Never let the French handle coffee, Bridie. It's the one thing they can't do.'

'Can they not? I didn't know it. But I am not so ignorant of other things that would help me, out in the world. No harm would come to me now in a town, be sure of it. I have well in mind the things to avoid — and understand more of them than Father Keith believes I do, indeed. But isn't it the same everywhere — those that have known you too long will never allow that you can look after yourself?'

'That's so, Bridie,' said Tom, thinking of Mrs. Mott in London, worrying over his accommodation, every night of his leave, as she seldom worried when he was on operations.

Denyse having pulled on a skirt and sweater, Bridie felt more at ease, and grew confidential as she helped them to get breakfast.

'I couldn't say that it was always so with me. Years ago, I was walking home with a girl from the school at Comines, and she was after telling me the way of women getting their children. I said to her, "Away, nonsense!" I said. "Are you thinking my Aunt Agnes — she that had one from each husband — Now I ask you, would she ever be doing the likes of that? Or my own mother either? Or yours? Surely to goodness," I said, "you've heard women complaining and crying out, in this very village, against the trouble they have in finding food for a great crowd of children? Proclaiming want and worse will be upon them with another mouth to feed? And as like as not, aren't they the very ones that go on to have several more? What you say doesn't seem likely," I told her. "Except, of course, for the cows and pigs and the other bastes — I've seen that myself." (For she was always one to think you had never noticed the rain till she pointed out the wet you had from it. I wouldn't have her think I didn't know about the bastes). But she found no answer at all when I said, "Why would people be doing that, and they with more than enough children already? Apart from the curious taste they'd need to be doing it at all! Answer me this!" I said. (Mind you, I was very young at the time, though I'd not be calling it a sensible process to this day.) And you couldn't be putting Aunt Agnes and the very idea into the same thought. "A child is the gift of God," I told her, "and I'll not be hearing otherwise." Though why He should be giving two to my

Aunt Agnes and none to my Aunt Mary, I don't know. But my Aunt Mary doesn't always be telling everything she has in her mind, though it's plenty she does tell. "And there may well be a good reason without my knowing of it," I said. "But as to the other — !" And then it got me laughing, thinking of Aunt Agnes and that, till I couldn't be ashamed as I should have been, for my friend to imagine such terrible things! Every time it came back in my mind after that, I went off laughing in the same way — and wasn't that nearly the ruin of me —' Bridie turned suddenly dramatic, waving their saucepan of scrambled eggs in the air — 'one Saturday evening on the road to Ardrinath, not believing the things the girl had told me, and meeting two coastguards with a bit of drink in them? Still, I managed them.'

'How did you manage them, Bridie?' asked Denyse, taking the saucepan from her; but the girl had turned shy again. She lowered her funny sandy eyelashes and murmured something about riding in a cart to be shown the light at Drumross — 'or that's what they said they would show me. Then all of a sudden I thought, And if she was right after all! So I having shown no fear of them, they put me down when I said, "Wait now, for a minute, will you, while I go into that wood." Mr. Fairburn, how long do you think they waited on the road, while I walked home through the back of the wood?'

'I've no idea, Bridie,' he said, delighted. 'Depends how much drink they had taken. But I'll tell anyone who asks my opinion, that after that I think you could hold your own with Dublin.'

'Oh, will you? Will you tell Father Keith?'

'I'm afraid he isn't likely to ask my opinion, and if I gave it, he still wouldn't be impressed. Except perhaps in the wrong way. After all, we're strangers here. Will you do something for us?'

'Oh, I'll do that — but will you tell my mother and my aunts, then, and Sean?'

'Only if they ask. And they won't. Why should they?' said Tom, sorry now that he had made this light remark, which was taken so seriously. Denyse's pledge to the priest was in his mind: 'They shall not be worse off, by anything we say!' 'Will you catch Mr. Wallace at home, Bridie, before he starts for the shop, and tell him we'd like to hear the 1 o'clock English news on his wireless, if he'd leave the house open for us, as he kindly suggested?'

'But you listened yesterday at Father Keith's.'

'That was to Athlone. We want the London bulletin.'

'They give that too, from the Eire station. Father Keith says so.'

'Yes, I know, but—' He stopped, not knowing what explanation to offer of the fact that now they felt unable to go back to the priest's house; and then a wave of irritation ran over his mind that any rational explanation should be required of him by an inhabitant of neutral Ireland, at such a moment in the world's history. The last time they had heard the score, the daylight cost of the attack on Britain had been 83 raiders to 21 British fighters, with 5 pilots saved. At any time the balance of losses might change. If the attack could be made worth while to the enemy—if it could be prolonged beyond the endurance of the defenders' supreme effort, beyond that pitch of brilliance which no amount of courage could replace—then the air was lost, and the last phase of fighting had come; nothing remained but the overwhelming horror of an invasion which would be resisted while anything remained with which to resist, though its success became certain from the moment the air was lost.

'Father Keith's house would never be shut up like that old crow's.'

'No, I daresay not. Mr. Wallace told us he'd need warning if we wanted to use his set. That's why we'd be grateful if you'd run along now—'

'But didn't you hear all right on Father Keith's? Once we got it going? Isn't it a good enough machine?' asked Bridie anxiously.

'Quite good enough.'

'Then why wouldn't you be listening again on Father Keith's, if you want to listen?' Bridie demanded. 'You'll be hurting his feelings.'

Tom looked helplessly at Denyse. Denyse rose from her knees by the stoves, gave Bridie's bottom a friendly smack and said, 'Go *now*, Bridie dear, and ask Mr. Wallace,' offering no explanation at all.

Bridie ran grinning down the hill, waving to them at every turn.

'Admirable woman,' said Tom, settling down to an extensive breakfast: all of it, except the coffee and the bread, had been provided free by the infuriating country, with which it was impossible to stay out of temper for more than a moment at a time, surrounded by proof of so much generosity. The coffee the campers had brought with them from Belfast, the bread they had been allowed to buy from the Sullivans after much argument; but the fish, eggs, butter, milk, even the stewed plums with which they finished the meal, were part of the Kildooey tribute of hospitality that must not be paid back in money, but only in conversation, or occasional gifts of slab chocolate to Mrs. Mary.

In a little while Bridie came racing up the hill again to say that Mr. Wallace was delighted, everything was unlocked, they would find the radio by the fire in the parlour, tuned in to London, and he had left out his sherry for them, trusting that they would help themselves. 'But don't you touch it,' she warned them. 'Didn't he give some to my mother and my Aunt Agnes when he was arranging the land purchase for Sean's new cabin. And for weeks after, wasn't everything in the shop a ha-penny dearer to both families till he got back the price of the bottle?'

'Oh, now look, Bridie, are you sure?'

' — An Ulsterman!' said the girl, unwilling to demean her case with further evidence.

Several other people had wandered up the hill by this time; lads with some live bait for Tom, and an old couple, ostensibly come to ask the campers if they had noticed a straying calf, black with a white foot. The purpose of their visit was obviously to see the cooking and sleeping arrangements in the quarry; they were shown round in a proprietorial way by Bridie, who returned to the village with them. Before she left she gave Denyse a brown paper packet: it contained a set of picture postcards of Boston. 'These are what Helen would have shown you the other night. She says, to tell you she was sorry she didn't see you again, but she didn't feel well when she got home to fetch them.' No flicker in Bridie's face showed whether she believed what she was saying, or not. 'Will you keep them, please, for she says she has been to Boston later than you, so she can remember without them.'

They accepted the heartrending little present, and went off to fish, landing later in the morning to bathe from one of the coves along the coast. There the secret feeling of the early day still lingered: it was as if no one had ever before walked on its sands or looked into its caves. After the bathe they passed through the village on their way to Mr. Wallace's; Sean hailed them as they stopped on the bridge to look at the snapdragons. (Father Keith was nowhere to be seen, but the flowers he loved nodded to the wind in a blaze of double-sunshine; lovely indeed they looked, with light falling on them from above, and reflecting back to them again from the surface of the stream, so that they quivered and exulted in this special radiance of their own, the yellow blooms like small flames, and the red glowing as if blood had splashed on the crumbling stonework.)

Sean shouted peremptorily to the campers to wait, and came running after them, without his shoes or his coat. Bridie had told them that he usually slept all the morning after one of the night-meetings in the bog; despite the long rest, his fervent, pale face still held a drawn look. Sean marched and drilled, it seemed, with all the exhausting vigour of his dreams, for which his body was no match at all. Lanky and ill-conditioned, it was a poor housing for so much burning spirit. From the tone of his hail, Tom and Denyse expected something far less friendly than the request he made when he caught up with them. The bridge road was rough, and his mother's cabin a hundred yards away; one foot, as he explained later, was already blistered from the night's activity—by the time he reached them, hobbling over the stones, he was amused at his own discomfort, and native good manners had softened his angry air. He suggested that if it were not too much trouble, the car should be moved a little some time during the day, so that he could get at the stones he had already loosened. They had the impression that he had changed his mind, as he ran, about what he was going to say.

'Of course. I'll shift her as soon as we're back from Wallace's,' Tom told him. 'In about an hour. I meant what I said, that I'd be glad to give you a hand. I'll get the car half out on the road, just clear of your stuff; then we can load in all the stone you've got ready, and run it down to wherever you've chosen to build. It'll save your donkeys a trip or two.'

'No, no,' said Sean vehemently. 'I don't want that at all. The place where I'll build isn't settled for certain. Just pull your car out, that's all.'

When they were half a mile beyond the village, on the way to Mr. Wallace's, they met Helen's man, Michael, who pointed out to them

the site of Sean's future home. All the digging was done already, and
the foundation course had been laid in heavy stone. Their mild
curiosity to know why Sean had bothered to lie to them — and to lie
so that he was bound to be found out — was swallowed up at once
by a far greater curiosity when they pushed open the door of Mr.
Wallace's parlour — What possible motive could have prompted him
to collect the things with which it was stuffed?

They had been prepared by the outside of the house for ornate
ugliness within, knowing from Bridie that he was the designer and
builder himself, so that presumably the inlaid glass-work on the
doorposts represented his own jackdaw taste for anything shiny. But
the ugliness of the exterior could be matched in most places in Ireland,
where a local tradesman had made money and built to satisfy his
hankering for grandeur; nothing they had ever seen had prepared them
for this room.

It was an over-crowded museum of everything connected with himself, the fantastic monument to a singularly uninteresting past. Little
space remained on the walls between enlarged snapshots of Mr. Wallace at all ages — baby pictures and photographs of choir-outings and
army groups in which he figured — and an assortment of framed
certificates proving that he had joined the Derry branch of the Prim-
rose League in 1909, maintained an unbroken attendance at choir
practice in the same town during 1911, and completed a course in first-
aid, prior to taking out a druggist's licence to sell patent medicines
as well as groceries in 1912. In that year he had also moved over the
Border to Kildooey; several photographs testified to this, all were
dated and bore explanations: 'Day of Arrival. R.J.W. approaching
shop', 'R.J.W. by Kildooey bridge. The first Sunday.' At this period
Mr. Wallace's camera had evidently been fitted with one of the at-
tachments which allowed the owner to set it and then walk in front
in time to be taken; but only just in time. A slight blurring of the
legs was common to several pictures, and a harassed expression.
Shortly after his establishment in Kildooey it must have broken: there
were not many pictures of himself of later date. Instead, the few
inches of the wall-space which remained, round about eye level, had
been filled by tacked-up showcards; on these were gummed a series
of apparently pointless souvenirs. 'A pretty sea-shell. Picked up by

R.J.W. at Drumross Head, Whitsun, 1913,' or a piece of bog-oak,
'Found by R.J.W. on a walk near Kilcar, August Bank Holiday,
1913'. In group-photographs, where other people had crowded nearer
the camera, partly eclipsing him, he had identified himself with an
arrow or a cross as well as his initials; lest he should fail to be recognized by the unknown spectator for whom this display was arranged.
There were many pictures in which he was only half visible: a burning diffidence seemed to keep him always hanging about the outskirts
of any little assembly, so that he was easily pushed aside. No other
names or initials were given in his records of days gone by. And into
this house, Bridie had said, no one but himself came, from month's
end to month's end. While none at all ever came willingly, without
a business intention.

Dating from after the last war there were many photographic records
of local transactions. 'Barn, in good repair, and 2 fields, negotiated
from Philip Clancy to Philip Riordan, on the marriage of their children, May 6th, 1920.' But no wedding picture accompanied this snap,
torn at the edges and curling off the wall like many others — Mr.
Wallace, presumably, had not been asked to the festivities, though his
help had been sought for the marriage settlement, he being a better
bargainer than Father Keith. The newest-looking card in the room
had been bent to fit into a corner; it bore a rough drawing of the
signpost by the quarry, with the measurements, the wording on the
arm and the date of erection written underneath.

Anything which he had ever touched seemed eligible for a place in
this gallery of unflattering self-portraits, the composite picture of a
man with no friend but himself, the one person for whom, out of
loneliness, he had conceived a passionately preserving love.

'I think it's the most horrible room I've ever seen,' Denyse said.
'And the most pathetic. Everything he's known seems to have been
dull, including his particular war. Here's his hospital sheet. Nearly a
year at Millbank, and then invalided out. Such a dreary life, you
wouldn't think anyone could bear to live it more than once, even in
imagination.'

'I can't find the radio among all this junk. He said it was by the
fireplace.' The floor was crowded with miscellaneous furniture as
though for an auction. There were standard lamps, with new and

very fancy shades, heavily fringed and beaded; and many mirrors, in keeping with the outside style of the house, but there was also a tiny, low old chair in which Mr. Wallace could only have sat as a very little boy, and in a glass-fronted cupboard they noticed other relics, such as an old Meccano set and a stamp-album—obviously Mr. Wallace had never thrown away anything. 'For Crissakes open the window, Denyse. I don't know what it all smells of, but it smells.'

'There's the set. With a special fretwork front, to make it look like part of the overmantel. Both of his own design, I think. And the smell is just dust and unhandledness,' she said. 'There's a sort of unoccupied smell—nothing to do with the state of cleaning, though of course this room could do with a lot. But you get it at Versailles and Hampton Court, and I recognize it. I doubt if he often comes in here, except to remind himself that there really is such a person as R.J.W. —there must be, if he can be photographed and pick up shells.' She got the window open with a struggle.

Immediately the cheerful day-breeze from the sea threatened havoc in the room, tearing at the tacked-up snapshots and cards. They were forced to close the window again, and listened to the London programme in musty discomfort for about ten minutes before the reading of the news; neither of them daring to trust their watches, which had not been checked for some time, for fear of missing the important item. As the radio brought them the sound of English voices, anxiety returned with a sense of the reality of the outside world, though the voices were singing in a variety feature of exceptional inanity. The close atmosphere added to their feeling of mounting tension, so did the irrelevance of the music; and then the extraordinary room grew dim around them as the B.B.C. announcer's voice began reading the latest figures of air casualties.

The news was nothing like so good as it had been when they last heard it. Proportionately, the British losses had mounted by nearly half as much again. Was it just the luck of the day—new tactics on the part of the aggressor, which could be met with new methods of defence, or a more decisive change than that? It occurred to Tom, switching off the machine, that all over the civilized world, whose future existence probably depended on that answer, men were thinking exactly his thoughts, with the same tightening of muscles in stomach and throat.

'We'll come back to-night for the late news,' he said.

They returned to the quarry and shifted the car, and Denyse made sandwiches to eat while they fished. Throughout the afternoon, Tom devoted himself to pollock, fishing from the long spine of rocks which ran out to sea at the end of their headland. He perched on overhanging ledges, with his eyes on the swirls of water rising and falling mesmerically below him, and baited and rebaited methodically, scarcely aware of what he did. Denyse, who absorbed sunshine like a plant, basked nearby, considered the lovely sweep of coast, and occasionally took his spare line. They did not talk much.

When he reeled in for the last time, at Denyse's suggestion of tea, Tom could not have said whether the catch had been good or bad without looking round at the fish in the crevice behind him. It was a first-class flying day, favouring the bomber, not the fighter, with thin deceptive haze at about five thousand feet, and three-tenth cloud-cover above.

They noticed, while getting the meal, that Sean had taken away none of his building material, though he had now had access to it for several hours.

Bridie came panting up the hill with a new-laid egg in each hand, as a contribution to their meal. 'I thought she would never lay in time, the crayture!' she called as she approached, one arm raised to show an enormous double-yolker. 'Egg-bound, that's all she was this morning, the sick red hen, and heaven send it's the same with the old grey. We've been clucking at her whenever we were near, mother and I, to make her think we shared the burden. It helps,' she protested, in reply to Tom's surprised expression. 'Everyone knows it helps, when a hen is egg-bound. Can't you feel, yourself, how terrible it must have been for the poor red hen — she no bigger than a pullet — with an egg the size of this inside? It isn't so bad for the grey, she's full grown.'

'Tell you the truth, I find it very hard to put myself in the place of either of them,' Tom said, to the mermaid eyes fixed upon him expectantly.

'Ah, well, you're a man,' Bridie excused him at once. 'There's scarcely a woman, I think, but knows the feeling when she wants to say something and can't — like me, when the old people are talking of the wickedness of the towns! They who've forgotten what it is to want something with all their hearts!' In a moment she took the sleeve of Denyse's sweater between her fingers and bent over to examine it, so that they should not see tears in her eyes. 'Mrs. Fairburn, there's something I've found out I don't like — I should have guessed, but I didn't — ' The voice came muffled. Denyse put an arm round the girl. 'There was someone in America Helen fancied more than Michael. He hadn't spoken, when the letter came, fetching her home. But maybe, she thinks, he would have asked her if she'd stayed. I knew she didn't want to leave America, but I just thought, well, wasn't it reasonable, with all the excitement of the town about her? Till we went home, last night, and found her with the pictures in her hand. The ones she gave you to-day, to be rid of them. She looked so that I said to her, wasn't she glad, at least, to be among her own people again, even if it meant leaving her friends? Then she told me. Michael knows too. For he put it to her when they left my Aunt Mary's, do you remember? — was there someone else? But still, he thinks it's her duty to keep her word to him. An Irish girl should marry at home when she can — that's what they all say, the old ones. If he didn't think that, surely he wouldn't be wanting her still? Knowing there's another more to her fancy?'

'Well, that, my dear, is a thing one can never know for certain.'

'It's beyond belief to me now that I didn't see for myself how it was with her. And she my own sister. I've known other things that have passed in Kildooey though the old ones thought I didn't! But this — ' In her distress, Bridie turned to philosophy, which sat oddly upon her. 'Isn't it strange, now, the way two people will be coming along the road together, and one says, "You can smell the hay strong from here", and the other says, "I don't get anything but the turf burning", and they walking within a few inches of each other? So it was with us. I should have known what she meant when she said about liking the wind to blow from the west. Maybe I was too taken up with myself and Dublin. But Mrs. Fairburn, don't you think it's hard on her?'

'Very hard, Bridie.'

'But it is her duty, isn't it? You'd say the same as Father Keith?'

Discomfited in her turn by the girl's insistence, Denyse looked to Tom for a way out of the question. The promise to the priest was again in both their minds. The form of words Denyse had used, 'They shall be no worse off through anything we say' might easily be interpreted to mean, 'No worse off, in our view of good and evil'. Loosened somewhat from her dogmatic faith, Bridie would probably become a much better person from their standpoint, more intelligent, honester in mind; the words, however, had been neither spoken nor heard in that sense, but in the priest's own meaning of them. If Bridie's new friends attacked this one point of his teaching, they would weaken his whole authority. There could be no question whether or not he would consider that a step down in grace for the girl.

Tom wriggled, mentally, feeling contemptible as he did so. 'Well, your duty is what you yourself believe it to be, isn't it? So it doesn't matter what we think, but only what Helen thinks. If she hadn't been convinced that it was right to come back and marry Michael, wouldn't she have stayed where she was happy?' To his relief, Bridie accepted this reasoning with a mournful little nod, and sniffed till the tears stopped. 'Maybe I think too much of myself, and Dublin,' she said again, 'to keep my eyes open at home and see how it is with other people. At least, that's what they all say to me.'

'What makes you sure of liking Dublin so much?' asked Denyse, to cheer her still more by distraction.

The sandy wet lashes flashed up with a smile. 'Oh, everything I've heard, my dearest! The lights — they say that looking down at night from the hills around, you might well be thinking all the stars had fallen out of the sky on to the city, you might indeed! So beautifully it shines. And by day the people there — in such numbers — coming and going, not always living in the place, do you see. Why, you might be standing in one of the great squares or roadways they have, and thinking, Surely there must be some end to the different ways a nose and a mouth and two eyes can be arranged! And telling yourself, Without doubt the next face to pass will be one that's a bit familiar. (You standing there for hours, maybe, just looking at the people going by.) But let you watch never so long and it mightn't be. Or if indeed it was someone you knew, coming towards you — even an old friend, maybe — wouldn't there be a grand pleasure in the very astonishment of that, among all the unknown faces? And if a stranger spoke to you, just wanting the time, there'd be no telling he hadn't just come from Persia, or India, or anywhere, or seen the Pope. Don't they say — those who know it — there's better company in that town than anywhere else on earth? The way you'd think it almost a waste to sleep at night for fear of missing the jokes, and the rare, informing talk? Streets and streets of great houses — isn't it like that?' She broke off, waited a moment for his answer, and then went on without it. 'So many have told me. Margaret Clancy, that's just gone for a nurse, she was trained in Dublin. And Sean's brother that died, and my cousin Shamus went there, too. (Though he says there's more money to be made in London. But I wouldn't be thinking of money.) They told me Dublin was like that. Even when they said, to be ending with — some of them! — I shouldn't look beyond Kildooey yet awhile. And yourself has been there too — isn't it like that, now?'

'Yes, I suppose so,' said Tom unwillingly. It troubled him, even through his deeper concern with the issues of the day, to think of the disappointment that might be waiting for this passionate child among the bedraggled Georgian finery of Merrion Square, in the midst of people hurrying by on one of Dublin's bleakest mornings, when pinched faces looked mean, and good-fellowship hid behind closed doors, if it existed anywhere in that particularly cruel city. But from his own early days he remembered a hatred of those who tried to destroy bright visions by the assurance that one day youth would see through them. Older people had told him then that flying would not satisfy him for ever. How right they had been, and how stupid, since no such warning could ever destroy hope, but only tarnish it.

'Of course, Bridie,' he said, warmly, and used his deepest Cork brogue to please her, because she considered it funnier in him than an English accent. 'Yourself has the rights of it entirely, and there's great doings there in peace-time. What with the Horse Shows and the Easter processions and all, they haven't told you half of it, the people you've met! But wait, you, till the war's over — you said yourself, that would be soon enough now. For devil a bit of fun and jollity will you find in the streets, or the grand houses either, till that time comes.' ('And when that time comes', he added in his thoughts, 'you may be lucky if you can find Dublin.')

'I could wait here till then,' Bridie agreed. Having won her point about the glories of her dream, she turned to nearer marvels. 'When you went into Mr. Wallace's,' she asked, 'did you see that he has water just where he'd want it in the kitchen, running at the touch of a tap?'

'Well, actually, I didn't notice that,' said Denyse. 'I wasn't in the kitchen.'

'It's there.' Bridie nodded her head in emphasis. 'My mother says so. He doesn't have to pump above once a week. Maybe that wouldn't be anything very great in Dublin' — the grave young voice turned wistful again — 'but it's the only house here that has such an arrangement. Even at Father Keith's, they have to bring in the water for the day from the pump in front. And at the farm that will be Helen's —'

'Bridie,' said Tom on a sudden impulse. 'If it's possible to arrange it while I'm here, there shall be water laid on, just the same, in the cabin that Sean's building for you. Get him to hurry a bit, and decide where the kitchen's to be, and I'll see what I can do. Would you like that?'

'Oh, Mr. Fairburn, you mean — you mean you can do things like that? Putting water into people's houses?'

'That's what I earned money by doing, before the war,' he told her, and ignored Denyse's cocked eyebrow. They had talked of his work that afternoon, to avoid talking of the battle over England in the rare moments when they talked at all, and Denyse knew, by now, that designing a viaduct was the nearest he had ever come to what she herself had called 'putting up municipal washhouses'. The suggestion that he had been a plumber was even less dignified; Tom, however, had gone some way towards eminence in his own line, and was therefore not inclined to be touchy about his professional status.

'Oh, Holy Mother of God,' said Bridie. 'Oh, may all the saints —' She stopped for want of any suggestion as to how the saints could adequately reward such goodness. The prospect of owning the second house in Kildooey to have water laid on was obviously an enchanting one, and all the more enchanting because it was distant: the prestige could be enjoyed now without any of the drawbacks of housekeeping. This thought would compensate for almost anything, even for a postponement of the great experience of Dublin.

'Why hasn't Sean taken away all this stuff?'

'One of his donkeys has gone lame. To-day. Wouldn't it!' said Bridie in a fever of excitement and irritation against her man. 'Oh, wouldn't it now.'

'Doesn't matter. The car can take it down after tea — and we'll help to build,' he said to Denyse, when Bridie had gone flying long-legged down the hill, to report the splendours in store for her, not first of all to her mother or Sean, but to that far more important person, Mrs. Mary. 'I must tell me aunt. Even she, not a drop of water has she ever had in the house but was brought by hand! Though of course it isn't often brought in by hers,' she added fairly.

'I want something to do,' said Tom. 'Very badly, just now. Making something, I mean. Quite hard work but simple. Just so I can't think much, except about what I'm doing. There's no point in fishing as things are.'

'I was afraid there wasn't.'

He turned to her quickly. 'Ah, but yesterday was lovely. You and the fishing and everything! Don't misunderstand. It's been grand for me, just being with you. You're still lovely to-day, and it's only the fishing that's gone! This sort of anxiety — it isn't the same at all as the state I was talking about in the ship. It's not personal. But it's just — that I know too much of what's going on. What must be going on. I know what it's like when men are asked to fly too often. They'll do it. But I know what it's like, you see. Four and five times a day — and to be doing nothing myself — well, I'd rather be devising gadgets to make that nice little girl envied by her neighbours in due course. There's a trick I had before we met, that's come back, too.' He looked at her apologetically — 'I keep finding myself holding my breath. Try. ing to hold it back indefinitely. I think it's some half-baked idea at the back of my mind of waiting for the worst to be over; everyone has the same reaction when they're expecting to be hit. But I'm not, now; and as I say, it isn't the stranger in charge again. (You remember that, too? When I tried to explain — ') Was it true, what he was saying, that the stranger was no longer in control? He was not sure.

'Yes, of course I remember. Tom, dear, you shall certainly have your busman's holiday — we'll build. I'll enjoy lending a hand. I don't think I'll be much good. But at least I can do what I'm told.'

'An ex-busman's holiday,' he corrected, 'which is much more satisfy-ing. It's like this — ' He paused and began to frown. 'I don't know if I made it clear — no, I'm sure I didn't — '

'You don't need to explain anything more about fear to me,' she said urgently. 'Really, my dear, you don't!'

'To you?' He laughed quite naturally. 'I wasn't thinking of ex-plaining anything more to you. I'd gone a long way beyond that! I was just wishing I'd made it plain to Bridie that all I can do in the circumstances depends on the slope of the ground. I hope to heaven it does slope enough to let us run some kind of primitive water-supply into the house. Before I suggested it I ought to have looked.' They enjoyed together the fact that her affection for him had made her rather ridiculous; it did not occur to him until long afterwards that he had never met another woman who would have appreciated this. 'What else can we think of, in the way of amenities for Bridie?' he said. 'Her taste is likely to be awful from our point of view. With Mr. Wallace's house as a model of elegance. But it isn't our business to reform. Only to pander. Come and help me get this stuff into the back of the car, and we'll go down and pander with the greatest in-genuity — at least, I hope we will.'

CHAPTER X

BUILDING

THEY found that the land sloped excellently, both before and behind Sean's site.

For hours the campers carted stone, made experimental dams in various trickles of water which seeped down from the hills, and prospected the contours of the land for sumps and runaways, till Denyse was soaked and tired.

They knocked off for a consultation when Sean appeared. Sean had heard through Mrs. Mary of the offer to Bridie, and the panniers of his one sound donkey were laden with a few choice slabs from the quarry which the others had overlooked in their loading.

'A grand job of carrying you've done for me,' he called cheerfully, unloading the new stone on to the considerable dump which they had piled up in several hours of hard work. He appeared to have lost his opposition to the idea of their help with the building.

''Tis too kind of you altogether,' he said several times while Tom outlined his suggestions. They were made tentatively; a notion was dropped at once if Sean did not seem taken by it. One such discarded plan was for a separate water supply to the sink and the copper (even Mr. Wallace had only one tap) to save Bridie the lifting of kettles on wash-day. 'She would never remember to keep more than one tap shut off at a time,' said Sean firmly. 'We should be flooded out.'

Inventiveness had not suffered from disuse; Tom's wilder fancies, thrown out for fun, amused them both. Sean had never seemed so normal and pleasant: the deep-set, visionary eyes closed with laughter at an idea for letting out the chickens in the morning without getting up from bed. 'It's a practical scheme,' Tom told him. 'I worked it out as a boy at home, for use on Sundays, because I was put in charge of the chickens and I loathed looking after them. The principle's an electro-magnet, with a battery and an alarm clock. To this day my mother won't let anyone touch the thing while I'm not there, because she thinks it's magic.'

'Well, now, I'd be fearing Bridie might feel the same.'

'I'm afraid she might. Women—!' said Tom confidentially, and smiled at Denyse. She noted and liked his manner to the younger man; never forgetting that the cabin was Sean's project, not his. It would have been easy enough to forget for the moment, with Irish courtesy leaving all decisions to the newcomer—'Are you going to have your main room this side or the other, Sean?'

'It's as you think best. You have more knowledge of such things.'

'Oh no, I've never built a house before. It's for you to say: I'm only asking so as to know where the pipe should run. You're going to have two rooms, aren't you, one big, one small?'

'That's so.'

'And you'd find the tap handiest in the big room, wouldn't you?'

'Maybe we would.'

'Well, it makes no difference to the water supply which side the pipe comes in. It's just a question for you to decide, so I can get some idea of the lay-out, and what length of piping will be wanted.'

'Which side would you be advising?'

'I don't know, really. You'd get more sun on the south, of course. But perhaps Bridie has some idea of her own?'

'Ah, no, she'll be pleased whichever way you say. She's washing the church linen to-night, and can't be along with us; and sorry she'll be, I've no doubt, to be missing the occasion. But Father Keith's house-keeper asked her, and she wouldn't care to displease him by refusing.'

'No. Of course. Would you rather wait and get her opinion before making up your mind about the big room?'

'Not at all.'

'You see, if we bring the pipe round to *this* wall —' (In his normal moods, and particularly on anything remotely connected with his real job, Tom's patience and good temper were inexhaustible.) 'Well, that means two more angle joints, but less piping. And if you'd rather it came through the other wall, it means a longer carrying line, but straighter. So there's nothing in it. It's for you to choose.'

'I want to pay for the piping, of course.'

'Heavens, man, there's no point in your buying it. A stack of the stuff is just wasting itself in our backyard at Cork, and has been for over a year. My father owns a printing works; it was rebuilt just before the war. There's enough scrap of all kinds from the old building for anything we can think of. It's no use where it lies. I've only to send word of how much we need.' This assurance, though founded on fact, was not wholly true. It would be far less trouble to drive over to Sligo or Donegal and buy the piping than to get it sent up from the South, with all the explanations that would be required. Whatever he spent would be in the nature of a wedding present to Bridie, but the demolished type-foundry, he surmised, might come in useful more than once for the saving of Sean's pride. He had also resolved to pro-vide Bridie with a lamp on a counterweight, a simple contrivance apparently unknown in this district: at any rate Mr. Wallace had not got one.

'Will you settle for the south side, then, Sean? The big room to run from about here, say, to the second clump of nettles?'

'That'll be it, exactly.'

A feeling of sudden and extreme cold, which she remembered later, came over Denyse while the two men were talking. But the daylight was dying; she had plenty of reason for chilliness, sitting still after exertion, on a soggy bank, in the evening, wearing very wet shoes, and stockings which were clammy to the knee; it did not seem surprising to her that she shivered. Noticing it, Tom said, 'We'll be going now. Back some time to-morrow. Now I know the layout you want, I can get on with it.'

'You'll find me here, whenever you come. I'll be getting on with the job myself now. And thank you. You should never be putting yourself out like this, all the same.' No reference was made on either side to the fact that he had tried to deceive them about the site. Tortuous kindliness would be enough to account for it, Tom concluded, as they drove the car back towards the quarry and a change of clothes. The explanation might well be as simple as that: since Mrs. Mary's remark about 'the English Forces' everyone had assumed that Tom was a soldier, and even if he were in the wrong army, Sean still wanted him to enjoy his leave, without interference from Kildooey affairs.

The car, which had behaved gallantly as an overweighted truck, now broke its near back spring, without provocation, when there were only the two of them inside. The chassis jammed down on the wheel, and they had the greatest difficulty in persuading it into the quarry, with a lump of wood wedged between the axle and the body to lift the weight off the wheel. By the time they had manœuvred into the entrance there was no time to rummage for spare shoes and trousers, and also reach Mr. Wallace's in time for the late news; they went over as they were.

Mr. Wallace was in, with a peat fire burning in the kitchen. He insisted that Denyse should change her mud-soaked stockings for a pair of his socks—and admire the darns in them; these he had done himself, he explained, as he did everything else for himself. He would take no refusal in his pressing hospitality; they had only the choice of drinking his appalling sherry or of offending him, as they listened through the open door to the wireless already playing in the dark cavern of the next room. Bremen was on the air. 'Seriously now, I always have the German station at this hour,' he said; 'they have the best choral music.' He tittered malignantly. 'They cannot make me pay a penny for it! Much as it would please them if they could, I've no doubt! For that reason I play it even when there is no choral music, which is what I really enjoy. I am one of the very few in these parts, Mr. Fairburn, who sees the Germans for what they are. Haven't I fought against them before? Hereabouts, people hold it against me that I did my best for England. For that, and for belonging across the border, they don't like me! But the Germans have the best music, so they do, and every night I listen to it, free! Every night, and how can they prevent it?'

It was indeed a curious experience, Tom found, to be entertained, in this odd pocket of neutral ground, by the station to which he had previously only listened in the air. Then he had been waiting tensely for its shutting off, as a signal that the enemy was aware of the approach of hostile aircraft, and below and ahead of him the defences were going into action. In the same circumstances, he supposed, he would soon be listening to it again: well, he would try to fix his thoughts on Mr. Wallace, listening assiduously in Kildooey whether he liked the music or not, in order that his old enemies should provide him with something for nothing.

Mr. Wallace moved about his own home as he had done about Mrs. Mary's cabin, giving the impression that he was levering himself round chairs and other objects against a strong gravitational pull from one side or the other. But he moved, too, with great sureness in the dark, threading his way noiselessly through the maze of furniture in the other room, to turn the wireless to Athlone when Bremen lapsed into talk, or to fetch for them some little treasure which had been overlooked on the earlier visit.

'My first shop. Did you see the photograph of the first shop I had in Kildooey?'

'Oh, yes. The one with you just outside.'

'But there's another. Better. With myself in the doorway this time. You didn't observe that one? To think the Black-and-Tans should choose to burn my first shop, when there were plenty I.R.A. roofs they might have burned within a mile of it. Aye, and all of them standing to this day. Sheltering the same heads as they sheltered then, for the most part. You must see: wait, now, till I get the picture . . . And I'll show you, too, the warrant I had from the Army for the repair of it . . . There, that's it. Do you see, twenty-three pounds, it says . . .' Scuttling to and fro like a crab, he clawed out of the darkness for them little decaying pieces of his dead life. He seemed excited by the chance of talking to people who could be expected to listen sympathetically to his English army experiences in the last war; but try as he would, he could tell them little more than the relevant dates, and the names of the places where he had been taken ill, or treated, or sent up for medical boards. (Even his ailment had been dull: chronic enteritis.) Yet he plainly tried hard to get into touch with the visitors: the deforming pride of the man, aware that he was uniquely himself — the R.J.W. whom no one else appreciated — longed for an outlet in companionship or boasting; but he had no companions, and of what could he boast?

As the time of the news bulletin came near Tom grew taut with nerves and scarcely replied to his conversation. Mr. Wallace either could not or would not get London for them to-night on his machine. 'You shall see how Athlone handles the news,' he said. 'You shall just see!' But this they knew already, from listening to the last part of the service at Father Keith's. Mr. Wallace, moved by darkly complicated motives, was not to be influenced by their wishes.

Denyse, too, found it difficult to keep up a pretence of attention, to a stream of hints about what would happen if Mr. Wallace ever chose to tell all that he had learnt in his eighteen years of local trading. Might there not be some in Kildooey less inclined to pass on their way with a nod of the head and a careless air? Father Keith's beloved parishioners: Father Keith himself — 'So good, ye'd be hard put to it to strangle an unkind word out of him. Or a truly kind deed either! Look at his harsh treatment of the young folk. Really, the case of Helen Sullivan, now! You, coming from civilized places, what a condemnation of this country it must seem to you! A poor girl fetched back from a place where she was happy! Where she was finding her merriment — making very merry indeed, I shouldn't be surprised!' Mr. Wallace leant forward, almost with a leer; and when he came close, he was inclined to spray. 'Those Sullivans, they are capable of anything, if you take my meaning, eh? If you take my meaning! And what does the good Father bring her back for? To raise more children in an overpopulated country.' Denyse gave up her efforts to be convincing in her interest, and said 'Yes', and 'No', at intervals, watching Tom's face for the last few minutes while he studied his wrist-watch, below the level of the kitchen table. But Mr. Wallace was no longer capable of noticing whether his hearers listened or not, he had found his outlet, in hatred; a hatred that he would not dare express to any-one else in Kildooey, for he was still nominally one of Father Keith's flock — he could not otherwise have kept his shop in the village. He talked on venomously of Father Keith, and all that he stood for.

'The Irish priesthood — aren't they holding down the Irish people? More than poverty. More than ignorance. They who want the present ignorance to go on, lest the people get beyond them. Loutish micks from the farms. Seriously, now, haven't they fought every reform that's been suggested in the country in the past fifty years? Aren't they behind every effort to keep the people where their fathers were before them — thinking of England as the enemy? Aye, and aren't they eager to push them further back still — talking their old, useless language, with not a book to read in it but is translated from the English! And for what? So there'll be easier misunderstandings with their neighbours!' His voice rose, shrill with pent-up rage. Athlone began giving the German High Command communique, which came first this time. Tom and Denyse looked at one another in a blank torment of apprehension; the figures of the day's air combats, if true, were disastrous: but were they anywhere near the truth? There was no reason to suppose so. Yet if they were — 'Ah, now, you want to pay no attention to that,' said Mr. Wallace, and talked on. 'I've no patience myself with this Government, allowing the like of that on the wireless. But that's how they are, these people. There's no sense or justice in the temperament of the Eire folk. No sense or justice at all.'

'. . . the Luftwaffe, pressing home another extremely successful at-tack . . . met by a second defence line of British fighters, thirty-three of which were sent down in flames, making a day's total in all of 88 . . .'

'Father Keith, of course, he's for neutrality stronger than most of them. Weren't the priests in with the I.R.A. during the Troubles? And wouldn't they be again, it's more than likely, if the fools that be drill-ing in the bogs, every moonlight night, should have their way?'

The conclusions he reached were often right, and always he reached them for unsound reasons: blinded by his personal hostility towards Father Keith, he stumbled on the truth by accident. Through all he said showed a lifelong need of trust and affection; and, as plainly, the fact that he had never had, in himself, the smallest amount of either of these qualities to give. So, giving and receiving nothing, he had acquired a grudge against the smiling, easy people who denied him the intimacy to which in any case he could not have responded. Constantly he saw the figure of Father Keith between himself and the only compensation possible to him, power over those who would not love him as they ought. 'I put down the dancing-floor at the foot of the hill when I first came — and I moved into Donegal from Ulster for the sake of the reputation they have in these parts — for good-heartedness! Will you believe it, now, that's why I came! And what did I find? With my own money I put down that floor. For the young folk, so they should have their pleasure on the summer nights. Not a penny have I ever made out of it. Nothing did I ever intend to make out of it, but just to see the young people happy. And because I came from the north they said it was to get goodwill for the business. And what did *he* do when he came? Stopped the use of the floor. Many and many a year before the Church as a whole came out against the village dancing. Ah, the little nun-like Irish girls, that would come riding down on their bicycles from over the hills, to dance so nicely in the summer dusk with their lads, while the older people watched, and all as it should be to the decent eye, of God or man. And then away with them up into the mist of the hills again — and maybe the lads accompanying them some of the way, and maybe all of the way, ah, Mr. Fairburn; who should go prying into that?' He looked knowing again, glancing eagerly from one to the other. 'Really, the prettiest sight it was. Though I'm no man for that sort of thing, it pleased me. And I had gone to great expense with the floor. But he must stop it. Are your feet warm and dry now, Mrs. Fairburn? . . . I said, are your feet warm?'

'What? — Oh, yes, thank you. Very comfortable, thank you. I think my stockings are nearly dry, too.'

'Ah, you'll not be let out of this house till it's fine and dry they are,' said Mr. Wallace with a heavy playfulness. 'You must have some more sherry.'

'No, thank you. I never — '

'Ah, but you must.' He poured out two more glasses. 'Seriously now, 'tis most refreshing to me to meet with cultivated people.' (This car-

ried an uncomfortable echo of the conversation with Father Keith.)
'Though it would open more than one mind, I've no doubt, if I were
to speak out —'

'One minute. I came to listen to this,' said Tom, strained beyond the
observance of Irish social standards. Athlone had switched to the
English bulletin.

On this day 103 of the invaders had fallen to the British defences at
a cost of 13 fighter-pilots and 22 machines: it was one of the most
successful days since the attack began. Denyse kept the enormous relief
out of her voice with difficulty as she said, 'Tom, it's all right still!'
Mr. Wallace was one of the unfortunate people before whom, instinctively, no one would betray either joy or sorrow if this could possibly
be avoided.

'England will win, there's no doubt of it — and who will be sorriest?'
he said, returning to his obsession. 'His Reverence, hoping for the
uplifting of his people through suffering!'

Tom, wiping his face, said something about the heat of the kitchen
after hours of humping stones; Mr. Wallace, however, was further
than before from noticing anything but his wrongs. Having brooded
through the bulletin, he broke out again vehemently: 'Never a smile
on their faces here but is false in some way! As I've found out to my
cost, over and over. But now I'm not taken in. I'm a match for them.
And have been for many a year —'

The peculiar work of the gombeen-man, feared and secret ruler of
many Irish villages, was then laid before them: Tom had been right
about Mr. Wallace.

Nothing was too much trouble, no negotiation too poor in profits
for him to undertake, if by so doing he could gather closer into his
hands the strings of the life of Kildooey. They were given a thorough
and oddly revolting exposition of this profession.

If a man sold three cows for more than their worth, through Mr.
Wallace's efforts, sooner or later he would be required to conclude
another deal in which he would not be the gainer. Someone else must
be put under an obligation to the shopkeeper, in order that in the
fullness of time he too might pay for it dearly. Before making the
second and less satisfactory proposal to the seller of the cows, Mr.
Wallace would wait patiently, for years if necessary, till the purchaser

of the cows was on the verge of marrying the seller's daughter, also
with Mr. Wallace's help. (His assistance in matrimonial affairs often
looked entirely benevolent. He lent money and gave credit on security
which was spiritual rather than physical: a young married man who
owed more than he could pay at short notice was always a potential
source of strength, a bargaining point against Father Keith in their
long struggles for supremacy in the control of communal life.) No man
would wish his son-in-law to suspect that two of the three cows in the
original deal were known, at the time of the sale, to have slipped their
calves — a damning piece of information shared by the owner, and
just one neighbour who had helped to bury them. But over this neighbour Mr. Wallace would have obtained influence in the meanwhile, by
another series of bargains, and so induced him to pass on what he
knew.

It did not appear likely that Mr. Wallace actually resorted to black-
mail at any time: it was, as ever, the guilty conscience of those who
had dealings with him which established the gombeen-man's position.
He was not often called what he was, by those who dealt with him,
for to admit that he was the gombeen-man would also be to admit the
guilty conscience of the bargainers. As in the case of the cows, made
profitable to him by a village wedding, it was never a coincidence that
a marriage — or a death — should enable him to turn over his money:
so many linked negotiations were always waiting to be concluded that
any shifting, separating or joining of people and their possessions
would, almost inevitably, advance one or other of them. Change was
the sun which ripened his sour little fruit.

In the next room the radio went on with a talk by a member of
the Dail, urging people to cut more turf because England, for her own
purposes, had almost stopped the sending of coal to Eire.

The main feeling which Mr. Wallace aroused was not so much
disgust as pity. Disgust, however, was there, and the visitors wanted
to get away. Mr. Wallace felt the stockings which Denyse had taken
off and hung from the mantelpiece: he pronounced that they would
be dry in a couple of minutes.

It was difficult to insist on leaving at once, and they stayed on. Mr.
Wallace was possessed with spite: his eyes, alive with their nearest
approach to gaiety, fixed on the half-full glass of sherry which he

twirled round and round before him, as though fascinated by the danger of spilling a few drops, yet he always managed to avoid this. (They noticed that he did not drink his own sherry, and wondered uneasily whether anything left in the glasses always went back into the bottle. Bridie had warned them that it did; in which case, whose dregs were they politely drinking now?)

'Ah, if they knew how much I'd kept to myself, all these years! With barely a "thank you", save when they were in need of something —' Mr. Wallace suddenly leant towards them across the table, and dropped his voice: 'How did he die, Mrs. Mary's man? Who knows that, eh? "At the hands of the Black-and-Tans", you'll say; "everyone knows that!" Ah, but who was he? Just a poor innocent labourer on a farm, and they killing the wrong man as usual? Some would say yes to that too, some would. But some know better!' They moved back as he mouthed the words at them with intense satisfaction. 'Wouldn't they like to boast of it now, the Sullivans! Wouldn't they — that he was the schemingest man of these parts in the dirty Republican army. So he was! It suited him well enough in life to be thought nothing but a simple farm-worker, while he planned the way for a few of his own kind to set on a coastguard's hut at night. That was but one of his brave deeds! To burn it down, and get the rifles, and shoot an unarmed man in the scrimmage. So a humble man he must remain in death, for it wouldn't do to have his memory connected with the dirtiest trick of all, the drunken tinker ambush. Oh, no; even Eire wouldn't be praising that! Oh, it wouldn't do at all, with his widow so thick with the priest — so thick that maybe tongues should have wagged more than they have, when the two were younger. But of that I'm saying nothing.' He leered at them, hoisted himself away from the table, and almost ran to shut off the wireless, so that he could speak softly and be sure of a hearing. Some of the tale floated back to them in the darkness: he could not wait till he had rejoined them to go on with it.

'Well-liked he was in these parts, the old tinker. In and out of the houses, mending pots for the women, with a "No, bless your sweet eyes. I'll be taking no money from a flower of a girl like yourself". (And she maybe with four children, and thick as could be with another.) You know how they crave for fair words hereabouts. Fair words meaning nothing! "Just a drop of tea I'll have with you now,"

he'd say, "and maybe some food to take on the road." Except on some
Fridays, when he'd consent to be paid. For he reckoned to be drunk
on Saturday, about once a month, and a long-standing trouble he was
to the police of all the places around. One lot or another would have
to be going out with the car, just when they'd want to sit in the station
and talk of the hurling scores. But there'd come a call from somewhere
to fetch the tinker from the middle of the road, he having the habit
of falling dead drunk in the highway, and they were always afraid that
one night the traffic would fail to divert itself round him.' Mr. Wallace
reappeared in the room, darting to the fire to turn Denyse's stockings,
and to the turf-box for more peat, talking all the while.

'Really, the constables had a fondness for the old tinker, do you see,
despite the nuisance he was. So they went out as usual, cursing him
but willing enough, when the message came one Saturday. Who gave
the message? I'm thinking it was Mrs. Agnes herself. Mrs. Agnes
Kearney, then, and already the mother of Sean. For her first husband
was one of the men with Sullivan, though he didn't amount to anything, and died in his bed. (And she jealous of Mrs. Mary from the
beginning of her days! Didn't she marry Sullivan's brother when both
were widowed, for no better reason than that Mrs. Mary couldn't,
because of the laws of the Church and the closeness of blood? And he
died on her too, within six months, Te, he! Te, he!).'

Mr. Wallace was now scrambling on to his chair again, using his
short legs as though to save himself from being dragged back into
the room behind him, by his private force of gravity. Spit and words
came with a rush. 'The police were after Sullivan for the coast-guard
killing, but they weren't thinking of that, the five young constables
who came out in the station vehicle to gather up the tinker, in the
gloom of the evening. They found him spread out in the road four
miles from here, with his horse eating from the hedge. Your side of
the village, not mine. 'Tis always on your side that things happen.
That's why I built here. Te, he! Lying the same as usual, he was,
from what they could see in the failing light. Only not dead drunk this
time, but just dead. Shot through the back of the head and laid out
there as a bait. And a fine bait he made, seriously now, for the constables got out of the car, to lift the old man, leaving their rifles inside.
And not one of them lived to get back into the van.'

'What a vile business,' said Denyse, crossing to the fire herself to feel the feet of her stockings. Surely they could go soon!

'It's the real Ireland you're getting all the same,' said Tom regretfully. 'With the fair speaking and the sudden incredible savagery, never more than a tinker's journey apart.'

' 'Tis! 'Tis!' said Mr. Wallace with satisfaction.

'How can you be sure it was Sullivan's doing?' asked Denyse. The atmosphere in the kitchen had been strange before: it was macabre now, with this man unstirred by the news of to-day, but almost beside himself in excitement over an event many years old, with all the actors dead.

'I have my ways of knowing. And there's more, there's more!' he said, trembling with an impersonal glee of hatred. He put his hands on her arms and pressed her back into the chair.

'Sullivan was on the run then, and Mrs. Agnes' man grew frightened of his company, and went back to his fishing. Though many said that Kearney had done his share in the shooting, too—while it was safe. (Mrs. Agnes never forgave him for leaving herself an ordinary fisherman's wife, the while Mrs. Mary was that of a bold patriot.) For it wasn't the killing of the tinker got Sullivan hunted. Nothing was ever proved on that. Not really proved, do you see. It was the coast-guard affray. An armed Republican against a fellow off duty, with empty hands—that's the idea, in these parts, of a noble blow struck for the old country! Still, they couldn't have stomached the tinker, even so. Yet I know who killed him. And others besides me. But not all know it; oh no, not all!

' "Ah, but how did he die?" you ask me again—' The visitors, who asked nothing but to get away, made assenting sounds in the pause, while he looked again from one to the other, very cunningly. It was, they thought, the quickest means of escaping from the presence of so much evil. Let him get to the end of his story.

'It was a proud and careless word of Mrs. Mary's which set the men who were after him on the right track. When he'd been on the run for six months. They went back to his cabin. Where you were yesterday! Very well accustomed, they were, to hearing a man's wife swearing by all the saints that she'd forgotten his very existence—so long it was since he'd set foot in his own place. With the remains of his last meal just cooling on the table, as evidence! But this one taunted them while they searched the cabin again, to see if he'd been home of late. She said, "You should have been along five minutes ago. Wasn't I telling my friend here" — which was Agnes — "there's not a snugger place in the hills than he has now. And wasn't she after replying, 'Indeed there is not.' So why should he be wanting to come here, with all the comforts of the home where he lies hid?" And not a trace of him could they find. But they noticed the boy Sean, peering round her skirts at the uniforms he'd been taught to fear. He'd been listening to the women talk. He'd been in the cabin often enough before, from the way he didn't care which of the two he hid behind, Mrs. Mary or his mother. Maybe he'd been elsewhere, too. Not above five or six, he was then.' Mr. Wallace put aside his untouched sherry and leant further across the table, resting on his arms; he looked obscenely like some animal about to spring.

'Soon, do you see, there's a new tinker's van stopping on bridge, where the children play, reaching for the flowers. And the driver asks Sean, in a kind voice, would he like to drive the horse? There's no uniform about a tinker, and the gossoon says yes, he would that. And when he's up the driver says, kinder still, there's none but Sean, among all the boys in Kildooey, that he'd allow to drive his horse. And all because Harry Sullivan speaks well of him. "Him that's on the run, up in the hills," says the driver, in a careless way. "See this kettle? It's what I'm taking him as a present. For he's a grand fellow and a great friend of mine, is Harry Sullivan!"

'"You going now?" says Sean.

'"Now," says the driver. "Would you be wanting to drive the horse all the way? Maybe it's a bit far. I doubt there's a boy your age in Kildooey has driven a van for the half of that distance."

'"Well, it isn't so far," says Sean. "But you can't go all the way by road. For there's the bog in between."

'"Maybe we could walk that bit," says the driver. "You carrying the kettle. He'd be glad to see you this day, would Harry Sullivan. 'A boyo that'll be ready to step in my footsteps, all in good time,'" he says.'

The unloosing of feeling, long pent up, gave Mr. Wallace the lilt and turn of phrase which the Ulsterman normally lacked. Reporting something which he could only know by hearsay, however the facts had come into his possession, he spoke with imagination, almost with laughter in his voice. 'They didn't go all the way. "Look, now, he's from home—if he calls it home," says the driver, when Sean has pointed out the old farm buildings, away beyond the bog on the other side of the hill. "He told me he'd hang a sack over the gate to show me when he was there by day. To save me a journey for nothing. And there's no sack, is there? You'd see it well against the white gate?"

' "No, there's no sack," says Sean, disappointed, for Harry Sullivan was the hero of all the Kildooey boys. Down to the smallest ones, that didn't know why it was a fine thing to be on the run. But they believed it, from listening to their mothers, or else from hearing the priest praying for the murderers! So the two of them went back. "Another day, when he's there, we'll take him the kettle. And you'll show him the way you can drive the horse."

'The Black-and-Tans, do you see, had taken over the case from the police by then. They killed Sullivan that night, in his hiding place. Shot him down like a dog, the way he'd shot others.'

Full laughter broke out from Mr. Wallace's lips with a spatter. 'The fools there are in Dooey! Not a moment of sleep would they know this night, those two women, if they guessed what I could say, did I choose! For they've kept his part in it from the boy, all these years. To be silent about that—'tis the only pact on earth they could keep together, those two! All that he knows is what everyone knows: Sullivan died as an Irish martyr! (Him that never did a hand's-turn of work in his life. And even when he was on the run, his wife was turning her eyes elsewhere, so little she cared!) Oh, yes, that's how he died, Mrs. Mary's man. But they've kept it from Sean. And both of them have good reason for that—his mother always afraid, now, if he knew what he'd done, the shame of it would send him out into the open with his activities, knowing no bounds, and he'd end as Sullivan ended. And the other—oh, the other has her reasons, too—' He slipped from his chair and hurried round the table to them, peering into their faces. 'Hasn't she been paid all these years, by the comrades of the man she sent to his death for the sake of a joke? Would they go on paying, if they were aware who it was that put it into the heads of his enemies to coax the way of his hiding place out of a child?'

Instantly, to both the visitors, came fear on behalf of the little com-

munity which had received them so friendlily. It was very different
from the vague unease which Denyse had known earlier in the evening,
by the site of the new cabin — that had been a snatching of the mind
at half-remembered memories and similarities and warnings: this fear
was rational enough, and plain to understand; indeed, it was all too
reasonable. Ill-balanced and spite-driven, Mr. Wallace had an unsuspected advantage over his fellows; it was vain to hope that he would
not try to use it, one day.

The visitors stayed on for a few minutes more, no longer against
their wills, trying as best they could to impress upon him the fact that
his private kingdom of power would last only so long as he kept his
knowledge to himself. Tom used reason, Denyse flattery. ('Of course,
Mr. Wallace, it must be very amusing to you, going about among the
Kildooey people, and thinking that all their lives they'll be deceived as
to what you know! How it would spoil everything if they suspected!')
It seemed intolerable to both of them that Mrs. Mary's surprising contentment, and Sean's life, and through him Bridie's — even Mrs.
Agnes's dour self-satisfaction — should all be in such pitiless hands.
The conversation was a difficult one to maintain, however, for Mr.
Wallace constantly agreed with them: under no circumstances would
he speak out now, he told them. They heard him, and doubted him, but
there was nothing more that they could say. In a little while they left.
It was delightful to get out into the cool darkness which had fallen
while they were inside.

'The room was unpleasant enough this morning,' said Denyse, when
the ornamented iron gate had locked itself behind them, squealing a
protest at being used at all. 'I'd no idea the man could be so much
more frightening than his room. Was the whole of that ghastly story
true, Tom?'

'Yes, I'm afraid so. Not that he wouldn't be capable of inventing it.
But it's got the flavour of the Troubles, all right. Those were the things
that really were done on both sides.'

'Then sooner or later, some little imaginary slight will sting, more
than the rest of his grievances, and he won't be able to resist the
pleasure of seeing just how much harm one word can do.'

'I'm afraid that's true, too.'

'But how could he know what happened to Mrs. Mary's husband?

He wasn't in the cabin when she spoke. Even if the betrayal story sounds true, it mayn't be.'

'We both knew it was, while he was talking. It isn't hard to imagine that diseased little mind of Wallace's ferreting back along a stale blood trail, however old it was when he first smelt it. Till he'd got what he was after. But the point is, neither of us had any doubt that he was telling the truth, when he spoke of Sean as a boy. Everyone's mind seems able to leap to danger more certainly than to anything else, I think. If it's not one's own danger, after a bit one usually begins to doubt if there's anything in the idea of intuition. Sometimes it's possible to doubt even when it is one's own danger. But if the feeling comes strongly — and you got it at the same moment as I did, because I was watching you — then that's the time when second-thoughts aren't any good. It's the only sort of non-reasoning I trust.'

'I had a moment of sheer horror,' she admitted. 'I was surprised that anything could grip me like that, so soon after the relief of the radio news — Oh, Tom, that's marvellous, isn't it! If the figures tomorrow can be as good, or better — But Mr. Wallace so loved what he was telling us that he made it vivid, and I saw it all happen.'

'Incidentally,' said Tom, 'the last part of that story makes sense of something said between the Sullivan women, when you were talking to Helen —'

He repeated it as well as he could remember . . . ' "Though one died in his bed". — "Mary, be quiet, now". — "Sean's out!" ' And ' "Reason? Would you still be looking for reason? That's not the way things happen." — "Or so you're pleased to think!" '

'The bitterness there must be between those two!' said Denyse. 'Sharing that secret and — luckily! — not knowing that Mr. Wallace shares it too. By the way, Bridie also knows, I believe. "I've known things that have passed in Kildooey, though the old ones think I don't! — " Do you remember?'

'Yes, but it doesn't matter if Bridie knows. She's good and sweet and Sean is safe with her. She's probably as secretive, too, as only the smiling Irish can be.' He began to talk in general terms to lessen the tension he sensed in Denyse's mind, disturbed by the passion of vindictiveness which had been poured out before them. 'It's a strange thing about village life over here; in the places where the people seem most open-hearted, you find these dark secrets in plenty, kept safely for generations by whole groups of neighbours and relations. There's elephant's blood in every family: nothing's forgotten or forgiven. Nor spoken about, if it's serious, except just enough to keep the memory alive. It's my impression that if three people in any English village know something against a fourth, in a week everyone knows. And in five years, nobody cares as a rule. But in Ireland, five years after the whispers begin about anyone in a small parish, they're still confined to the same ears. But by then the person whispered about has probably broken his neck, in the most innocent-seeming way, through falling off a ladder. And no one else knows, to the end of time, which of the whisperers cut through a rung of the ladder, in order to finish with the need to whisper. Roughly, that's the temperamental difference.'

'I wish someone would finish off Wallace before he makes trouble,' she said.

'Somehow though — and I don't know why — gombeen-men never do end that way. Perhaps because they're careful never to go up ladders, or walk at random too near the edge of wells.'

'It was such a relief for him to tell us! It was like the bursting of some very slow-gathering abscess of hatred in his mind. Only it'll re-form. In a way, we may have done Kildooey an ill turn already, just by being here to be told. Having had that relief once, he'll want it again, more than before.'

'Poor devil — that's for both him and Sean.'

They spoke of other things; of the air figures and the possibility that the Luftwaffe could afford these losses; even at the present rate of exchange, the whittling down of the British fighter-power might still be worth while, so that sheer weight of numbers should tell in the end. Tom went into technicalities at some length.

'Stop playing the accomplished hostess to me, Denyse! ("Always draw a man out on his own subject.") You're asking the right questions at the right intervals, but really, you're not listening! What are you thinking about?'

' "Random," ' she said. 'I'm sorry. It was a word you used a little while ago, and suddenly it brought back a lot of things I'd forgotten or tried to forget. You're quite right, I only half-heard what you've just been saying. But before that, when I *was* listening, it was your remark about danger that started up the echoes, "Random" came into it — "walk at random". It was what you said about the mind recognizing danger, and then pushing the recognition away by thought — You know, Tom, I wouldn't marry you!'

'When have I asked you to?' he said ungallantly, kissing her as they walked.

'No, you haven't, have you? But I don't think I need consider it a delicate subject and keep off it, do you, seeing that I'm not free anyway? What I meant was that a husband who always knew when his wife had stopped attending would be a considerable strain — Paul was usually much too interested in what he was saying to notice.'

He was amused, in a wry way, at the pleasure he took in hearing her mention another man's name; she used it so much more casually than before. He said, 'I'm in love with you, and you know it. But if you were available I still shouldn't ask you to marry me. Because I don't want a wife who's in love with someone else.'

She did not answer.

'Tell me about "random",' he said.

'It was a joke people made in Paris. Or rather, the Germans made it, by accident, in their bulletins, and the French took it up with delight. At the time when England first reported the deliberate bombing of her civilians. "The killing of women and children at random by the Luftwaffe." The Germans translated this as an enemy admission that "Damage to military objectives was done in the neighbourhood of Random". It was the sort of gaffe which was very popular, that first winter. In cultured circles. When I heard it I got the feeling which made all my visits to Paris so miserable at that time — while we were still waiting safely behind the Maginot line. Not only a sort of foreboding that I couldn't explain, though there was that too, but also the idea that I was losing touch with my world. Didn't people realize any more that death at random was still death? — the end of a universe for whoever it was that died? — even if "random" didn't happen to be a place? Then as I told you, it was impressed on me by Paul that people needed to be trivial-minded during a war, and I helped to argue myself out of the fear. The same thing happened just after the break-through at Sedan. Before we knew what that meant. Only this time the mistake was made by the other side. The French bulletin said somthing like: "Même que la position n'est pas au claire il faut renfermer que les forces Françaises n'ont pas perdu cohésion," and the English gave it out that though the position was somewhat confused, Cohésion was known to be still in the hands of the French. I was frightened again, because the French laughed so much. The cosmopolitan ones who could understand. The cosmopolitan ones who were always entertained by bêtises. Who went on right to the end finding the whole of our civilization far too amusing to defend. It was a great relief just then to talk to a high officer we knew, because he didn't laugh at either of these jokes. He was very grave, and he said, "The soul of France is immortal, Madame. Never forget that. Whatever happens, she will rise again". And hearing a soldier say that, I managed to push away the fear with reason, once more. Just as you said. Someone was being serious. A man with great responsibilities. And he wasn't alone. Others were saying the same thing, too, behind the giggles of the blâgueurs. But that was when I should have been most afraid. Because what he said at that moment was the deepest defeatism of all. A faith so complete that it called for no action whatever. The soul of France was immortal; what did it matter if she died?'

Two figures, just discernible in the darkness, leant on the coping of the bridge, watching the starlight on the stream. There was the murmur of a young man's voice, talking very softly for no ear but a girl's. The murmur stopped when Tom and Denyse approached. Bridie called good night to them as they passed.

They returned the greeting and went on in silence for a moment, hearing Sean's voice again, followed by Bridie's laugh.

'That's interesting!' Tom said, when they reached the other side of the bridge.

'You mean, because so far those two have taken each other for granted?'

'Yes—' Their voices had been as low as Sean's; Mrs. Mary's sharp ears, however, had pounced on the sound of unfamiliar footsteps passing her cabin. It took her some time to struggle up from her settee and reach the door; from the other side of the bridge they could pretend they did not hear her shouting. Getting no answer, she summoned Sean and sent him after them. It seemed too ungracious, then, to refuse to return with him: 'My Aunt Mary wants a word with you.' He shepherded them back to her doorstep before rejoining Bridie.

'There's nothing special I have to say,' she told them unblushingly. 'But come in, the both of you, for a cup of tea.'

Denyse, however, was anxious to get back to the car; it had been an exhausting evening. They made the excuse of being wet about the feet, which was no longer true, and refused to come in.

'I'm deserted this night by you all,' said Mrs. Mary crossly. 'Even the young have gone out courting, they who never troubled themselves about it before! Father Keith's off consoling Mrs. Clancy for the loss of her daughter, sailing back to-night to her nursing in England; and even Agnes has gone home to sit on her hair.'

'To do what?' they asked together. This was the joy of Mrs. Mary's society—that in it one saw the outside world, even the dreariest objects, like Mrs. Agnes, from an unexpected angle. A deplorable woman, Mrs. Mary—they looked at her with a new curiosity to-night, after Mr. Wallace's story; havoc indeed had been wrought by her irresponsibility, even to the death of a man whose safety lay in her keeping, but it was hard not to oblige with an ear if she had a mind to talk. They found themselves nearer the threshold, and twitched one another back. If they were drawn inside, an hour at least would pass before they could get away.

'Wasn't it the regular boast, in her generation and mine, that a girl could sit on her hair, so well it grew?' Mrs. Mary turned artfully from the door in order that they should follow her in, and be trapped. 'Never a notable aunt you had, the two of you, I'll be bound, but could sit on her hair. (And she known at all, that is, for the looks she had.) Wasn't it so?'

'Come to think of it, yes!' said Tom, with the gloom of the last hour or two lifting from him. 'I was told in childhood about two beautiful aunts I never saw. And the only thing I can remember is just that: they could sit on their hair.'

'I was sure of it. And you, my dearest?'

'Well, I don't think it was ever a French fashion for aunts.' Denyse excused her relations with the sense of guilt which Mrs. Mary often induced in those who failed to agree with her. 'But I've certainly heard it about other people's aunts, in England.' She and Tom held on to one another firmly, and stayed where they were while Mrs. Mary patted the settle invitingly.

Having failed to entice them over the threshold, she waddled back to the doorway. 'With the beautiful hair you have yourself,' she said, 'there's no doubt the ladies of your family could have sat on theirs if they wished. But they had too much sense, maybe. Though it's not for me to say, for I never measured my own hair that way. There's nothing wrong in it, of course, but the attitude of mind it gives you after a time, just like Agnes; not seeing the interesting things that must be happening under your nose at every minute. For there was never hair that would reach to where you could sit on it, without you gave it all the help you could by the tilt of your head. In the whole of my time, I've met no woman could sit on her hair that did anything else worth doing! "Mary," said Agnes to me this evening, while we still hoped you'd be taking a cup of tea with us later, "Mary," she said, "It brings back old days, when we were that age, so it does, to see Sean and Bridie walking together in the dusk. And, talking of those days, do you know," she said, "I can still sit on my hair as I used to then!"' (Mrs. Mary's own hair was now a thin, short, grey fuzz, looking the less because of the size of the face it should have framed) but her eyes were as young as ever, flashing with irritation. '"Away home, then," I said, "and uncoil and sit on the few hairs that are long enough! May it do you as much good as ever it did—and what was that?" So now I'm alone, and Father Keith would be letting you know it's my own fault! But you'll be having a cup of tea with me after all, won't you? Then I can tell Agnes in the morning what she missed, sitting on her hair at her age!'

'No, thank you very much indeed, Mrs. Mary. Not to-night.'

'To-morrow then? I'll have some fresh bread baked for you, or Bridie will, or Kathie or someone. And it'll be waiting for you here.'

'Well, that's very kind of you. But don't actually count on us, because we may be too late to stop, after giving Sean a bit of a hand at building his new place.'

'Ah, I heard of the wonderful plan you have for the water. Wonderful indeed. But I shall count on you all the same,' said Mrs. Mary, giving words to the spirit which had made her such an improbably happy woman. 'Then if you don't come, at least I will have had all day the pleasure of the expectation.'

CHAPTER XI

WARNING

The flapping sound of heel-less shoes echoed on the road behind them as they turned up the hill after leaving Mrs. Mary. Father Keith, they had noticed, wore flat, stout sandals; and they increased their pace. But the sound gained on them, and then ceased in the grass verge as he cut a corner, knowing the rough hillside well enough to avoid the ditches by night. When he returned to the road he was close beside them.

'Tom?'

'Yes?'

'Wait, now. Have you no more concern for old age than to set it tearing up a hillside, like one of the voles I was telling you about, with the owls after him! And all for the sake of a private word.' Under the professional joviality of the priest, which could turn so quickly to harshness with his young people, there sounded the extreme embarrassment of the man.

'I'd no idea you wanted to speak to us.'

'Why else would I be coming all this way up in the dark? It was just — ' He stopped, panting. Even when he had recovered his breath, he still hesitated to give his reason. 'Ah, I'll be coming up to the top with you, anyway. I fancy I'll find Kenny Clancy there, and give him a line of my mind for leaving his mother alone to-night. With his sister travelling on the sea, back to one of the bombed English towns! I heard him start up this way, a few minutes before you parted from Mrs. Mary — I keep a watch on you all, you see!' He gave the beginnings of a laugh, and then changed his mind. 'Ken Clancy, you know him. One of the lads who digs bait for you. A good boy, but thoughtless of his mother — poor soul, with her girl in peril.'

'Yes, do come,' they said, but the discomfort he showed was shared by all three.

A bat, squeaking overhead, provided the priest with a subject of which he could talk without anxiety — the untainted, non-human world that had given him all the pleasure he had been able to know of late. He told them several things about bats which were not new to them, and for something to say in return, Tom related the rather pointless story of a dead bat, taken into a training plane as part of an elaborate practical joke; it had turned out to be not dead, but a considerable nuisance in the air. From awkwardness he slipped back into the use of Service slang which he avoided with Denyse.

'Is that what you are? You had not told me. Part of an air-crew?'

'Yes, I fly a bomber.'

'Then God forgive you, my son, for what you do now! I had not meant to speak of this again — it was for something else I came — but you must know well enough that time for you may be very brief? How can you live as you do, knowing this? Knowing that perhaps even now you stand on the threshold of death?'

'Just because the time may be scarce.'

'No,' said Denyse. 'Not only that, Father Keith. Or not for me, at least. But because we have a great need of each other — more than I think we could make you understand. Our fault, not yours, I mean, that we couldn't make you understand. There would be so much to explain — and now won't you tell us, please, what it was you were going to say?' She swung suddenly into a former manner, the social technique which, had the priest been less sincere, would have set Tom laughing enormously, in this incongruous setting. She had charge of the situation immediately.

'Only this. I heard you went up to Mr. Wallace's for the wireless news to-night — because you are strangers, nothing you do, or say can escape notice in Kildooey; you are doubtless prepared for that in a small village! — and I couldn't have you thinking that my house was shut to you because of anything said last night. Or just now, for that matter. Myself, I'm rarely at home in the evenings. Indeed, while you remain in Kildooey I'll make a point of not being in, if you'll agree to come sometimes, so that you shall feel undisturbed. A priest's room is meant to be a place which is barred to no man, whatever load may be upon his conscience. It will make no difference to the feel of my home, to me, if you come. But if you don't come, having been there once for the news, all Kildooey will want to know why. Please make use of my house.'

'Thank you. I think we will, won't we, Denyse?'

'Yes. I would much rather,' she said, even more relieved than Tom to think that they need not go back to the depressing museum of self-love on the other side of Kildooey.

'Now that I have fallen in with you for another purpose,' said Father Keith stiffly, 'I see no harm in asking you, just briefly, what I would have liked to discuss with you at length, in happier circumstances. As I am walking your way in any case, do you see — are you, by any chance, readers of Dickens?'

'Are we — ?'

'Readers — and admirers — of Dickens?'

There was a rather long pause.

'Well, yes.'

'You are, Denyse? (I am still calling you that, remember, because I can think of nothing else to call you. Not from discourtesy. I hope I say it right.) But not you, Tom?'

'No.'

'Why not?'

Tom had been less successful than Denyse in keeping the note of surprise out of his voice. Obligingly he tried to marshall his views, distracted by memories of that equally irrelevant first conversation with Denyse in the ship. But the effort to talk with detachment, then, had at least had a purpose, to ignore an air raid. There was no purpose, so far as he could see, in discussing Dickens with Father Keith on a Shee-ridden hillside at night; he found it extremely difficult.

'Because he always seemed to me to be much too ready to accept any system of his time as right. Provided only that the men who ran it were a bit kinder. It was always men he blamed — individual men. Not the state in which they were forced to live — the things that had made them what they were. Oh, and the fact of his leaving sex right out of the picture — well, it made it an incomplete sort of picture. But mainly I shied off him because he appeared to feel that if men were better, conditions would do, however awful.' (Quite a creditable performance, he felt, with mild satisfaction, for someone who had just been discovered on the short road to damnation.)

'I haven't read anything of Dickens's for years,' said Denyse. 'As a girl, though, I found my introduction to him very exciting.'

But Father Keith, they found, did not really want their views. He longed to pay homage to something which he had loved with an un-troubled heart.

'And to me, he is the one writer on the affairs of this world who has never failed me when I needed his help! Someone to whom I can always turn in safety for refreshment. He sees humanity as it is. With anger, yes, but with tenderness, and great forgiveness — such great forgiveness! It is that which moves me most. Yet he does not deny the depths of humanity even in his passages of hope. There is no wavering and no fear in him, and I can draw strength from that. He will set no traps for my lack of his greater knowledge, and out of his compassion he endangers nothing which I hold dear. Nor does he do like other writers, and plunge his pen into slime — for what? For the pleasure of proving again that no man's heart may know a secret thought, too base for his fellow to share it with him, willingly! There have been other writers who have given me much help in time gone by. But now it is as if we have drifted apart like human companions, not sharing the same interests any longer.' For the rest of the way up the hill, scarcely pausing for their comments, he poured out his grati-tude to the few books which had remained his friends through the years, while life had slowly contracted for him into a tormenting aware-ness of evil.

'Kenny!' he called as they reached the quarry and the level ground.

'Yes, Father,' answered a voice from just beyond the signpost. A boy slipped down from the top of the piled wall on which he had been sitting. Here the road dipped again as it ran inland; below him was spread mile upon mile of the dark countryside, over which the glim-mering finger of the signpost pointed to Dublin. He padded towards them silently on bare feet.

'What are you doing up here?'

'Nothing, Father,' he said, sounding scared. The ever-guilty con-science of twelve years old responded to the severity of the voice break-ing in on his reverie.

'Then why aren't you where you could be some use to your poor mother for once? This night of all! Leaving her troubled and praying alone by the fire for the safety of the ship that may be in danger as we speak.'

'I didn't think of it, Father.'

'You didn't think! And when, Kenny — when will you be starting to think of others? Answer me that!'

'I dug worms for himself at midday,' said the boy, now thoroughly alarmed. 'I have them in a can, and the can's by the thrickle of water where Bridie Sullivan does be washing the jug in the morning. I thought, if himself didn't come back soon, I could tell her to give them to him then. Lively and fresh they should be,' he urged, in extenuation of whatever wrong he was doing, 'by reason of the coldness from the thrickle of water around the can, do you see, Father?'

'You could have brought them up at a time when your mother had less need of you.'

'Yes, Father, I could have done that,' said the boy. 'But — '

'But what?' asked the priest, brushing aside the campers' attempt to thank the boy for his kindness over the bait.

"There was a bit of an argument to-night, between Peadar McQuire and Danny Hughes,' he said, naming two older lads who had lent their boat to Tom. 'That is, Peadar, he says it has "To Dublin, so many miles" on the new signpost. And Dan, he says no, it hasn't. Only "To Dublin". But they were mending the boat, so they gave me their matches, the way I could climb up and see for them, when I had put down the bait. Danny has the rights of it,' he added. 'And I was just sitting, myself, and wondering, how far is it, then, after all?'

'Away down and tell them to think of less nonsense!' said the priest angrily. 'And if ill comes to your sister on the crossing, you can blame yourself all your life you were not doing your best for her safety, praying beside your mother.'

As the boy trotted past, Tom stopped him and added a bar of chocolate to his thanks. A pile of this rare bliss for the children of Kildooey lay in the back of the car, in full view of all who came daily to stare at the encampment. There was no means of fastening the doors of the car, but none of it was ever taken without leave.

'I am hopeful of one thing, over this building of Sean's!' Father Keith turned to them explosively when the boy had gone. 'One day, when it's a fine heavy load of stone you have on board, I trust you will back into that signpost without damage to yourselves! I am a man of peace and order, as indeed I must be, or I would uproot it myself! — but now, I have no excuse to talk with you any more.' He wished them an abrupt good-bye, and left them to a night of acute discomfort on the floor of the broken-springed car, with the person on the upper side sliding down slowly and helplessly on to the one who lay hard against the angle of the chassis, whenever sleep had relaxed their efforts to stay apart. 'To think that this is called sin!' said Tom, after Denyse had wakened him for the third time, protesting that she was being crushed. He was a tall, spare but heavily-boned man, weighing nearly half as much again as she did. But if she took the upper side she tended to roll with unbearable suddenness on to his damaged arm. The jack, which might have righted the tilt, turned out to be defective; it was the only thing over which the horse-coper who sold the car had been dishonest, and it had been thrown into the sale quite unnecessarily as an afterthought, when the price was already settled.

All the next day Tom built with tremendous energy, either alone or working alongside Sean; but Sean showed a tendency to drift back to the village at intervals during the later afternoon and evening, to see whether Bridie were yet available to come and admire the progress of the cabin.

She had set off with Denyse to go to Donegal Town, where the broken spring might be mended. By standing on the running board of the car, and leaning out as far as possible, she could weigh down the chassis on the opposite side, while Denyse drove at a snail's pace, negotiating potholes with infinite care. The roads were appalling, and the chock of wood jammed in over the axle gradually worked out and had to be hammered back at intervals; it seemed to the campers an uninviting ride, but Bridie had jumped at the offer with alacrity.

After an hour or so of crawling she gave her reason: 'We've no means of knowing when my cousin Shamus will be in Donegal. "Soon", he said to Mr. Fairburn — so himself told me when we met. Well, "soon" might be to-day, mightn't it? I would like him to see me riding in a car,' she admitted, with the surprising yellow lashes sweeping down over her beautiful eyes, in one of her fits of shyness.

'Then come inside, quickly, if you do see him,' said Denyse sympathetically. 'Never mind the spring. We can stop till he's gone by. But it'll look more impressive that way.'

'It's not that I'm drawn to Shamus himself,' Bridie explained, at their next halt to bash in the chock. 'It's just I'd like to stop him thinking there's no one else in the family can get about from place to place! He's no stay-at-home, that one! He's been all around, the same as yourselves.' Denyse was relieved; she had been wondering with considerable anxiety whether the girl were really in love with Shamus, and hopelessly, as it would appear. It was impossible to be with Bridie for long without taking her concerns to heart: the position of Helen, forced into an unwanted marriage, seemed more than enough of such tragedies for one village. Bridie went on ecstatically: 'I'd like him to call me to the attention of any companion he might have in Donegal. Why, look, he'd say, if it isn't my cousin Bridie, now! And she in a private vehicle! And then he might say, Where will we be seeing her next, I'm asking you, if it isn't in the very capital of Eire itself?' She laughed gaily, half in mockery of herself, half in pleasure at the notion; Bridie was in love with her own creation alone, the mythical city to whose existence the signpost bore witness so solidly, so enchantingly. 'Father Keith says it was always winter, and always raining when he was in Dublin,' she continued, 'and you know he hasn't a good word to say for the place.' She swung out at a perilous angle, with one foot only on the edge of the step, as they went over a series of bumps; and the words were jerked out in breathless rushes. 'But why should it matter if it rains there? When so much of the pleasure is to be found indoors in the evenings? The entertainments and such (in peace-time of course),' she added, in deference to what himself had said. 'Surely the people wouldn't want to stay out long in the streets on a winter night, with plenty of houses to visit? And winter or summer, there's nothing like rain on the windows for making the company inside feel happy at being out of the weather. Oh, when you and Helen were talking at my Aunt Mary's, the other night, I thought, Now if only it would come on to thunder and lighten, wouldn't we have the best evening! Hearing of foreign places, and a storm outside to make me glad for once to be safe in Kildooey!'

Luck was not with Bridie; Shamus failed to appear, by splendid coincidence, in the central square of the charming old town as they drove into Donegal; but luck was certainly with Denyse. A spare spring, which could be made to fit, was found at the local garage, as well as an excellent mechanic who was fascinated by the oddities of the car; he did his best for her, in half an hour less than he had estimated at first. (Tom had said when they left, 'Now remember, if the man says two hours, it means four at least. And if he says "Ah, sure, it'll be done be tea-time", go and book rooms at the hotel. Bridie will love the adventure of sleeping in a strange bed, and I'll ask Mrs. Kathie to put me up, instead.')

As it turned out, they were back in Kildooey by dusk, and before they left Donegal, by sending Bridie along to buy stores, Denyse had made an opportunity to slip into an ironmonger's, and order all the piping and other material needed for the water supply to the new cabin — even if the stuff had really been sent up from the south by train, it would have had to come via Donegal, as the nearest railway town. There would be nothing suspicious, to Sean, in its arrival by the local carrier's van.

Sean met the car at the outskirts of the village, where he had obviously been hanging about, waiting for Bridie. 'I thought you were never coming! And I wondered, had you lost the way, with the dark threatening?' He spoke in the grudging voice of a man aware that he was showing a ridiculous concern. 'It was a pity to waste a whole day, going to Donegal,' he pointed out to Bridie.

'Waste, is it?' Bridie answered with spirit. 'What else is there to do with time in Kildooey?'

'I've been working all the while on the cabin. One of the walls is up to your shoulder.'

'Then I fancy it's Mr. Fairburn we should be thanking for it.' Sean's attention to her was something so new that she could not take it seriously. 'Did you think that the rest of the L.D.F. had risen without you and marched for the Border?' she asked teasingly. 'And maybe trampled us underfoot on the way?' But they went off together amiably enough, to do chores for Mrs. Mary.

Denyse found Tom hot and tired and happier than she had yet known him. He was pleased with the progress of the work, pleased with the way his arm was standing the strain, and still more pleased

—infinitely more pleased—by the behaviour of his temper. He had felt no resentment when Sean had made successive excuses to wander off to the village, leaving him to labour alone, on Sean's behalf. A few days ago the stranger would have taken charge, if not to the extent of angry words, at least to that of stopping work himself. He had gone on, lost to more personal feeling in the pleasure of making something.

The news, to which they listened at Father Keith's, was fairly reassuring. Later—attracted by a smell of fresh bread and by extraordinary noises coming out of the door—they looked in at Mrs. Mary's, and found her at supper, surrounded by her family, in the throes of choking violently on a fishbone. Few could have risen with more dignity to an awkward situation. Flapping her hands in distress, she was purple in the face when they put their heads round the half-door; and the sounds from her throat became rapidly more and more alarming. Her court fussed about her, offering her water which she could not drink, and patting the vast expanses of her back. Nevertheless, she was conscious of social obligations, and waved the visitors to the fire, signing to someone to draw up the settle for them.

"'Tis from one of the rock-fish you gave her yourself!' Mrs. Agnes stopped her ministrations to inform Tom of his responsibility, with an idea of spreading the general discomfort.

'Oh, now, it wouldn't be his doing at all!' said Mrs. Kathie, quickly.

Mrs. Mary glared at Mrs. Agnes, hawked up the obstruction with a supreme effort and laid it placidly beside her plate. 'Wouldn't you think,' she said, 'that a creature living in the sea would be needing all its available agility? And not go cluttering up its body with loose bones?' Having transferred the blame to the fish, she sent Bridie for a cloth with which to mop her face. Even before it arrived, she had embarked on a series of anecdotes about local fish and fishermen as though nothing had disturbed her composure. They were diverting tales, and all bore one resemblance to the famous ghost story; they were free of probable motive or any normal sequence of cause and effect.

Mrs. Agnes said an early good night, and nagged at Sean to come home with her. He was engrossed in Bridie's account of her shopping experiences in Donegal, and anxious to hear the end of her dilemma in the big store, where a man had offered her five different kinds of saucepan cleaner—'Would anyone believe the like of that, who had only been in Mr. Wallace's?' A scratchy glove, a ball of metal shavings, a long wire brush, a short wire brush, and some steel wool. 'Meanwhile,' said Bridie, 'herself had disappeared, leaving only a written list — on which, do you see, was no guidance at all, at all! But only the words "Saucepan Cleaner" underlined' — Bridie's delightful voice could make high drama out of almost any occurrence. 'Maybe it isn't any of those she wants! I thought. But just a scouring powder. So I asked him, had he any of that? "Oh," he said, "is it Vim you're meaning, or Old Dutch Cleanser, or White Cat, or any of four other kinds beside?" And I overwhelmed with the uncertainty of it, and the time running out, and the money running out, and so many things remaining to buy.' Around this hearth, the standard of technique was exacting for anyone who would heighten life by a little art; but Mrs. Mary, the adept, was nodding her head approvingly, while Mrs. Kathie murmured that it was indeed hard to reach a decision with someone else's money. Together, the two older women provided a background for the girl, like a Greek chorus, against which her story stood out with considerable suspense. Mrs. Agnes's voice cut into it, raised against Sean: 'It's not as if I would always be having your company on my way back to the old cabin! And empty indeed it will seem then — ' She whined on till her son submitted and followed her out, without hearing what Bridie had actually bought in the end from this bewildering selection.

'It will be sad for her when he marries,' observed Mrs. Kathie, after the door had closed on them. 'The last of the family left to her, she having lost so much!'

'She's grieving over it well ahead, then!' said Mrs. Mary. 'Distress and foreboding from beginning to end, that's all Agnes has got out of motherhood. And I doubt she will ever be able to appreciate the comfort there is in having nothing more to lose.' She smiled round on the fewness of her possessions. 'Some women are more concerned by motherhood than others. I mean' — she elaborated the subject for the visitors — 'they give themselves over to it, and relish even the nastiness for its own sake. In fact, if himself will not mind the mention of the thing, there are women that take the diaper as others take the veil, and Agnes was always one of them.'

It was never certain at the moment of speaking whether Mrs. Mary

would treat her own observations seriously or not; this one she elected
to find an enormous joke. A peal of laughter, in which everyone joined,
rang round the cabin. Mrs. Mary rocked about on the settee, repeating
the phrase which fascinated her, till her laughter reminded the muscles
of her throat of their recent spasm, and she began to whoop and choke
again. She was soon too weak to make her usual effort to detain her
visitors when they gathered up their bread and prepared to leave.

'Ah, now, that's how it is with Agnes,' she said at the door, wiping
her eyes with one hand, and patting her friends good-bye with the
other. 'Just like some of them take the veil—I wish I could tell that
to Father Keith!'

'I wouldn't put it past you, Aunt Mary!' declared Bridie, also con-
vulsed by such daring wit in the presence of himself. Her enjoyment
of it was such that she was indifferent to her own failure that evening
—not once had she managed to get the conversation round to the
signpost and its legend, and so on to Dublin.

'Well, I wouldn't put it past me, either,' Mrs. Mary agreed modestly.

'The dear people!' said Tom on the walk back to the quarry. 'The
incredibly silly people, too, in some ways. But they're dear people
all the same. What a lot I owe them already. For being able to
produce themselves so beautifully. It must be one of the quickest
and cheapest nerve-cures that has ever been discovered: getting absorbed in the life of an Irish village. To the point where you can
almost sing "Here we go round the mulberry bush" with the children.
Forgetting it isn't a mulberry bush, even for them, but a bomb. D.A.'

For some while, before going to bed, they sat on the wall opposite
the signpost, near the place where Kenny had sat, and listened to the
slow breathing of the sea below them. He found himself telling her
at last, without effort, of the episode of the burning chemical factory,
and the journey home, and the way it ended; of the reasons why that
particular bombing stood out in his mind in horror from other raid
incidents, no different in intention, the intention to destroy. It seemed
to him, as he spoke, an all-important moment; he could trust someone again. Surely this also meant that he could trust himself—he
had been right, then, when he said that the stranger was no longer
in charge! A surge of thankfulness swept through him—that night,
for the first time, he awakened Denyse by crying out in his sleep,

in the grip of a nightmare of detailed, uncontrollable fear; of fire and of falling; of the curtain of steel through which 'they' required him to go again; even of small and apparently unrelated sensations now imbued with the boundless terror of a dream—the stretching of new silk, a difficulty in reading the maker's name on the corner of an instrument board. Not till the next day was he able to work out that he had used a pair of spare lining-gloves for the first time on the night of the crash, which must have taken place just after dawn. Presumably he had been watching longingly for daylight, testing visibility by the writing on the little metal plaque. He could actually remember nothing at all of the last hour of the flight. It was as if the stranger were laughing at him, and his recent delusion of freedom; deliberately choosing sleep, as the time of helplessness, for this demonstration of the strength of the invader still in possession of his mind.

Denyse roused him, whispering reassuringly, stroking his face. He put out a hand towards her, thankful to find her lying beside him in the darkness; and ran it over her breast and shoulder and neck to comfort himself with her presence. She turned her head away from him sharply as his fingers touched her cheek, and he felt that they were wet.

'Denyse! I didn't know you could cry?'

'I thought I'd forgotten how. But you were sleeping so deeply, I couldn't wake you at first—couldn't reach you where you were. And I knew then that when you go—Oh, the things I try not to know, for both of us.'

He said, self-woundingly, 'Is it because I'm behaving like a child —as your child might—calling for help, in a panic, at night?'

'No, I don't think so. No. It's just because you're you, Tom.'

He held her for a moment, till the world of Kildooey grew real and steady about him again, and he could hear the rhythm of the waves through the beating of his heart, and hers; and then the tiny night-sounds of the quarry reasserted themselves—crumbs of earth falling from the overhanging bank, insect-small shrillings and rustles from the ground—and the night became only the gentle loneliness of the Donegal coast. The endless, aimless noise of the sea was soothing; so was the call of plovers keeping vigil over the hill behind them; soon he relaxed and sleep returned, to be broken again by violent dreams.

After this he lay awake for a long while, wretched and worried to an extent that he had not known for some days, and when at last he achieved sleep once more, it seemed no more than a minute before Bridie was standing beside the car, beaming at them an hour earlier than usual.

'I thought I would make sure to catch you before you dressed,' she said. 'To tell you I would like to give some return for the enjoyable ride I had yesterday. The copper is to be lit in our cabin this morning. Will you be trusting me with any clothes you have, that would be the better of a washing? It would give me great pleasure to be very careful with them. I will be as quick as I can. Maybe you could wear your bathing dresses underneath for a bit, if you haven't enough else?'

It was useless for them to protest that no return was necessary for the chance of standing on the running board all the way to Donegal —Bridie had made up her mind. And it seemed too unkind to explain that Denyse had already delivered a bundle of clothes to the laundry in the town, and arranged for the carrier to collect and return them when he brought out the piping; the girl was eager to handle the kind of silk and embroidery which she had seen for the first time on Denyse; even Tom's unspectacular pants and singlet could be invested with a certain glamour; they had possibly been worn in Dublin.

They let her take away several garments which were not yet really dirty by camping standards. These came back in a remarkably short time, Tom's being excellently washed. The quality of the material, however, had scared Mrs. Kathie as much as Bridie when they came to examine Denyse's things beside the copper. No damage had been done, but nothing looked fresher than before, after a nervous dip into luke-warm water, without rubbing or squeezing.

Helen came with Bridie to return the washing, surprising the campers by her visit. They had not seen her since the moment when she left them to fetch her postcards; nor had she gone to Mrs. Mary's again, at any hour in which they might be expected to call at the cabin. They had done what they could to help her to avoid them; in a place of the size of Kildooey it was hard not to see all the inhabitants daily. There was no means by which Denyse could help being a reminder—more disturbing than the west wind—of the life beyond the sea which Helen was required to forget.

Loitering till the younger girl had gone, she said, 'I am ashamed that

Bridie should have done your things so badly, Mrs. Fairburn. But I couldn't tell her, or my mother, for fear of hurting their feelings.'

'Of course not. They're fine.'

'No. Please give them to me, now, to do over. I'll be up at Michael's farm this afternoon, and they won't see if I wash them again there.'

'My dear girl, of course we won't let you bother to do that! My stuff's splendid,' said Tom. 'It looks most professional. And I'm sure my wife's quite happy about hers, aren't you, Denyse?' (A matter of ill-done laundry! he thought. That was enough to make Helen come to us, against her will. I must remember that this is almost as important to her as the possession of the stranger to me. A matter of laundry and proportion. She is fussing too much about washing, as I am about dying, and neither counts very much just now.)

'Why, of course, everything is all right as it is,' said Denyse. 'It was sweet of Bridie to want to help us at all.'

'I would like to do that just as much as Bridie,' said Helen. 'Only I'd like it for a different reason. She told me she had never touched anything so delicate before. Where I was in service in America I looked after all the personal things, those that were too nice to send out. They said I had clever hands. I had much appreciation out there, and it was a good house, you understand. Oh, it was, indeed. They knew how everything should be done.' Her eyes left their faces and looked past the signpost, past the nodding grasses on the quarry's edge, and an eddy of butterflies blown off the hill, along the road that wound through the valleys to be lost in the distance. 'I know I shouldn't be thinking back so much. I know I was right when I wanted you to take away the photographs I brought home; I'd always be poring over them if I kept them, wishing myself away. But just for once—to do what I used to do—it can't be wrong, do you think, to take pleasure in showing you the skill I have, with the prettiest things? It isn't to be expected that anyone like you will stop here again.' Still with her eyes on the far stretches of the road, she smiled slightly: 'To think I couldn't see for tears when I left Kildooey by this same way, three years ago! The signpost wasn't there then, but a man took me and my box in a cart to the railway station at Donegal, and where the road went after that, I didn't know nor care. Now let me have your things, please, and say nothing of it to Bridie.'

Embarrassed with pity, they thanked her and allowed her to have her way.

'Irish homes must be the kindliest in the world,' said Denyse, to please her with praise of the one thing she would find plentiful in Kildooey — courtesy. 'I didn't know that people in families could be so considerate of each other's feelings! Anywhere else a sister would have told Bridie exactly what she thought of her efforts. But not here. It must sweeten life very much, that sort of gentleness between relations. We have precious little of it in France.'

'I missed it at first when I went to America,' Helen admitted. 'The thought we give to each other. But though we're kind, there are other things we have, to balance the kindness.' She turned at the sound of steps on the road behind them. A heavy, middle-aged woman was toiling slowly up the hill towards the quarry, waving a piece of paper. 'Ah, now, I'll not be spoiling the occasion for Mrs. Clancy by stopping. She showed me her telegram down in the village, and she'll enjoy reading it over to you by herself.' She smiled at them both. 'That's what you meant, wasn't it, by the sort of kindness we have in our homes? You'd say, there's none but an Irishwoman would thraipse all the way up here, of a hot morning, to tell you her daughter was safe at the end of her journey! When you've never even spoken to her Margaret. Well, it's true. But there's a kind of cruelty we have as well as kindliness. Do you know what made Margaret go for a nurse? Not once could my aunt Mary Sullivan pass her on the bridge without gawstering her — "And when will we be hearing of your wedding, Margaret?" or the like of that. With Margaret the plainest girl in Kildooey, too homely for any man. "Ah, now, I've no mind for that sort of thing!" she'd say. "Never a girl turned twenty that hadn't!" my Aunt Mary would tell her. "There's more than one heart you'll be breaking, if you hold to that attitude. No doubt about it. No doubt at all. And the lads all sick with sighing!" Before I went away myself I heard my mother gawster her the same — she that wouldn't hurt anyone. And there's another thing we have, under the kindness — jealousy. Not just of people, of everything. But you know that yourself, without my saying it. Look now, be careful with Sean . . .' She broke off, as if she had said too much.

'In what way?' said Tom. ' "Fianna Fail?" He thinks I'm Cromwell's nephew, more or less, and I've told him I think he's a damn fool, and we're quite amiable about our opinions!'

'Ah, then, sure it's all right,' said Helen at once, anxious to agree, to be convinced, or to appear to be convinced, at least; and tucking her bundle under her coat she went away quickly, not to interfere with Mrs. Clancy's pleasure.

CHAPTER XII

WIPING A JOINT

'I KNEW you'd be glad,' repeated Mrs. Clancy, beaming at them. 'I said, I'll not rest till I've shown them the message, up in the quarry! "Safe and well Margaret", and the official mark, you see, showing where it comes from, so there was no need to pay more to tell me she had got over the water.' She gave the telegram to Denyse to feel. 'Ah, well, my dearest, I told myself, it's true my legs are older than yours, but at the shop Mr. Wallace was telling me you couldn't be doing with long walks at all. So I thought — '

'Mr. Wallace told you what?' interrupted Denyse curiously. Pottering about the site of Sean's cabin was more tiring to her than to Tom, but on each occasion when they had set out to walk across the hills, where nothing else ever went except the wind and the blue butterflies, Tom had complained bitterly that she forgot he was a sedentary worker; she always wanted to keep on longer than he did.

'Indeed, wasn't he after saying it was reasonable enough for one like yourself, used to the pavements of towns. The winter rains have the roads entirely destroyed hereabouts, and thanks to the war there's no money for mending them — This terrible war, the way it gets into everything! — A long pull-up, it is, to his house, and bad going all the way, so you wouldn't be risking your car on it in the dark. He told me it was a pitiful state you were in, what with the wet and the weariness, the time you managed to walk over in the evening. Maybe it was your shoes to blame as well as the road, he said; the dear little town shoes, not man enough for the country.'

'My "dear little town shoes" were these,' said Denyse, displaying serviceable English brogues, thicker in the sole than anything worn by the women of Kildooey. 'What on earth got hold of Mr. Wallace, to make him invent such an extraordinary story? I was a bit wet and a bit tired. I wasn't on the verge of collapse!'

'Were you not? Well, it would make you giddy, so it would, trying to follow the divagations of a mind like his, to understand what is in it. Maybe it was some joke you made, and he thinking you meant it. He takes everything in earnest, that one, with his "Really", and "Seriously, now".'

Father Keith came by at the moment, taking a lift home in a cart from one of his other villages. He had not yet seen the telegram, and Mrs. Clancy rode away with him, reading triumphantly.

In the course of the day, which was Sunday, the walls of the cabin rose by about a foot. Sean went off to Mass with Bridie in the morning, and in the afternoon was summoned away twice by Mrs. Agnes, but Tom took from the work only a short interval for lunch and tea combined, so that by the time he knocked off for the day, the building was ready for the door and window-frames.

In the green-gold dusk, while the campers were eating the pleasantest meal of the day, Helen managed to smuggle back Denyse's clothes, undetected. They were indeed beautifully finished, and praise from the visitors seemed to give the girl a moment of real pleasure, out of all proportion to the occasion. She too mentioned the legend about Denyse's exhaustion, which was being put about by Mr. Wallace.

At Father Keith's, later in the evening, they heard that the casualties in the air on both sides, during the last twenty-four hours, had been the heaviest yet sustained in the battle; there was no sign of slackening in the weight of the attack. Denyse was thankful that Tom turned in to sleep too well drugged with labour and fresh air to dream.

Mrs. Clancy visited them again the next morning, to ask a favour. 'Out of the kindness of your hearts, let you not be giving any more chocolate to my Kenny! For it doubles my work on wash-day, so it does. The bit he had from you, for the bait, he kept in his trousers pocket between licks, to make it last the longer, and to feel the comfort of its presence there in church, when he couldn't be getting at it. A little wisp of a bar it was yesterday, well dwindled by sucking.

You'd never think it could spread so far through his clothes in the short time there was for sitting on it during the early service. I'm away now to shut him in Mrs. Mary's, where it'll be warm for his bareness by the fire, while I get the trousers off him to scrape them with a knife, the way they are. He'd be badgering me all the time not to waste a chew of the pocket-lining if I had him loose in our cabin while I was cleaning them—Ah, Mrs. Mary, now! Wasn't she hearing the same story from Mr. Wallace about the notable exhaustion you had upon you the night you walked over to his place?'

'Tom, I'm rather worried about this,' said Denyse when Mrs. Clancy had gone. 'It looks as if we didn't provide anything like a good enough save-face for Mr. Wallace, after we stopped going to his house for the news. All Kildooey knows our movements, as Father Keith said. And so this silly explanation to Mrs. Clancy, about my finding the distance too great to walk—half a mile on from Sean's building site! But it's Father Keith's house we prefer to his—we ought to have realized how he'd mind that. While his pride and hatred are gnawing at him, nothing's too trivial to be resented, thought about and thought about, among those appalling bits of shell, and bog-oak and all the photographs. Father Keith came into it, and that was enough.'

'Bridie gave him quite a good reason for our going back to the priest's. I told her to say that, after all, Father Keith had invited us first, and it was only because we couldn't get the hang of his set at once that we came to listen to the other radio. Now we've discovered the trick of Father Keith's, we needn't bother Wallace any more—Thanks very much; we're very grateful, and so on. I said "Be flowery", and I'm sure she was.'

'Well, evidently he can't accept that reason. Or he's afraid the Kildooey people won't, and Father Keith will have another little triumph over him. Is this going to be serious, Tom? I suppose we'd better back up his story for the sake of his pride. Officially, I'll be a very poor walker!'

The sense of danger to the small community of people they liked came drifting across the valley from the unhappy house on the farther hill. It made no difference to the way it could poison the earth-sweet morning for the campers, to recognize that it was unimportant compared with the apprehension which loaded every thought they sent over the narrow sea. At its strongest it could make them wholly forget for the moment the greater, more abiding anxiety.

But in spite of Denyse's resolve to humour him, they were driven to use Mr. Wallace's invention against him, when he stopped them in the car, later in the morning, just as they had started down the hill with another load of stone for Sean.

Had they yet been in the seal cave, a few miles along the coast? Whatever they did in Kildooey, he said, they must not miss that. True, he had not yet visited it himself, but it was believed that half the seals in the Western Irish waters were bred in that cave. Wasn't there more pleasure, and profit too, in seeing the wonders of nature, than in saving a fellow with nothing better to do, the trouble of building his own house?

'The more such hands are occupied in harmless ways, the less likely they are to be used against us and our cause.' Since those moments in which venom had spurted from him by his own fireside, the idea of Mr. Wallace as an ally had become more and more unattractive. His use of 'us' and 'our' aroused instant annoyance, all the more because they knew it to be unjustified; a Londonderry man, he had better right than Denyse to mean by 'our cause', that for which the Battle of Britain was being fought. In an effort to get rid of him, they offered him a lift in the car as far as the cabin site, if he cared to squeeze in on top of the stone, but Mr. Wallace had come for a purpose, and refused to be shifted. With his head poked in round the side of the window, he held them as the stranger had held Tom during the thunderstorm on the Ballinfaddy road.

He spoke at last of the reason for his visit, pressing them to come to his house for the news, questioning their motive and their excuses. Father Keith's set would only get Athlone; wasn't his the better? Wasn't it? Wasn't it, now? He was determined to make them agree. 'We could have such interesting talks,' he said wistfully. 'It was a treat to me, a great treat, when you came.'

Denyse looked at him blankly when he became insistent, far beyond the usage of Kildooey manners. 'I'm sorry,' she said, 'but it's too far for me to walk—as you know!'

'Ah, now, I only said that to quiet those who might be asking questions!' Mr. Wallace was unabashed. 'From the great way you help him-

self and Sean at the building, toiling about with the stones, it's fine
and strong you must be on your feet.'

'All the same, it's a rough road.'

'But you do the first part every day. So why will you not face the
little bit more? You with the car at your disposal, too.' Arguing,
pleading in the end, he drove them into corners from which the
only logical escape was by way of admitting that they did not come
because they did not want to come: they struggled to avoid saying
this. Both of them became exasperated by his refusal to let them spare
his feelings, along with their own.

'We've no wish to seem rude to Father Keith. After all — Bridie told
you, I think? — his was the first invitation.'

'To think you should choose to go to his house rather than mine!'
The voice rose unpleasantly to the shrill note they had heard in his
kitchen. 'What consideration has he shown to others — Helen Sullivan,
for example — I'm asking you, what kindness has he shown to her
or anyone else, that you should feel obliged to consider him?'

They could find nothing more to say. Tom's brake-foot was growing
numb from holding the car on the steep slope, because the hand-brake
was inadequate. It occurred to him longingly that if he took his foot
off the pedal, without warning, Mr. Wallace might almost be de-
capitated, he was leaning further and further in at the window. From
the moment the thought took shape, cramp seized his ankle. As if
sensing the impulse, Mr. Wallace climbed on to the running-board,
and his head, now protruding into the car at a seemingly impossible
angle, looked as though it grew downwards from the top hinge of the
door. 'Has he troubled himself to think of this, I wonder — ' he went
on. 'Has he troubled himself at all to think of one thing before calling
her home — 'Tis more than her agreement he's taken for granted, in
marrying her off, like that! Mine, too! Oh, yes, mine, too! There's
money owing from Michael's family for the new milking barn. And
for other things besides, from before the old man died, when the farm
was in a bad way, through his infirmity. There are several things I
have arranged for them without seeing a shilling of what's due. But
in this place they think the man at the shop can always wait for his
money! Not only wait; no, but advance more, without further security!
There's this and that a young couple must have, to set them up in

housekeeping. Oh, he'd agree to that, would Father Keith; but where's the credit to come from? The shopkeeper must whistle for his payment, so long as his reverence can have his way, and another cruel act be done for the good of the Holy Church!'

In the sunshine, with the sea wind blowing about him, Mr. Wallace still managed to give the impression of exhaling mustiness. He spoke with indignation of cruelty, and the effect was as though the forces of cruelty were strengthened by his anger. Again the thought came to the two who listened, that never before had they met a man forced to so many just conclusions by such unworthy motives.

'One day, maybe, he'll find that he's assumed a little too much. A little too much!' The tempo of his talk changed, his glance shuttled back and forth from one to the other as his words quickened. 'You'll be coming over, now, some of the evenings, won't you? Ah, you will. Not all, but some? You'll manage it. There's things I could tell you, Mrs. Fairburn, would astonish you greatly. Of wider concern than Kildooey and its people. You, too, Mr. Fairburn, for all that you've lived in the south. For instance, now, did you hear of the case there was lately in a Dublin hospital? Oh, I have it in detail. A perfect case, and typical!' He began to laugh with excitement. 'With the world as it is to-day, of course it wouldn't do for a priest-ridden country, like this, to recognize the existence of a disease that has scourged mankind for a thousand years or more! No, no. Wish it away and don't be polluting the purity of Eire with the thought of it! — so there's no test for the safety of the blood as part of the service of transfusion. They pumped infected blood into a man —' He spluttered with the enjoyment of another's tragedy which seemed more obscene here than it had done in his own surroundings — 'Into a good young man that was after falling off his bicycle and losing two innocent pints of his own to a passing tram! Not a case could he bring; who should he find to argue it for him in Dublin? A lawyer with a reputation to lose? No, indeed, in a land where so much trouble can be admitted! That's the mentality of your friend and his kind.'

He was beside himself with hatred once more, entreating them not to put what he considered an affront upon him, in favour of Father Keith; all restraint thrown aside in his anxiety that they should return to his house.

'Why will you not come to-night?' he demanded once more.

'Too far.' They felt despairingly that this argument was going on, repeating itself, for ever.

'Ah, we know there's nothing in that talk of mine about the distance!'

'Look here'—a taste of the black rage which he had known so often in the past came back into Tom's mouth. 'We aren't coming to-night. Or any other night. And frankly, we don't see why we should.'

Before Mr. Wallace could answer, the acute pins and needles in Tom's right leg had taken charge. Without his intending it, the car moved forward, carrying Mr. Wallace on the running-board. The passenger extricated the top part of himself from the window, his face wearing a look of alarm which was irresistibly funny. The engine had stopped; Tom jammed it into low gear because the hill happened to be steepest at the bends and the brakes too worn to be trusted alone. Mr. Wallace hopped off while the car, which always resented this method of starting, progressed down the slope in a series of bounds like a bucking horse. It looked as if the driver were doing his best to ensure an accident.

Tom and Denyse laughed. 'I wish this hadn't happened, all the same!' she said, sobering up as the engine took hold again smoothly. Mr. Wallace was now out of sight round the curve. He had kept his balance on landing, but with difficulty. They could not bear the thought of stopping to apologize, and perhaps reopening the whole discussion.

At the site of the cabin, a knot of people waited for them eagerly: Sean was there, Peadar and Dan had come up from the beach, and Kenny had escaped from Mrs. Mary's with a towel round him in place of his trousers. As the campers approached, Helen's young farmer, and one of the old ladies, chanced to be going by on the road, leading two cows to the bull; they, too, stopped when someone pointed out to them the stack of piping which the carrier had just delivered.

'Oh, lord,' said Tom, despondently, 'I hadn't bargained for an audience! After Wallace just now, this is too much.'

'An audience for what?'

'Wiping a joint, I'm afraid.' He had mentioned at Mrs. Mary's, a day or two before, that as soon as the material arrived he intended to make a union for the tap. In that atmosphere, where trivial events were the stuff of drama, he had extravagantly described the pleasure of handling, squeezing and persuading molten metal as though it were putty. 'I suppose that's what they've come to see.'

'Well, why shouldn't they?' asked Denyse as they slowed down. 'You made it sound enchanting. I'm looking forward to it myself.'

'Well, you may be! I've never done it before.'

'But, Tom, the way you spoke of it — !'

'I know. I wish I hadn't. It was — well, the atmosphere of the cabin. Conversational competition. No, not competition so much as obligation. Bridie had just made a grand story of choosing a saucepan cleaner. I've always wanted to wipe a joint — so I let them think — Damn, isn't that Mrs. Mary coming, too? Getting a ride down in a turf cart?'

In the infinite leisure of Irish life (which made poverty so bearable, if inevitable) those who had heard him describe the feat were ready to take time off from the boat, the byre or the field to come and watch him perform it, together with friends who had only learnt of the promise at second hand. The driver of the turf cart stopped as well. As the audience grew, Tom was assailed by more and more doubts of his own competence.

A small fire was built for him, inexorably, between stones, in the shelter of the cabin walls, the first fire in the new house. The grave attention of the onlookers gave the whole proceedings a feeling of mystical significance. 'I'm certain I'm going to make a mess of this!' he said, as he and Denyse stood apart, like priest and priestess of some initiatory rite, waiting for the turf soaked in paraffin to burn red. 'I've only seen the thing done once, by a professional.'

'Then whatever possessed you to talk about it so lyrically?'

'I've tried to explain! And you see, it's been my secret ambition for years. I've always felt that wiping a joint would be quite intoxicating. A glorious experience. Really a sensual sort of pleasure. But when I was a boy everyone thought it was beyond me, and since I became an engineer everyone thought it was beneath me. So I've never had my fun. And now I'm going to ball it up properly with all these people looking on. I know I am.'

'Is it really so difficult?' She fell in love with him then, because he was worried — a man who had lived too closely with death, and was now concerned, to the exclusion of all else, with the possibility of fail-

ing in a little act of kindness, before a group of people, none of whom
he would be likely to see again after the next few days. The single-
mindedness of this she knew to be characteristic; absurd though it was
at the moment, it was more moving than any need for her that he had
shown.

'"Difficult!"' he said. 'Listen, any fool who can drive a car can fly
a plane. After a fashion. My usual observer, who is a Scot, points out
every time he gets a chance, that the larger the crate the more the pilot
is just a taxi-driver. But wiping a joint is something extremely skilful,
which a good workman won't even let you watch, if he can help it.
It's a sort of guild secret.'

'Then it's beyond belief that you boasted of it that way!'

It was essential to laugh at him, to keep some part of herself at a
distance from him, if that were still possible, till the first moment of
panic had passed. Dismay seized upon her; this overwhelming emotion
was indeed a second and unwelcome giving of hostages to life, from
which she had felt herself safe, being empty of heart. Before, the sense
of her loss of everything worth while had at least been absolute; such
sorrow carried with it a measure of relief, in freedom from hope. From
now on she would walk between the twin torments of dread and
hope.

'Well, I don't know,' he said, frowning. 'I didn't expect to be watched
like this. Here comes Mrs. Agnes, too! If she starts criticizing and puts
me off—'

'—Flight Lieutenant Fairburn, D.F.C., is likely to be wholly dis-
credited as a plumber's mate. And covered with shame as a result.'

'A plumber, darling,' he corrected. 'No self-respecting plumber would
be likely to let his mate touch a wipe. Anyway, why shouldn't I be
embarrassed?'

Tenderness flooded out all the unhappiness in her mind. If he could
be so wholehearted, over something of such unimportance to his own
future, then he was indeed making progress at last in his private
battle, out of the closed ring of self into which fear could shut a
man. And beside this, nothing mattered.

'Tom, I've discovered something I want to tell you.'

'Then don't tell me now, if it's about Wallace. He'll be nosing round,
too, in a minute, I'm sure.'

'It's not. It's about me.'

'Well, that can wait, too!' he said, and grinned at her briefly. 'What I want is something that'll do instead of the proper ladle for this job. You forgot to buy that, and I told you about it twice!'

Plumbers' metal and a square of canvas had been ordered at the same time as the piping, and brought over by the carrier. A heavy iron pot was gladly sacrificed to the melting of the metal by Michael, who sent his mother scurrying across fields and ditches to fetch it from the farm when Tom explained what was wanted. She returned with the other beautiful old woman as well; to the group of spectators had been added, by then, the police constable from Comines; he stood for some time leaning on his bicycle in the road, plainly trying to think of an official reason for joining the watchers. In the end he approached with the excuse that wherever Sean happened to be, he expected to find trouble, a pleasantry which was not well received. Mrs. Mary led the others in a steady stream of compliments on the ingenuity of the visitors, able to live in a car yet experts in the comforts of civilization — a display of goodwill which Tom for once found wholly unwelcome. 'Never a man in Kildooey, since himself was here last' — pleasant voices were raised purposely, so that he should overhear — 'Never a one his equal in using his head or his hands as if he wouldn't be knowing which!'

'I wonder if I get charged with S-I.W. at the end of my leave, supposing I slop melted solder over my hand, trying to pour the stuff without a ladle? As I probably shall!'

'You do remember, at least, how a joint is meant to be wiped?'

'Don't go making this any worse, Denyse! It's quite bad enough — waiting to make a fool of myself. Yes, I think I do. When the stuff's liquid, it's poured on to four thicknesses of greased canvas, held like a cup, with the hand as a saucer. And then worked at awful speed into one of those neat, pregnant little bulges you've probably never admired before! I suppose you thought they grew naturally on pipes?'

' — Bridie will be blessing him, many a year from now, so she will.' For the moment even Mrs. Agnes forebore to say anything disparaging about the plan for laying on water, or the structure of the cabin, though she pointed out to Sean that he might as well be getting on

with the job of mending her gate, for all the need of him there seemed
to be on his own ground.

In a neighbouring field the bull, which had smelt the cows, set up
an unnerving, intermittent bellow; and in the midst of this scene,
Denyse's heart sang. The pain of feeling, running back into the once
numb spirit, was nothing compared with the joy, the splendour of
richness and roundness that had overtaken the early autumn world,
from one moment to the next. Nothing seemed to be too big nor too
small to be affected by the sudden transformation of everything in
sight. All day, the mountains had lain flat against the horizon; they
had depths to them now, and the wildest colours, and she could believe in a further side even more fantastically beautiful than the side
which she could see. She looked about the group and loved, not only
Tom, but all of them, particularly the constable, a loyal man who remembered to speak Gaelic to the younger people; as there was, however,
no vernacular for 'solder', 'flux' or 'wiping a joint', and he wanted the
job explained to him, conversation lapsed into English.

'I came over from the Post,' he told her, 'to make sure that you have
your driving licences for Eire? And also your other documents. But I'll
not be troubling himself at a responsible moment like this; no, indeed.' He ticked them off in his record book. Denyse had brought
to Ireland no official papers of any kind except her passport, and this
was not valid for the Free State. It occurred to her that as an alien she
was probably liable to imprisonment for unlawful entry; and in the
same instant, that being in love with Tom, she was somehow quite
safe; this irrelevance would not happen to her, whatever else did.

'To save your coming over again,' she suggested, 'perhaps we could
drop in with all our papers, at the Comines Post? One morning when
my husband isn't so busy?' They would be gone in four days' time.

'Do that,' said the constable warmly. 'And I'll introduce you to a
man who could be useful to you, maybe, if the restrictions press upon
you at all in the matter of petrol? My cousin has more than he needs.
We've so few cars in these parts, it's a shame not to use up the petrol
we have, before it is taken from us, one way or another, as no doubt
England will be bound to take it for her own use, with the war turning
so badly for her — I am sorry to hear about that.' (Petrol, like other
commodities, had been rationed for some time; but, in their experience,

only as yet in theory. The pinch which was soon to be felt everywhere in Eire was not even guessed at by most people in the country.)

'Thank you, we'll hope to see you one day next week, then,' said Denyse's voice, lying — Whatever the cost of the days to come, said Denyse's heart, truly, they will be worth living; for the anxiety will be mine now, more than his.

Tom was kneeling by the fire, testing the heat of the metal, supremely absorbed. The surface of the pot began to shiver and cloud.

Mr. Wallace walked by, in the midst of the hush which followed Mrs. Mary's awed injunction, 'Mother of heaven, will you look at that!' while a shining stream of hot metal poured steadily out of the pot into the folded canvas on Tom's palm. Few turned to greet the shopman; he scarcely acknowledged the waves of those who did. No one suggested that he should stop and enjoy the spectacle, too.

'Now what's wrong with him?' asked Mrs. Agnes suspiciously. 'Going by like an east wind! There's something he has on his mind, depend on it!' Everyone else, however, was too enthralled by Tom's efforts to notice Mr. Wallace's demeanour. With a circling movement of the canvas, Tom began coaxing the soft metal over the end of the pipe and the base of the brass tap-socket; it ran too fast, and he caught and checked the flow, stroking, pressing, his hand moving with a caressing lightness, smoothing the growing bulge into symmetry when it sagged out of shape or swelled too fast on one side. Once the metal threatened to get the better of him, cooling and sticking unevenly where it met the socket; it was like toffee in consistency, and rapidly becoming unmanageable: he worked over it still more swiftly, and ruin was averted just before the wipe hardened. Beginners' luck was with him; when finished, it was a beautiful specimen, its fashioning had indeed been an indulgence of flesh and spirit alike. 'Oh, I would love to do that, I would!' Kenny kept muttering.

Tom was enchanted with his success. Mrs. Mary summed up the general feeling: 'The neatness of it! And the rotundity! By a man of education, too; it is wonderful.'

Regrets were expressed that Bridie should have been away on an errand, taking the grey hen to be dosed, and so had missed the most impressive part of all that was being done for her. The little group showed no inclination to break up when the exhibition was over; in-

stead, while the older people talked, the younger ones took a hand
in unloading the car of the stone which the campers had brought, and
completed another course for Sean all round the walls. Still flushed
with his triumph, Tom laid out the piping, savouring the performer's
triumph in having given so much pleasure that his audience remained
loath to return to ordinary life.

Pleasure, however, was short-lived in Kildooey. Helen came running
down from Michael's farm with news which startled the whole village.
Mr. Wallace had called while she was churning, in the absence of the
old ladies. He had spoken of the debt outstanding on the milking shed,
and announced that no further credit would be given to Michael or
his family until it had been paid.

Here was spite of the most unusual kind. It meant, in effect, that
Michael could not afford to marry yet awhile; and marriage, until
now, was something which Mr. Wallace had always encouraged.
Helen's man, like most of the small-holders in the neighbourhood,
could not put his hand on so much as five pounds of ready cash, and
the withdrawal of credit at the shop was serious for the family; flour,
tea, sugar — all the necessities which his meagre acres did not produce,
came through Mr. Wallace, as well as the boots, the new clothes, the
pots and pans and small household improvements which must be
bought in honour of Helen. Uneasiness spread; people went home
angrily discussing this thunderbolt; there was scarcely anyone in
Kildooey who was not in debt to the shopman — had not been encouraged to some such commitment as Michael's, over a loan for the
purchase of stock, or the mortgaging of a field on which the payments
had fallen behind. The term, 'gombeen-man', was applied to Mr. Wallace openly for the first time, in the visitors' hearing.

'All the same, I'm glad he's turned on Michael, not the Sullivans —
it's safer,' said Tom, when they had returned Mrs. Mary to her own
doorstep and were again alone in the car.

'I suppose we could advance Michael the money?'

'We could, but I'm not going to! Not to help Father Keith in keeping his hold over people like Helen.'

'No, I think he can fight his own battles, too. He's got all the desperate strength of the Church behind him. And I'd no idea it was
still so strong anywhere in northern Europe.'

But for a little while Kildooey's collective troubles became insignificant, along with those of the outside world. Tom said, 'What was it you wanted to tell me?' as they drove back to the quarry for a further load of stone.

'Well, is it still the wrong moment for saying I love you?'

He stopped the car, in the middle of the road, in order to have both arms free for Denyse — to the horror of Bridie, who came upon them suddenly round the bend of the hill; Bridie was still too young to like her gods to be human. She walked past with scarlet face averted, talking to the hen under her arm.

Later in the day, Father Keith strode into his living-room while they were listening to the radio there; again, the losses just announced — in the London bulletin, quoted by Athlone — were in the neighbourhood of four to one against the attackers; but the casualties among the British fighters were still heavy enough to be unbearable for long, at such a rate of attrition. Finding them holding hands, like children, he seemed almost as embarrassed as Bridie had been at seeing them kiss. 'I promised you, I know, that I would not disturb you here in the evening,' he said. 'You must forgive me. I want to ask your help. Indeed, I need it. It is a strange position I am in, that twice I have come to you, since our first talk, to say "Help me, if you will". But you were understanding, the first time — ' He spoke to Tom, nervously ignoring Denyse. She was aware that he found it still more disturbing to talk to her than to her lover, enveloped as they both were in an atmosphere which he dared not breathe more than need be, for fear that it should come to smell to him less like a cesspool than a library; but of the two, she was the one who could have given him the more precious companionship, and he was aware of it. Tom kept her hand in his for a moment or two, because this seemed slightly less undignified than the hasty letting-go which Bridie had forced upon them.

'What do you want us to do?'

'Wallace might listen to you. To no one else in the place but to you. Because you are not of my flock. Speak to him, as I cannot with any hope of success! Ask him not to stand in the way of this marriage of Helen and Michael. What wrong have my young people done him that he should hit at me through them?' He walked up and down his uncomfortable, office-like room, his soutane brushing Denyse as he turned. 'To you it may seem a small thing; a village wedding put off for a while. But who knows for how long, or what may happen if it is postponed? In a community like this, it is not a small thing. I am afraid of the consequences. I am afraid of what may happen to Wallace himself. Anger rises quickly in this country, as you know. For all I can say, to keep them from violence, the lads here may not take it quietly if he chooses such a moment to make a victim out of Michael, who is well liked. Wallace has had his shop burned once; this time it may be his house, and over his head. Tell him that, if he will listen to no other appeal.'

'No, I'm sorry. We can't do that. Neither of us will do anything to help in forcing that marriage on a girl who doesn't want it!'

Father Keith's heavy face took on its most unyielding expression, but he kept his temper. He slumped into a broken armchair, and sat with his head resting on his hand, half turned away from them. 'We look on marriage and duty somewhat differently!' he said dryly. 'But even judging by your standards, it seems to me, after twenty years among them, I am likely to know the needs and characters of my own people better than someone who has been here a little over a week! And I had the girl's own interests at heart when I called her home, as well as the wishes of her family — to leave out altogether the considerations of faith, which you will not allow. I have made many mistakes here in Kildooey, in times of perplexity — God forgive me for them all. No doubt I shall make more. For once, though, the way is plain, and I can only follow my conscience, thankful that I believe with all my heart that this marriage is good, and will bring a blessing on them both.'

'Father Keith,' said Denyse, 'you've been as kind to us as your conscience allows you to be. I think we both feel rather mean, refusing to do something for you in return. But not as mean as we'd feel, backing up your effort to imprison Helen in a world she isn't fitted for any longer. In order to satisfy that conscience of yours, and for no other reason which we can see!' The friendliness of her voice took some of the sting out of the words.

'— Your conscience, and a taste for power! I've wanted to have this out with you for some time. I was just too lazy before.' Tom spoke without any such disarming manner. The realization that, henceforward, Denyse would be at the mercy of any chance which assailed him had produced a process of feeling exactly the opposite of hers; wild joy had come to him in the first instant, followed by a sober counting of the cost to her. He was ready for an encounter with Father Keith's vole-sacrificing god, who would choose such a moment to give him, whole-heartedly, the woman he wanted.

But it was not possible to come to grips, they found, with either Father Keith or his equally pitiless god. 'If it's a real attempt at understanding you're ready to make,' he said, 'I'm willing to argue. But not for the sake of arguing, mind you, Tom.' He would not face the possibility that on this one occasion, in the matter of Helen, perplexity might have become his soul better than faith. Instead, he repeated again and again the assertions with which he held at bay — valiantly, it seemed, even to them — the threatening uncertainties that lurked behind human sympathy. 'We are here to fulfil God's will, not to seek our own happiness.' 'She will find comfort in the sense of well-doing, in keeping her given word.' 'I will remind you of a saying, "He that loseth his life for my sake — ".' And in reply to Tom's angry question, 'Suppose it's the only life she has, the one you're asking her to throw away?' he said, with a simple curiosity which was strangely touching, 'you who are prepared to sacrifice your own life — is it possible you can believe that, and still be willing?'

'Yes,' said Tom. 'Not easy, but possible. Well, supposing we are right?'

'That is absurd, and I told you, I will not argue for the sake of an argument.'

'As a man — remember you said this about me yourself — a man for whom time may be very short, I'm also not inclined to argue for the sake of argument. Suppose it's all she has, this life?'

There came then the answer of supreme, age-old despair. 'It would still be better spent, my son, as if in the hope of eternity.'

'That is the most terrible condemnation of human nature I've ever heard,' said Denyse. 'From anyone. If I thought it could be justified — if I thought mankind not strong enough or good enough to be given the truth — then indeed I shouldn't consider it was worth salvation of any kind. Either here and now, or in any conceivable after-life.

Certainly nothing on earth would be worth Tom's dying for, if you were right!'

Father Keith looked at her, startled, and did not reply for a moment. When he did, it was with another, sweeping assertion of faith. Once more, in the conversation that followed, everything he said was pervaded by the consciousness of evil, the feeling that all but a few sterile human activities were unclean, the preoccupation with forgiveness and the need to be forgiven. Even so, through the exasperation of getting no satisfaction from him, no real answer to any question save that cry of profound pessimism, both Tom and Denyse were conscious of their liking for Father Keith. Mr. Wallace was right in so many of his views that he should have deserved respect, and instead he was contemptible; the priest, it seemed to them, was wrong in almost everything—wilfully and timorously blind to an extent which Denyse described to him, in the heat of the talk, as wicked. Father Keith smiled at her then; so did Tom, and in a moment Denyse smiled herself: Father Keith's admirable quality as a man was something that could not possibly be denied.

The old problem, thought Tom—the confusing effect of words which cannot mean the same thing to the users. He was listening to Denyse attacking hopelessly, when he himself had tried in vain every form of appeal which might touch that conviction of sin and the need for its only remedy, sacrifice. By early training, she knew more than Tom of Christian dogma, and could argue from Catholic practice in France; but not even on sexual grounds, he reflected, hearing the priest parry her questions, could a man and woman have failed more completely to understand one another. 'It is her duty,' said Father Keith of Helen's submission, after half an hour's talk, as though nothing had been said at all on the other side. He spoke in the tired, sad voice with which he had used the same words on the campers' first visit together to Mrs. Mary's. 'She knows it is her duty.'

Mrs. Mary came in, on the heel of the sentence, as though conjured up by the repetition.

The priest finished what he was saying: 'If you'll not help me, I must do the best I can by myself. Though I cannot think he'll listen to me.'

'Is it Mr. Wallace you're after speaking of?' Mrs. Mary's eyes snapped with interest in their dead grey casing. 'Just now I gave him something to take home with him, so I did! And may it echo in his ear all the way.' She sat down puffing.

The campers turned to her anxiously. One word from her might unleash so much; yet to such irresponsibility as hers, a warning of what Mr. Wallace knew seemed likely to increase, rather than lessen, the likelihood of that word being spoken. She enjoyed the feeling of interest focusing upon her, and was not prepared to satisfy their curiosity at once, by telling them what she had said or done. She produced the cake of maize and currant bread which was the excuse for the visit.

'For your birthday, Father, dear,' she said. 'Knowing how you like the stuff, and the way it is with Mrs. Omaney, that she can never let herself go with the dried fruit, even on occasions.'

'Thank you, thank you,' said the priest absently. 'Though my house-keeper bakes very well, so she does. My birthday is not till the day after to-morrow.' His gravest fear he had only hinted, not expressed, to Tom and Denyse; it was that now the young couple might not wait for the wedding. Something dreadful might happen, he felt, not because this was likely but because it was almost unthinkable to him in its dreadfulness. It was a possibility which was not likely to occur to anyone else; least of all, in Ireland, to the two concerned.

'Ah, well,' said Mrs. Mary comfortably, 'you know how I am with carrying my weight about. There's days when it mightn't be there at all, and days when it's all over me. I thought I'd try and get along with my cake, in case I wouldn't have the co-operation of my feet, to-morrow or the next day.' She had brought a fine cartwheel of bread, of the size which Mrs. Kathie always baked. 'And now I'll give you what I said to Mr. Wallace, in the hearing of the lads. It's a queer thing' — she went off at a tangent again, at the last minute, to save up the revelation. 'I've often said to Agnes — both of us being widows — you never really know how much you dislike a man till he's dead! For there's something about daily living, it gets you used to anything. Even the very things that afterwards will have you saying, "Now how did I ever put up with that!" But it isn't so with Mr. Wallace, no, it's not. He might be gone these five years, for the feeling

I have against him, turning on Michael just now, of all times, over the price of a cow-shed.'

'You're an uncharitable woman, Mary Sullivan, even in your memories. It's not the first time I've called you that. In his day, I fancy, Harry Sullivan had much to put up with from you, too—God rest his soul!'

'God rest his soul, and those of all who die by the hands of Ireland's enemies—though it's only by accident,' she added quickly. Then the wide mouth widened further with happy malice; in losing most of her teeth, Mrs. Mary seemed to have lost more than other people ever had. 'But why would you be naming that one, in particular, Father, because of what I said? Did I mention him? No, I did not. Was I thinking of him? Why should I be? True it is, we didn't see eye to eye in everything, Harry Sullivan and I. There's few couples that do, with spirit on both sides. It's all so long ago, I'll not pretend now that we were closer than we were. I was never one, like Agnes, to spoil to-day with harping on the sunshine of yesterday. But I am astonished at your words, Father, and so will our good friends be, to hear you wanting marriage for Helen and Michael in one breath, and running to such conclusions in the next about my own! It's as if you didn't believe in the blessed institution? I called out to Mr. Wallace as he went by my door, with the lads on the bridge, watching him pass. (All but Sean, who was with Bridie, as ever in these days!) I said, "Lucky for you the lads of to-day aren't the lads that used to be in these parts! In the times when neighbourly feeling was worth something!" I said, "Worth a broken window, it was, in those days", I said. "Or even a broken head."'

'God help you, woman—you said that!' exclaimed the priest in alarm.

'Ah, what difference does it make! Either they'll do it or they'll not.'

'Haven't you the sense to know there's always a time before a fire is well alight, when no more than a breath is wanted to make the flames take hold?'

'Or it may just blow the thing out,' suggested Mrs. Mary placidly.

'Nothing you ever said has blown out trouble!' answered the priest shortly. 'All the afternoon I've been talking to the lads, and the older people, too, who should know better. Telling them that a man's heart is not to be softened by violence. The way they're breathing it now around Wallace, he must be fully aware of the ill-wishing there is in Kildooey, without your help! And you choose this moment to try exciting a pack of silly youngsters, who are idle enough, anyway, to be ready for trouble!'

He got up and went out. They heard him leave the house, without returning to bid them goodnight. The lamp light, shining through the window, caught his intent face for a second as he stood hesitating in the street outside, having taken a few steps in the direction of Wallace's house, and then paused to think.

'Ah, the dear man!' said Mrs. Mary with interested detachment. 'Deciding — you can see it — would he be more likely to gain his way by going the rounds of the houses, urging all to keep the peace? Or would he be better speaking his mind to that Wallace, to make him relent? And for all he says about ill-wishing, there's not a priest in these parts to touch Father Keith for breathing fire and spirit together, when he puts his mind to do a bit of it himself. 'Tis no use at all, though, for him to waste his time appealing to that old crow. But maybe his presence up at the house would keep the lads away.'

Father Keith made up his mind and went resolutely towards Wallace's.

'I'd be glad of your company, back to my own cabin. As I was saying' — Mrs. Mary put on her wheedling manner — 'I can never really trust my legs nowadays, even on a short journey, for fear of their coming faint with the effort required of them. So I don't care to be out alone. If you'd walk as far as my cabin with me, maybe we'd have a cup of tea afterwards?'

'Well, that's a very nice offer, Mrs. Mary, but for one thing, we've drunk a lot of your tea, and tea is going to be scarce in Eire soon —'

'Ah, but it isn't scarce yet. And while we have it, we'll share it, or what use is it? Have you ever considered a curious thing —' She hurried on, feeling that they were about to refuse. 'In a manner of speaking a fat woman walks farther than a thin woman, over the same distance? It's true, though you may well laugh' — she was laughing herself, applauding her own fancy — 'for her bones do be sliding forward through her flesh at every step. Before the leg is seen to be moving, you understand. And afterwards, at the end of the step, doesn't the flesh come sliding forward, past the bones again, to catch up? It does indeed; I can feel it happen in myself. So that altogether she is longer in motion at every step. May you long be spared the feel of the muscles plucking and plucking at the bones, this way and that, which is the worst of carrying a great load of flesh.'

'You know, Mrs. Mary, dear,' said Denyse, 'you're the only woman I've ever met who was worth hearing on the subject of her weight. Of course we'll see you home, but I think, if you don't mind—'

'Ah, don't say it. We'll see how you feel when you get to the door.'

She yearned to prise out of them some explanation of the mysterious sentence she had caught from Father Keith: 'If you'll not help me—' Twice she tried to approach the subject on the way to her cabin, throwing an artless-seeming question into her long account of what each of the Sullivan family had said about the shop-keeper in the course of the day. But the visitors were not to be drawn, and she went back to the general topic of Kildooey's indignation. Nor were they to be lured beyond her door. It seemed to them both that for many hours—ever since Denyse spoke in the car—they had been struggling vainly against ridiculous odds to be alone together, for more than just a few minutes at a time.

'I hope to goodness she hasn't succeeded! That the village won't make any move against Wallace!' Climbing the hill to the quarry, Tom would not yet speak of their own personal concerns—not out on the sea-road at night, where the pure and revengeful Irish ghosts might well be listening—so bitterly angry was he still with Father Keith's savage deity and all the hierarchy of spirits, in whom, at the moment, he almost believed.

'Funny that this action of the gombeen-man's, which has got him so well hated, must be just about the best thing he can ever have done —giving Helen a reprieve.'

'Yes. I think Father Keith was right,' said Tom, 'in being afraid that if this marriage is postponed, it may never happen. I hope so, anyway.'

'—the best thing Wallace can ever have done, if he's doing it for Helen's sake. Which, of course, I doubt!'

'Oh, who can ever say how pure a man's motives are. I've never even been sure if I wasn't exaggerating in some way when I've talked to you about fear. So that there should be something worse than the reality — your picture of it.' He spoke more lightly than usual, almost in apology for things said in the past.

'Oh, don't, Tom. Darling, don't.'

Steps followed them up the hill in the darkness as they had done once before, but these were young and running despite its steepness, and they were only heard near the summit, as though someone had been waiting silently on the grass verge, hoping that they would speak as they went by, and be recognized. There was no moon now, and the night was intensely black, even to eyes which had grown accustomed to it.

'Mr. Fairburn?'

Tom switched his torch on to Danny Hughes. 'Hallo. What d'you want?' Annoyance seized both the campers; was there no time when they could count on being by themselves?

'I couldn't be sure it was you. I thought I must chance it and speak. Mr. Fairburn, I have to ask you, because I have no one else I can ask. Who would have the money at hand, I mean. Will you give me enough to get me to Dublin? I will pay you back from there when I get work, if you tell me where to send it. I will indeed, I swear it.'

'Never mind that. What's happened? Why d'you need it?' But both of them knew. So Father Keith had been too late at Mr. Wallace's.

The boy gave a shrill, slightly hysterical laugh. 'To get me away from here,' he said, 'before the police is after me! — he saw me, the old gombeen-man. There was others in it, too, but he caught me with the stone in my hand, and he'll swear to it. Though it wasn't I began it, he'll say it was.' Dan was obviously terrified by what he had done, and yet glorying in the action. 'We came close round his house, into his garden without his hearing us, because he had the wireless playing, do you see. Very loud he had it, on a station abroad. We could hear the foreign voice speaking between the tunes as we crept round. It was funny to hear it, and we so close we could have understood if it had been English. And then we let loose with the stones we had gathered. Into the room where the wireless was playing, because it was dark, and we didn't want to smash the kitchen window where the light was, for fear of what the glass might do to him. We could see him there. We didn't mean to hurt him, you see, only a bit of his property, for what he is doing to Michael. There was much damage done in that other room, I think, from the noise of it. But all the time the wireless was playing. And we supposed he wouldn't come out. We didn't think he had the courage, for how would he know we meant him no harm, not to himself? But he came running among us, out by the kitchen door. I was standing in the light of it as it opened, and he caught my arm, that was just going to throw, and he was crying, he was indeed, the old gombeen-man! Crying out for us not to break his beautiful things. "My things," he said, "Oh, Dan, not there, in that room!" As if we would be likely to listen to what he wished! And then I heard Father Keith's voice, and I pulled myself loose, for he's a weak little man, that other, and crying and all. So I ran, and was waiting for you here.' The boy's voice wavered from its bravado and fell silent.

To the hearers the scene sprang into moving clarity; Mr. Wallace, unaware of the enemies at hand, listening unhappily, gloatingly in his solitude to the enemy who could not help but entertain him. It seemed natural, and yet added to the distressing quality of the picture, that when the attack came Mr. Wallace had thought little of his personal safety, though he must have known how easily, in Ireland, men were injured or killed in affrays like this; it was not his life, but the proof that he had lived it, which must be preserved at any cost; and now, of the crowded lamp-shades and photographs and framed diplomas, which were all it had brought him, how many, they wondered, were broken or scarred by stones?

'Mr. Fairburn, will you lend me the train money to Dublin? Then I will walk all through this night, so I may be well beyond Comines when the day comes, and the hunt is up after me. I can take the train from somewhere the other side of Donegal. Maybe in the morning I can get a lift to a station further along the line. They will have warned the police at Comines already. Father Keith or Mr. Wallace will have done that. But I'll not be taken at night. Will you do that?'

'I suppose so. You idiot, Dan. What haven't you started!'

'Was Sean in this?' asked Denyse.

'No — he's too busy courting, all of a sudden, to take a part in such things.'

'What'll happen if you stay here?'

'I will go to prison,' he said, no trace of the former relish remaining.

'And it will be very hard for my mother. But Father Keith will see to it. Father Keith will say it is right I should go, for this.'

'And make the mistake of treating you like a man. How old are you?'

'Eighteen.'

'Good heavens. I thought you were sixteen at most! Is your father alive?'

'No.'

'Pity,' said Tom. He did not want the responsibility of sending this raw lad to Dublin — still less, however, of landing him in gaol. 'Do you a lot more good to be treated as if you were a fool of a boy — which you are — and given a damn good hiding.'

'Well, it won't be that.' By his voice they could tell that Dan was grinning in the darkness, relieved to find the seriousness of his offence minimized in this way. 'The constable at Comines, he knows that once before I was out with the others. When we fired a hayrick Mr. Wallace had taken over. Because we thought he was wrong to take it for a debt. It will be prison this time, unless I can hide away till the trouble is all blown over.'

'I see. Why d'you choose Dublin to hide in? Have you friends there?'

'No, but — no. Only it isn't a strange place, now, in a way. Seeing the name on the signpost here, I have often thought of it. And when I am there, I will think of "To Dublin", written up in Kildooey, and it will seem less of a way from the people I know.'

'Have you never been away from home before?' asked Denyse, still more perturbed than Tom at the responsibility thrust upon them.

'I haven't, no. But as I tell you, I've thought of it. Oh, I'm not like Bridie over Dublin! I know it will not be all pleasant! It is not the place itself — only — look — ' Hesitating, groping for words, half whispering in the night for fear of his voice echoing down the hill, Dan tried to express to them the frustration lying beneath the peace of so many Irish villages.

'I'm half glad of this chance,' he said vehemently. 'If it hadn't come in such a way, my mother would have held me back. And Father Keith. I would have wanted not to hurt her, she being alone but for me. I would have wished not to offend him. But it's sick and tired I am of knowing they say that Ireland is the land of the old! They have it all arranged here. Helen got away — they brought her back; well, that was right enough; she promised herself to Michael and he has waited for her three years. It's not the same for a girl. Bridie talks and talks — she will never see Dublin either! They have her tight. They had me the same. Peadar was with me to-night, and two others from Ardrinath you don't know. Cousins of Michael, as well as Kenny, but Kenny was only watching. It was Peadar's stone went first through the window. He wasn't seen, though. He'll stay and be told, till he's a man and after, "Let you be busy, the way the old are busy, living each day the same as the last!"' The note of hysteria rose again in the boy's voice; the unknown future, the journey on which he must embark now, at once, in the darkness, were terrifying to him. '"Fill your hands with your work," they'll say to him, "and your head with the thoughts that the old have thought before you. And then you will have no time for mischief." Have we not! You heard to-night! My father died at his fishing, and I have his boat. Well, I'm not afraid of dying in a boat, and I'm handy with one, you know. But now it's not such a good boat as it was when he had it. And if I have luck with fishing, maybe in time, here, I can get enough to buy another boat. Through Mr. Wallace! And that is about all. And once—you will think it doesn't matter—'

He was breathless with emotion and the difficulty of putting frustration into words, even for one brought up to speak his heart.

'I'll tell you; once, the few of us that are of an age in Kildooey, we had the idea of meeting those from Ardrinath of the same age — there's not above fifteen of us all told. Once a week we planned we would have a gathering, in a barn Michael was for lending us. The one he pulled down to build the cow-shed that isn't paid for. Oh, the fine plans we had! Maybe a bit of singing, one week, since dancing was disallowed. And another time we would be like the Dail — that was Sean's idea; no one else cared for it much — one village siding for Dev and the other for Cosgrave, to see who had the best of the argument; over the land holding, say. And we might have a play; they did that once in Comines; the girls were for that. We would be having a meeting anyway. With no one much over twenty in it, if we did talk foolishness, it would be our own foolishness, so who would be worse off? But he wouldn't have it — Father Keith — and the old ones were behind him. They didn't want us meeting, the boys and girls together.

In case, when the time came, we mightn't be listening to them, about marriage. I think it was that. Anyway, he stopped it. Told Michael not to let us have the barn. And now it's "To Dublin" for me.' There was an attempt at bravado again in the voice, but it fell flat. 'How much will it cost, in the train, do you think?'

'Under a pound, I should say. Come up to the car and I'll give you that and another pound as well, and if you run through the money before you find work, well, you can always join the Eirean army. Or you might even scrounge your way up north again and join one of the fighting services!'

'How shall I send it back to you?'

'While the war lasts, don't bother. I don't think you can send money from Ireland to England. And afterwards' — Denyse's arm had remained in his, and he felt her stiffen — 'perhaps we'll come back here again. I'll look up your mother, supposing I want the money, and ask her where you are. You'd better keep in touch with her, even if you stay in Dublin. And if we don't turn up again when the war's over, well then, it doesn't matter.'

'It is very kind of you, Mr. Fairburn, not to be in a hurry. But I would rather pay it back as soon as I can.'

'All right, then, if Dev will let you, which I doubt, send it to a friend of mine, a Madame Messagère. Write out Madame Messagère's bank address for him, will you, Denyse? It's no use telling you my London address, Dan, because I'm going to give up my flat.' (He had no intention of subjecting Denyse, on the occasions when they might still be together, in England, to the scrutiny of that strangely assorted couple, Mr. and Mrs. Mott — poor Mottie!) 'Madame Messagère will look after it for me.'

Aware of the thought behind the suggestion, Denyse scribbled on a scrap of paper, held against the bonnet of the car, the means by which two pounds might be made available to her without further trouble — some day — if Tom were dead by then. Surely this is one of the strangest things women do in war, she reflected — agreeing to their men's arrangements for them to go on living when it no longer matters if they do. He will want to give me everything, even the trivial things like this; and I must let him. I must listen to what he would like me to do, and have — in case the end of the world comes. 'That figure's meant to be a seven,' she said. ' "South-west, seven." I crossed it by mistake. Would you like something to eat before you go, Dan?'

'I would that. I missed my supper.'

They gave him a stiffish whisky, and some of the endless bouillabaise. 'If I had known your food was so good,' he said gallantly, 'I would have been on the run every night you were here!'

'You aren't "on the run" now,' Tom told him brusquely. 'And don't start thinking of yourself in those terms. Or you won't even reach Dublin. You'll be so taken up, expanding yourself into a national hero, you'll be run over by an old woman in a turf cart, through walking, regardless, in the middle of the road. All you're doing is skipping out of a gaol sentence, for hurling rocks through windows. I'm rather sorry I didn't make it a condition of keeping you from prison that you crossed the Border and joined up!'

'Oh, I couldn't have agreed to that,' said Dan, shocked.

'You needn't worry, it wouldn't have done any good to England if you had,' said Tom. 'But what a few months as an Erk, say, might have done for you!'

'My brother and a cousin have gone from Kildooey to the English Forces,' Dan admitted. 'They tell me Eire has sent more men than Ulster, all told. But I have always listened to Sean rather than to them.' If he were losing stature in his own eyes, the future seemed to be gaining in stability in the most comforting way, through the older man's refusal to see him as a tragic figure. This and the whisky had banished all trace of hysteria by now.

'Off you go, then. Before I change my mind altogether about helping you!'

'All right. Good-bye. And thanks — in a way.'

'Good-bye. Thanks for the use of your boat. And good luck — in a way.'

'Tom, weren't you uncalled-for nasty to him?' said Denyse, when the steps had died away into the night, along the improbable little road to Dublin.

'No,' he told her. 'Nothing to what I felt. Wait and see what harm he's done! He, and behind him Mrs. Mary, refusing to connect cause and effect. And behind Mrs. Mary, of course, you and me — that unlucky incident with Wallace in the car this morning!'

'But Dan did say, didn't he, that Sean had nothing to do with this affair.'

'You think that's going to make any difference to Wallace after to-night? Like a miser, with his gold touched — that's how he'll be. Why did they have to choose that queer room to damage, the bloody young fools who aren't going to pay for it! He knows where he can hurt, more than he's suffered himself — and nothing else is going to count with Wallace.'

'Well, let's sleep on it anyway,' she said. 'Perhaps the whole business won't look quite so black to-morrow.'

In a few minutes his mood changed. 'Of course, they're right, these people, about many things. Bridie particularly,' he went on, in his Cork voice, lying tired and contented in her arms, ' "I wouldn't be call-ing it a sensible process to this day".'

CHAPTER XIII

CONFLICT

THE milk did not arrive the next morning, nor any of the other cus-tomary tributes. Kildooey was too full of its own affairs to think of the campers; so full that even Bridie, though she forgave them for being human, forgot that they had human needs, in the new excitement of Dan's disappearance. A great coming and going of visitors to the quarry started shortly after dawn.

The lovely opening of the day at Kildooey was something which Tom and Denyse could have wished to keep for themselves; there would only be two more dawns before his leave ended; and a habit had sprung from the morning of the gulls, by which one of them would stir in the half-light, and rouse the other, so that together they might watch the first shafts of sunshine reaching down over the hill's high shoulder to touch the sea, and the sudden glowing of the white walls of the cabins in the village, when the earth woke, long after the air and the water were in full possession of the day. But this morning they had only a few good moments to enjoy undisturbed. A gusty, salt-

laden wind, presage of a rough day, was blowing up the hill; the dew
of the night before had been heavy; the strong scent of wet, new-cut
hay from the valley swept up to them, between the nearer smells of
heather and the earthy freshness of the quarry. Tom lit a cigarette in
his own mouth, and twisted it gently between Denyse's sleeping lips.
'Mouillé — dégoûtant,' she murmured serenely, floating on the warm
half-tide of consciousness, as remote from him as the gulls riding the
morning sea.

'The wrong husband. You lose a cigarette for that,' he said, and took
it back to smoke himself. Nor would he let her have another when
they began to receive their untimely callers in procession; starting with
the Comines constable, who stood and coughed for some time in the
road, before wheeling his bicycle into the quarry. He had already heard,
by telephone from Father Keith, that Dan Hughes had not been seen
at home after the attack; he wanted to know from the campers whether
anyone had passed late in the evening along that road. (In the absorbing
interest of the case he did not think of asking to see their personal
papers.)

But it was more than a compensation to Tom for missing the tip
of the day, in the distraction of talk, to realize that he did not care
at all, now, if Denyse still dreamed in another world. A little while
ago he would have minded, but awake she belonged to him; and
securely, too, since the enchanted moment on the way back from his
vindication as a plumber. So did he himself return in dreams to
another world, of yesterday and to-morrow, in which she had no part,
but that other world had not profoundly troubled him of late.

The constable noted in a little book their shameless assurance that
they had seen and heard no one on the Dublin road, after leaving Mrs.
Mary Sullivan's. As soon as he had ridden away, the lad's distracted
mother arrived, to ask if they could even guess where her son might
be; she had already been questioned by the constable who had arrived
in Kildooey before cock-crow.

Denyse was reduced to stealing cigarettes from Tom's case while
he was talking to Peadar and Bridie; they came just as Mrs. Hughes
turned disconsolately down the hill. 'I told the constable that you
wouldn't know about Dannie at all,' she said in parting. 'But, of
course, the whole night through, I was hoping you'd have a message

for me in the morning. For I said to myself, how would he get the money to go, except from them?'

'Is it true, then, what you told the constable?' asked Bridie in surprise. 'And you didn't see anything of Dan?' Both she and Peadar assumed, in the Irish fashion, that as friends the Fairburns would automatically lie to the police, and freely admit it afterwards to other friends. The campers, however, lied in the English fashion — stolidly, to everyone — once they had started. It seemed to them simpler to tell one story and stick to it, than to sort out truth and fiction for a series of overlapping visitors.

The news of Dan's flight, and the occasion of it, had reached every house in Kildooey before midnight. According to Bridie, several of the women, including Mrs. Agnes, had sat up all night with Dan's mother — 'Urging the poor soul, whenever the tea got low in the pot, could she not try for a wink of sleep, now? Or would they just boil up another brew first?' In moments of malice, Bridie had more than a touch of her notable aunt in her tongue.

Early as it was, both she and Peadar had already been prowling round Mr. Wallace's to see, if they could, how much damage had been done. They reported that he had evidently been at work all night. By first daylight, his spoiled treasures had been carried out of the house, even to the chairs and occasional tables and fretwork articles which had merely been scratched by the stones. They were now ranged along the kitchen path, with a mass of broken frames and bric-à-brac piled on top, so that the constable might examine them on the ground outside the shattered window. It was comprehensible, to the campers, that he did not want to let anyone into the chaos of that pitiful room if he could help it; like a lover, he was unwilling that the object of his devotion, the shadow of himself, should be seen at a disadvantage by any eye, even for the purpose of securing revenge. He shouted angrily at Bridie to stop her spying, when she climbed over his wall to help herself to a drink of water from the ornamental pump, as she had often done before. Peadar had been more careful not to be seen skulking near the scene of the attack.

'Strange it is that you didn't hear Dan go by,' said Bridie. 'Even if he didn't speak to you. With you lying in a car so close to the road! He must have gone ahead of you, or else you were already sleeping when he passed.'

'I'm a very light sleeper,' Denyse told them. 'I don't think anyone could come along that flint road in the night without my knowing.'

Bridie said firmly, 'Then he climbed the hill, to go round the back of the quarry, so you wouldn't hear, and joined the road away beyond. That's what he did.'

'Maybe he didn't at all, then,' said Peadar. 'There's more roads than this, lead out of Kildooey. He could be making for Killibegs, or Dunfanahy. Hasn't he a sister married in one or the other? Why should he be travelling by this road?'

(Everyone except Mr. Wallace, Father Keith and the constable knew that Peadar had led the attack, but it was convenient to forget this, with Dan in flight and the blame already attached to him. Kenny was reported to be getting a belting at the moment from his father, officially for staying out late at night, actually in order that authority, baulked of a scapegoat, might not pick on him as a substitute.)

'"Killibegs or Dunfanahy!"' Bridie turned her gold-fringed eyes upon Peadar and then to the signpost. 'Where would you be heading yourself, this minute, if you'd taken the chance to be away out of Kildooey?'

'I don't know,' said Peadar.

'You don't know! Holy Mother of God, you don't know!' The sea-blue eyes lingered on the signpost and returned to Peadar. Peadar blustered, because of the scorn in them.

'Well, there's more towns than one where a fellow can hide, all the same! One day,' he said, making a resolve, 'I've no doubt I'll be going to Dublin myself. But not that way. Not slipping out, like Dan. 'Tis silly. I'll tell my people I'm going — and Father Keith — and how will they be stopping me?'

'Oh, one day — !' said Bridie. 'But I haven't a doubt that Dan is half-way there this minute!' She spoke like a child, desolate with envy of someone else's treat.

'Well, if he is,' said Tom, 'isn't it nice to think that, when the fuss is over, he'll be able to come back and give you the very latest news of the place? And that's more than I can.' Bridie must be consoled. No such eyes should mourn.

'If I'm still here,' she agreed sadly. 'But surely the war will be finished by then, and I'll have gone, myself? Or else I'll have married, and it'll be too late to hear about Dublin. With profit, I mean. For I think, don't you, it would be best for me to do all my travelling before I marry, and then put it right out of my mind? I've been thinking it over these last few days, and that's how it seems to me. I'll never be content, if I don't, even with the beautiful things you're after arranging for me in the new house.'

Sean appeared, displeased at finding Bridie beside the car.

'I'll be down at the building in about an hour,' Tom told him, determined that this day, one way or another, Sean should be kept from meeting Wallace alone. 'You and Peadar, now you're here, you might stack up some stone for me to drive down. I'll move the car out on the road while we have breakfast. I've got to start home, you know, on Thursday. I think, though, if we really go at it between this and then, we can get everything done except the actual thatching.'

'And for that, of course, I'll have to get an expert!' It was said in Sean's most ungracious tone. A fanatical mood was upon him; his face was drawn as though he had not slept that night. Despite his insignificant frame, Sean had a gaunt handsomeness which was brought out by ill health. The skin over the prominent bones of forehead and cheek and jaw gave the impression of being stretched tight by the effort to contain such turmoil of spirit. To him, the whole episode of the attack on Wallace was part of the problem of Irish disunity. 'North against South. Do you tell me Irishmen would be hunting Irishmen at this minute — do you tell me that a good lad would be forced from his home. From the place where he belongs! — if we had finished with partition as we should have done, years ago? No, I'm telling you, No!'

Passion increased in him because of Bridie's biting frivolity. 'I wonder now, Sean, could you ever be shaping a question so the answer was yes? To the everlasting surprise of us all!' Her glance swept round the company, taking into complicity against him Peadar and Denyse and Tom, and Mrs. Kathie who had just arrived with a message from Mrs. Mary. (It was practically a command: Would the visitors call in without fail, please, on their way to wherever they might be going that morning? She had killed and cooked a chicken for them as a present.) Even at what was, for her, considerable cost, Mrs. Mary intended to ensure that this new excitement did not go stale before she had a chance to enjoy it fully. A chicken could not possibly be accepted in exchange for less than half an hour's discussion of the whole affair.

'Now Bridie!' said her mother, trying to stifle laughter, 'how can you be so unkind, when you see Sean has the matter at heart!'

'Ah, let her be. What she says doesn't count! They were long overdue, a few Eire stones, banged through a rotten Ulster window — for that's how it was! An Ulsterman Wallace remains. Would he have turned on Michael, else? While the Border stands, shame on all of us, this side of it, who call ourselves men! While the Border stands, such things are bound to happen, and the best of our lads will suffer for it. I wish I had been with Dan last night! One act, however small, is worth a hundred pious thoughts for Ireland. I wish I had been with Dan instead of wasting my time — !'

Sean was white with anger which he could not direct more openly against his sweetheart; contempt for her opinion on any subject was a long-standing habit of mind, not yet affected by the change in his feelings towards her. He argued hotly with Tom and Denyse in defence of political violence, and they found it tiresome to search for reasoned replies, knowing that he was not attending to what they said. As once before, in the priest's manner, he paused for them to speak at intervals, and then went on with his own train of thought, as though they had not spoken. Bridie stood, sweet and coltish, rubbing a shoulder against the signpost, gazing at fold upon fold of coloured hills, through which she could picture Dan making his way towards the far-off city.

'Well, I'm sorry to stop this discussion,' said Tom, when physical need left him no alternative. 'But my wife and I would like to get up and dress now!'

Mrs. Kathie hurried Bridie away, murmuring about the poor cow unmilked and the poor chickens unfed, with the grey hen still uneasy inside herself — lest the campers should be embarrassed by a feeling of churlishness after they had gone. The other two withdrew some distance up the road and sat down out of sight, waiting till they could get at the stone in the quarry.

'Thank goodness!' said Tom, heaving himself out of the car. 'And you'd better dress, fast, if you don't want to be immobilized again, for hours. Here come another lot of footsteps up the road. If they're women, Peadar and Sean won't like to say why we drove them out. But they're still some way off. You've got about three minutes. Never mind about washing, we can have a bathe later.'

Denyse had been right in saying the situation would look less menacing after a night's sleep; they felt absurdly cheerful, racing into garments which the wind tried to snatch out of their hands. 'I shouldn't
think,' she said, 'that Mrs. Kathie's "bastes" have ever been attended to
so early in the morning! It'll be a notable day for them, as well as for
the rest of the village. Whenever I look down at Kildooey, while I'm
washing up the breakfast, I see the old cow standing by the back door,
throwing a meaning glance at her udder.'

'Gallic overstatement, darling. You can't see that from here.'

'I can. She's just a little black and white square, with a long neck at
one end that comes curving round, in the most appealing way.'

'I expect she's more elastic than we are,' he said. 'Seeing she's of
the country. You really needn't be so concerned about local times of
milking.'

They managed the business of getting up with several seconds to
spare, and, if unsecurely fastened, were fully dressed, to outward ap-
pearances, when Helen and Mrs. Agnes came into the quarry. They
had walked up the hill together, but once again Helen seemed anxious
to speak to the campers alone. Prepared to wait, till the other should
have said her say and gone, she helped them to get breakfast, and to
push the car out on to the road, so that the young men might get on
with the digging while they ate. Mrs. Agnes's reason for coming was
unexpected — to boast about Sean as a good son.

'He took no part in it all, last night, and I can tell you what it was
holding him back! For the way it is with Sean, he'd be up the first of
them all, for the sake of a friend like Michael, if he'd only himself to
consider, so he would. But he didn't want to be bringing distress on
his mother; no, not he! Knowing how it would be for me if they took
him away. And the constable down in the village this very minute,
questioning every household that has a lad in it! To know his where-
abouts while the stones were flying. Didn't that one come to my door
before any of the others? He did, indeed. Before he came to you.
With his certainty that Sean must have his hand in any disturbances
in Kildooey! But "No," I said, "No. Here's a lad with too much regard
for his mother. Not like some!" I told him. "There's many a widow's
boy will leave her without compunction, but not Sean. And luckily,"

I said, "there's others can testify he wasn't at Wallace's throughout the evening".'

'Very luckily!' said Denyse. One incredulous eyebrow had shot up as far as it could, without the other, at this explanation of Sean's behaviour. 'Bridie was with him, wasn't she?'

'She may have been,' admitted Mrs. Agnes, taking no notice of the loose eyebrow. 'But that wouldn't have been the influence on him at all. Well I remember the tears that came into his eyes one day — he'd have been about Dan's age then — Dan Hughes that didn't even stop to bid his mother good-bye before thraipsing off! Well I remember Sean saying, "Mother, never a step will I take without thinking first, how will it bear upon you? For there's not enough consideration I can ever give you," he says, "in return for the care and the love I've had from you, all these years".'

'Really,' said Tom, embarrassed with fellow-feeling for Sean. It was the sort of disclosure his own mother enjoyed dragging out of the defenceless past for comparative strangers — which in turn was one of the reasons why he kept away from Cork for most of his leaves. Sean and Peadar, however, were working with a good deal of noise in the quarry, using the communal pickaxe in turn; it could be hoped that Mrs. Agnes was inaudible to her son at this distance.

Heavy rain clouds, trailing a long grey veil over Kildooey, drove towards them before the wind; Mrs. Agnes hurried away down the hill at the first spatter of big drops, but Helen stayed on. 'I doubt if one word of the same ever crossed his lips!' she said. 'Sean of all people!' She climbed into the car with them and sat, very still and giving out a feeling of uneasiness, looking through the window at the rain, which blotted out in a moment the white houses in the valley. For a while she could find no words for what she had come to say. She was not wearing her bright incongruous town clothes any longer; with nothing on her head, and her blown hair curling about her face, she looked prettier than they had ever seen her before, but no longer distinguished in any way from other fresh-faced girls in Donegal. Something of urgency, they knew, had brought her to them again. Tom talked to Denyse, to give Helen time to get up whatever courage she needed. 'How Mrs. Agnes reminds me of Mottie — !'

'Mottie — ?' began Denyse. 'Who —'

'Mottie,' he said eyeing her severely — a wife should recognize the name of the cook-housekeeper.

'Oh, yes. Yes, Mottie!' said Denyse meekly.

'Mottie always boasts that Mott won't let her do a hand's turn of work for him on a Sunday. "Now sit you down," he's supposed to say — rather archly, judging by her tone — "and let *me* wait on you, old girl." Not only a lie, but one that Mott would be deeply ashamed of her telling.'

'I wonder,' said Denyse, 'why so many of us choose to boast of things said to us that either a man couldn't have said, if he happened to be middle-aged, or would so much rather not have said, if he happened to be young? But I know who it is that *I* think Mrs. Agnes is like. Of the people I used to know, I mean. An English maiden lady in Paris; she was so delighted with the war, for a few days after the invasion of Belgium. She said, "Now *this* will stop the worn-out horse traffic! See if it doesn't!" (And it did, of course.) They've got the same kind of single-mindedness.'

'Oh, Mother of God, what am I to do? What can I do?'

The cry broke so suddenly into their amused conversation that the silence afterwards seemed as though it had been torn out of the hushing sound of the rain. They could hear that, down in the village, a few belated cocks were still crowing the day, the sound coming to them faint and far off, muffled by the downpour.

Helen said, in a low, desperate voice, 'The winter here — the grey days and the long nights, and always the same faces! And no word spoken of anything that goes on beyond Comines, or maybe Ardrinath — and that treated as if it came from the world's end! You think it's beautiful here in Kildooey, because you've only come at this time of year. I've spent twenty winters here already. But I didn't mind when I didn't know anything else! Before I came back here from America I thought, It'll be different, when I have my own home, with Michael! (I am fond of Michael really; I've always been fond of him.) But it isn't going to be different. It's Kildooey I mind, not marrying Michael, you understand. It's hating Kildooey I dread.'

Denyse said, 'But actually there is someone else in America?'

'Yes, there is — there was. But he isn't a Catholic. We quarrelled when I said I must come home. He has another girl now. It's over. It was that, even before I left.'

'You don't want to go back then? That wouldn't solve things? We'd do whatever we could to help you to get back, if it would?'

'No. I'm promised to Michael. It's my duty to marry him.'

'Girl, don't do it if it's only your duty! You're asking too much of Michael as well as of yourself, starting life together like that.' Talking to Helen now, they felt none of the restrictions which had hampered them in talking to Bridie on the same subject. Whether or not Father Keith would consider that they were breaking their word to him, it was not possible for them to twist aside or remain dumb before Helen's dry-eyed, anxious misery. But arguing with her was like arguing with Father Keith himself.

'It is right I should marry him,' she said, when they had put forward every reason against it. 'Though I'd rather it had been the other, if that had been possible. It's strange, now; you go so far beyond what I was thinking as I came up the hill! I was meaning to ask you only —would it be wrong of me to beg Michael to sell his farm, when he's waited so long to share it with me? I should be getting advice from Father Keith about this, not you; but I know what he'd say, and I can't bear it. He'd say, I mustn't think first of myself. The farm doesn't pay, hardly at all, you know. 'Tis a poor place, but it was his father's, and the old women have given their life to it, and they cling to it. The fields are big, for these parts, but they're undrained. It's too much for one man to work. Well, you can tell it doesn't pay; Michael can't even get out of debt to Mr. Wallace. The ground is sour for want of the lime he can't afford to buy for it. Land here is in demand, all the same; there's little enough can be cultivated on this coast, and with the pressure of the population we have in this country it's likely enough he'd find a buyer, if I dared to urge the sale on him — after he's built the new milking shed for me. I don't know what right I have to do that, when he's met with such trouble already over the shed? But if he moved south, off this coast — Oh, I wouldn't care how small the new place might be. Not if we were somewhere that — well, maybe it would have a bus running nearby, going into town. So I wouldn't be so much cut off. It wouldn't be like Boston, but still —'

'It wouldn't be like Boston' — Denyse's heart ached for the littleness of the girl's demand on life, just something less than the living burial offered by Kildooey to the returning traveller. 'If you're sure you could be reasonably happy like that,' she said, 'I think you should tell Michael. Milking shed or no milking shed. And see how he feels about it.'

'You think I could? You think the disappointment of it wouldn't be cruel, after the way he's waited?'

'Of course, it'll be hard on him being asked to sell his father's farm. Possibly he'll refuse. He may say that the money he'd get for it wouldn't buy enough land to live on, down in the south. But give him the chance. It won't be so hard to be asked, now, as to see very plainly that you aren't happy, soon after marriage. And no one on earth could conceal that, living as close as you'd be living on the farm, working and eating and sleeping together, all the year round. Besides, Helen, he knows already that you didn't want to come back.'

She said, like a child repeating a well-learnt lesson, 'Father Keith says that self-sacrifice is blessed in itself.'

'Oh, damn that, my dear,' said Tom. 'When it's pointless it's just about on a par with jealousy — something really poisonous to be anywhere near!' Seeing that Helen had not followed this, he came down to the concrete example. 'Just look at your Aunt Agnes. A woman given to sacrifice if ever I saw one!'

'She is that,' Helen agreed, gazing out steadfastly into the blur of the downpour. 'We would have to take the old people with us.' She shivered, partly with the cold which came in the early morning rain. 'It is wicked, but I hate them! With their bare feet and their talk of nothing but the calves and chickens they feed. And their oldness. And their content. Just their oldness — it is wicked, I know. They must live with us till they die. But if we were near a town, I could go in alone to the shops at times. I could do the marketing there every week. And there'd be other people I'd get to know, if I did that. It is strange,' she told them again, 'I supposed you would think ill of me for wanting Michael to upset his life for me. And now you say I shouldn't even be marrying him if I don't wish it myself!'

'But didn't anyone in America say that, too?' asked Tom. 'Your friends there. Apart from the man who was interested in you himself, I mean?'

'Oh, no. You see, I was always with people from this country. They were sorry for me, but they knew I must go when I showed them the priest's letter.'

A gust of wind forced the last of the downpour through a slit of open window into the car, sprinkling their faces. Helen pulled her mother's shawl over her head in a purely peasant gesture. 'If we moved away from this coast,' she said, 'maybe inland, or right over to the east, I wouldn't be thinking any more of the wet wind as the one that blows from him straight over the sea to me. Even if I noticed it was coming from the west, I'd think it had gone over other houses in this country — blowing round other people's lives, you understand — and not come to me without hindrance, all the way from the farther side. Now, when the rain comes — you'll be thinking I'm fanciful; mostly, I'm not; but it's different when you're unhappy, you look for things that seem unhappy too — it's like tears.' This was spoken so simply that they knew it was not said for effect. Almost in the same breath she added wistfully, 'There's good farm land in the pockets of the Wicklow Hills; Shamus talked of it once, I remember.'

Denyse looked at her curiously. 'Was it the signpost made you think of moving across Ireland?'

Helen nodded. 'Father Keith knew it would prove a troubling thing to Kildooey,' she said, 'seeing that notice so often. He is very wise. Well, I will ask Michael and tell you what he says.'

With the suddenness of Irish weather, the clouds parted over the village, tearing to the ground their veils of falling rain. The edges swept by on either side, brushing the sea on one hand, and the bogland behind the quarry on the other. Even before the sun struggled through the gap, it was as if all the miraculous lamps were lit at once inside the green and purple hills.

Helen got out of the car, into the flash of September glory; she answered a comment they had made only in thought as she stood blinking in the brilliance of the new-washed morning: 'I know there's nothing as lovely as Donegal to-day,' she said, 'in the place where I've just come from, but you can't live on the memory of such times. Not in winter, you can't. Sitting alone with those whose words you know by heart, listening to the rain coming down, and wondering what they're doing in the places where there's life.'

Father Keith was their next visitor; he appeared, high above the car, perched beside the driver of a hay wagon bound for Ardrinath. The priest visited his outlying districts as often as he could: with a pleasant indifference to his own dignity, or rather a certainty that it could not be assailed, he was accustomed to demand a lift in anything on wheels which happened to be going in the direction he wanted. The driver was a stranger to the campers, a more prosperous looking farmer than any in Kildooey. In an effort to pay off Mr. Wallace, at least in part, Michael was selling a rick which he would badly need for his own beasts later on, and getting less than the market price for it because he could not manage the carting himself.

Father Keith stopped the hay wagon when he saw that Helen was with the campers, and called down to her some trivial request which would take her back to the village at once. Then he hesitated, before beckoning to Tom to come up beside him: the climb down was something of an ordeal for a corpulent man of his years.

'So you don't trust us!' Tom grinned as he swung up on to the wagon. He was rather pleased, in view of their recent advice to Helen, that the anxious Father so obviously did not. 'Well, maybe you're right!'

The farmer from Ardrinath took this, as Tom had known he would, for a gallant joke. 'And who would be trusting a gay young fellow in a fine car,' he said, speaking to Helen's back, 'with a girl as sweet as the morning?'

She turned, managed a smile and waved to him as she went obediently down the hill, to deliver the unnecessary message to Mrs. Omaney. Denyse put her head out of the car and looked up at them on the wagon. 'Ah now, if I'd seen your wife was so beautiful,' said the farmer, unabashed, 'I'd have known that you couldn't be aware of temptation at all, if his Reverence will excuse the mention of it!'

Father Keith, deep in gloom, took no notice of this sally; he ignored Tom's remark as well, and signed to the farmer to drive on. 'It won't hurt you to walk back a pace or two,' he said to Tom. 'For I, alas, am not on holiday, with all the day before me.' It occurred to Tom that Father Keith was unconsciously trying to steal a few minutes of the time which the campers might spend in building the new cabin; everything they touched, down to pipes and door-posts yet unused, they defiled by their handling still more than other people did by theirs; in his view, even the stones of Sean's house were becoming polluted. If the two had been alone, Tom would have put this idea to the priest, in the certainty that Father Keith was a good enough man to laugh at himself, if he were charged with an absurdity which did not threaten his defences. To-day, his sombre spirit could not be lightened by the beauty of the inanimate things he trusted, the singing of birds after rain, the cleanness of the shining air. The following wind rollicked along the road, making the cheerful smell of the hay almost overpowering at times, but he spoke only of his cares. 'Mark you, I'm not asking anything of you now. I'm just telling you this, and leaving the rest to your good sense — I'm deeply hopeful, for his own sake, that Dan Hughes will be caught. For his own sake: I put it no higher. For what he did to go unpunished, at his age, might well be tragedy. It would be enough to settle him all his life in lawless ways. The constable tells me you say you haven't seen him. If that's so, it's likely he's still in the neighbourhood, for he wouldn't have the money to get far. If he comes to you to-night — well, as I say, I'll ask you nothing, but to bear in mind that many an outcast from society has no more than this to thank for the worthlessness of his whole life — no more than this — that he was "lucky", as he'd say, in some early escape from the law.'

'True, Father. True indeed,' said the farmer sociably, as Tom made no comment beyond a nod.

'Terence Hogan!' said Father Keith. 'There's not a soul for twenty miles but knows your farm is the meeting place for the lads drilling in the bogs! And has been, ever since the worst days. You're no support to those who would see peace in this poor land!'

'Ah, but that's my old mother's doing, not mine! A wonderful woman she is, too.' The farmer turned proudly to Tom. 'Eighty-seven this month, and you know what keeps her going in these sad days? The interest she has in Mrs. Simpson, and what will be happening to the woman after the war.'

'I don't think I know Mrs. Simpson?' Tom believed himself acquainted, by name at least, with everyone of note in the parish. This Mrs. Hogan was the one at whose house the fat-tailed sheep had been mentioned, probably during an I.R.A. gathering. There were several anecdotes about her in Mrs. Mary's store; Mrs. Mary was too big a

woman herself to be jealous of a member of her own sex who had encouraged even more men to add zest to life with occasional shooting.

'Do you not?' said the farmer in surprise. 'And she married to your
old King. They told me at Michael's farm that you were English?'

'Oh, that Mrs. Simpson — Yes, I am — No, I'm afraid I don't know
her, even so. But good heavens, all that business was such a long time
ago. Years and years. Before the war.'

'What's a few years when you're eighty-seven? It's yesterday still to
my mother. The conjecture and trouble there was!' — the farmer threw
a sly look sideways — 'with those like his Reverence trying to keep the
fuss of it out of the Irish papers!'

'It didn't sully any but the worst of our rags,' said Father Keith.

How infinitely remote and restful such interest seemed — strangely
nostalgic, too, at such a moment, thought Tom. So medieval martyrs
may have recalled, at the stake, the academic discussions of former
days; heated arguments about the number of angels who could stand
on the point of a pin.

'Scarcely a week passes but my mother listens to the news on the
wireless. The English news or the Irish news or the German news; she
has all her senses with her, you see, God be praised, and she doesn't
confuse them at all. "And I wonder," she says, over and over, "will the
English be recognizing Mrs. Simpson as their rightful queen, in the
end, as the price of America coming to help them with the war?"'

'A woman so close to her last days!' Father Keith spoke bitterly. 'And
she wastes her thoughts on such unworthiness!'

'Ah, now, begging your pardon, 'tis not that at all,' said the man
from Ardrinath. 'One little woman, no bigger than my mother, and
didn't she do what the whole of Ireland has failed to do — shake the
British throne? Why wouldn't my mother be thinking of it still, with
satisfaction, after the years she spent in that very cause, she with little
enough satisfaction left to her at her life's close?'

'She'll have less when I've done with her this morning!' said Father
Keith, turning human at last. It was said in Kildooey that his only
weakness was the pleasure he took in the stubbornness of his old ladies.

'That's as may be,' said the farmer, stopping to let Tom get off, before another deluge swept up from the west. 'It will do her heart good
to see you anyway, Father. It always does. Her heart, that is. I'm think-

ing nothing on earth could affect her soul, not even you. A grand woman she is, indeed,' he leant over perilously to shake hands with Tom in the road. 'Let you be coming over to see her yourself one of these days, with your beautiful wife. For it's hardly a step from our farm to the Seal Cave as well, and the likes of the two of them is something in Nature you never saw outside of Ardrinath.'

'We'll come with pleasure, if we have time. Unfortunately we've only two days more.'

'Ah, the pity of it. Well, come if you can.'

'We will that.'

'And you'll just bear in mind what I've said about Daniel Hughes?' Father Keith came near to pleading with him in the end.

'I'll bear it in mind, yes,' said Tom, and went back along the road, to be met by Denyse, hatless and coatless, oblivious to the rain beginning to fall on her bright fair head.

'Tom, I wish we could get right away from Kildooey! Just for these last two days.'

'My dear —'

'So many people — So much on top of us. Can't we? Oh, I know we've got ourselves absurdly involved with their lives, till it's become a kind of duty to stand by, between Wallace and Sean, if we can. But after all, we really aren't responsible.' She looked at him apprehensively, as though the desire to get away quickly was stronger than she could explain, or even understand. 'My papers: you know they aren't in order. It's quite possible the constable will remember he hasn't seen them, and come back to the quarry, just because he happens to be around Kildooey.' Both of them knew that she was not really worried about this.

'Funny woman,' he said, linking his arm with hers. 'You'd be the one to say we couldn't possibly get from under, just at this moment, if I suggested it! And there's another reason besides Wallace — No, two — Well, two bits of the same reason, really — why I don't want to be pulled out of Kildooey sooner than I've got to be. I want to finish the job on Sean's cabin as well as I can. Such an unimportant bit of building. I know it's ridiculous to feel so pleased about it just because it's the first thing I've put together instead of knocking apart, for over a year. But I do feel pleased with it. And unless I've got something to do with my hands — something quite enthralling, like building — well — I'm a lot better, but I'm not yet capable of being content to be just on leave, with the thought of what's going on over the other side.' He looked up into the flying, broken sky, which was already showing signs of clearing again. Along the English coast it might be cloudless: fighters' weather. Or it might not. How could one tell, in Ireland? But over that familiar coast the bombers were flying now. He knew at this moment that except for the small, pleasant job he had chosen to do, he was ready to leave Ireland; he would be easier in mind nearer the battle, taking his part again when the time came.

'All right,' she said, bending to scratch her chin with his fingers. 'Finish off as much as you can, before we have to go. I won't interfere. I know what's the matter with me, really. I'm frightened of seeing any more stupid hurting. Any more human damage. I'm not wanting to run away from Kildooey so much as from the road to Bordeaux. And that can't be done, of course. So go and build, darling. We'll try to keep Sean with us as much as possible, all day. For his safety, while the outrage is burning-fresh in Wallace's mind. I've an idea he'll only vent his malice on someone he can catch alone. He couldn't tell Sean that story of the tinker's van with us standing by. Not after what he said about never letting anyone else know.'

'No. Almost certainly not. It's a queer kind of enemy to be holding at bay, though — the chance for one man in a village to talk to another alone!'

'Just while his hatred of all Kildooey is at its most vicious,' she said. 'And that probably means, just to-day. To-morrow, I don't suppose he'll have forgiven or forgotten anything, but at least it's likely the first edge will have gone from his temper. Anyway, we'll do what we can. Build with Sean all the morning. We've got him secure in the quarry now. We'll take him and Peadar and the stone, all together, down to the site in the car. Then we'll get him to come along to the Seal Cave in the afternoon by inviting Bridie — he'll follow her anywhere, because we've taken her heart. And we'll give a sort of pre-farewell party to all the Sullivans and their relations in the evening, getting rid of our spare stores. To-morrow will be another day and another problem. But much less urgent — I hope.'

'It's the same, fighting in any war,' said Tom. 'No good looking beyond the day. If you're the person doing the fighting.'

'That isn't you speaking, but the genius of the English race — such as it is!' said Denyse, half in mockery, half in profound, aching affection. 'You must remember it's not in my blood. If we'd felt like that, in France, there'd have been no Dunkerque; Reynaud would have found the miracles he needed to save the country — several million men who could fight without hope. And we'd still be fighting. There might even be hope!'

He knew well by now the note of agonized bitterness that came into her voice when she spoke of the tragedy of the last few months in France. 'It's my turn to say, "Darling, don't!" ' He brushed the raindrops from her hair with hands that gave some comfort just by touching her — the kindest of silly gestures; he had no coat to put over her, and the rain was still falling. They went back towards the quarry. 'We'll manage for now, anyway,' he said. So they planned, and nothing turned out as they intended.

Sean had worked like a demon, loosening about twice as much stone as Peadar; more was ready to be lifted than the car could take in one load. 'Carry what you can. I'll fetch the rest by donkey,' he said. 'Dan's mother, in her distress, won't be thinking to use her own this morning, and I'll borrow him if my own beast is still lame.' He was off down the road on foot before they could think of an excuse to stop him, leaving them to load in the stone with Peadar before they could start in pursuit.

Mrs. Mary had her own way of preventing them from catching up with him when they reached the village. As the car approached the bridge, she waddled through the rain into the centre of the road, waving her cooked chicken by the drumsticks. She kept it in her hand, under her coat, while she held them up to discuss the jolliest aspect of Dan's escapade — the questioning by police, and how it brought back old times, the full, important days, when the constabulary in force were always nosing about in the neighbourhood. Like the meeting with the ghost, this outbreak of violence in the village was in process of becoming entirely her own adventure. Had she not played her part in it by shouting at Mr. Wallace, before the listening lads? With Father

Keith out of the way, she could boast of her share in wrecking the gombeen-man's peculiar room.

In imagination the campers saw once more this treasure-house of loneliness, not as it must be now but as it would never be again, with all its irreplaceable rubbish intact. The feeling of cold distress which they had known there came back to them as they listened to her up-roarious laughter, coming out of a funnel of tattered trench-coat. The garment she wore over her head and the top of her body must have belonged to her husband; was it the same gunman's uniform, they wondered, in which Harry Sullivan had waited for the constables who came, unsuspecting, to collect the old tinker? In some ways the gay, fat woman, whose joking had led to his death, seemed more sinister than the unhappy man who might yet be prevented from turning the affair to his own purpose.

They tried to get on, and failed. It seemed to them both that they had spent an astonishing proportion of their time in Ireland in these circumstances. But by now Bridie had hurried on to the bridge with a milking stool for her aunt to sit on, it being a bad day for Mrs. Mary's feet.

'My right knows when it's going to rain,' said the huge creature merrily. 'My left knows when it's been raining, even if it's only a shower during the night. Thank you, child. Thank you — and devil a bit of willing service can I get out of either of them while it's actually coming down.' She settled herself so that they could not proceed across the narrow bridge without moving her. Not even the promise of a party in the evening could achieve this yet awhile.

Bridie pointed out with interest that Mrs. Mary appeared to sit much lower than the stool. To Bridie, built with the strong, arrowy grace of one of the swallows which skimmed about them, over and under the bridge, her aunt's soft bulk was something to be prized and extolled; it had, indeed, a rarity value in the land which bred the leanest and loveliest of old woman. 'There would be many fine big people in Dublin?' she said softly to Tom, while Mrs. Mary squeezed the utmost of reminiscence out of the new upset in Kildooey. 'With all the vehicles in the street, and the company close at hand, there'd hardly be reason to move about as much as the most of us do, here, running the flesh off us?'

'They were both in Dublin, the two fattest women I've seen in Ireland,' he assured her. 'Barring your aunt. But honestly, Bridie, they couldn't hold a candle to her.'

'Mother of God, you don't tell me? Not in Dublin itself! You know, I've been thinking over what you were after saying about Dan, earlier in the morning. When Peadar and I were by the car together.' The long, tawny lashes lifted to him in the look of melting attention which could affect Tom's heart a little, even with Denyse, who was much handsomer, sitting close beside him. High time I went! he thought cheerfully; how hopelessly polygamous men are! — and how is it possible that Sean has waited till the coming of strangers to fall in love with this enchanting girl?

'I always start thinking again about what I've heard,' Bridie went on, 'when I reach the bend in the road on the way home. For at the time of first hearing there's often too much to consider. You were asking, wasn't it a fine and quietening reflection that Dan has gone on ahead of me, to bring back the tale of whatever is new in the town since yourself was there last? And at the moment I was doubtful. But not now. Not a question of it, with yourself going away to break the link, 'tis nothing but luck on my side. I will feel all the more at ease when I do go, for it's Dan will tell me, too, in due course, the things you wouldn't be thinking of mentioning; they'd be so familiar to you from other big places. But not to us. Like, what do you pay for milk?'

'Mrs. Mary,' Denyse protested, 'if you don't let us go on down to the building, Bridie won't get her embellishment!' 'Embellishment' was a term first applied by Mrs. Agnes, in a slighting manner, to the water piping. Shocked, the other Sullivans with their exquisite manners had immediately changed the sense by their own use of it; the word now included, in an admiring way, all Tom's ingenious contrivances, especially the pulley and ring in which an oil lamp would swing, when there was a roof from which to swing it. This had given the greatest pleasure in anticipation. 'But you'd wonder how his father's business would get on without it, especially in winter,' said Mrs. Kathie admiringly. Not even Denyse had been accepted more easily than the myth that all the material was discarded stuff from the printing works in Cork.

'Ah, now, don't be detaining them. With the evening in store for us.' Bridie went at once to her aunt, to help her up from the stool. Dublin was a goal, a dream to be realized, a tickling excitement of the fancy, but the envy of neighbours was an immediate good.

'Father Keith would be glad on the whole if she didn't get it,' said Mrs. Mary, letting herself be persuaded to her feet, but she did not yet move aside for the car.

'Comfort being more disturbing to him than sin?' Denyse suggested. 'I dare say it's stranger anyway. For sin is always in the front of his thoughts; but comfort, I imagine, he's never known at all?'

Mrs. Mary went off into paroxysms of mirth, her quick mind seized on the truth of this irreverence, and her enjoyment of it threatened to force her back on to the stool for support; while Peadar from outside the car, and Bridie in the road, looked on with grave disapproval. They were devout young people, and did not like the idea.

'You have it. Oh, my dearest, you have it!' crowed Mrs. Mary. 'The one is a familiar thing, but the other he mistrusts, and no wonder — the dear, good, poor man — and haven't you just the way of thinking that I have myself?' Her regard for a kindred spirit prevailed over her delight in such talk, and at last she let them pass, adding a packet of bread and salt to the chicken, in order that they might go on building for Bridie without interruption from hunger.

Again the sun lunged through the clouds and bred a million flashing reflections, on puddles and stones and blades of grass, so that the day became dazzlingly bright in a few seconds. Before they reached the cabin site they met Sean, leading two panniered donkeys back towards the quarry; and beside him walked Mr. Wallace, talking — whispering, rather, at intervals, though there was no one else near enough to hear. From time to time he twisted his neck so as to look up as closely as possible into the drawn, angry face of the young man beside him, and mouthed at him; every gesture, every attitude of the older man's was somehow instinct with darkness, a darkness in which crawled twisted things which should never have been born. The sunlight haloed the group; the figures shone with the richness of the scene.

Sean held up his hand to stop them, curtly interrupting the gombeen-man. His manner to Tom was as short. 'The wall on the north side is higher than I want it. I said, let the place be lower at the back than the front. Many of the cabins here, they have that slope, because of the wind. You or another, I don't know who, added at least three courses too many. I didn't.'

'I expect I did,' Tom spoke mildly; he was worried beyond any resentment of Sean's tone. How much had Wallace managed to tell, in the brief time in which their guardianship had failed? It was impossible to guess by Sean's face. 'I don't remember hearing you say that about the slope,' Tom went on. 'Good idea, though. It'll take no time to pull a few stones off again, with Peadar to help.'

'Well, I did say it!'

'All right. Come over to the site and show me exactly how much lower you want it, and we'll trim the side walls to meet the slope.'

'But the donkeys —'

'Let me have them,' said Denyse, with inspiration, hopping out of the car. 'I'll take them up to the quarry and load them, and I hope Mr. Wallace will come with me, to show me how much they ought to carry? As he's walking in that direction, anyway.' It was spoken in her firmest voice.

'Well, I wasn't thinking of going so far —' began Mr. Wallace. He seemed dazed, like a man snatched suddenly from another world; but presently, looking greatly surprised, he found himself leading one of the donkeys beside her, away from Sean, Peadar and Tom, who settled down to work at lowering the wall.

'What was he saying to you, Sean?' Tom came straight to the point when the shopkeeper was out of earshot. It was a bad mannered question, by Kildooey standards, but more hung in the balance, he thought, than courtesy.

'Ah, some damn nonsense about his own concerns —' (Tom drew a breath of relief.) 'To show the cleverness of him, no doubt! — about the secrets he has in his keeping. And the little that Kildooey knows. "Of what?" I was tempted to ask. But it seemed he was waiting for that, so I thought, No, let him find his own way, to get out whatever it is that's plaguing him. And I let him run on, till he was almost choking on his own words! Dear knows, did he look so clever against Kildooey last night, with his window in smithereens? But in the end, "Say what you have to, man," I told him, to be finished with his squinting at me and his grinning at me. For I hate the face of him today more than I ever have. But he wouldn't be hurried. "There's a nice long road before us," he says, walking alongside with the dribble coming out of the corner of his mouth. "So there was on another occasion. A long road before you—"' Sean stopped pulling down Tom's work and frowned, looking puzzled. 'That's what he said!'

'A bit touched in the head, he sounds—and well he may be,' suggested Peadar vaingloriously, 'after the happenings of last night! We have him shaken. Maybe he'll go from Kildooey now. "To Dublin", as his own board says. Or back over the Border. Good riddance either way to the gombeen-man. Why did we stand him so long?'

'I don't know,' said Sean absently. 'I don't know!' The look of bewilderment deepened on his face, as though some part of him were trying urgently to bring back a lost memory, against the fierce resistance of the rest. He burst out suddenly in temper: 'He started to talk to me about the Troubles. That Ulsterman! It was just before the car came. I was ready and ripe to tell him what was in my mind when you drove up.'

Tom knew a certain tempering of his relief; Sean would now tell him instead of Wallace, and he was in no mood himself for another political harangue on the evils of Partition. It was odd to remember that only ten days ago he had been looking forward to this sort of talk as refreshing. Well, even so, it was a hundred times better that Sean should let go to him than to Wallace.

Sean squinted along the wall. 'That's low enough now. Level her up —I would have said to him, "Dear send that the Fenian dead may know that we're coming! That it's not for ever the shame of disunity will lie on the land—the Fenian dead who gave us—"'

'The Fenian dead', reflected Tom, would certainly have given the gombeen-man the opening he wanted.

The vehemence with which Sean had talked in Mrs. Mary's cabin, with the priest present and his family about him, was nothing compared with the force of the words which broke from him now; all his personal loves and hatreds dissolved into a torrent of speech, so that his spirit was eased. Partition—neutrality—and the old, unavenged, unavengeable grievances; the course of the flow was inevitable. Several times, when the talk turned to the war, there came into Tom's mind the cruel simile he had used before, of Eire as a young girl at her first party, proud of her decision to drink lemonade instead of something stronger — it was such a rough party. But to-day he had the kindness not to repeat it. Sean was touching in his anxiety that his country should be worthy of her new adult status. 'And we will take other decisions, as important as that of standing aside!' he said, gazing dazzled at the sun seeking out rifts in the scudding clouds. 'We are not afraid of responsibility here.

'We will think for ourselves, I tell you!'

The sun disappeared and the sun blazed out again, in the patchy local weather which gave no idea of what the fighters were facing — sixty, eighty, a hundred miles away — where men who, if they thought in the hour of battle, did not think for themselves, were shouldering instead the responsibility for the whole world.

'I think I will go and set a lobster pot.' Peadar spoke with indifference, over the unabated rush of Sean's eloquence. He approved the gist of what was being said but had also heard it rather too often before. 'So I will have one of the creatures for yourself and Mrs. Fairburn to carry away with you. A good lobster, now, it takes so long in dying, it will travel nice and fresh to your journey's end.'

'I'm sure my wife will be very grateful,' said Tom, doubtfully, wondering what even the efficiency of Denyse would make of a live lobster as a parting present. 'Why isn't the constable bothering about you, Peadar? You who really ought to be in gaol? He's supposed to be questioning every household with a lad in it, and the lad himself.'

'There's seven in our cabin. I told them all what to say beforehand. Ours is the only household,' said Peadar with satisfaction, 'where everyone had the same story right from the start: about me in bed with a shouting colic. So he isn't bothering about me. The innocent ones — the tales they do be concocting in the agitation of the moment, why, they can't be expected to hang together at all.'

Tom laughed; and Peadar strolled away; and the angry voice went on. 'We are of age — let "Mother" England remember that. Let her like it or not, that is her concern, not ours! Only, let her remember!' To this motif they finished the wedging of the door frame — it was a nice bit of rough carpentry, over which Tom had enjoyed himself — and the casing of the chimney.

'Mind you,' Sean admitted, 'there are things for which I am sorry that England is losing.'

'And what would those be, eh? What would those be?' With a laden donkey in tow, Mr. Wallace came upon them unawares round the corner of the wall, through which Tom was running the pipe with the wiped joint. The sense of crisis returned.

From the road, Denyse called for help with the other donkey, which would not negotiate the ditch, and Sean went off to help her, with a short bit of piping in place of a stick. The donkey saw him coming and jumped, breaking the pannier girth; the stones fell into the ditch and on the bank, one of them slightly injuring the beast's pastern. 'I am always unlucky. A borrowed donkey, too,' said Sean, examining the damage.

'Some might say yes, but some, ah, some might say, no. No, not so unlucky!' Mr. Wallace had scuttled back to join them, his crabwise movements through the rough grass taking him from one place to another faster than seemed possible for someone with such short legs. Thereafter, while they prepared the rafters, he hung about them, darting from one to the other like some predatory little animal, longing yet afraid to attack.

The spilled donkey-load was left where it fell for the time being; these stones were only for the outhouses, the byre and pigstye; the cabin itself wanted nothing but the roof, and the lining of the walls, for the actual construction to be complete; the immediate jobs were mainly carpentry. Odd lengths of wood had been contributed by many people: the news that Sean's cabin was being built for him by English campers had gone out widely, and small gifts or the loan of tools had come from places as far away as Ardrinath, in order that Kildooey should have full use of its alien visitors.

Tom and Sean climbed up and sat perched on the gable-ends, fitting the roof-tree into place, while Denyse handed up to them whatever they wanted. As soon as the gombeen-man reappeared, Sean had relapsed into sullen silence. Mr. Wallace, not to be discouraged, talked up at them, or talked at Sean under the pretence of talking to Denyse.

To the two who knew his purpose, it was a situation of half unreal, half sickening suspense. He hinted at his revelation, skirting round the subject, trying to exchange understanding glances with those who were aware of what he could not quite bring himself to say, titillating himself with their knowledge. But they had been right, it seemed, in their surmise that he could do no more, before an audience. Yet what he could accomplish was disturbing enough. When he stood still for a moment they could see that as once before, in their company, he was shaking with excitement. He had been almost incoherent in his talk, on the way to the quarry and back with Denyse. Now his remarks became more and more meaningless to an outsider, in his efforts to drag in obscure references to the past, which none of the others would follow up. No one replied at all to most of his interjections.

But he remained, unable to tear himself away, unable to make himself clear, while shower after shower swept up the sky, drenched them to the skin, and passed on. He did not appear to feel the rain falling on his venomous upturned face. While he was silent, casting around in his mind for a fresh approach, the three at work on the cabin spoke among themselves. After a time they did not answer him any more, whatever questions he asked. The feeling of unreality grew. The consciousness of evil at hand was so strong, upon Tom and Denyse, that each observed how intolerable it became to the other to know Wallace behind and out of sight, as though the danger he represented were physical: both of them shifted about to keep him in view. This was easy enough for Denyse but presented considerable difficulties for Tom, now astride the ridge pole, marking out the spacing of the rafters.

He was a much more experienced carpenter than Sean, who left the scarfing-in of the rafters and tie-beams entirely to the visitor, acting, himself, only as a measurer. Even if there had been no tension between the four of them, it would have been exasperating to hear the obsessional voice calling their thoughts elsewhere while they were trying to bear in mind a series of different lengths and spaces recorded by knots in a piece of string; there would only be enough timber to finish the frame of the roof if the best possible use were made of each piece, without regard for regularity.

'There's some things scarcer than others in Kildooey, eh, Mr. Fairburn? Eh? Wood, now — or is it knowledge? Knowledge of things that have happened? For the things that have happened in Kildooey, who would believe them unless they were told? But some day, someone will believe them, eh, Mr. Fairburn? What do you say?'

Gradually, however, despite the fantastic atmosphere of menace, the impression grew upon them that this was all Mr. Wallace would do —

now. Hint, and skirt-round, and not quite manage to speak. His opportunity had passed at the moment when the car slowed down beside him and Sean. He had lived too long with his spiteful advantage,
fondling it with his mind, keeping it to himself as something precious,
like the hoard of possessions in the wrecked room. Having failed when
the chance was his, it was likely that he would not try again to share
what he knew with Sean.

Bridie came down, to exclaim in charming awe at the progress of
her embellishment. She agreed with delight to the proposed visit to the
Seal Cave, and ran away to wash and iron herself a clean dress for the
occasion — by the time she had gone they were almost sure that their
hope was justified. The obscure, irrelevant remarks of the gombeen-
man came further apart; they remained as tenuous as before, in their
connection between the realities of the moment and those of long ago,
but they seemed to hold less pent-up fury; if he were tired out by
emotion which could not reach a climax.

One moment, without looking away from the join he was hammer-
ing, Tom was acutely aware of Mr. Wallace walking rapidly round the
cabin, in one of his bouts of movement; and in the next Denyse said,
'Look! Oh, at last!' very softly. Having reached the corner of the wall
nearest the road, the gombeen-man was going straight on, without a
word, undulating over the broken ground, making his way back towards his own desolate dwelling.

'Good,' said Tom with less thankfulness in his voice than he actually
felt. Sean grunted in reply; the taciturn state induced by Mr. Wallace
lasted through the meal they made, off Mrs. Mary's chicken and
bread. Tom's superior skill in woodwork had discouraged him altogether by the time they went back to the work; he no longer helped
in measuring, or by holding rafter and tie in place to be joggled in,
but pottered at odd jobs on the ground instead. With a splitting head-
ache, Denyse also gave up, and sat down on the dry side of a half-door
which someone had brought along. Tom carried on alone.

'I had meant to take years over this job,' Sean observed in a flat, ex-
pressionless tone after a long period in which no one had spoken at all.
'Years, do you see; and now it's almost done!' A great change had
come over him from the period of daemonic energy in the quarry during the early morning.

Down the road towards Kildooey walked a dapper figure in a town suit, with a soft felt hat worn at a tremendous angle. While still at a distance the man began to wave.

'Who's that?' asked Tom.

'How should I know, any more than you? 'Tis no one from Kildooey.'

In a few seconds Sean added, 'My cousin Shamus from England,' in a yet more surly voice.

No one could have looked more alien to the soil of Donegal than this native son as he picked his way towards them through the puddles. 'Ah, now, I see you found your way along the Ballinfaddy road,' he called amiably to Tom, in the rich accent which suited him admirably in London, but not here.

'Thanks to your excellent friends, yes. I — we are very grateful. I have to introduce you from up here: Mr. — I never got your second name: you're not a Sullivan are you? — My wife.'

'Shamus is enough, as you found.'

'From all I've heard, your name's much better than a passport,' said Denyse. She rose to extend a hand. (It grew noticeably dirtier as it advanced towards the immaculate newcomer.) 'There's a policeman prowling around Kildooey and my papers aren't in order. I'll rely on you to get me out of trouble if he finds out.'

'Lay your mind at rest,' he said cheerfully. 'Is it the officer from Comines? There's plenty I have against him, and he against me, from the days when I was as eager as Sean, here, to be running around the bogs at night, in innocent pursuit of the honour of Eire and the ruin of my trousers. There'll be no trouble! Why didn't you bring your lady with you,' he called up to Tom on the roof, 'when you came in to say you were wishful of visiting Ireland? I wouldn't have wasted so much of your time, before coming to an understanding!'

'And what brings you back to Ireland anyway?' asked Sean. 'Now you're no longer willing to fray the legs of your fine suit in the bogs — nothing but the seat of the same on an English stool?'

Shamus, the friend of everyone, was not to be ruffled. 'Ah, now, it's still *"Eire le h-aghaid na eireannactha"* for me, the same as ever,' he said. 'And moreover *he* knows it' — wagging his head towards Tom — 'For I said as much when we first met, and he wouldn't have it at all.

But I've grown to think there's better ways than the old ways. Haven't they always been apt to hang on a bit too long in this country, the way grown people cling to their childhood? The lad with the gun was yesterday's hero; and to-day it's the lad with the wireless transmitter who counts. And maybe, to-morrow, it'll be the lad with the parachute that does the greatest service to Ireland.' He examined his nails as he spoke, in the manner Tom remembered from their first meeting — a hundred years ago, it seemed. 'So why should I be running around the bogs, in uncomfortable search of yesterday's fame? Did you remember to tell my Aunt Mary Sullivan that I'm as loyal as ever?' He cocked his head up at Tom. 'The way you promised you would?'

'I'm really ashamed to say I forgot, after all you did for me!'

'Never mind. I'll tell her myself to-morrow. Will you take a word for me to all the Sullivans, Sean?'

'All right.'

'Tell them, Shamus will be along in the morning. I've a thousand and one things to attend to, for the rest of to-day. And a friend's car waiting for me round the corner to take me back to Donegal Town. But I wanted to see, could it really be true what they told me — weren't they speaking of it this morning as far abroad as Killibegs! That you, of all men, were letting those from across the water put up your future home for you!' He laughed, not ill-humouredly. 'Well, I would never have believed it, if I hadn't observed with my own eye. And you just standing by.'

Rain threatened again; the three from Kildooey were too wet to take shelter when the showers came; Shamus in his nice clothes ran to a thick tree, and from its protection called back to them inquiries about everyone in the village. 'Your mother, Sean, is she in good health? Or as good as she ever was, dear soul? And Bridie? Is it true that Helen is back, but there is a hitch to her marriage? Tell her, then, I've half a mind to stay and cut out Michael altogether!' The downpour lasted too long for his patience; he took off his coat, turned it inside out, and wrapped it round his hat before legging it up the road out of sight.

''Tis about all he would be good for, that one!' said Sean dourly. 'To do a man an ill turn when his luck is already against him.' He picked up the borrowed maul which Tom had been using on the rafters, and made as if to work again.

'Oh, I don't know!' Tom protested. 'He worked wonders for me — us — in London and Belfast, when there was no obligation at all. We shouldn't be here if he hadn't.'

'I daresay!' To Sean, at the moment, this was plainly no recommendation of Shamus's good nature. The rain slackened; he threw the tool on to a heap of sacking in a corner of the cabin. 'I'll be off, now, to take Bridie round to the Seal Cave by boat, if she's ready. The tide will be setting that way; it makes southerly. And the ebb will bring us back.'

'By boat! But surely it's rough for rowing a curragh?' The suggestion had been that they should all go together in the car at about 5; it was now only 3 o'clock.

'It won't rain any more.' Sean looked up into the wind. 'And the sea will flatten with the turn of the tide. She likes the boat in all weathers. Let you watch our progress from the coast-road. And you'll see where the cave is by noticing where we go. We'll meet by the opening. There's an old track down from the cliff top.' He spoke impatiently, and was gone.

'Well, we evidently aren't wanted. And, praise be, I don't think we're needed any more, either! We'll go for pleasure only, on our own!'

They hugged one another like jubilant children, in the dripping concealment of the cabin. 'I think we'll jack-up, now, too!' said Tom. 'What a morning — and afternoon! Wallace had slugs crawling all around my spine! Sweetheart, how's your head?'

'Getting better so quickly it's almost a pleasure to feel the bit of ache that's left! It's throbbing delightfully to a rhythm like a train's — "I-*think*-we've-won; I-*think*-we've-won; I-don't-know-why, but-*think*-we've-won."'

'So do I. You were masterly, leading him off with the donkeys! Just at the right moment.'

'But my heart sank when I couldn't get rid of him in the village on the way back. No one would speak to him, poor devil. When they saw who was with me, even people like Mrs. Mary went into their cabins and shut the door.' For a long while — Denyse babbling light-heartedly — they fought their curious battle over again, comparing the moments when each of them had begun to feel safe on Sean's behalf, to believe that the ghastly revelation would be forever postponed.

'Drive me back to the quarry now,' she said, 'and I'll slap together something to eat at the Seal Cave; Mrs. Mary's chicken was just wasted on me. My mouth was still so dry, I felt I was chewing the Sahara desert. Chewed and chewed but it wouldn't go down. This is certainly the loveliest head-ache I've ever had, because of the way it's lifting.'

CHAPTER XIV

THE SEAL CAVE

The pain had gone entirely by the time they were back in the quarry, where they had left the primus stoves. Whenever they went away from their site they arranged a ground-sheet over all belongings which would not be spoilt by a little exposure, and hoped that if the Kildooey children came up to play with their things in their absence, the older ones would remember to rearrange the ground-sheet afterwards; otherwise the stoves became hard to light. To-day it was too much to expect that anyone should be as considerate as usual, with the distraction of police visits going on in the village; but after ten minutes of blue smoke and fume, one of the primus stoves sputtered up the water which had got through the nozzle, and Denyse produced the speciality which delighted Tom — an omelette, hot and squashy, slipped into a hollowed-out segment of a loaf of bread, which was then sealed up again with heavily buttered crust; the thin flat Irish loaves were ideally shaped for this purpose.

They ate, in messy comfort, lying on their backs in the steaming grass of the cliff at Ardrinath, above the place where they guessed the entrance to the Seal Cave must be. Sean and Bridie had been left far behind: the passage in the small boat through the rough sea turned out to be much slower than Sean had anticipated. But he was right when he prophesied that the wet squalls would not come again; the late afternoon became gloriously hot; the whole countryside, however, was saturated with rain; to reach the spot where they spread Tom's mackintosh they had walked among rainbows, a great arc overhead, and small ones in the spray about their feet at every step. Lying on the mackintosh was a gesture to convention; they were as wet as the grass beneath it. From their bodies, their clothes and the whole visible world rose little wisps and curls of vapour.

The wind went mad, and ran unsteadily in circles, bringing back to them, one after another, heady reminders of the valleys on three sides; peat smoke from one direction, hay from another, and in the third, lime trees must have been late in flower, though they could not be seen. The sea sent up its salt tang as the waves burst on the rocks below in clouds of spray. The small birds on the top of the cliff went mad, and sang after the rain as though it were spring; all the butterflies and grasshoppers, even some of the sober bees went mad; the butterflies with love and the grasshoppers with activity, while several bees appeared to take the fallen scraps of egg for yellow flowers and bumbled about them. Tom, prone, had tried to slither his half of the omelette into his mouth, without much success. He had picked most of it out of the grass afterwards. In the entire scene only the gulls were at all sensible, and they, too, were at play; nothing could be wholly serious in this extraordinary, irresponsible hour. Over and over again they launched themselves from the cliff face in discouraging example to a flock of rock-pigeons, who persisted in trying to float as far over the sea as the gulls without moving their wings, but the gulls soared in a huge circle, returning to their ledges without flapping, and each time the pigeons failed as they banked on the turn, and came fluttering back ignominiously to settle, and then to try again in the wake of the gulls. There could be no purpose save pleasure in this flight. There seemed no other purpose worth considering. Down on the white-capped sea, the boat with Sean and Bridie in it crept nearer the watchers on the cliff, who sat up at intervals to mark its progress. It was tossing wildly, and even with the tide bearing it on, would take at least another half-hour to draw level with the spot where they lay. Denyse turned over on her stomach towards him and finished up at the last of his spilt crumbs. 'Out of kindness to the bees,' she said. 'I can't bear them to be disappointed just now. One of the things you've given me back, Tom, is greed. Before we met I'd got to the stage of not noticing what I was eating. But when I was at school, I remember I had a discussion with another child — we must have been thirteen or so — wondering what on earth we could find to do when we were thirty. Because by then, of course, we didn't expect to be still concerned with careers, clothes, mar-

riage, bringing up families, or travel. We should have been everywhere and done everything, draining life to the dregs. The question
was how to fill in the few remaining years of anti-climax. After a lot
of talk we decided that probably we'd still be interested in food. And
how right we were. I wish I'd used six eggs instead of four.'

There were long gaps in the talk, while they considered with approval the madness of every living thing in sight except themselves. 'I
know nothing at all about your childhood, except the dreary school
part,' he said. 'You know mine — how I came to fly; what my father
does. How do you come to be the daughter of a priest? You did say
you were, didn't you?' He spoke lazily; after the stress and threat of
the early part of the day it was heaven to lie in the sun in a mood of
indifference to everything — everything but the varying noise of the
wind in the grass, which just kept him awake, and the slope of the
ground, which almost sent him to sleep in spite of it — it was so con-
veniently steep that he need not raise himself fully to keep a half-closed
eye on the bobbing black curragh. That was indeed having a rough
passage; it was much better to be sprawled out on the rounded top of
the down.

'Come of a family always in love with the improbable,' she said as
lazily. She sounded half asleep. 'Living in the tradition of the English
eccentrics. But France has never been able to throw up eccentrics as
comfortably as England. Ours tended to be unfortunate people. Tiresome by comparison. We were burnt for our doubts and our heresies
in the centuries when every reasonable man knew there was a god, and
exactly how he liked to be worshipped. It convinced us, after a time.
We produced really pious bishops, and ecclesiastical authors, in the
period of the great French Rationalists. (France turned to free-thinking
rather earlier in the nineteenth century than England.) The Rationalists
convinced us as well, but too late, of course. We were staunch atheists
again by the time that Materialism had crumbled, and the only certainty left was that however you explained the Universe, it couldn't be
as simple as all that. Our atheism went on down to my father's day.
He was sent to school in Britain, too. French people don't have their
children educated abroad as a rule. That must have been the reason
they sent him. After my own education, it's the only one I can think
of anyway. He went to a glum Scottish public school, Presbyterian

enough to make him insist on being confirmed there in the Church of England, by way of protest; it seemed so skittish in that atmosphere. I'd like to be able to say he went to the right school at the right time to be in the famous confirmation class, caned by the headmaster because the man couldn't imagine what so many boys were doing, waiting outside his study, if they hadn't come for that. But unluckily he didn't — spiritually, it was the sort of thing that always did happen to my father. He'd have appreciated it, too, and it might have turned him seriously to religion at a much earlier age. Actually, he took confirmation as a joke. He might even have got his Call before he married, and then everything would have been simpler for his family — it would just have been someone else's. As it was, he didn't join the Roman Catholic Church till after he'd gone up to the University. He walked out of a lecture on Determinism, saying loudly, "To hell with the probabilities, I'm going back to God." We'd been converted again.'

'Love, this is an admirable story. But I'm afraid it can't be true. Because Determinism wasn't thought of in your father's day.'

'It is true!' said Denyse indignantly. 'True in the only sense that matters. Of course not in detail, because I wasn't there to see, but dreadfully true in outline.' Wide awake now, she propped herself up on one elbow, to free the other hand and talk with a wealth of cheerful gesture. 'I mean Evolution, then, or whatever it was at the time. There are moments when you're English in the worst sense, Tom. And you had the nerve to glower at me when I said the wrong and practical thing about Mrs. Mary's ghost story! You remind me of the awful school where I learnt to be superficially English, too — "No, Denyse, here we don't play *at* hockey: this is the deplorable French way of thinking" (all right, they didn't in fact *say* "deplorable"; they conveyed it). "We *play hockey*. That is quite, quite different".'

'So it is,' said Tom, and turned over on his front, because that was now dry. Immediately he felt the warm, soft hands of the sun and wind taking hold of his clammy clothes and drawing them away from the sodden skin. Denyse's hand, much less gentle, thumped him as Bridie had thumped the donkey; instead of dust there flew up a surprising cloud of steam, and she desisted.

'The interesting thing is that my father said "Going back to God", meaning that particular Church. You know I'm still close enough to my childhood to feel that of course he was right; if you're going to think in terms of God, you must think in terms of the Roman Catholic Church. The odd thing is that anyone of his character should think in those terms at all. But the desire for the priesthood didn't get hold of him till after he'd married my mother and I was born. He prayed vehemently for our safety for ten years; and we were safe. That's almost all I remember of him; his praying, and a nice rabbit hutch he made me. We all got influenza in the 1922 epidemic, and he prayed still more vehemently for our safety; but most vehemently of all for my mother. She didn't seem as ill as we were, but it was her existence which stood in the way of his ambition. She died, and that convinced him of the efficacy of prayer. He rushed into retreat in one of the contemplative orders and through it into the priesthood. I was sent to England because it was a nice long way off; officially, it was because I had a Catholic cousin in the school, and we were expected to strengthen one another's faith in our isolation. But she, lucky girl, was in a position to leave the next term, by threatening all the things she would do if they didn't take her away. I wasn't. If I'd done them I'd only have gone to another school, where they also played at life but not at hockey.'

Tom, wrapped in layer after layer of ease — of the body, and the mind — knew as well the immense pleasure of the creator. This was the Denyse he had made, this woman who had come alive under his hands. Sooner than he had hoped. There was the long heartbreak of a child, he knew, behind that story, but it came bubbling out with the same sun-drunk exuberance with which the pigeons tried to be gulls, and the wind spent itself in circles, and the grasshoppers bounded prodigiously from one patch of grass in order to sit idly in another. A woman so happy and near and glowing bore no resemblance, save in feature, to the remote automaton he had met in the Irish boat. A few inches from his eyes, a chrysalis on a stem of charlock had split open in the heat, and the black and red butterfly inside was beginning to spread crumpled wings, expanding jerkily in the sun. He watched it as though it were a clock, ticking away this madly contented hour; an hour to be held, and delayed by consciousness, and hoarded in the mind more jealously than those moments between night and day at Kildooey through which the gulls fought over the fish. Each sudden quiver and stretch of the delicate veined membrane, hardening as it dried, flicked away into the past another instant; but there could be no fitter measurement of such time than the spasmodic unfolding of an insect's wings. The world had grown fragile with joy; he felt that it might break when the butterfly grew strong enough to fly.

'How much in love with the improbable are you yourself?'

'Not in the least. I've had my glut,' said Denyse emphatically. 'On the road to Bordeaux in June, in Stepney during August. In one case, walking out of my own drawing-room into chaos; and in the other, walking out of chaos into the Underground, where the incredible sleepers had put their hair into curl-papers. (And then we all went back into fresh chaos in the morning.) You've got to believe in a fundamentally orderly world, as my family always did, deep down, before the unlikely becomes really attractive. At heart, they felt you only had to accept a First Cause, or reject it entirely, for the Universe to make sense. It won't do that for me, either way.'

'D'you want to come back with me to England? Where I gather you've had the two unhappiest periods of your life?'

'Why do you ask me?' she said, surprised. 'You know I do.'

'Then you are in love with the improbable,' he said gravely, 'for I think I'm offering you the smallest possible chance of happiness. I've always wondered how the wives of air crews managed to stand their life. Listen, either you'll live at a distance from the airfield, and I'll see you occasionally, and you'll wish you were near enough to hear the bombers go out at night, and count them, and wait, and count them again coming in towards morning, for the sake of knowing the odds — I must tell you this, my dear, before you decide to come — I suppose the law about friendly aliens will change in time, and you'll be allowed to work again; till then you'll just have to do nothing and get through time, somehow. (As an alien, of course, you'll be suspected of worming R.A.F. secrets from a besotted dupe every time I visit you, but that part I don't suppose you'll mind, and certainly I shan't.) Or I may be sent to one of the easy-going stations, where you can live fairly near, so I can see you more often; and then you *will* be able to listen, and count, and wait, and count again; not knowing for certain whether I'm actually on operations or not. And then wait another few hours to find out. You're also liable to get bombed again, near an airfield, but I know this is like the suspicion you'll arouse — something you won't mind. Only I shall.'

'I must be my father's daughter after all,' she said, the new life gone for the moment from her voice, but it remained light and level. 'I'm still tremendously glad we've met, even in this war. Even with that prospect ahead.'

'You must be indeed!' It did not seem possible, in that atmosphere to go further — to thank her for being so.

'Did you really expect me to say I'd rather stay in Belfast?'

'Well, honestly, no.' He smiled at her, noticing again, on a different level of gratitude, how rarely beautiful her mouth was when she smiled. To most women's faces a smile was unbecoming, one liked them smiling only from associations of pleasure. Her lips had the rare quality of looking as though they were originally made as a pair, and had not come together by accident; the lower was the same width as the upper. It was by far the most important balance in a human face, he thought, and not one person in twenty had anything near it — he would remember to tell her about it one day when there was time. He was pleased that he had remembered to ask her if she were returning with him. 'As a matter of fact,' he said, 'I wired for both our reservations in the ship two days ago. I knew you'd want to come, but the fact that you do is amazing all the same. You've got this in common with a peculiar man I know very well, because I've flown with him a lot. I know exactly what he'll do, which is always admirable; but why he does it, goodness knows. There the resemblance stops. He's my usual navigator, only whole and at large still because he was on leave the night of my last flight. Of the three who baled out, one's dead, and two are prisoners — ' He began giving her sketches of the people she would probably meet; Ireland faded away from around them. 'He knows what the flying life is really like, of course; the genuine and un-avoidable dramatic quality. But the real courage and horror aren't enough, apparently; or else they're too much. He hankers for the sort of emotional falsity which turns the stomach for most of us — he's a Scot; I think I told you, and a good man on the job. What he enjoys reading are picture-paper versions of our doings. "That's interesting, isn't it?" he says, handing me the *Daily Mirror* with his thumb on the headline "Jilted — So he Shot Down Two Messerschmitts". And the films he recommends are obscenely embarrassing productions, in which flying personnel are apt to run bloodsweeps on their chances of survival, saying throatily, "It's you or me to-night, Ole Man! You—or Me!" (When really it would almost certainly be both or neither, which he's just as well aware of as I am. Apart from the fact that death can't be discussed.) I rather fancy he thinks of himself in secret as a Dare-Devil of the Skies. Or else an Intrepid Bird-Man. In fact, or I wouldn't have him in the crew, he never takes a risk he can avoid, though he'll stand anything he's got to, and—Oh, damn Sean! See that?'

The curragh had come close inshore, under the cliff, almost level with them, and then turned, and was now heading straight out to sea, where there was an island inhabited only by gannets.

'Well, if he wants to show her the nesting-grounds we'll look for the Seal Cave ourselves, and not wait for them. They may be any time, messing about out there—he's just being bloody-minded, he knows we're standing by for him. That's probably why he's doing it. I want to go on afterwards and see the notable Mrs. Hogan.'

'I want to go on and do everything in the world to-day,' she said. 'What a world!' They started arm in arm down the steep cliff path, but in the end it turned into a mixture of slippery climb and slide, taking them twenty minutes to reach the rocks at sea level.

There was the mouth of the cave. They made their way in along a fin of rocks jutting out from one side of the entrance, their rubber soled shoes making little noise as they came. The tide flowed deeply through a clear, narrow channel between the rocks and the farther side of the cave. Inside, to their sun-dazzled eyes, it was dark and empty; pale patches and streaks which might have been veins of marble showed faintly on the rock walls. From the invisible vaulting overhead water dripped steadily; there was no other sound but the rush and gurgle of the sea.

'This can't be the place,' said Denyse, despite a strong smell of fishy decay. Her voice echoed loudly. Instantly there was a noise like that of a dozen cats mewing to their young, of a hundred sows grunting to theirs, and an uproar of flopping and splashing as the pale patches came alive on the breeding-ledges just above tide-level. The mothers tried to bunt the babies off into the water, and the young seals resisted piteously, protesting their fear of the drop. They did not mind the strange voice; they felt secure and comfortable on the familiar ledges, but the mothers were terrified of human beings; occasionally, on this coast, the fishermen shot at seals when they seemed to be taking a more than usually heavy toll of the fish. The struggle lasted some minutes; the young were so soft and fat that their weight slipped easily to one side or the other of the shoving noses, and the old seals found it hard to get a purchase. Gradually the old seals won, getting their noses further and further under the wriggling stomachs and heaving. A procession of little seals came wallowing down the channel, chivvied and guided from behind. They were without fear, and stared at the human beings as they passed, but they did not like the sun, and tried in vain to turn around in the entrance. There was another tussle, which the mothers won. The young were white and almost round with fluff and good-living, and their expressions were so infinitely mournful, when they were pushed on towards the glittering breakers, that the intruders were stricken with remorse at having disturbed them. A fat furrow on either side of the nose marked the youngest faces as if with tears. This accidental look of appeal gave way, among the mothers, to an equally meaningless look of disgust. The sleek, mottled bodies of the adults made a line of flashing safety between the young and the sharp rocks against which they might be dashed. The old seals dived and turned, and herded, never offering a steady target for a moment, till the little seals were out in quieter water, beyond the first line of waves; here the whole flock hung about, submerging every few seconds, to come up and gaze at the menacing creatures on the rocks out of one eye, before submerging again to come up and study them surreptitiously with the other, giving the impression that down in their own element the seals were unable to believe in the existence of anything so repulsive, and returned to the surface every few seconds to amaze themselves with the reality.

'I think we ought to let them go back now,' said Denyse, 'to have a little peace before Sean and Bridie come to bother them too! Actually I'd love to kidnap one. If you say we're going to have a live lobster with us on the journey, why not a small seal, which wouldn't be much more trouble, but a great deal more fun? Still, I suppose it wouldn't do, since we don't even know where we're going. I seem to remember hearing that very young ones can drown, if they're rolled about too much in rough water; let's move along a bit. As a matter of fact the fish-taint here is getting me down a bit.'

They retired a few hundred yards along the shore, and watched the whole procession of old and young return to the cave. The boat was nearly a mile away, tossing about in the troubled sea by the gannet island, over which skeins of birds hung like banners swirling in the wind.

They bathed, using Tom's shirt as a towel.

'Either you really do stink of fish, darling,' she told him, 'or the seal smell is stuck in my nose, and maybe we were wise not to take a young one back with us.'

'I expect I stink of fish,' he said. 'Goodness knows I've eaten plenty and washed little enough, this last week. I'm really tempted to go and kidnap you one. A small seal is the only thing I've felt parental about! One thing I know, we're both going to be sick and sore and bad tempered to-morrow, from too much sun!'

'But I don't mind about to-morrow, to-day!' said Denyse.

'Remember,' he said abruptly, 'this is my armour. All this. You, and the kindness we've found in Kildooey. The good things that remain.'

A longer, less arduous path brought them back to the top of the down; there, by the car, Michael was waiting. He walked across to them, moving heavily as though he could not see the rainbows in the spray, nor that the world had gone admirably mad. His kind, young face was set in the lines of puzzled unhappiness it had worn during Denyse's first evening at Mrs. Mary's. Now, as then, it seemed that he did not understand why he should suffer, having done no wrong that he could recognize, but when disappointment came to him he accepted it without complaint. Absurdly, his expression struck both of them as something like that of the young seals; yet his very real dignity was not lessened by the resemblance.

'I am on my way to the man who took over my hay this morning,' he said. 'To ask, will he let me have it back, if somehow I can arrange for the carting. For look, there is no hurry now to pay off Wallace, and it is wrong the beasts should go short in the winter, if it can be helped. I thought I would tell you—she spoke to me, the way you said. About selling the farm.' At once they felt guilty, before his unaccusing sadness; yet the council they had given to Helen had been forced from them, in honesty, and they could not have offered any other. He showed no resentment. 'You know, I did think of her feeling the place terrible quiet, in winter,' he said. 'Before I spoke to her family about calling her home, and they to the priest, I thought of it. I mean, I feared my place might seem a good way from the village, for it's a rough walk over the fields in bad weather. I didn't think of Kildooey itself seeming too small. It's hard to fancy how it must look to some-one fresh from a town, for I've always been in Kildooey myself, so it's neither one thing nor the other to me, you understand — not big nor small. But I wondered about the farm. For there's many a better farm round here. Well, Hogan's for one. Still, I hoped —' He did not say what he had hoped: that love had survived, and love would be enough. 'I see how it is for her, now. And with yourselves going away, so there'll be no one can share the thoughts she has of the things she has seen —'

'Oh, Michael, I'm sorry if it's our being here that has made things worse! Reminded Helen too much of what's going on outside Kildooey.'

He said, 'You shouldn't be looking at it that way at all. You were right in what you said to her. Much better she told me now she wasn't content to settle here. Rather than after we married. For I can't move, not yet awhile. That's why I said, there's no hurry about the payments to Wallace. With land-prices down because of the war, there'd not be enough coming in from the sale of the place to provide for the old ones as well as ourselves. You guessed that, didn't you? She told me. Helen and I, we could manage by ourselves, anywhere. I could get a job on someone else's farm if there wasn't a bit of land going cheap enough for me to buy. For a while, anyway. But my mother and her sister would be lost entirely without the beasts to tend, and feeling themselves a terrible burden to us, and I wouldn't have that for them. Maybe when the war is over, land prices will be up again, and I could do a deal with someone. They say it was so last time; there were many bargains to be had, because of the men that didn't come back; and the end can't be far off now, do you suppose? Even if we could, I think we shouldn't marry till then. 'Tis too far and expensive for Helen to go back to America in the meantime, and dangerous as well, with the sinkings they have now among the big liners. (We hadn't been considering the danger at all, before she came back, but only when she got here we were thankful, hearing how it was with people in other ships, and realizing the risk she had run.) She doesn't want to go back, either. But she would like to find a place again, somewhere in a town. I think it would be hard for her, having come home to get married at once, to wait about in Kildooey. And Father Keith would not object to her going away, for a bit, because he knows it was Wallace's doing, not ours, that we couldn't marry yet. So I was thinking, would you be keeping your eyes open in London, if you do be going there, and tell us should you hear of a place that would suit Helen? She being very good with her hands, and at all fine work.'

'Oh, Michael, of course we will, if you're sure that's the best thing —for her to go?'

'I'm sure,' he said. 'And I'm only asking you because she wouldn't be liking to bother you herself.' It was as though he were apologizing to them, with his sweet, slow smile, for the breaking up of all his plans. 'Wallace will be gone, too, no doubt, by the time peace comes,' he said. 'He has told the police constable he'll be out of here as soon as he can collect the most of his monies. Maybe he'll not wait for mine. I'll be letting the beasts eat it in the meantimes anyway. We'll not be marrying by his leave, then.'

He said nothing to suggest that he realized how small had grown the chance of his ever marrying Helen — pretty Helen, with a dread of Kildooey in her heart, who was going back to a town, just for a month, or perhaps two — till the war ended. They sensed that he knew, if not that the war would last for years, at any rate that he had lost her for ever, by his generosity.

'Wallace! So there's another one shifted from Kildooey by the signpost!' said Tom, really for something to say: the lack of reproach in Michael's attitude made it almost unbearably touching.

'Ah, now, if it takes so little to shift them,' he said, 'isn't it best they should be able to go? Well, I'll be seeing about the hay. Will I tell Mrs. Hogan you're coming? At her age, she likes to expect people. It makes the visit seem longer, without tiring her.'

They did not answer, and instead of repeating the question about Mrs. Hogan he, too, stared down at the curragh, which was once more well under the cliff. It was coming in fast through the rough water just off the shore, under the urging of both pairs of oars; but now something strange was happening down there. Bridie, who was forward, stopped rowing and bent over her raised oars, as though she were doubled up with sudden laughter at something she or Sean had just said. In a moment he shipped his oars, leapt up and turned to face her, standing in the stern of the frail craft, rocking it, with a foot on either gunwale. A sea caught it, and with the weight high, shot it over. It righted itself, half submerged. The two in the water clung to the side, and the light curragh turned over on them. Only one figure reappeared, clear of the boat, struggling to right it.

'Can they swim?' Tom and Michael together raced down the steep path, with Denyse following.

'He can. I don't know for Bridie.' The cliff was maddeningly difficult to negotiate at speed. There were places where, if the men threw themselves over small drops, instead of lowering themselves carefully, they missed the overhung track and fell among thick scrub and brambles, wasting time in clambering back to the path. It took them only a few minutes less to reach the bottom than it had taken Tom and Denyse, descending at leisure.

The upturned boat floated several hundred yards out to sea, in the tumbled patch in which the waves, running obliquely to the shore, curled over and began to break. The second figure was visible now. Neither made any further effort to right the boat; one supporting the other, they clung to the stern. Here the movement was extreme; they were constantly submerged as the scend of the water flung up the light bow. A heavy surge lifted the stern clear for a second, and one of the two no longer had the strength to hold on; the other needed both hands for himself as the buoyant end was wrenched upwards.

Bridie was unconscious, having been in the water about twenty minutes, when the men got her ashore. The curragh as it turned over must have struck her a glancing blow on the head; there was a small trickle of blood oozing through the wetness of her hair.

Long after hope had gone, Michael and Tom and Sean kept on with artificial respiration, while Denyse took the car in search of the nearest doctor. He lived eight miles away and was out when she arrived, but she brought him back within an hour. He knelt down by the girl, and in a moment told the men that there was no need to go on.

'She'll never see Dublin now,' said Sean, in a far-off, contemplative tone, lifting his head from his hands as he sat exhausted beside the body. 'But I shall.'

He bent over and kissed her cheek, below the smear of blood spreading down from her hair, and the wide fringe of the seaweed coloured lashes. It was likely enough that he had never kissed her before.

CHAPTER XV

LEAVING KILDOOEY

THEY took the body back to Kildooey in the car. Sean talked quite freely on the way, of the pleasure he and Bridie had known, that day, in watching the flying of the old gannets, and the antics of the late broods on the crowded breeding ground. Coming back in the boat towards the cave, he said, he had told Bridie of Shamus's remark at the cabin site — of his surprise that anyone with Sean's opinions should let his house be built for him by strangers from the other side of the water. Bridie had made fun of him and his beliefs.

'I'd felt, somehow, she wouldn't laugh at me; not just then,' he said. 'Nor at the things I cared about. I turned the boat over deliberately, you understand. Because she made me angry. She has always laughed at what Ireland means to me.'

'Nonsense. I was watching. It was an accident,' said Denyse quickly. The doctor was with them in the car, holding Bridie on the back seat with the help of Michael. The back seat had been put into the car again for the jaunt to the Seal Cave; they were grimly crowded about the dead girl, with Sean and Denyse crushed in beside Tom, who was driving. 'I also saw it was an accident,' he said. With the tally of the young dead rising in the fighting lands, what was the use of letting yet another pointless death be added here, by legal vengeance, when Bridie had already died without purpose?

Michael hesitated a moment. Then, 'I say that too,' he said. 'It just happened, by chance. The sea was wild.'

'People are often distracted out of their minds, after an accident,

and accuse themselves unjustly.' The doctor spoke soothingly. 'If there
are three of you, as witnesses —'

'But it's what I meant — that she'll not go to Dublin now, but I
will, at the Assizes. And so I will!' said Sean. 'It's true, I tried to help
her, after the boat was over, but when I turned it, I did it to kill.
I knew she couldn't swim. We were joking about that near the gannet
island — what would we do, she said, if she fell out, the way the
boat was jumping? I meant her to die.' As he spoke, they were driving
through Comines. 'I want to say good-bye to my mother first, before
I give myself up. Or I'd be asking you to stop here. Perhaps you'd
be driving me back later? Since the war they have no vehicle, I think,
at the police station.' He was composed, far more so than they had
seen him on other occasions, when they had argued with him on
politics, or he was discussing the attack on Wallace. He had taken his
decision. For all they could do, Sean, stubborn and fanatical to the
end, would see to it that Ireland accepted another fruitless sacrifice.

In Kildooey there was fatalistic acceptance of this. Even his mother
did not protest when he asked Tom and Denyse not to testify on his
behalf, speaking just as he got into the car to be carried back to
Comines.

At his request they had left him with Mrs. Agnes for half an hour,
while they took Bridie on, not to her own home, for fear of the shock
to Mrs. Kathie, but to Mrs. Mary's, setting out afterwards to find
Father Keith. Then they returned to his mother's cabin, with the
priest; Sean was standing in the road with Mrs. Agnes, waiting for
them. He seemed numbed with the horror of what he had done, and
it was plain that with what remained alive of his heart, he desired
nothing but the fullest penalty, and minded only the inevitable delays
of the law. He would not even change his wet clothes, and was still
without a coat when he set out again for Comines. Doubled up to make
a pad under the girl's stomach, it had been left behind on the rocks
when they carried Bridie the roundabout way to the cliff top. He and
Father Keith sat silently together on the back seat, where the leather
was sodden with the water which had run out of her hair, and the
frock which had been ironed for the occasion.

For the flower-like girl, who had been everyone's favourite, there
was no wailing in Kildooey, none of the great outward show of grief

which Denyse as a stranger to the country had been led to expect. These people, who dramatized life as much as possible, took death and disaster very simply. By the time the car came back from Comines for the second time, Bridie had been transferred to her own home. She lay in Mrs. Kathie's cabin; and Mrs. Kathie, standing with Helen beside the bed, no longer looked anxious; dry-eyed and calm, she listened attentively, nodding her head in agreement, to the tender and heartfelt things said by those who came to tell her that nothing would ever fill the place which her daughter had held in their affections — she with the bluest eyes anyone could recall — or they spoke of some small incident from Bridie's childhood which they had remembered with love for years; or they said nothing much but crossed themselves and prayed in Bridie's presence, and kissed Mrs. Kathie and Helen, or held their hands, for a moment, before they went quietly away again.

Late in the evening, Denyse and Tom packed their gear, leaving little trace of their stay in the quarry where, if things had been otherwise, they would now be giving their party to the Sullivans and their other friends; the weather was still glorious.

In a week the impression of their tyres on the ground would be gone, and the ledge they had levelled up for the cooking stoves would look as though it were natural; rain would soon obliterate the mark of their small fire of burning rubbish. They had two days in hand, but it would be intolerable to remain on in Kildooey even overnight. It was Denyse's suggestion that they should get back into Northern Ireland before daylight. Part of those two days would be spent in Belfast, making a deposition in Sean's favour, whether he wanted it or not. The fact that they would be lying, when they swore to the accident, would matter little to either of them beside the conviction, which they shared, that it was the last thing they could do for Bridie; she would not have wished Sean to pay with his life for that moment of blind anger. He could hang himself still, if he wanted to; but he should have the chance to change his mind.

They were dead-tired, and they packed slowly, by the light of the headlamps. 'The news was good again — in fact, definitely reassuring,' said Tom, making desultory conversation because she was staring down so fixedly at the lights in Kildooey; standing motionless with her hands full of plates and mugs. In the village the lights shone with a heartrending illusion of tranquillity and happiness.

'The news? Oh, yes. You heard it when you took Father Keith home?'

'I did. It's steadily good. I think we've won this particular battle. Too early to be certain, but I'm as nearly sure as one ever dares to be, before the end of an attack.'

The progress of the great fight beyond the channel, which had been in the front of their minds, standing between them and the enjoyment of Kildooey, seemed infinitely remote now; it would not stand between them and the sorrow of Kildooey.

Effort was needed before they could talk or think of anything but the drowned girl lying behind one of those gleaming squares; but the effort must be made, and they were people recently, fiercely schooled in turning their minds from the dead.

'Yes.' She looked down at the mugs in her hand. 'I want to take these with me, wherever it is we're going. Let's sell everything else back to the ex-horse coper, for whatever he'll give, but keep these. Places get into things: they hold the nicest part of Kildooey — the grand mornings and evenings. The breakfasts Bridie got, and the suppers in the dark that were best of all.'

'If you like,' he said, 'we'll send the proceeds from the rest to Mrs. Mary, anonymously. She'll think it's from the I.R.A. and be glad of it. Though I don't expect more than five pounds back for this "experienced vehicle", in spite of his promise.'

'Yes. I'd like us to do that. Tom, what a bad day it was for this village when we chose to come here. Or you chose, and I chose to go with you, wherever you wanted to be.'

He said: 'I think with Michael, "You shouldn't be looking at it that way".' He took their gear from her and stowed it, and then with an arm round her shoulders walked her over to the low wall, where they sat as Kenny had sat, under the signpost, listening to the sea. 'We did our best to hold off from Kildooey a threat we recognized: something that had nothing to do with us. And we failed to see another that was of our own making. Perhaps we ought to have guessed what jealousy could do. Perhaps we should have, if we hadn't been too taken up with what Wallace could do. But I don't think so. We did our best. There's one thing Bridie would have been pleased about — '

He broke off. Father Keith's heavy, flapping footsteps were coming up the hill. They went to meet him.

'I came to say something I forgot, my son, when you drove me back from Comines. For I imagine, with this dreadful thing happening among us — God's will, though it must be, I cannot yet pray in resignation as I should. It is a dreadful, dreadful waste of dear young lives — I imagine you will not be staying out your holiday in Kildooey, in the midst of grief?' The priest sounded very old and weary, and his voice was primmer than usual, as though the things which pressed in upon him had moved closer, the shadows of doubts and fears which he dared not face.

'We'll be gone in about half an hour. Will you say good-bye to all our friends for us? We don't want to intrude on them now. We'll write, I expect, later on, to thank them for everything. But it'd be kind if you'd give them all our love, when you see them.'

'I'll do that. I came to say, thank you for keeping your word to me.'

Through the darkness they looked at the glimmer of his face in amazement. Denyse pointed out, 'We can hardly say none of your young people is the worse for our coming! Which is what we promised. You realize that it was because we built Sean's cabin for him — ?'

'I know, I know. But you are not to be blamed for that. I am sure of it, myself. Though I know those who would say, if they knew, it was because you live as you do that this calamity has followed your good wishes. Many would hold that view — men I respect for a faith less questioning than mine. But I cannot think so.'

'He really would have to be seen to be believed, wouldn't he — ' Tom spoke, gently, 'the supreme being who killed Bridie in Ireland because, unknown to her, Denyse was married to someone else, in France?'

'Maybe. Maybe, I don't know,' said Father Keith, who had always worshipped exactly this God, not without effort and suffering. He put his hand on Tom's shoulder, as he had done when they first talked on the bridge. 'Good luck go with you, anyway.' His hand dropped and he stood silent. The loud booming of the sea came up to them on the dying wind. Then he said something which echoed in their minds for a long time, because of its quality of extreme spiritual fear. 'But I wonder, now, if I have missed anything? If I could have prevented it?'

In a moment, his voice returning to its normal, rather commanding tone, he asked them to take from him a small leaving present. Father Keith, too, was practised in turning his mind from the dead. It was, he said, a book of Dickens'. 'I think this work is my favourite,' he told them. 'But you must not think you are depriving me by accepting for, on my word, I believe I have it all by heart. And I will like to think of you reading it, Denyse, because you say you've been away from Dickens for a long time. And you must make Tom read it, too — I'll rely on you! — so he sees what he's missed all these years. I'm sure he will if he goes back to Dickens. The substance of him is strong and pure and sweet.' He pressed the volume into their hands; they could not see which book it was. Denyse guessed that either Pip or David Copperfield would be his most cherished friend. 'You'll find in it moving descriptions of the natural loveliness of the earth. Do you know what I thought when the owls came from Norway, all that long, dangerous way for the love of their young, that they might be reared on a rare plenty? It ran into my mind at once that I would like to tell Dickens, walking around Kildooey with him! I could see him leaning over the bridge, with his black beard waving in the wind, to look at the snapdragon, and he'd be pleased by it too. But it was the nests we had — everywhere the owls could find a hole — that would be setting me asking him, "Did you ever see the like of that?" For I know it was the clean kind of queerness he would appreciate — that somehow they knew of the voles! Well, it's a queer old man you'll be thinking me now, and maybe I wouldn't have said so much before, but you are going, and I see no harm in a timely fancy. For what we have here, to-day, and what you return to face, perhaps to-morrow — that is the reality of the world.' He murmured a blessing, almost inaudibly, and left them with the abruptness he had always shown in parting.

After the noise of his sandals had faded into the persistent sound of the sea they took the dog-eared, much-read book into the light of the headlamps: it was *Great Expectations*.

Denyse stowed it carefully in the car, where it would keep the two mugs from rattling against the metal map-case. In a moment she asked, 'You were saying Bridie would have been glad of something if she'd known. Known what?"

'Just that she's given me the thing I needed. She even more than the rest of her people — time in which I wasn't concerned with my own affairs. It isn't much to have bought at such an awful price, but for what it's worth, she'd have been glad, if she'd understood, that there was anything at all — I know now that I can go on. I'm all right.'

'You're sure?'

'I was pretty sure before. I'm quite sure now. There's a sort of perspective gets lost when one's very worried in a personal way: the sort that makes it possible to believe someone else's death might really be as tragic as one's own! You couldn't help me much there: you came so close, so soon; thinking about you was like thinking about myself. I could worry nearly as well, wondering if Father Keith's owl-God was going to hit at you again through me. But Bridie and Sean were right outside my world. And until a few minutes ago, I hadn't really thought of anything but the two of them for a long while. That's the sort of perspective I meant. I'm all right — I can go on now, for as long as is necessary.'

'How long? How long may it be necessary? It looks, as you say, as if our side had come out on top in just one battle. But . . .' She was touching him, clinging to him. With the feeling of physical communion between them, a flow of understanding running from nerve to nerve, there was no need for her to say anything to what he had just told her of his own problem. Thankfulness and an enduring love were in her hands, and her lips.

'Do you mean, are we going to win the war?' he said. 'Almost certainly not.' In their close companionship this was the one question which, so far, neither of them had cared to put into exact words. It was generally avoided by those who saw without sentiment, and were prepared to mind with their lives, in the autumn of 1940; but having been put, in this moment of barriers-down, it was answered in the spirit of autumn 1940, when Britain, fighting alone, stood strangely, stupidly, magnificently undismayed on the brink of defeat. He thought of the two laughing women in the bus: 'If you must talk nonsense —'

'What chance can there be,' he said, 'unless the nearly unthinkable happens, and Germany's unwise enough to attack Russia, and America sees her own interest in time to come in with us, while we can still stand? Then we shall almost certainly win; but not otherwise. And at present neither of these things looks in the least likely to happen. But no man's responsible for more than his own behaviour up to and through death. His decorum, I think the Romans called it. Well, whatever happens you can believe with absolute certainty that I was all right. I told you, "This is my armour". I meant it. It'll last as long as I need it — come on, my dear, get in; we've got that farce of the Ballinfaddy road to get through before morning.'

... **Reprinted from the December Book-of-the-Month Club News** ...

THE SIGNPOST
By E. ARNOT ROBERTSON

IT is hard to describe this novel, for what the reader expects it to become, it definitely is not—and the central theme of the story, which is a love affair, is used for quite different purposes, so that, actually, you get two excellent novels in close combination instead of one.

Tom Fairburn is an airman on brief leave from the Battle of London. He is suffering from what we hear too little about, the shock of an essential but particularly terrible bombing, which was his job and under his leadership, and from which he escaped with a damaged plane and got home only by a heroism which brought him a decoration and the leave. He is Irish by provenance, and to neutral Ireland he goes, hoping to find at least a momentary escape from the war. On the way he meets Denyse, wife of a French banker who has gone collaborationist, leaving her to escape through the horrors of the refugee crowded road. The story then becomes a gypsy love story between the two in an old car headed for Donegal. It is fresh, strong, and charming.

But Donegal takes over the narrative. They camp on the outskirts of a little sea village, inhabited chiefly by Sullivans of whom Fairburn had met one. And the village adopts them, and soon with the desperate war for England, to which Tom must return, always in the background, they are enmeshed in a village story. It is Irish, truly Irish, with the fascination, the desperation, the wit, the hard realism of Ireland.

There is a signpost in the village which points toward Dublin, and that is the symbol of the whole tragi-comedy. The young long to escape the narrowness of their environment, which, nevertheless, they love. Bridie, one of the most poignant studies of a young girl in recent literature, is to be married to Sean, the fanatical Irish nationalist, but she wants to see the great world, which is Dublin, first. Helen, her sister, is back from America, ordered by the priest to fulfill her marriage promise, and she is longing for a Boston which was her Utopia. Wallace, the Gambeen man (loan shark we should call him), sits like a spider on the village web, getting them all in his power, fighting the priest. But he is not a spider, only an unhappy egoist, who wants to lift them all out of poverty to satisfy his own hurt vanity.

Such Irish folk! Aunt Mary Sullivan, infinitely prefers talk to food or money. She tempts Tom and Denyse with chickens and tea to come to her cabin, where everyone follows, and the conversation is like Dublin in the Irish Renaissance for whimsical brilliance. But underlying it all is tragedy —the tragic memories of what happened in the "bad times" of the Black and Tans, in which even Aunt Mary was involved; the tragedy of an almost maniacal patriotism, eating Sean's heart out for love of Ireland, so that the vast war beyond the sea is a shadow beside the great need to unify his country.

And there is Father Keith. A good man, a kind man, a stern man, to whom the morality of his village is more important than health or happiness, more important than the crisis in the world outside. He learns that Tom and Denyse are "living in sin," does not expose them, does not relent toward them, begs only that they do not harm his village by their example. Here, in this little Donegal scene, the author manages to present one of those eternal conflicts between different kinds, irreconcilable kinds of the good. For Tom and Denyse have brought life to the cramped existence of the village, set Bridie on the right path, won even Sean's respect, protected the helpless against the Gambeen man. The scenes in which this plot develops are so fresh, so unexpected, so full of wit and charm and the sense of rich if suffering human nature, that they could be played almost verbatim on any stage. But you cannot upset the balance of nature by bringing in a new plant or animal to a strange environment without terrible risk and so it is in this story.

Whose fault? The unbending priest who is both the good angel and the implacable fiery sword of village life? Tom and Denyse? The world, which has left this tragic idyll of Ireland behind it, yet threatens with its immense powers of attraction to draw into ruin this little speck near its orbit? The reader can anwer; this is not a story with a moral as I read it; it is an imaginative transcript of very real life.

However, who wishes to be charmed and amused, who wishes to be moved by the distresses none the less vital because they happen to simple people, should read *The Signpost*. And also those who need to understand the neutrality of Ireland in the great war; and the distinction of Ireland which has made her drama, and the personality of the Irish race, and Irish emotions, notorious in a modern society.

HENRY SEIDEL CANBY